Warriors of Epona

A Novel of the Roman Empire

Adam Alexander Haviaras

Warriors of Epona and the Eagles and Dragons series

Eagles and Dragons Publishing, Toronto, Ontario, Canada

ISBN: 978-0-9918873-8-5

First Paperback Edition

Cover designed by LLPix Designs

*Please note: To enhance the reader's experience, there is a glossary of Latin words at the back of this book.

Join the Legions!

Sign-up for the Eagles and Dragons Publishing Newsletter and get a FREE BOOK today.

Subscribers get first access to new releases, special offers, and much more.

Go to:
www.eaglesanddragonspublishing.com

For my parents, Stefanos and Jeanette.

My love and gratitude always,

for putting a sword in my hand, and a horse beneath me.

Για τους γονείς μου, τον Στέφανο και την Jeanette.

Έχουν την αγάπη και την ευγνωμοσύνη μου πάντα,

γιατί μου έδωσαν ένα σπαθί, και μ'έβαλαν στην πλάτη ενός αλόγου.

Warriors of Epona

Eagles and Dragons

Book III

PROLOGUS

A.D. 208

In the dawn mist, at the edge of a far, northern wood, a white stallion caroused, revelling in life, in the moment. His neighing and the sound of his hooves cut through the air to penetrate the ancient forest, heralding the day to the darkness within. He cut right and left and jumped and leaned to full gallop, his footing always sure. Power surged in the muscles beneath his shimmery coat, his mane silver and wild, untamed.

Then there was laughter, laughter to lighten the heart of the darkest recesses of the world. A ringing voice of spring rain and sunlight both. The stallion stopped, ears forward, eyes turned to the wood and the growing light that approached.

As dawn's pink light finally laced the mist, She came: the mistress of horses, a goddess in shining robes of white and gold. She was tall and slender with red-gold hair, her eyes alight with life from beyond the veil of worlds.

The stallion approached and kneeled, his magnificent head bowed to her.

She sang to him, and he rose to meet her loving hand which caressed his muzzle and neck. On the branches above her were perched three white birds, and about her feet were three white hounds with red-tipped ears, her loyal sentries of earth and air.

Her presence was music, but in a moment the music changed, her demeanour darkened. Her eyes narrowed to dark tidal pools, and the stallion reared in front of her toward the field and down the valley. Calming him with a word of the otherworld, she waited as a wind was born in the West and clouds descended. She smiled, terrible and beautiful at once.

They are here...

The stallion entered the wood at her side as they came, horses and men clad in iron and bronze, clenching sword and spear and shield for war, for the kill. Above these riders soared the dragons, their howls ushering in the battle to come.

She watched the leader, and his head turned quickly to her as he flew past, his war mask brilliant across the green field. At his signal, the riders split into three columns, their mounts beautifully disciplined.

At a word from the goddess, the three birds followed, shot from tree to sky as arrows on the wind. She sighed, her lithe hand outstretched, fingers wrapped about a swaying branch of rowan as though clasping the hand of an old friend.

A moment later, the light of dawn returned and she sat atop the stallion to gallop soundlessly back into the wood, trailed by her running hounds whose ears swayed like field poppies in a spring breeze.

Part I

THE KILLING FIELDS

A.D. 208

I

ANGUIS ET APER

'The Dragon and the Boar'

The chieftain was waiting around the last embers of his night fire when the voice echoed down the glen. He rose slowly when the others jumped. The swirling designs that covered his body came to life with his movement, and the blue boar across his massive chest bristled in anticipation. He had dreamt last night that this was the day on which he would etch his name on the stone of time. His ancestors would not let him down, they demanded he fight.

"Lord!" screamed the chieftain's scout as he flung himself onto his knees from his pony's back, lungs heaving. "It is the Dragon, my lord. He is coming in at the western end of the glen!"

The chieftain looked at the ground beneath his feet, the sky above. He could feel his warriors' eyes upon him, expectant and itching for battle. They were the mightiest of his clan, nine hundred strong, their ponies sturdy and swift.

"How many?" He allowed himself a smile.

"Eight dragons, lord. About two-hundred and fifty riders in all."

"Against our nine hundred?" the chieftain's voice erupted and he pumped his powerful arms to the sky. "Today we finish this, and I will kill the Dragon with these bare hands!" His warriors roared their approval and adulation. "Mount up! We go now to the kill!"

With that, nine hundred fighting men bounded onto their mounts, the chieftain in his war chariot, and thundered westward down the glen, eating up the earth before them.

Mist hung loosely in the valley, forced back by the growing light of day and more than two hundred and fifty horses and riders of the Ala III Britannorum who trounced the muddy green of the land as they rode to meet their quarry, the Boar of the Selgovae. Each man knew his role and that of his comrade so that they moved as one, a force of nature rushing to battle as a wave to the shore.

Above the riders, the draconaria howled terribly, their long tails fluting back over their ranks when they were hoisted and the force split into three as they entered the valley, one down the centre and two smaller ones on either of the flanking hillsides among the trees. At the crest of this wave of howling scales and teeth rode their praefectus, the 'Dragon', his long, crimson cloak flowing behind him like a river of blood. His face was masked by his crested war helm with the mark of the dragon, rampant also upon his black armour and his red and gold vexillum standard mounted on a spear carried by one of his men.

The praefectus picked up the pace of the charge when he spotted the sacred birds above his three columns, guiding them to battle. He hefted his twelve-foot kontos lance and a rush of warm wind seemed to push them on from behind to meet the dark wave of the enemy as it appeared in the distance, small at first, but the size of the force coming at them quickly became more apparent. Beneath the deathly cold demeanour of his war mask the praefectus smiled as he noticed the disarray of the enemy forces coming toward them, each individual hero of the Selgovae fighting for his own glory. In their centre, churning up the earth, came an ancient war chariot skillfully-driven. On the small fighting platform stood a giant of a man gripping three ash spears, a golden torc about his brawny neck.

The praefectus now knew his target and focussed on it, his every limb tingling, pulsing with the fight to come and he pushed straight at the warrior chieftain who was pulling back an arm to launch a spear. The praefectus did not need to look to know his men were exactly where they should be; he could feel them. As the two waves approached in a body of screams and battle cries, the praefectus transferred his lance to his other hand and unslung the golden-hilted sword at his back.

"Anguis!" roared the riders behind him.

The Boar of the Selgovae let fly his spear at the winging Dragon's heart only to be hacked away in the air before it struck home. A second spear flew on, farther than most men could throw, and was parried to land harmlessly on the ground amidst the riders behind. The chieftain roared and his warriors surged at the smaller force, covering the entire valley. Before he realized it, the chariot was swerving, its driver at his feet, impaled on the Dragon's tooth. The chieftain grabbed for the reins with his free hand and braced himself defiantly on the prow of his ancestors' chariot. In a moment he was swept away through the red air as the Dragon leapt from his horse amidst the crashing armies and chaos.

The Dragon and the Boar soared out the back of the chariot to land heavily on the already bloodied earth.

"Ahh!" the chieftain raged as he felt the blood leaking from his side where the Dragon had already sunk his tooth into his flesh. He regained his feet only to find his bodyguards writhing on the ground about him, daggers protruding from their guts. In front of him stood the Dragon, his bloody cloak blowing in the rushing wind, his steel face cold and blank, the only trace of emotion the golden sword that was pointed at him, dripping with the blood of his people.

The Boar rushed at his enemy with his long hacking sword but the Dragon moved with ethereal speed, behind him when he should have been in front of him, cutting at his back, inflicting weakening wounds about his body. The boar writhed, but would not abate his attacks, and the two fought on.

The praefectus moved instinctively, as though with foresight, unaware of the ring of fighting warriors that had formed about him and the chieftain. About the circle swirled his riders, in a maelstrom of death as they hacked away at the enemy forces, on the killing field and on the hillsides where the other columns had engaged. At the back of his mind, he was only vaguely aware of the thunder further down the valley. His other eight dragons had come to join the battle at the rear of the enemy.

The Dragon and the Boar fought on, circling, swirling and biting. They slashed at each other remorselessly, the voices of their gods ringing in their ears.

"Morrigan!" the Boar screamed the name of the war goddess as he leapt and rolled to slam into the Dragon's guts and lift him into the air to the delight of his warriors. His prey would not be held long, having climbed over him in the rush of his attack to land on his feet behind the chieftain.

The Dragon roared like one of his draconaria when he felt hot blood pouring from a gash in his thigh inflicted by the Boar in his attack.

"The Dragon is bloodied!" the chieftain goaded, but before he knew it his enemy was upon him, and he felt one of the Dragon's teeth sink into the muscle of his leg, lancing with pain. His massive arms reached out to grab but met only air as the Dragon wrapped an iron arm about his neck from behind and began to squeeze.

Immediately the Boar's vision failed as he began to succumb to the death grip, his tired, wounded arms flailing backward helplessly. Now the remainder of his bodyguards moved in to help, but as quickly as they neared, just as quickly were they swept away, impaled on the lances of the unseen second wave of dragons that was finishing off the desperate remnants of his warriors.

Wanting nothing but death now, the Boar heaved with a last effort so that the Dragon was thrown over his head, the death grip broken. The Dragon swirled in a flurry of red before him and the Boar charged to skewer him on his long sword as he came down. The Dragon landed on his feet and immediately lowered and spun, his armoured leg crashing into the Boar's knee, the golden sword flashing up to slice through and shatter the Boar's ancestral blade.

The Boar tried to raise himself on the corpses of his clansmen where they lay about him, to meet his death on his feet, but he felt burning fire in his leg and fell back down again, agony ripping at his throat. His arms shaking he looked up to see the Dragon staring down at him, his expressionless mask cold, a god of death whose glowing sword now extended to his throat.

"Kill me!" the Boar raged at his enemy. "I am not afraid of death. Kill me!" The Dragon's arm steadied for a moment and the fallen chieftain readied himself for the blow that would send him to his ancestors, but it was not meant to be. The Dragon shook his armoured head once, turned and walked away. "Kill me, you demon! Coward!" the chieftain roared, disappointed and bereft. "Why won't you kill me?" he asked, but all that met him was the billowing crimson cloak amidst the carnage.

The chieftain made to grab a nearby dagger to do it himself, but strong, scaled arms grabbed him and the world went black.

From the top of his dapple-grey stallion, the praefectus surveyed the killing field, finally allowing himself a deep, calming breath to bring himself back to humanity. Behind him, his vexillarius and princeps waited atop their own mounts. He remained silent a moment, stroking his stallion's neck softly, contemplating the scene about him. The valley floor was churned and hacked and bloodied, as though the earth itself had been disembowelled by sword and spear, trampled. His men did not address him, waited, as they knew he had come to wish for silence immediately after every engagement. His second-in-command, his princeps, waited, knowing how much Britannia had changed him. In a short time they had fought and defeated thirty chieftains and thousands of warriors of the various rebel tribes, for the emperor, for Rome. As the

'Dragon', the praefectus had become something of a legend among the tribes, something to be feared and challenged by the bravest.

The praefectus shook his head and closed his eyes beneath his mask. It was all blood now, on the road to Hades. He did not notice the three white birds in the branches of a tree far up the hillside, watching. He motioned subtly to his princeps who trotted over to his side.

"Praefectus?" the head decurion noticed the blood flowing from his commander's thigh and spoke so no one could hear him. "Anguis," he addressed him by his name, the ancient word for dragon that only his friends used. "You are wounded."

The praefectus looked down at where his old wound from the assassins in Africa had reopened. He covered it quickly with the edge of his crimson cloak.

"I'm fine, Dagon," he assured him. "It's nothing new. I'll have it stitched up back at base."

The princeps nodded and spoke louder. "What are your orders, Praefectus?"

The praefectus looked at the rows of captured enemy warriors where they were hobbled with ropes about the cart where their chieftain had been tied and was still unconscious.

"Marching formation back to base with four turmae surrounding the captives. We'll hold them under tight guard in Trimontium until a detachment from the sixth legion can come to take them to the slave yards at Eburacum." He looked at the bulky form of the chieftain again. "I want the Boar held apart from his people, secretly. Have the physicians bind his wounds."

"It shall be done as you command, Praefectus."

II

TRIMONTIUM

'The Place of Three Hills'

The column of armoured horsemen and captives snaked for miles among the bulbous hills and rushing rivers of the war zone north of the Wall. The dragon banners fluted above the mounted warriors at whose head rode the praefectus, Lucius Metellus Anguis and the princeps, Dagon, the Sarmatian king. Accompanying the praefectus and princeps as always, was Barta, the praefectus' vexillarius and bodyguard. Dagon had assigned the giant Sarmatian to be Lucius' shadow when his friend had been given command of the quingeniary ala over a year ago.

Barta was the tallest of the over five hundred Sarmatians in the ala, his loyalty and sense of duty as sturdy and rock-hard as himself. From his head of dark hair, icy eyes were ever searching, watchful for threats to his commander and his king. On his shoulders were the skins of wolves he had killed, which added to his ferocity; a good thing, as the Celts, in battle, always went for the vexillum that was Barta's charge. His long sword was lightning-quick, and much of the time, before attackers got close enough to attack the praefectus or Sarmatian king, they would be on the ground clutching at one of Barta's many throwing knives.

In truth however, every bronze-scaled, fighting man of the ala was loyal to the praefectus to their death. Half of the

Sarmatians had known him since the days in Numidia when they had fought the desert tribes together on the sands of Africa.

Lucius Metellus Anguis had been a tribune then, subsequently recalled to Rome when the Romans of the III Augustan legion had seen him as god-abandoned. The strange and tragic murder of the tribune's visiting sister in the midst of the legionary base at Lambaesis had fostered great unease among the troops there.

Shortly after the tribune's departure from Numidia, Mar, the former Sarmatian king, and Dagon's uncle, had, on his death bed, recommended Lucius to Imperial Command as the new Praefectus of the Sarmatian ala. He had also commanded his warriors and his nephew to follow Lucius Metellus Anguis, warrior and friend of his people, who carried the mark of the dragon and the favour of the Gods.

King Dagon and his Sarmatian warriors had become family to Lucius, had given him their loyalty, their love and their blood. It was a gift for which the Roman dragon was grateful, a burden which he felt acutely every day when atop his horse and leading them to yet another battle beneath the howling draconaria.

The three peaks of the hills overlooking the refurbished base at Trimontium loomed larger now in Lucius' field of vision as they approached the patched-up ditches and walls of the fort from the West, following the line of the river below. From the time that Rome first invaded and conquered the southern reaches of Caledonia, Trimontium had been a choice stopping point for travellers and a base for operations north of Hadrianus' great wall.

Beneath his expressionless cavalry mask, Lucius felt the usual oppressiveness of the three peaks' shadows upon him, like angry Titans ready to crush them without hesitation. Those hills had been sacred to the Selgovae, and now he returned with one of their greatest chiefs in chains. The small Roman signal station at the top seemed a meagre presence, one that could be extinguished, flung from the heights to the valley below. The troops assigned to the station up on the northern peak complained of spectral harassment, and a loud keening from what the local Celts called banshees, a sort of Celtic fury that wailed upon rooftops in the middle of the night. Lucius believed it, but could not say so in front of his men. Soldiers of all nations were extremely superstitious, and Romans were no exception. Lucius made as if he were not bothered, but in reality, in that faraway land, the shadows moved all too often in the mists of night.

Still, in addition to being strategically useful, Trimontium had proved useful to Lucius' persona as the 'Dragon' in the region. The indigenous Celts believed the Dragon had taken the hills as his own; the peaks were his horns and the signal station at the top became his poisonous fire. Rumour had its uses in a war of re-conquest, and Lucius used it to his advantage. At the very least, it kept the war bands at a safer distance.

As the marching column came parallel with the fort's walls, Lucius observed the defences again, as was his habit. They would need to be solid with their new intake of prisoners, especially the Boar of the Selgovae, whose people might try to free him. Lucius made a mental note to keep the chieftain apart from the other prisoners and to double the sentries until troops from Eburacum came to take them all away. For now at least, the defences were solid, having been rebuilt by the men of VI Victrix prior to the arrival of Lucius and his Sarmatian ala. The stone and timber wall stood dark and imposing behind three consecutive rows of deep ditches that surrounded the fort, western and eastern annexes. The latter two areas contained a bath house, a mansio for visitors, and a small civilian vicus where traders and camp followers had set up temporary homes.

When the praefectus acknowledged the sentries at the Decumana gate, a cornu rang out, deep and groaning, to signal the Dragons' return. The oak and iron gates lurched inward and Lucius, Dagon, and Barta turned in beneath a massive stone block reading:

ALA III BRITANNORUM
Quingenaria Sarmatiana

The cornu continued to sound as rank upon rank of Sarmatian warriors came through the gates, the chained prisoners and the cart carrying the defeated chieftain in their midst. The Boar was conscious again, standing straight and defiant, the muscles of his tattooed body strained against his chains. His eyes met Lucius', but they were not full of hate, or resignation, simply a sort of calm defiance that belied his angry body.

The Boar saw the praefectus give his princeps an order that was passed along, and soon after the chieftain was led away from his people to a building farther down the Via

Decumana. The rest of the prisoners were taken to various holding cells at the north-eastern corner of the fort where they were kept under tight guard by infantry auxiliaries and archers. Lucius watched the chieftain disappear into the lower levels of the Principia-turned-exercise hall before giving his mount to Dagon and heading to the commander's house at the southern end of the fort. As always, Barta followed.

As Lucius made his way to his quarters, the familiar sounds of the base began to ring out - the chink of Sarmatian scale armour, the neighing of hundreds of war horses, the call of the sentries atop the walls. Added to this was the angry groaning of the Selgovan prisoners, the shuffling of their manacled feet. But Lucius had become inured to the latter after so many battles.

Lucius and Barta walked through the wide doorway into the commander's house, returning the salute given by the guards flanking the entrance. Of all the refurbished structures in the fort, after the defences, the commander's house had received the most attention from VIth Legion. They crossed the courtyard of the square structure, hobnails scratching on the weathered stone surface. Before entering his personal rooms, Lucius turned to Barta.

"Barta, you may go now. Rest and eat."

The massive Sarmatian stood tall, but bowed his head as he replied.

"I am content Praefectus," he answered in his deeply guttural, accented Latin. "I will remain here until Lord Dagon arrives. The enemy are among us now..."

"And they are all chained and under guard. You need not worry."

Barta looked up then, at the darkening sky, a shadow blanketing his features.

"Nevertheless, Praefectus, I would prefer to stay."

Lucius knew the man would not be moved. His loyalty was sometimes uncomfortably stringent, but it was admirable too.

"Very well, my friend." Lucius smiled for the first time that day, and placed his hand up on Barta's shoulder. Barta looked down again, eyes trained on the dragon image across Lucius' black cuirass. Lucius gripped more tightly to get his message across. "You fought well these last days, Barta. Lord Mar and your people would be proud."

The man said nothing, merely tensed his jaw in pride, but also in a sort of fought-off sadness. Despite being a brutal giant, a deep pain harassed his soul, a pain at the loss of his former king and kinsman, and the loss of his own family on the great plains north of Pontus, far away. It was the same for almost every Sarmatian under Lucius' command. Having lost almost everything, Lucius Metellus Anguis, the 'Dragon', was now the keeper of their loyalties, and their lives, which they gave willingly.

Lucius released his hold and turned into his rooms. Barta stood outside his door, despite the fact that his own room was just across the courtyard.

The door closed and Lucius stood in the middle of his rooms, alone for the first time in days. He closed his eyes and breathed deeply of the scent of pine that yet emanated from the new beams that held up the tile roof. It was beginning to rain outside, as it always did in that far corner of the Empire. His armour and weapons, his crimson-crested helmet, all felt three times as heavy in that moment as exhaustion finally clawed up his body. His head began to pound and he felt his guts twist.

When the feeling abated, Lucius Metellus Anguis, Praefectus of the Ala III Brittanorum, sat on a stool in the middle of his quarters feeling more alone than ever, though surrounded by friends. This latest battle flashed again in his mind, every cut and thrust of sword and spear, screams of triumph and of pain and the thundering of horses' hooves. The dragons' howling and…birds, white birds in the barren branches. Three of them, watching…

He looked to a niche in one of the walls where three small oil lamps illuminated three statuettes, the first a pink marble representation of Venus, beautiful and serene. Another, Apollo, his family patron and protector. And the third, a newly carved image of Epona, Goddess of Horses who was now his constant companion and the mother of their camp. Lucius moved to a table in a corner and picked up a small branch of rosemarinus, a chunk of frankincense and a small sheaf of wheat, one of many such he had tied with lengths of dyed thread.

Standing before the immortal renderings, blood encrusted on his person, Lucius laid the rosemarinus at the feet of Venus. He then set the frankincense alight in the flame of a lamp and laid it in a dish before Apollo. Lastly, he offered the sheaf of wheat with both hands to Epona, who stood with a strong stallion at her shoulder. The warrior said not a word but fell to his knees as his heart screamed out for help. Every battle he had engaged in from the beginning of the war had been successively easier. The Dragon and his iron warriors vanquished all comers. This last battle had been too easy, Lucius thought. He had actually enjoyed it, defeating and humiliating the Boar, and it sickened and frightened him to his depths. He felt more machine now than man, an engine of war hurtling against flesh and bone foes, unrelenting. He was haunted by Mars and his iron laughter.

Then, a light dawned within, thoughts of his wife, Adara, and his twin son and daughter, Phoebus and Calliope. They would be over four years old now. It had been over a year since he had left them, an eternity, and he struggled to remember their faces amidst the countless dark memories of battle. Rallying himself, Lucius Metellus Anguis rose, felt the dried mud and gore on his ancestral armour and set about disarming himself to clean and polish it all, to remove all traces of the death of others.

It was strange, the peace that a menial task could blanket upon the mind. With the mud and blood wiped away, the cloth floating in the crimson water of a basin, Lucius dipped a piece of doeskin in oil and set about polishing his bull's hide cuirass, rubbing the grain of the hardened leather in a calm, circular motion. That done, he moved on to the image of the dragon, its wings outstretched, powerful and wise. As ever, it took on a light of its own, that ancient symbol given to his ancestors over four hundred years ago by Apollo himself, who slew the great Python at Delphi. He often thought of the irony that he, Lucius Metellus *Anguis*, a Roman, should be given command of the Sarmatians, a people who venerated the dragon. Just as the symbol appeared on their banners and bodies, so it adorned his cuirass, the cheek pieces of his masked war helmet, his greaves and the sword given him by Adara and shown to him by Apollo at the ends of the world. *The Gods are a mystery to me.*

The Dragon was a part of him as much as he a part of it. It used to frighten and confuse him, as it did his friends long ago. But now, he had come to accept the gift of ancient power and skill, and the curse of loneliness it gave in return. He looked down at the tattooed dragons that now coiled about the muscles of his forearms, a long scroll in the left claw and a red-tipped spear clutched in the right. He smiled fleetingly, remembered when Dagon, himself a king, had given him the tattoo after their first, crushing victory under Lucius' command. The men had been awed by their praefectus' skill and power.

Every Sarmatian warrior had images of animals upon his person; wolves, bears, horses, falcons, centaurs, griffins, sphinxes and dragons. Lucius had not protested when Dagon insisted upon this singular honour for a Roman commander. Even Lucius' dapple-grey stallion, Lunaris, had been branded with a similar image on his rear hind quarter to further bind him to his master, his friend. For the Sarmatians, horses were most sacred, honoured as family members, even to the extent that upon their death, they were burned upon pyres next to their riders.

Perhaps, Lucius thought, that is why Epona had taken notice of him. The goddess had entered into his dreams, or as flashes in his waking hours. From the time he arrived in Britannia, he had felt her presence, seen the white birds in a nearby tree, specks on a hillside boulder, or winging through the sky before an engagement. He thought he might have been going mad, but a few times between wakefulness and sleep did he spy her, smiling, laughter in flashes of white and red-gold. But she had never spoken in words, only feelings and reassurances. Lucius would wake with a remnant sense of extreme beauty laced with terrible possibilities. She was to be honoured, not lightly, and so was now one of his personal triad of deities.

When Lucius finished polishing his armour, and a sense of peace had come back to him, he stood up, running a hand through his dark hair and sighed. His hand caught in the grime matting his hair. He took the sword his wife had given him, for it never left his side, and stood. He made his way to the baths of the commander's house to clean and soak in the caldarium where the furnaces had been stoked since their return.

After washing with strigil and oil, Lucius sat in the hot water pool, allowing the steam to envelop him for a spell. He leaned back, rolling his neck and shoulders, raised a hand to touch the dragon-hilted sword. He had promised Adara he would always keep it with him.

I miss you, my love, he thought. *Venus, goddess, bring her to me soon.*

Since arriving in Britannia, he often struggled out of the violence of his everyday existence to wrangle some memory of his family, of happiness, before it faded again. His wife, her black curling locks, the green of her eyes, all of her. He could not imagine how much his children had changed. The last time he had seen any children was when the ala had stopped at the Wall to re-supply for the journey at Coriosopitum. Some of the Wall officers and troops had had families, wives with babes in arms and older children toddling about their mothers' and fathers' legs as they had all gathered to watch the Sarmatians ride into the settlement. Seeing those families had only served to make Lucius angry at not being able to see, to hold, his own. Children had waved to him, and cheered, but he had lowered his iron mask and ignored them.

The door to the baths creaked and Lucius' arm slipped out of the water, silent, to take the handle of his sword. Nobody spoke. The blade's tip scratched the stone floor as Lucius stood up naked in the misty pool and pointed the blade at the shadowy figure coming through the steam. The dragon on his arm strained then settled.

"Anguis?"

"I'm here, Dagon." Lucius lowered the blade.

"I can barely see you for all this heat." Dagon waved the steam in front of him away momentarily. He always skipped the hot pool, opting only for the tepidarium and frigidarium when he visited the baths. He was not bathing, however. He was dressed. Dagon looked down at his friend's thigh where the water about was darkening. "Your wound is bleeding again."

Lucius looked down and wiped away the clotting about his old wound. "I'll have the surgeon put some new staples on it. He looked back at Dagon. "Is something wrong?"

"No. Nothing's wrong. The Selgovan chieftain has been asking to speak with you."

Lucius stepped out of the pool, past Dagon, to the cold room. "Not yet," he said before splashing into the cold water in the next room.

Dagon knew it was still too soon to have brought the message, realized he should have waited until after Lucius had finished. He would bring it up again later.

Night had fallen and the rain continued to drench the fort, sluicing along the buildings' roof tiles to splash on the paving slabs. The commander's house was alight with conversation and permeated with the scent of roasted meat as Lucius shared a meal with several of his decurions. He had converted one of the larger rooms into a triclinium with rough benches and couches where he and the men under his command could talk and eat in peace. They drank only beer, for wine was more difficult to come by, and they all wanted their wits about them with the constant threat of attack. The Sarmatians rarely lost control of themselves the way Romans tended to do.

Lucius listened to a friendly argument between Brencis and Vaclar about the merits of the Selgovae in battle. He ate sparingly of some roasted boar that some of the hunters had brought back out of the hills that evening.

"Vaclar, you listen here." Brencis, who was Dagon's younger royal cousin, sat up and faced the other decurion who mimicked large ears the better to hear. Brencis, jovial as ever, shook his sandy head of hair, grey eyes dancing as he smiled and pulled at the long moustache he had recently grown. "You look ridiculous!" The others laughed. "You say the Selgovae were so easy to beat, that they are bad fighters. But I tell you that that battle could easily have gone the other way, for they are a fierce tribe." Several of the others nodded in agreement. Though Brencis was all of twenty-four years, even younger than Dagon, he was a fierce fighter, astute observer, and strategist. He had the respect of his people, his cousin, and Lucius. "No. They outnumbered us greatly. The reason we won that battle with seemingly so little effort is because our preafectus, our *Anguis*, planned his strategy carefully and did not lead us into danger without being fully prepared. Not like some of the puffball commanders my men and I served under in Germania. If we won that battle easily, it was because Anguis knows how to win battles and has the ears of the Gods." Brencis raised his cup, and Dagon, Vaclar and the others followed, all of them in agreement as they looked to Lucius who now sat upright. "We drink to you, Anguis, our commander, our friend, our lord of war."

"Anguis!" they toasted in unison.

Lucius put up his hands, humbled by their devotion, awkward. "And I drink to you all, my defenders," he glanced at Barta who towered next to the door, "my brothers. Every victory we have been granted in this land since we arrived has been because of your discipline, your skill, our fleet-footed mounts, and the inspiration that your ancestors whisper to you with every breath. I drink in turn, to you, Ala Sarmatiana!"

"Ala Sarmatiana!" they echoed. Only Dagon, did not echo the call, for he was too busy looking at his friend and wondering at the personal darkness behind the bright words.

"Praefectus, I wonder if we might question the captive chieftain to find out what kind of training in war his people undergo? It might help us in future battles." This was asked by Hippogriff, the Greco-Sarmatian decurion. His braided blond locks were tied back from his bearded face. The others always teased him that it was the Greek in him that always wanted to gather information which he then wrote down on papyrus scrolls he thought would be useful in war planning. "We could try and get as much information out of the Boar as possible."

Lucius stood up then and went to the window. He wore his black cuirass, pteruges, high boots and his long black, wool cloak. He held the sword in his hand, a part of his arm. The others all watched him, curious.

Lucius remembered his dream the night before the battle. It was of the Boar, before all his people, holding out his sword for Lucius to take, no complaint in his eyes. Even as he bowed his head to Lucius, a massive stallion had appeared behind him. The chieftain had done everything but give up his sword in the battle, so Lucius had taken the dream to be a sign from the Gods, from Epona, that his cavalry was to be victorious. It had seemed the Selgovae's gods were not with them. So, he had relayed the order of battle that morning when it had come to him. The signs were not to be ignored.

"I would not humiliate the Boar by asking him to betray the people for whom he fought such a battle." Hippogriff looked humbled. Lucius turned from the window and put his hand on Hippogriff's shoulder. "It's a good idea, and worthy intelligence. But I believe these people are born to war, sword in hand, and that they train as they fight, all-out, no order, no discipline." Lucius went to the door. "The Gods were with us, and not with them. Sometimes, it's that simple. I go now, to see Lunaris, for without him, I might not have come this far." The Sarmatians all nodded for each of them carried out the same act every night, of feeding and brushing down their own brave mounts in thanks for their service and undying loyalty. Barta followed Lucius out as the others fell back into conversation.

The Sarmatian stable block was situated at the northern end of the base. It was quiet inside, all sound muffled by thick carpets of fresh straw and rain on the roof tiles. The gentle huffing of hundreds of horses was broken only by the occasional neighing. Lucius and Barta entered the southern end which was closest to Lunaris' stable on the left. Immediately to the right was a wooden image of Epona surrounded by horses, dragons, gryphons and other creatures.

The scent of the place gave pause and comfort, the mixed smells of horse dung and sweet smelling hay combined with the silence of the place. Lucius inhaled and looked to the image of the mother of their camp and then went to Lunaris' stable. The stallion had been waiting and stretched his muscular neck over the stable wall to meet Lucius as he approached. As always, Barta moved slowly the length of the stable block to look for intruders. Lucius pulled back the heavy hood of his cloak and smiled as Lunaris searched for the hand that always bore some kind of vegetable or fruit. As the horse picked up the apple, his teeth clicking on Lucius' ring of entwined dragons, the Roman ruffled his jet mane and chuckled lightly.

"My friend," Lucius whispered, entering the stable to stand beside the big Iberian. He picked up a horse brush and began running it over the stallion's flanks in long downward strokes. Lunaris' dappled coat twitched with each sweep. The trooper that had taken Lunaris to the stable earlier had already brushed down the praefectus' mount thoroughly, but Lucius always wanted to do so himself. In a sense the Iberian was his best friend. In Africa, friends had betrayed him and the memory of it still haunted him in some ways, walled him against new, close and uninhibited ties with others. He placed his hand over the dragon brand on Lunaris' flank that mirrored the tattoo on his arm. The stallion's tale whisked in a circle; he had not liked it when they pressed the custom iron into his skin. It had taken Lucius some time to calm him afterward, to win back his trust, but he had. Lucius sometimes thought that he would be better off if he was able to be as forgiving as his horse.

Barta's footsteps were returning from the other end of the stable block, but stopped some distance away so as not to disturb Lucius. The Sarmatian had no idea what troubled the praefectus so, but he respected him and honoured him as a man and warrior-commander. He knew these moments of solitude were needed, and stayed back as far as his conscience would safely allow.

Lucius leaned on the worn oak rail and gripped it until his knuckles whitened, not letting go. His war-torn self longed for the past, the enveloping embrace of his love-filled wife, the two smiling suns of his children's faces. Like a tortured winter sea, he was crashing in on himself and just when his surface would begin to settle, another surge of anger would break.

"I miss them, Lunaris." His grip on the rail weakened. "I feel adrift without them. They are my purpose." Lucius struggled not to allow his sad frustration and self-pity to overtake his rage. He knew that if he allowed himself these moments of weakness, he would be dead. It was that simple, that terrifying. "What am I doing here?" his voice was a hoarse croak. Lunaris nudged him and leaned his thick neck over Lucius' shoulder. "At least I have you...and the Dragons."

He stopped abruptly as the outside door opened and closed, noise invading the space for a few, brief seconds. Barta was approaching from the opposite direction.

"Anguis. Barta." Dagon nodded to both men. "Thought I would find you still here." The young king looked at the tall Sarmatian for something, but Barta shook his head slightly, looked down. Dagon turned back to Lucius. "Anguis, an Imperial dispatch rider has just arrived from Eburacum. Orders from the emperor."

"Where is he now?" Lucius pet Lunaris one more time and stepped out of the stable.

"I've left him with some of the men at the drill hall office. He's a Praetorian."

"Then we shouldn't keep him waiting." Lucius pulled his hood back over his head and the three men strode out into the rain.

III

CULTRI IN TENEBRIS

'Knives in the Dark'

The exercise hall that had been the former Principia was a large, covered space with an observation platform at the eastern entrance. The air was humid and scented of mould. Rainwater dripped in the dark corners of the rafters, but the structure was solid enough and well-used. At that late hour it was dark, with only a few torches providing flickering orange light where they protruded from braces on the surrounding columns.

Lucius, Dagon and Barta entered briskly through the tall oak doors. Ten guards stood at intervals in the half-light, and in the centre of the dirt floor of the hall stood the Praetorian messenger. The man was calm, infused with confidence in the imagined invincibility his position afforded him. Lucius suppressed his annoyance; apart from his friend Alerio Cornelius Kasen, who had been made a Praetorian centurion, he trusted none of the Imperial Guard. Lucius strode straight up to the messenger, flanked by Dagon and Barta.

"You have dispatches for me?" He held out his hand for the leather carrying tube, but the man did not offer it.

"Praefectus Lucius Metellus Anguis?" He looked Lucius up and down.

"Of course. Who else?" Lucius still held out his hand.

"Just checking, sir. You are not known to me personally." He finally handed Lucius the tube. "I have only heard you spoken of by Centurion Cornelius."

Lucius looked up. "Did Alerio send you? What is your name, soldier?"

"I am Crato. Caesar Caracalla sent me via Centurion Cornelius."

"How nice for you." Lucius replied, unimpressed. "Where is the imperial force now?"

"I have heard that you have apprehended the Boar of the Selgovae."

Dagon looked at Lucius, not succeeding in hiding his surprise very well. Lucius studied the man more closely.

"We have, yes. I have dispatches for you to carry back, requesting a detachment to pick up all the prisoners."

Dagon handed the messenger a sealed scroll. The man nodded and tucked it beneath his cloak. He stared at Lucius."

"May I see the prisoner?"

"Which one? There are many."

"The Boar, of course. I-"

"I'm afraid that's not possible," Lucius cut him short. "He's surrounded not only by my men, but by hundreds of his warriors. I have him in a secret place. Secure until he is moved to Eburacum. I'm sure the emperor would like to meet him."

"Is he in this building?" the man persisted.

"A *secret* place. You understand, I'm sure. We can't risk him being rescued. The walls have ears… and I wouldn't want you to be disciplined for going beyond your messenger's duties."

"Of course," the man relented and turned to go.

"You haven't answered my question. Where is the imperial army?"

"Still in Eburacum. But there is movement." The man put his hood on and made to leave. "Just read the dispatches, Praefectus. It's all in there."

Lucius knew he would get no information from the man. He could feel Barta tense behind his shoulder.

"Do you require quarters? We have a couple spare beds in the barracks, I believe."

"I don't think so, Praefectus. I've taken rooms in the mansio for the night."

"Very well." Lucius paused, remembered his duty as host commander. "If you require anything else, notify my men."

Without another word, the messenger withdrew quickly out of the doors and into the rain. Lucius watched, silent, where the firelight splashed on the wet flagstones outside.

"Have him watched, Dagon."

"The messenger?"

"He's no messenger." Lucius looked at Barta. "See the string of blades beneath his cloak?" Barta nodded. "No mail messenger carries weapons like that. He's a Praetorian spy."

The three men went back into the night to the commander's house and the Sarmatian guards inside the exercise hall shut the doors and barred them from the inside.

Lamplight licked the darkness about the disarrayed campaign table where Lucius sat in his quarters. It was well past the sixth hour of darkness and the rain had finally taken its ease. Harvest moonlight breached the small windows at his back as he stared at the remaining unopened message – the one from his wife.

He had left that one for last, partly because it was the one he most looked forward to, but also because his warring self was fearful of weakness. They had been apart for a long while now. Had Adara changed? He knew he had, and that alone caused him apprehension.

There had been two dispatches from Eburacum. The first was from Caesar Caracalla relaying the emperor's plans and praising the Sarmatian cavalry under Lucius' command. Caracalla always said more in person, but his tone was oddly congenial and full of camaraderie as he stated his eagerness to join the men of the Legions on the campaign march. Despite Caesar's tone, however, Lucius knew better than to fall into a false sense of security. The man was a chimera of emotion.

The other letter was from Alerio and it filled the gaps left by the Caesar's generalities. The emperor was pleased with the progress the Ala III Britannorum was making, and he promised a long furlough for Lucius and his men once they had secured a position far enough to the North. Which was where they were to push on to. Lucius was being commanded to push hard up to the very edges of the Caledonian highlands, moving in conjunction with the VI and XX Legions. Supply lines would be secured by re-establishing some of the old marching camps including the iron Gask frontier forts. Once that was done, supplies and more troops could be brought in easily by sea.

Before any of that could happen, Lucius knew he had to renew the treaty and oaths of the Votadini to the East. They had been strong Roman supporters for many years, trained in Roman tactics, and had been the only ones to keep the

Selgovae in check. Sentiment however, was useless. Rome had left the Votadini to fend for themselves while it pulled back to the Great Wall. They would need reassurances, and rightly so. Lucius had sent word to their leader, Coilus, some days ago, and expected an embassy any time. The Votadini were fierce warriors and expert cavalrymen. Much depended on their support.

The rest of Alerio's message remained official in detail and tone, and Lucius wondered at what might remain of their old, once-iron friendship. There had been no assurance of Adara and the children's safety in Alerio's missive.

Having escaped into the military details for long enough, Lucius reached for the scroll from Adara and held it to his forehead briefly. Then he broke the seal, which did not appear to have been tampered with, and read.

Lucius Metellus Anguis
Praefectus, Ala III Britannorum

My beloved Lucius, husband,

It seems an age since I last looked upon you. It has been an age! It is late into the night now and I am writing as the children sleep – for it is the only time I have to myself. I hope that this message actually reaches you, my love.

First of all, though you may already know this, we are safe in Eburacum. This has been an arduous journey, the sea voyage from Ostia to Massilia was trying, but the crossing from Gesoriacum was positively terrifying, despite our offerings to Poseidon. Perhaps the waters surrounding Britannia are less known to him? It was even worse than my crossing to Africa years ago when I was pregnant with the children, and Alene was still with us. Do you remember that blackened sky?

It was good to have broken the journey over land from Massilia to Lugdunum on the way to Gesoriacum. Gaul really is quite beautiful in places and as I said in my last letters, I still think you would love seeing Alesia which I know you read about in your copy of the Divine Julius' memoirs.

I am rambling now. I know. I just miss you so much I need to tell you everything that is in my mind. The children listen as best as they can but are eventually drawn from their mama's reminiscences to their toys. Who can blame them, really? They are so grown up, Lucius, so smart. I hear all the other mothers following the Imperial court, as I am, expounding on the virtues of their advancing offspring but I am convinced that ours are truly blessed, touched by the Gods. Dare I say it? I must smile at my own pride but they are truly wonderful and take after you and I both. Phoebus has many questions about you and is always practicing with the wooden gladius you gave him before leaving. It is still heavy for him but he is improving, his movements smooth and swift. Calliope is dreamy as ever and full of questions about the stars, the Gods and all manner of things. She loves bedtime stories, especially the one you used to tell her about Perseus and Andromeda. I try but it is not the same, I think. She still sings ever so sweetly. Alene's songs...always singing. They miss you so much but I think I do most of all, Lucius. There is a painful void in the recesses of my heart while we are apart. I must get back to you, the other half of my soul, as Plato said. I can not explain it well. I have had nightmares, so many that I have made offerings to

Morpheus regularly – the dreams have abated but I still fear. Calliope assures me you are well and with such utter certainty she gives me great comfort. But, Lucius, my love, some images haunt me. Beware of fire, round fire. I can not find other words, nor do I wish to dwell on it. I prefer to live in Phoebus and Calliope's bright optimism.

News from home. It seems it is easy to get letters to me where I am in the imperial train and so your mother has been sending word to me of the family. Your brother, Caecilius, is well and learning to run the estate in Etruria, helping out your mother. Our sculptor friend, Emrys, has been helping a great deal too and has been an invaluable support to your mother. He's even figured out how to deal with Numa and Prisca. What a sight! I think Prisca has begun to idolize Emrys whose warm charm never ceases to make her smile. Actually, Emrys is heading to Athens for a special commission and has offered to bring your mother with him so she can take up my parents' offer to come and visit them. They would love to have her and I know she would love to see all that Alene, Gods keep her, had described in her letters when we were there together long ago.

You see? I reminisce, something I do overmuch. Oh how I can not wait to be with you in the present, to live together and look forward rather than back. The children are my saving grace and I enjoy teaching them. Letters, painting, philosophy. I'm afraid, my strong Roman, that they are more Greek at this point.

But I do not know when we shall see you and that is a torment I can no longer bear. Alerio tells me, for I see him once in a while, that the only safe place for us is in Eburacum with the empress and her household. The army will be moving north for the war – I try not to think of you caught in the middle of it as I know you must be. My only comfort is that Dagon and his men love you and follow you. They will not tell me much, only that once your ala has secured one of the Caledonian frontier lines will the children and I be able to join you. The empress has been kind to us and we lack nothing. In fact all the officers' wives and children are well taken care of. However, I can not help feeling we are always being watched. Thankfully, my only wish is that this campaign ends so that we can be together.

I will stop now, for I know you are likely reading this into the late hours of darkness. For now, my Lucius, know that I love you and long for you with all of my being. You have all my, and the children's, love. Please also give my wishes to Dagon, Barta and the rest of the men. I too am offering to Epona for all of you. But most of all, I pray to Venus and Apollo. May they watch over you every moment.

Goodbye for now, my truest love.

Adara

Lucius closed his eyes, buried his face in the parchment to allow the scent of Adara's perfume to take hold of him. His mind stood on a precipice of collapse as soft emotions clung to his aching heart. His eyes began to burn beneath his tired lids. How he missed her, his young growing children, their family life back in soft, green, sunny Etruria.

Then, with a jerk, he ripped his face from the letter, remembering some of Adara's words. He scanned the script again, worry mounting, and found it. *Dagon and his men love you and follow you.* Lucius flipped the scroll over again to inspect the seal, but it did not appear to have been tampered with. Nevertheless, a skilled person would be able to heat it slightly, open the seal and re-adhere it without anyone being the wiser. That one phrase, written by his wife in a personal letter could endanger them all. Emperors did not want commanders who were loved by their troops above themselves. Too many usurpers and mutinies had been borne out of such sentiment among the soldiers.

Lucius slammed his fist on the table, breathed deeply to crush his rising panic. He had been in the imperial favour for some years now, especially since he had helped rid the emperor of Plautianus, the brutal Praetorian Prefect. Now, in far-off Britannia, at war, there were far too many military men itching to gain favour over their comrades, who would not hesitate to inform on anyone they saw as competition. Lucius Metellus Anguis, the *Dragon*, was indeed 'competition'.

"Gods protect us," Lucius whispered, casting a glance at the niche where he prayed. "Grant us swift victories as we move northward, so that I may bring my family closer to me all the sooner."

Darkness and the cold commingled perfectly in the night. There was a pervading sense of uneasiness when all nocturnal motion ceased, insects, birds and other predators. Lucius stood in the middle of a vast, barren field. The crops were burned to charred stubble, still glowing and yet, that biting cold. His feet froze in the mud, a sense of ice climbing up through his veins like roots fastening him to the ground. He was naked but for his dragon ring and he fidgeted with it as whispers pierced the darkness about him, the night littered with wraiths approaching him more with every utterance.

He shook for cold, for fear, but fought back the urge to scream. *I am not afraid! I am not afraid! I am not afraid!* He cursed to the dark, feeling heat within.

Then the ground released his feet. In that moment a note sounded, and a light pulsed. The moon, full and luminous, began to blaze where it hovered behind smoky clouds like a fire in the night sky.

Ahead of him, not twenty paces in the darkness, a lone figure of muscled mass swayed on his feet staring at Lucius beneath matted locks. The two approached cautiously, then the other spoke…

"I asked to speak with you…" he said and paused. When next he opened his mouth, the Boar of the Selgovae stood still as a red cicatrice sliced across his neck before he was yanked back into the darkness, eyes gaping at Lucius.

A circle of flame sprang up from the earth, from the depths of Hades itself, to surround Lucius. The dragons on his forearms seemed to writhe. From deathly cold to unbearable heat, Lucius felt death near and only returned to hope at the sound of galloping, thunderous hooves blasting through the ring of fire in a burst of white and red.

The horsewoman released Lucius outside the fire in the darkness again. Lucius, on his back, looked up to see stars shooting down from the heavens to burn up the wraiths as if from some heavenly bow. Standing above him then, a slender arm of warmth and familiarity reached out to him, helped him up and…

"Wake up…Lucius…"

The parchment burned on Lucius' campaign table where he had fallen asleep, and as he jerked awake, Barta burst through the door and strode over to him with a blanket to smother the hem of Lucius' sleeve which had just caught. Lucius jumped up, disoriented and stared at the charred remains of Adara's letter. The images of his dream rushed back with a sense of panic.

"My Gods," he remembered. "The Boar!" Lucius grabbed his sword and ran outside.

"Praefectus! Anguis!" Barta called after him.

Lucius looked up at the night sky as he approached the structure of the exercise hall. The moon burned ivory behind the clouds.

"Open the doors!" he commanded the two guards as he approached the torch-lit entrance. The guards, trusted men, saluted sharply and knocked with the butt end of their pila on the oak doors, their signal to the guards inside to unbar. There was a return knock and the doors groaned open. "Has anyone been through here since we left earlier?" Lucius demanded.

The men looked puzzled and shook their heads, looking at their praefectus and Barta who had just come running up. "No, sir!" answered the optio, a man named Taboras. "Not a soul's been here. All's extremely quiet."

Lucius moved into the hall. "Close the doors behind me. I'm going to see the prisoner." With that, he plunged into the darkness of the hall to a stone staircase at the far end. Barta, Taboras and one other trooper followed.

“Praefectus? Do you suspect something?” Barta asked, fingering his throwing daggers.

“Maybe, Barta.” Lucius held his sword in front, rushed into the lower reaches of the hall where the cells were located.

They stopped when they reached the bottom, the sound of dripping water audible among the stone and iron cells. Lucius took in the scene with his accustomed quickness. There was a pained grunt at the far end and he rushed toward the guttering torches facing the Boar’s cell. A flash of steel and another grunt.

“Hold there!” Lucius commanded, but the flicker of a shadow darted toward a far corner just ahead of one of Barta’s daggers which crashed to the stone flagging. “Where is he?” Lucius asked out loud. There was another grunt and he turned with his torch to the cell.

There in the darkness knelt the Boar, chained at the neck and arms like a brawny circus bear before the mob. He looked up at Lucius momentarily and sat back against the wall to reveal two daggers, one protruding from his right shoulder, the other, which had cut the side of his head, lay red upon the ground.

“Mars’ balls!” Lucius raged. “Get more men,” he said to the trooper. I want this place searched top to bottom for whoever did this!”

“Yes, Praefectus!” the trooper snapped and headed back to the surface. Shortly thereafter a cornu sounded, raising the alarm.

Lucius opened the cell, waving Barta back. He knelt down before the Boar. Was it him or had the lifelike tattoos upon the warrior chieftain faded?

"What did you see?" Lucius asked him. "Who was it? One of your people? A rival?"

The Boar laughed. "My rivals are all dead, Roman. And imprisoned, I am as good as dead also, to my people."

"What did he look like?" Lucius pressed. He could see the blood seeping from the shoulder wound.

"I did not see anything other than a cloaked figure and a flash of a blade."

Lucius picked up the blade on the floor and held it up to the torch light. "Barta." Lucius handed the blade to the big Sarmatian and put his finger to his mouth, his expression dark. "Taboras," Lucius called to the optio.

"Sir!"

"Go to the mansio and see if our Praetorian messenger guest is in his bed."

"Yes, Praefectus!"

"Take extra men."

The optio paused, nodded and left.

Lucius turned to the Boar. "I'll have my medicus take care of this." Lucius yanked the blade out of the chieftain's shoulder. The warrior bit down as the blade scraped bone on the way out. Lucius tied a piece of cloth around the wound as a temporary tourniquet.

"Why help me, Roman? Is my fate not to die by Rome's hand anyway?"

"Quiet. Keep your strength," Lucius answered abruptly before standing up and backing out of the cell. The trooper returned then with ten more men. "Keep a tight watch. I don't want any harm to come to him. The physician will be here shortly." The men all saluted. Lucius moved to where Barta stared at the wall where the assassin had disappeared. “Anything?”

“Nothing, Praefectus. It’s as if he vanished into thin air.” Barta looked uneasy. Lucius showed him the matching knife.

“Things that vanish don’t carry these.”

“No, Praefectus. They do not.”

The two men went back up to the drill hall which was now full of armed men. There, Taboras told Lucius the Praetorian had been in his bed at the mansio, and that he had raged that he had been disturbed.

There were no more incidents that night. When day came, it dawned clear and crisp over Trimontium, with occasional puffs of white cloud. Lucius stood in the midst of the courtyard of the commander’s house surrounded by his decurions, Dagon and Barta. From where he stood, he could see hawks wheeling and diving around the distant peaks, revelling in the gusts of wind. His crimson cloak whipped about him, bringing him back to the Praetorian before him.

“Praefectus! Are you listening to me?” the man yelled and Barta stepped up. Lucius quickly put a hand out to stop him. Crato sneered.” Careful barbarian or I’ll have you flayed.”

“That’s enough!” Lucius boomed in his parade ground voice. He moved one step closer to the Praetorian who was much smaller but who did not bat a lid. “You may have special privileges with that uniform you’re wearing, but this is *my* command and nobody, *nobody*, threatens my men.”

“Your men? Yours? These are all men in the service of his Imperial Majesty Septimius Severus, your emperor. These are not *your* men!”

"We all serve the emperor and while the emperor is away, I command and guard this ala, these men, in his name. You would do well to remember that, Crato." Lucius stepped back a little, eyeing the man, "And," he added, "if I see fit to wake you in the middle of the night to carry out an investigation of a cowardly act, I will do so."

Crato was fuming and struggled to regain his composure under the gaze of the tattooed Sarmatian warriors about him. But he did, and managed to cloak his rage.

"Very well," he said. "Do you have any other dispatches?"

"Yes." Lucius held out a small, sealed scroll. "In addition to the one given you yesterday, this one outlining the incident last night." The Praetorian showed no sign of surprise. "I have a copy in our files as well. For the record."

"Of course, Praefectus." The man turned to leave. He seemed eager to be away.

"Wait. One more thing," Lucius said, Crato stopping and half turning toward him.

"What?" he snapped.

"You may want these." Lucius produced the throwing daggers that had been used on the Boar the night before and tossed them to the ground between himself and the messenger. The clang was ten times louder in the courtyard than it would have been elsewhere. Lucius and the Sarmatians all stared darkly at the Praetorian.

"Humph! I've never seen those in my life. You should be more careful, Praefectus," he spat. "Those look quite dangerous, wherever they came from." With that, he went out into the street where his horse was being held for him.

Dagon stepped up to Lucius as he stooped to pick up the daggers.

"You have a knack for making enemies, Anguis. That one will be back."

"Yes he will. I fear he is the small fish."

"Amongst my countrymen, it is a serious matter to lay a dagger down between two men. You have thrown two between yourself and one of Caesar Caracalla's men." Dagon sighed, struggling as he usually did when reconciling the superstitions of his homeland and the hard business of war. "Perhaps centurion Alerio will be able to give some insight?"

"Perhaps, Dagon." Lucius snapped to and addressed the assembled decurions. "I want the guard on all the Selgovae prisoners doubled at all hours. Tripled on the Boar. We should start preparing the entire ala to move out. I want to head northward as soon as the prisoners are picked up by VIth Legion and once we have met with the Votadini leaders. Make your preparations. You all know your business." Lucius raised his voice slightly. "Let's show these Praetorians how real warriors behave!"

The courtyard reverberated as the usually quiet men roared their agreement, chanting, "Anguis! Anguis! Anguis!" as they dispersed.

"His wounds have been bound and stapled. He is well now," Dagon added.

"It'll take more than a couple of daggers to kill the Boar, you can be sure of that. I'll go and speak with him."

"When?"

"Now. You take over for inspection."

Dagon saluted as Lucius went into the street, Barta several paces behind.

IV

SOCII

'Allies'

The stairs that led to the lower level cells of the exercise hall had dried considerably with all of the extra torches and the passage of guards. They watched over the Boar of the Selgovae on the other side of the final set of bars, at the end of the subterranean corridor.

The Boar was calm where he sat on the straw-covered floor, legs bent, elbows on his knees. He knew it was only a matter of time before he was taken to a public place to be strangled in front of the provincial populace. And yet, he was calm, ready. The Morrigan had seen him fight the Dragon in war. He had lost, and so his time on this land was at an end. But he knew his name would live, his deeds, as having stood against the Roman invaders rather than being bought for buckets of silver.

He would die their enemy, not one of them as Caractacus had, long before, when he was taken to Rome itself and made his case to the wretched Claudius. Caractacus had a path, and the Boar knew his own. He would not go to Rome an oddity, a freak. He would die on the island he loved.

Severus was not going to leave until all Caledonia was subdued, and the Boar knew it.

He was ready for when it came, death that is. But he would have liked to have held his wife once more, and played with his children, all nine of them. *The price of losing in battle? Perhaps.* He did wish to speak with the Dragon, however, an enemy that he had never seen the likes of, an enemy that sought to heal and protect him.

The footsteps coming slowly down the corridor told him that he would now be able to.

When Lucius came to the last cell, the Boar was waiting, looking up at him from between the lengths of his matted locks. It struck Lucius that the chieftain looked calm, almost confident, despite his incarceration.

"There is magic lighting your movement. Your gods love you," the Boar said.

"Leave us," Lucius said to the guards who stood in the shadows.

"Praefectus!" They saluted and moved to the end of the corridor to stand with a few more of their comrades. The Sarmatians watched warily as their commander approached the bars.

"For a while, I did not think you would come," the Boar said as he stood slowly, betraying the effects of his shackles.

"Well, I'm here now," Lucius replied, obviously uncomfortable. "How are you wounds?"

"Fine. I've had worse." The Boar stood straight, stretched his oak-like torso, the boar tattoo bristling. "How are my people? Giving you trouble, I hope."

"No end of it," Lucius eased a bit. "They're a constant headache. There have been three attempts to break out and free you. They're lucky none of them was killed."

"Hmm. You do not understand them, Dragon." He moved to lean on the bars not two feet from Lucius' face. "That is exactly what they want, not to break free, for they know that is now impossible, but to die fighting."

"They want to be hacked by a Sarmatian long-sword, or impaled on a kontos?"

"What is the alternative? To be sent away from our land to some inferno of a mine, a slave in darkness? To die entertaining Romans as they stuff their fat faces in the arena? No. Death now, with a sword or dagger in hand, or bare-fisted to strike a final blow. It is the only honourable way for a Selgovan warrior to leave this world."

"Many who survive the arena, if that is where they go, win their freedom eventually." Lucius knew this was empty, but tried to offer some hope. He felt ashamed for having even said it and stared at the floor. "Why did you want to speak to me?"

"Why did you let me live? Why heal my wounds?"

"You may yet be allowed to live."

"Come now. The weight that I see pressing down on your armoured shoulders tells me that you have had a taste of Roman politics. You know they will not let me live. They cannot. They have already tried to kill me, but you stopped them. You will wish you had not done that."

"If there is a chance that you live, you and your family might live under the Pax Romana."

"Like the tribes of the South? No. They sold their souls to Rome and lost their way of life. Now they dress and live as Romans."

"I have a good friend who is Dumnonian, and a sculptor of great renown about the Middle Sea."

"Pah!" the Boar scoffed. "Dumnonians are Romans now. I'm of the ancient Selgovae, and always will be. Until I die that is, which I hope will be soon."

"What of your family? Have you any children?" Lucius noticed the Boar relax at this and slump his shoulders ever so slightly.

"I fought for my family, my people. And yes, I have nine children."

"Nine?"

"Ha!" the Boar laughed proudly. "Yes, nine - five sons, and four daughters. Tell me, how would I inspire them by becoming a Roman? I would not. But by dying in battle, they would be able to hold their heads high, proud that their father, the Boar of the Selgovae, died for them and our people. My death will kindle a fire in their hearts that will not easily sputter."

The chieftain stood tall, strong and proud in that moment, looking to a time and place far beyond the confines of his dank cell.

Lucius could not help but admire the warrior's straight-forward thinking.

"What if…if you are executed in Eburacum? It will not be with a blade in your hand, but by strangulation. What then?"

This hit home.

"I do not believe the Morrigan will abandon me completely. In the end, she will grant me my warrior's death, for I have offered her many enemies."

"May that be so. I have a family too…what I would not do to be with them in peace."

"Peace? How can peace be had when you serve Rome? You are one of the greatest warriors I have ever met, Dragon. Your men are a true force of nature. Why would Rome allow you to withdraw when they can use you beside her legions of butchers?"

"You underestimate our legions."

"I do not, but what would we be but stalks of scythed wheat if we did not stand against Rome's might?"

"Futility is the word that springs to mind."

"Perhaps. But, mighty Dragon, is it not also futile to chain you and your family to Rome?"

Lucius stepped to the bars. "I am Roman," he said through gritted teeth. "My ancestors were Roman."

"Yes, but I have a sense you are more than that. This symbol," he pointed to the tattoo on Lucius' forearm where he gripped the bars, "and the symbols on your armour, your ring, the sword at your back, all of it sings of something more."

"What? Are you also a poet to your people?"

"Ha! No. Poetry is shit. I am, however, one to see that you have not yet found your place. If being with your family is your goal, if peace is your goal, fight your way free of Rome's iron grasp. A dragon should not be chained, but many free men would be led by one."

"Why are you telling me all of this? Fighting my way free to my family will mean crushing every tribe from here to your highlands."

"Futility for both sides then. It is the nature of the warrior's song, is it not?" The Boar stepped back, hands at his sides. "I tell you these things as one warrior, a leader of men, to another." He nodded and looked at Lucius again. "In the past, when I have sought to unchain myself of fear, of anger, of the burden of leadership, I have climbed to the peak of a tall mountain and screamed and yelled until my gods have given me a sign, until I have felt free."

"And that works?"

"When your Roman walls are closing in on you to crush your spirit, you should try it."

Just then, the sound of approaching hobnails echoed in the corridor.

Lucius recognized the sound of Dagon's sure step.

"Praefectus." Dagon saluted formally then glanced at the Boar.

"Yes, Princeps. What is it?" Lucius still stared at the caged Boar, disturbed by the chieftain's frankness.

"The Votadini are arriving." Dagon did not volunteer any more information in front of the Selgovan prisoner.

"Votadini?" The Boar smirked as he stared at Lucius and brushed back his hair, his expression dark. "Ah, the Roman sympathizers, or 'clients' as you call them. Good fighters." His gaze bore deep into Lucius' eyes. "You will need them in the bloody months to come." He spat, and Lucius turned to follow Dagon who was already on his way back down the corridor.

"Dragon!" The Boar jumped up, a hint of desperation upon him.

Lucius turned back. "What is it?"

"Think hard on what I have said. For both our sakes." He smiled, though sadly. "My parting gift to you as a brother-warrior."

Lucius turned and headed back to the surface, sunlight, and the sound of distant horns.

"What was that about?" Dagon asked as they made their way to the east gate. "Did the Boar plead for his life?" Dagon watched Lucius closely for any sign that his hard exterior might have cracked.

Silence.

"Not for his life," Lucius finally answered. He stopped at the bottom of the stairs leading up to the gatehouse tower. "He asked for a good death."

Lucius continued up the stairs, Dagon looking at his armoured back before he and Barta made their way up to join him on the battlements.

"What will you do?" Dagon pressed.

Lucius turned to face him. "I'll do what is expected. I'll hand the Boar over to sixth legion tomorrow."

"So that he can be taken in chains to Eburacum, and then thrown to the mob in Rome?"

"Since when do you care so much?" Lucius' voice had risen, and Barta glanced around at the surrounding men.

Dagon straightened to meet his praefectus' eyes. "How many battle lords have we killed since we came to Britannia, Anguis?" How many skilled warriors' bodies have we left for the crows when they would have made powerful allies who could help Rome hold this island?"

"They don't want Rome, Dagon." Lucius' voice was calm. "They're not our friends, and they don't want to be our allies."

"But we Sarmatians made our peace, didn't we? And we're a proud race."

Lucius could see Barta's neck straighten, his eyes closed momentarily to feel the wind and sun on his face. Lucius put his hands on his princeps' shoulders.

"Different times, under a different Caesar."

Dagon looked around nervously.

"You know what I mean," Lucius continued. "Severus has come to Britannia to wipe out the Caledonii and all else who stand against Rome. He's got thirty-five thousand men, his Praetorians, and auxiliaries like us to make sure it happens. We're not here to make friends. We're here to ensure our allies are still allies, and to wipe out our enemies."

Lucius turned abruptly to the East to watch the Votadini approach.

"Here come the only friends we have in this region." Lucius nodded for the cornu to sound from the opposite tower.

The sound was met by a similar signal from the other side of the river where the Votadini column made for the bridge.

"Looks like five hundred horse," Dagon said.

"Open the gates!" Lucius ordered before making his way down to where their horses were being held. "Easy, Lunaris," he soothed. He looked behind to see Dagon, and Barta hoisting the dragon vexillum high in the air. "Let's go meet out allies, then."

Dagon knew Lucius well. The look he saw was one of resigned sadness for the life he wished he was leading.

Lucius charged out of the fort's gates with Dagon and Barta behind him. Outside, on the muddy field, two hundred Sarmatians fell in behind them to go and meet the approaching Votadini. When they arrived at the bridge, Lucius ordered his cavalry to line up in two great semi-circles while he, Dagon, and Barta waited before them to meet with the Votadini chieftain.

"They look more Roman than I do," Dagon commented.

"Rome's provided them with weapons, armour, and horse harness since Antoninus built his wall. The Votadini have held this region on their own for a long time."

"They might not be happy to see us then." Dagon felt for the hilt of his long sword, that which had belonged to his uncle, Mar.

"You could be right. Let's see." Lucius did a mental check of all his weapons - the spatha at his saddle, the daggers about his waist, and Adara's sword which hung at his back. Part of him wished he had put the mask of his helmet down so as to observe the Votadini from safe anonymity.

A gust of wind licked at his red cloak, and Lunaris stomped his front hooves in the mud as the first horses approached their side of the bridge.

The Votadini were warriors, there could be no doubt, and though their arms and armour were slightly aged, they were polished and effective. Cuts and scars showed proudly beneath the outer sheen.

The lead rider carried a banner bearing a galloping white horse on a red background.

The sight gave Lucius pause as it reminded him of a dream, though he could not remember what.

The standard-bearer turned toward Lucius' own banner and stopped.

Then came the leader, an aged man whose grey hair was the only sign of advanced years. Otherwise, he was tall and proud, his bearing regal. He smiled.

"I am Coilus, Chief of the Votadini, and I welcome Rome back to the lands which are rightfully hers. Ave!" He saluted.

Lucius edged forward to get close. "Salve, Coilus of the Votadini!" Lucius saluted back. "I am Lucius Metellus Anguis, Praefectus of the Ala III Britannorum, Quingenaria Sarmatiana, serving Lucius Septimius Severus, Emperor of the Roman people and conqueror of the Parthians."

"We have been hearing much of your deeds against the Selgovae and the other rebel tribes, Praefectus. Your men are mighty upon the field."

"As have yours been in Rome's absence from these lands. Are you yet Rome's ally?"

The blunt question took Coilus by surprise, but only momentarily. The older man smiled and his laugh boomed in the valley.

"The Gods themselves could not make me turn from Rome, Praefectus!"

Lucius smiled back and the tension eased. "Then we can return to base, and break open the amphora of Falernian I've been saving."

"Oh, how I've missed the Empire," Coilus chuckled as he fell in beside Lucius and they led the way back to the fort. "This is my son, Afallach." Coilus nodded to his standard bearer, a young scowling man the same size as Lucius.

Lucius nodded to the younger man who simply stared back at him.

"I've got quarters for you and your men," he said turning back to Coilus. "Once you're settled, we can talk."

They passed beneath the gates and turned up the Via Decumana to the horse yards.

The fort erupted with noise.

"I see you've made improvements to the fortress since arriving," Coilus commented to Lucius as he looked around. "It hasn't looked this defensible in years."

"It required a lot of work, but we needed it as a secure point north of the wall. Sixth legion provided much of the man power."

"Feels like old times," Coilus smiled, removing his helmet.

Lucius removed his own and enjoyed a momentary ray of sunlight upon his face. He watched the Votadini chieftain stroke his horse's muzzle briefly and wondered if he could be trusted. He was inclined to like Coilus, his seemingly honest demeanour, but his son, Afallach, unnerved him. Lucius made a mental note to double the guard that night.

"Come," Lucius said to his guests. "Let me show you to your quarters where you can refresh yourselves before getting down to business and that wine." Lucius turned toward the southern end of the fort and the commander's house where rooms had been prepared for Coilus. "My decurion, Hippogriff, will see your men and horses taken care of."

A tall Sarmatian standing at attention nearby saluted and went about his task.

Lucius and Coilus kept walking, and Dagon, Barta, and Afallach followed.

That evening, as the Sarmatian and Votadini men ate and drank in their tents and what remained of the barrack blocks, Lucius, Coilus, Dagon, Brencis, and Afallach dined in the triclinium of the commander's house. Barta stood outside the door as usual, silent and imposing.

The plaster on the walls was old and bubbling, and the roughly hewn wood furniture not of the greatest comfort, but the room was dry thanks to the new roof, safe from the intermittent showers that seemed never to end in that region of war.

The fare was simple - fresh bread, roasted lamb shank with spiced millet, and greens.

Lucius watched his guests eat: Coilus appreciatively, Afallach slow and measured. Lucius found he was not hungry - thoughts of the Boar's words still lingered in his mind. He ate little and drank even less, and Dagon followed suit.

"How is life at, I forget the name of your fortress…" Brencis, clearly uncomfortable with the silence, tried to engage Afallach in conversation. "The 'Curia' is it? I've heard it called that."

The question was innocent enough, but it brought Afallach to a seated position.

"It is called Dunpendyrlaw, Roman."

Brencis held up his hands. At a look from Lucius, he dismissed the thought of reaching for his pugio.

"Peace, friend. I knew not of that name."

Afallach reclined again, his eyes on the young Sarmatian.

"And I am no more Roman than you," Brencis added. "Our praefectus here is the only Roman in this entire fort, I'll wager."

"Ha, but not in loyalty!" Coilus clapped his hands and shot an angry glance at his son. "All of us here are loyal to Rome, Praefectus. Have no doubt. Tomorrow, the Votadini will renew their sacramentum to the emperor before all your men. I see that this has been troubling you, and so I wish to put your mind at ease."

"I've been at war in these parts for many months," Lucius said, placing his cup on the squat table before them. "Allies have been few and far between."

"Understood. Well, we are here now."

"And we," Afallach jumped in, "have been fighting, alone, on Rome's behalf for years. Since Rome tucked tail and withdrew from Antoninus' wall, it has been us, and us alone who have held the Selgovae at bay."

"And Rome thanks you for it," Lucius said, low and evenly to the young Briton. "It may be that bad decisions were made in the past, but this is a new emperor. Severus intends to take all of Caledonia by storm and put an end to the rebellions that plague this frontier."

Coilus and his son were silent.

Lucius realized he may have spoken out of turn, but he could not stop now.

"You'll enjoy your Pax Romana soon. The emperor conquered the Parthian Empire where every Roman who tried had failed. The Caledonii will prove much easier a conquest," he said, but as he did so, a chill ran the length of his spine.

"Fine words, Praefectus," Afallach scoffed. "I fear you will dine on them."

"Peace!" Coilus' fist grabbed hold of his son's wrist. "You insult our hosts." He turned back to Lucius and Dagon. "Ever since we have heard you defeated and captured the Boar of the Selgovae, he's been of a foul disposition."

“Why’s that?” Dagon asked. “I’d heard he was a nightmare for the Votadini. Surely you must be happy he’s to die?”

“No.” Afallach stood then, his strong frame’s shadow dancing on the wall behind him as the brazier crackled. “It has been my aim to defeat him on the field once and for all.”

“He’s a great warrior,” Lucius commented.

“And he was to be mine,” Afallach stated. He looked wounded, truly disappointed. “Tell me, Praefectus, how many of your cataphracts did it take to bring him down? Five? Ten?”

“Didn’t you know?” Brencis smiled behind his cup. “The Dragon ate the Boar on his own.”

Afallach looked crestfallen.

Dagon watched Lucius rise and stand before Afallach. That look again…sadness.

“It was quite sad, really,” Brencis continued. “A short battle unworthy of the stories we’d heard.”

That’s enough!” Lucius barked over his shoulder. “I’ll not have a great warrior have humiliation heaped upon him when he fought so bravely.” Lucius turned back to Afallach. “What’s done is done. There will be plenty of other enemies to kill.”

Then Afallach grabbed Lucius’ forearm and pleaded.

“Let me meet him in single combat tomorrow, Praefectus.”

“What? Sit down!” Coilus demanded, but his son ignored him.

“I can’t do that,” Lucius answered.

“There used to be an amphitheatre down by the river,” Afallach continued. “Let me meet him there to fight as our ancestors fought. Let me gain this glory for my people!”

Everyone stared at the young man, his eyes burning with a fervour they could all understand in some way.

"Don't be ridiculous!" his father bellowed, embarrassed. "The Boar would tear you to pieces. Do you forget the great Votadini warriors he's sent to the Underworld, the settlements he's burned?"

"I don't forget, Father. Do you?"

"Get out!" Coilus growled.

Lucius watched the young man go and nodded to Barta to make sure he returned to his quarters. He then sat down and took a sip of wine. It was a minute before Coilus gathered himself again.

"I must apologize, Praefectus. I had no idea he would say such a thing. Afallach clings to our old ways much as I cling to Rome. He lost two brothers to the Boar, and his sister, Lucretia, was taken as a slave. Some say she was sent to the Ulstermen across the sea..." Coilus hung his head and then drained his cup.

"Drink, friend," Dagon said as he refilled the aged chieftain's cup.

"Our people are proud," Coilus continued. "The Votadini are the finest horsemen in Britannia, erm...until you arrived." He nodded to the Sarmatians. "We have a great past, and I've no doubt that our future, however long that may be, will be greater. But...I will not lie. Our loyalty to Rome has cost us dearly."

"Why did you remain loyal to Rome?" Lucius asked. "There was no guarantee of another campaign north of the wall."

Coilus looked Lucius in the eyes.

"The world is different when you have children to hand it to. In a way, you fight more fiercely to preserve it. Our people thrived under the Pax Romana. I wanted my children to grow up in a world guided by Rome's light."

Coilus rose and moved to stand beside the brazier and stare into the flames.

"I wanted my children to have an education, to see the Empire for all that it offers. I wanted them to know that the world is more than a grass and rock fortress at Dunpendyrlaw."

Before turning, Coilus wiped a tear from his cheek, and Lucius realized the hardship that Rome had given the Votadini for a few bits of bloody silver and gold.

"Most of my children are dead now. Only Afallach remains. He is the only one that I can pass my dreams to now… And the Selgovae and Caledonii would take that away from me as well." He sat down heavily. "That is why I remain loyal to Rome, Praefectus."

Lucius had no words of comfort, for any attempt would be an insult. He raised his cup, as did Dagon and Brencis.

"To you, Coilus, and the Votadini. We are honoured to fight alongside you with Epona herself whispering on the wind."

They all drank and were silent for a while before going their separate ways for the night.

A short while later, with Hippogriff and Ferda guarding Lucius' door, the praefectus was finally allowed to shed his armoured skin and be alone. It had been a difficult evening.

Coilus' words had been upsetting, hard and real, and Afallach's plea disturbing. However, it was the Boar's words that still haunted Lucius. He splashed his face with water from a bronze bowl sitting atop an iron tripod beside his bed. After drying, he sat down rubbing his wrists and the coiled dragons that writhed about his forearms. He looked at the dragons wrapped about his finger, and upon the hilt of the sword beside his bed. His armour. His greaves…

It all sings of something more... the Boar had said. *A dragon should be chained by no one...*

Lucius closed his eyes and allowed himself to miss Adara and the children. They were in Britannia now, and yet, he could not get to them.

Severus' war machine moved only forward, and Lucius' ala was the probing spearhead of the van. In that land of low-lying cloud, it was almost impossible to see moon or stars, to speak his wife's name to the night sky, as he had in Africa, and know that she would hear and answer him.

He began to polish his armour and helmet slowly, his mind passing over the surfaces, searching for calm.

When he finished, Lucius went to the small stone altar beneath the high square window in the wall. The statues of Apollo and Venus stared down at him from their niche in the plaster. The new statue of Epona sitting atop her magical horse, hair blowing back, completed the triad.

He lit a chunk of incense and laid it on top of the stone altar. The room was dim with orange light, and the shadowed features of the gods shivered before him.

"Gods who watch over me," he began. "Please guide me in the time to come. My heart and mind are awash with doubt, and anger, and rage." He breathed, deeply, a shudder running through his body. "Please help me to end this war quickly so that I may rejoin my family all the sooner. I worry for them. Please let there be friendly eyes watching over them, that they may be safe. I would be with them soon, in peace. Already I feel this war has gone too long. And… I feel a shadow hanging over it. Please guide me, my mind, my sword, and spear… Gods, do you hear me? If you do, please whisper to Adara that I love her, and to Phoebus and Calliope that I will see them soon."

Lucius opened his eyes and felt alone. In the Temple of Apollo, on the Palatine Hill, he knew the god heard him. Beneath the full moon in the Numidian desert, the Gods would come to him and offer him comfort. But there, in Britannia, at the edge of the civilized world, he was unsure if the Gods even heard his prayers. Only Epona had appeared to him, on the fringes of battle.

He remembered the Boar again, and his talk of futility and making himself heard by the Gods.

Lucius backed away from the altar and looked out the high window. The sound of rain had stopped, and behind several teeth of cloud, a half moon struggled to be seen. The silver light called to him, and a moment later, he was strapping on his boots, pugio, and sword.

He considered the bull's hide cuirass for a minute, but opted for thick layers of wool beneath his long black cloak.

I'll be invisible tonight.

When Lucius opened the door to his rooms, Ferda and Hippogriff stood to attention.

"At ease," Lucius said. "I'm going out for some fresh air."

"Yes, Praefectus!" the Sarmatians answered and saluted.

"Stay here. No one is to enter my quarters."

The men nodded and watched Lucius head outside. They spotted Barta returning to relieve them, and nodded quickly in the direction Lucius had gone.

Barta followed. Dagon, his lord and king, had ordered him never to let Lucius out of his sight.

Lucius walked as quietly as he could past the stables and to the gate of the west annex. He saluted several guards who recognized him, and then silently cursed himself for having forgotten that he had doubled the guard that night.

With the Votadini, there were men everywhere, dicing, caring for the horses, and trading tales with off-duty Sarmatians. Their love of horses seemed to be the common ground. Lucius hoped that this would strengthen their battle bond when it came time to charge the Caledonii.

All the while, the large silent shape of Barta followed, his eyes taking in every scene that Lucius walked through until they were outside the walls, walking across the fields toward the sleeping peaks of Trimontium.

It was a long walk, but Lucius' stride never faltered. He pressed on for close to an hour until he reached the slopes of the north hill, and began to climb.

Stray moonlight caught Lucius' sword blade, and Barta drew his own spatha. Lucius stopped, head cocked beneath his cloak, before continuing. Barta shook his head and followed, looking out for Selgovan shadows, listening for slipping steps on the patchy areas of shale.

As he climbed, Lucius felt the world go quieter. The bustle of the base and neighing of over a thousand horses vanished, leaving him only with the beat of his heart, his footfalls, and the sighing of the wind. Finally, he reached the top and peered out over the edge, his sword out before him.

Patrols had reported activity up there previously, but at that moment it seemed quiet.

Lucius walked to the middle of the rock and grass area where a fire pit and a couple of structures had once stood. The air was thick, it seemed, with ghostly whispers of Celts and Romans who had made the climb for one reason or another. However, the round houses were long gone, and the signal station torn to the ground since the legions had last moved through. The wind began to pick up, and the clouds were brushed away.

Lucius paced like a caged animal, his sword swinging, his cloak whipping about his legs.

He resented being there in Britannia, and his anger began to boil inside.

"Gods!" he yelled into the wind. "Hear me!" his voice was lost.

Barta, who had just reached the top was about to charge up to Lucius' aid when Lucius called out his wife's name. The Sarmatian held back.

"Adara!" Lucius yelled.

The Boar had said that his gods heard him when he yelled from the heights, but Lucius' prayers had always been uttered in quiet confidence.

"Ahhhh!" he let out a desperate cry, his mind reeling with memories of bloody battles, of numerous enemies on the end of his sword or spear point. "Ahhhh! AHHHH!"

When he had exhausted his voice, Lucius fell to his knees in the windy dark, and gazed up at the moon and silvery stars.

A whining pierced his hearing then and the pit before him suddenly burst into intense flames of orange and then blue. Lucius stumbled back rubbing his eyes. When he opened them, what he saw made him shake.

Far-Shooting Apollo stood there, with Venus beside him.

The stars whirled in their eyes and the muted glow about them reflected the blueness of the sacred flames.

I knew you would come, said a voice that belonged to neither of the deities.

From out of the dark, beyond the ring of light, emerged Epona, her three white hounds at her heels. Her red-gold hair seemed to float about her wild eyes.

Then all three of the gods moved close to Lucius.

Why do you cry out in anger? Venus asked. The softness of her voice made Lucius want to weep. He bowed to her, wishing for her to touch him as she had so long ago.

But she stayed back.

Apollo instead stepped forward, the tip of his silver bow planted in the ashen earth beside the fire. He did not smile.

"My Lord," Lucius bowed.

Why do you doubt that we can hear you, Metellus? The god's muscled arm and hand hovered over Lucius' head and a wave of calm washed over the mortal man. *Do you forget us, after all these years?*

"No, Lord," Lucius answered, his eyes fixed on the blue flames, his mind straying to the bright goddesses beyond.

Do you forget the blessings of Eagles, of the fullness of a moon, and the promise of the stars above?

Lucius felt like a child then, and fought his tears of frustration, hurt, and loneliness. “Help me, oh Far-Shooting Apollo. I am lost…”

You are not! Apollo answered. *You are on the path you have chosen and we…* he glanced back at his heavenly sister and cousin, *We are there when you need us. But there are times when we must not alter the course of events in the life of man. You have always doubted yourself, your gifts. It is time to truly believe, no matter the consequences.*

The words were ominous and terrifying to Lucius, and he struggled to stand despite his shaking in the presence of the Gods.

Venus, her golden hair tumbling about her shoulders, brushed past her brother, despite Apollo’s move to stop her. The goddess’ hand reached out to Lucius’ face and closed eyes, stopping just short and passing over his brow and temple. *Remember your true love and children,* her voice whispered in his mind, a ray of light in a world of storm clouds. *Do not forget or forsake your greatest gifts, especially when the final test comes.*

Stop this! Apollo’s eyes blazed like comets in the night sky. *You go too far!*

Love must always go too far, Brother, she replied, though she did stand back.

“Please watch over my family,” Lucius asked, his eyes opening and finding Venus’.

She nodded, but said nothing.

Down in the valley, a cock crowed, signalling the coming of day.

We must go now, Metellus. The Charioteer is coming to light the world. Then, Apollo looked with compassion upon one of his favourites, as a father who realizes he has been too harsh. *Know that wherever you are, Lucius Metellus Anguis, there too shall our light follow.*

"Thank you," Lucius looked at them both and an instant later the blue flames exploded and Lucius was back on his knees, gripping his sword.

We are not all gone, Epona said, kneeling down beside the Roman. She reached out and laced her smooth, pale arm beneath Lucius' arm. *Stand now. And let your strength return for the coming battles.*

She was close, and her hair blew about Lucius' face like a soft spring rain. Her hounds circled them, a ring of white and red.

I am with you and your men, Dragon.

"I know, Goddess," Lucius managed. "I have felt you near."

And I have accepted your offerings, she replied. *Now accept my help as you and your horsemen go to war.*

"And my family?"

She smiled. *I said I would help.*

Lucius, not knowing what had come over him, took her lithe hand in his and made to bring it to his lips.

Epona stared intently at him and spoke before she vanished to the sounds of birds.

Behind you!

There was a shuffle of feet and Lucius spun with his sword out to slice off the leg of an attacking Selgovan warrior.

Two more rushed in.

"Kill the Dragon!" they yelled.

Lucius leapt back as his blade just cut the first man's windpipe, and the other fell behind with Barta's dagger planted in his chest.

On the other side of the peak, the big Sarmatian stood there breathless, the first rays of morning light glinting on his armour.

Lucius looked at him and nodded.

Barta strode over and dispatched the two writhing enemies. Then he spat on them.

"How long were you there?" Lucius asked.

"I followed you from camp, Praefectus."

Lucius looked at the three corpses. "I'm glad you did, my friend." He put his hand upon the Sarmatian's shoulder. "Anything else?" Lucius wondered how much Barta had heard of his weakness, if he had seen the Gods.

Barta looked at the ground, a minute trace of awe, or was it fear, on his bearded face?

"A man's prayers are his own, Praefectus. Wherever you lead us, there too shall we follow to fight at your side." He sheathed his sword and stood tall again.

Lucius smiled. *Such loyalty. I never imagined....*

They began the descent to the plain below and made their way back across the sodden field to the base. Smoke streamed from within the walls as the morning fires were kindled, and the cornu sounded the watch.

Many things were to happen at once that day.

As Dagon helped Lucius to arm himself in full armour in preparation for the Sacramentum ceremony, Brencis arrived to report that a patrol had spotted a cohort from VIth Legion. Apparently, they had been sent from Coriospitum to take the Boar back to Eburacum.

"Their tribune ordered that the prisoners be made ready," Brencis added sarcastically. "Oh, and our Praetorian messenger is with them."

"Perfect," Lucius worked his jaw. It was going to be a long day. He had wanted to speak further with the Boar, even though he did not know why. "Brencis, I want the prisoner fed and given a clean tunic and bracae."

"Praefectus?"

"You heard me."

"Yes, sir." Brencis saluted and spun.

"One more thing!" Lucius added, his heart beating faster. "I don't want him shackled. Just his arms tied in front. And tell him I'll speak with him before handing him over."

Brencis looked at Dagon, then went to carry out the orders.

"You sure that's wise?" Dagon asked as he fastened Lucius' crimson cloak with a blue and red enamelled brooch.

"As long as he is under my care, I'll not see him humiliated."

"Anguis, I never question your actions-"

"This is not the time to start."

"I trust you. The men trust you. I just wouldn't want them to lose faith in you."

"Have *you*, Dagon?" It was not accusatory.

"Never," Dagon answered immediately.

Lucius gripped his armoured forearm and turned to pick up his helmet. "Assemble the men and the Votadini outside the east gate for the Sacramentum."

"I will. You're not going back up the mountain, are you?"

Lucius smiled. "No. I'm going to see the Boar."

"I see we had a tunic that fit you," Lucius said as he approached the bars of the Boar's cell.

"Why you Romans constantly cover yourselves, I will never understand."

"It's a long journey to the Wall without clothing."

"Yes. So, the men of the legions have come with their chains, have they?"

Lucius nodded, then turned to the two guards. "Varkan. Akil. Leave us."

"Yes, Praefectus," the two Sarmatians answered before going back up to the drill hall.

"What do you want, Dragon?"

"To wish you well." Lucius paused awkwardly. "It has been an honour to fight you…and speak with you."

The Selgovan stood up then, looking Lucius over.

"You are strange."

"Yes." Lucius smiled and turned to go.

"Did the Gods speak to you?" the Boar asked, a hint of desperation in his voice.

Lucius stopped and turned back to him. "There will always be help," he said. "Farewell."

The Boar grabbed hold of the bars and watched Lucius march down the dark corridor. As the footsteps died away, he closed his eyes, thought of his own gods, and smiled hopefully.

The sun had broken through the low clouds by the time the Sarmatian and Votadini horsemen were assembled on the field to the East of the fortress. The wind howled from the gaping mouths of the Sarmatian draconaria, and the banners of the Votadini snapped sharply.

Lucius stood on a small dais before a rough stone altar, and Barta stood behind him holding the dragon vexillum in front of Dagon, Brencis, Coilus, and Afallach.

Above them all, a tall Sarmatian named Deva held the image of Emperor Severus on a double-length pole.

Hundreds of horses and riders fanned out before Lucius as he stepped before the altar with his pugio drawn. A thick sheaf of wheat had been laid upon the altar where Vaclar approached to lay a lamb. The beast did not struggle then but seemed to look into the eyes of the foremost horses who shuffled from hoof to hoof, snorted and tossed their manes.

Lucius placed his left hand on the lamb and stroked its soft wool.

Peace, he thought. *I shall be swift.*

The moment the wind died down, and calm washed over the assembly, Lucius brought up the beast's neck and sliced deep and sure across its throat.

The lamb bleated and trembled momentarily, and then settled into the pool of its own warm blood.

Lucius wiped his pugio on a cloth given to him by Vaclar, and sheathed it. He pressed his hand into the blood so that it was covered. He then raised his bloody hand to the troops, Sarmatians and Votadini, and spoke.

"Before the gods of war, the mother of our camp, and mighty Jupiter himself, I swear loyalty to our Emperor,

Septimius Severus, and to the eternal glory of the Roman Empire!"

At the bidding of the various optios and decurions spread out among the troops, the assembly repeated the words Lucius had spoken.

Then, he continued. "I swear to wage war for my emperor and Mars, who delights in battles. I will bleed for Rome, and for my emperor, and accept that the consequences of treason and cowardice are death, and the fury of Hades."

Blood had begun to trickle down Lucius' arm as he spoke but he held his arm high and turned to the image of the emperor as the troops repeated, including Dagon, Brencis, Barta, Coilus, and Afallach, the latter reluctantly.

When the echo of their voices receded and all was quiet, but for the wind, Lucius nodded to the cornicens who blew a long note signalling an end to the Sacramentum.

"We are ready to fight for Rome, Praefectus," Coilus said as they gathered on the grass. "What are the orders?"

"Depends if we have new orders from Eburacum," Lucius answered. "If things remain the same, we'll ride for Camelon and engage the Caledonii and their allies from there. We need to re-establish the line of defence from there to the Tava."

"To the Tava?" Coilus asked. "That will be no easy task."

"None of this will be easy, I think" Lucius replied, glancing at his bloody hands.

As if in answer, another cornu sounded from the South and they all turned to see the detachment of VIth Legion approaching.

"Looks like the first cohort," Dagon observed.

Lucius stepped forward, an ill feeling in his gut. Senatorial cursus-climbers always led the legions' first, double-strength cohorts. He hoped this one would be a reasonable person and not the usual sort of arrogant bastard who wore a thick purple stripe.

"Brencis," Lucius said to the young officer. "Assemble the Selgovan prisoners so that they are ready to go. Keep the Boar separate, until last."

"Yes, Praefectus!" Brencis saluted and rode off with two decurions.

Lucius watched the approaching bull banners of the VIth Victrix. At their head he could see a tribune with a high horse-hair crest. He rode straight, with one hand on his reins, and was flanked by a centurion, his vexillarius, and a rider dressed in black that could only have been the Praetorian messenger, Crato.

"Let's go and meet them" Lucius turned to Dagon, Coilus, and Afallach. "One turmae for each of us."

Dagon and Coilus mounted up, but before Afallach could mount his own horse with the Votadini banner, Lucius grabbed his elbow, Barta watching alertly.

"Stay alert, Afallach. Anything could happen."

"What do you mean?" The young Celt stared at Lucius.

"I gave you an order," Lucius said quietly. "Did you understand?"

"Yes, but-"

"Good. Now, let's go see who leads the sixth legion."

The five of them joined the sixty four men who had been assembled and cantered across the field to meet the newly-arrived legionaries and their tribune.

"Is that him?" the tribune asked the Praetorian, Crato, who rode beside him.

"Yes, Tribune. That's him, beneath the dragon banner."

The tribune of the sixth legion's first cohort looked up at the vexillum behind him with the charging bull upon it, and stared back at the approaching horsemen.

"He seems sure of himself, this dragon praefectus," the tribune said.

"Oh, he is," the Praetorian sneered.

"We'll break him of that. He's already had his glory."

He kneed his horse into a canter and the others followed. The nine-hundred plus legionaries behind them quickening their pace.

Lucius reined in Lunaris and watched the rows of crimson-cloaked troops approach.

"Do you know him?" Dagon asked.

"Not likely," Lucius answered. "Coilus?"

"So many new commanders have been brought to Britannia for this campaign…it's doubtful."

When the tribune finally stopped before Lucius, he said nothing. He looked over Lucius and the others, and yawned.

"You are all so heavily armoured, I do not know whom I should be addressing."

Lucius saw Crato staring at him.

"You ride quickly, Praetorian," he said before turning to the tribune. "Are you leading sixth legion?"

"No," the man replied. "That would be our legate."

"What's your name and rank, then?"

"Not sure I like your tone, Praefectus. I'm tribunus of the first cohort. My name is Marcus Claudius Picus. And you are?"

"Lucius Metellus Anguis, Praefectus of Cohort III Britannorum, Quingenaria Sarmatiana-"

"And so on and so forth... All very impressive." Claudius threw his cloak back over his shoulders.

Lucius noticed the new armour and pteruges without so much as a scratch upon them. *Pompous ass!* he thought. "Well Tribune Claudius, we have the Selgovan prisoners ready for you and your men to take back to Eburacum."

"Good. I don't want to waste time. The emperor and Caesar Caracalla are on the march."

Lucius glanced at Dagon who shrugged.

Claudius smiled. "Of course. You don't know. The army will be fully assembled soon."

"You have dispatches for me?"

"Of course." Claudius kneed his mount and pressed on toward the base, forcing Lucius and the others to get out of the way of the marching legionaries behind them. "I've heard of your many deeds, Metellus," Claudius said as they rode.

Lucius noticed he had completely ignored the Votadini. "Here in Britannia, of course, but also in Africa and, well, elsewhere."

When they arrived at the east gate, Lucius and Claudius dismounted while the remaining horsemen stood in orderly rows for the prisoner transfer.

Claudius accepted a cup of wine and turned to his primus pilus.

"Centurion, order the men to ready the chains and have their weapons out. We'll need to whip these dogs back to the wall."

"Yes, sir!" The centurion saluted and began mustering the troops.

"You're welcome to camp here tonight if you wish," Lucius offered.

"Oh, I don't think so," Claudius looked about at the Sarmatians, at Coilus, Afallach, and the Votadini. "I prefer the company of my own troops."

"I meant that you could camp together outside the walls, Tribune. The base is full."

Claudius ignored him and stared at Coilus and Afallach.

"Are these our Votadini allies then?"

"Yes, Tribune." Coilus stepped forward and saluted. "I am their chief, Coilus, and this is my son and princeps, Afallach."

"I won't even try to pronounce those names. So long as you have taken the Sacramentum. That is all we need."

"We have sworn to help Rome and the emperor," Coilus said sternly.

"I should hope so."

Afallach stepped forward, but Lucius' arm was out before he could take a second step.

Claudius removed his embossed helmet and watched as the Selgovae were marched out of the gates at the tips of Sarmatian cavalry spears.

"Ugly brutes, aren't they Crato?" he said to the Praetorian whose hands were hidden beneath his cloak."

"Animals, Tribune." They laughed, making disgusted faces as the prisoners passed by.

Lucius hated the man instantly. Claudius was trying to build a name for himself, that much was sure, but there was something else. Everything the man said was intended to insult and degrade. Lucius looked him over, assessing his strength as had become his habit.

Claudius was of about the same height as Lucius, with shortly-cropped, carefully placed, black hair. He had an arrogant, aquiline nose and his build was, from what Lucius could tell, carefully tailored in the gymnasium. He was not from the battlefield, and yet, his obvious wealth meant he would have had access to training that others might not have.

It was Claudius' eyes, however, that unnerved Lucius. They were bright and cold as ice. He had seen Libyan vipers that were more trustworthy than the Patrician officer before him.

"The Selgovae don't look so tough to me," said the returning centurion to Claudius.

"No, Centurion. They don't. I wonder that they gave our new Votadini allies so much trouble." The two men and Crato laughed, as did some of the legionaries.

Lucius could see Coilus swallowing his pride at the Roman's insults. He also kept close to Afallach.

Just as the tribune began to grumble at how long it was taking, the last of the Selgovae filed past them. The jingle of chains and curses could be heard from the group of legionaries who were preparing the prisoners for the march south.

Then, all eyes turned toward the gate and the warrior chief being led out.

The Boar of the Selgovae walked slowly, with his head high. He shielded his eyes from the brilliant sun that now shone down. Before and behind him marched two Sarmatians, and the road was flanked by the tall shapes of Sarmatian horsemen whose long scale armour shifted and scraped.

Ahead, the Boar could see the remnants of his warriors, chained neck to waist to feet. When they spotted their chieftain, they stopped jostling with their new captors and watched him. He had led them into battles and on raids for years, and they had loved him. Now, he had led them to imprisonment.

Yet they looked to him as if he might still hand them victory from oblivion.

To the right, the Boar spotted the Dragon standing with the two Votadini. He smiled. He knew Coilus and his son, the latter clenching and unclenching his fists even then. Beside them, the Boar spotted the Praetorian who had tried to kill him in his cell, as well as what looked like a Roman officer. His smile faded and he looked at the Dragon again.

The nod was minute, a silent farewell from one warrior to another. But it was the flash of the Morrigan and Epona behind Lucius that fired him.

The Boar lunged at the two Sarmatians in front of him and spun them into those behind him, taking a sword and dagger at the same time. He whirled, and a second later the Praetorian messenger was falling into the officer with the dagger buried in his throat, gasping and sputtering blood everywhere.

Lucius did not need to urge Afallach forward, for that last prince of the Votadini exploded onto the road with his cavalry sword seeking death for his family's enemy.

"Stand down!" Lucius commanded the Sarmatians and Votadini horsemen who began to press in to stop the engagement.

"My son!" Coilus yelled as Lucius held him fast.

The clang of metal and desperation was deafening as all watched the Boar and Afallach hack away at each other.

The Boar ripped off the tunic he had been forced to wear, and his brilliant blue tattoos writhed over his body. His men cheered from their chains, and he smiled in the moment.

Lucius feared he had over-estimated Afallach's skill, but the young man was possessed, and skilled in single combat. It was as if he had trained his mind to that sole moment of vengeance. Afallach's blade swung faster and drove deeper than in most fights Lucius had seen.

When the Boar's fist struck Afallach across the jaw, spinning him, the momentum was not wasted.

Afallach continued to spin until his long cavalry sword bit deep into the Boar's flesh on his right arm. No sooner had that happened than he pulled it out and hacked at the Boar's leg and sent the Selgovan to his knees.

The prince pulled back, panting, his black hair matted to his face. With a final roar he drove forward and plunged his blade into the Boar's chest with a thump.

Tears flowed down his face, mixing with sweat and spattered blood as he looked into the eyes of his people's long-time enemy.

Lucius watched the Boar sway, his glazing eyes looking to the sky, and then the play of a smile upon his peaceful face.

A good death, Lucius thought.

Coilus ran to his son and held him in his arms before raising his arm to the sky. The Votadini horsemen roared for their prince, chanting his name above the disdainful raging of the tribune beside Lucius.

Dagon helped the tribune up from beneath the dead Praetorian, and the man came straight at Lucius.

"What do you think you're doing, sending an unchained prisoner like that out of his cell? You're not fit to command, Metellus!"

"We'd had no trouble with this prisoner until you showed up with him," Lucius nodded toward the Praetorian corpse.

"That prisoner should have been fully shackled!" Claudius roared, his shiny armour spattered with blood.

"It's taken care of, Tribune," Lucius said, trying to sound casual. "Good thing our allies were here to kill the Boar for you."

"You have no idea what's going on, Metellus. The Boar was to be in the emperor's triumph. You, and our allies, have taken that away."

"You still have many Selgovan prisoners to sell as slaves, never fear."

"Oh, I don't, Praefectus," Claudius said suddenly, and disturbingly recomposed. "Centurion, give the praefectus his dispatches and ready the men to move out."

"Yes, Tribune!" the centurion answered, handing some scrolls to Dagon.

"I'll see you again soon, Metellus," Claudius hissed.

Lucius stared at the Patrician as he whirled around.

"I'll be sure to greet your family in Eburacum!" he called over his shoulder.

Lucius felt Barta and Dagon's strong hands grip him from behind, just as he prepared to go after Claudius.

"It's not worth it, Anguis," Dagon whispered. "Adara and the children are safe. He's just trying to provoke you."

Lucius stopped struggling and took a deep breath as he watched the Selgovan prisoners being marched away by the men of Sixth Legion. His mind reeled and struggled for control. He was glad no one noticed. They were all crowding around Afallach and the body at his feet.

"What should we do with the Boar's body?" Brencis asked as he rode up to them.

"How close is the nearest Selgovan settlement?" Lucius asked Dagon.

"I don't know. Perhaps twenty miles west to the first farmstead."

"I want two turmae to take the body on a light cart. Leave the Boar with his own people so that they can carry out the rites."

Dagon nodded and led Brencis away to gather some men to protect the body until the turmae could be assembled.

Lucius then walked through the crowd of Sarmatians and Votadini until he reached Coilus and Afallach.

"That was a dangerous situation, Praefectus," Coilus said, his nerves finally settling.

"Your son is a magnificent fighter, Coilus. You should be proud." Lucius forced a smile.

"I am proud, Praefectus. But I was not talking about the fight." Coilus looked to the South. "I was talking about the tribune." He turned to his horse and mounted, more at home in the saddle. "I hope being your ally does not endanger my men,

Praefectus." Coilus rode into the base, followed by his horsemen.

Behind Lucius, Barta was shaking Afallach's hand.

The young man muttered something and turned to Lucius.

"Praefectus, thank you for not stopping the fight. I… I…"

He was too overcome with emotion to speak.

Lucius put a hand on his shoulder. "The Gods favoured you today, Afallach. You have made your men proud, and avenged the lives of those you have lost. You can hold your head high now."

Afallach nodded, and did indeed stand taller.

As Lucius walked Lunaris back to the stables, he prayed that his family would be kept safe until he could be with them. When that would be, he could not say. He hoped that his prayers would reach the gods he had met on the mountain and that the smoke from his offerings, as well as his actions, would please them.

V

SOMNIUM DRUIDUM

'The Druid's Dream'

An aged man woke with a jerk on his bed. This was surprising because it was rare that he ever awoke so quickly, so suddenly.

From where he lay, his eyes scanned the interior of his round house. The central fire flickered in the hearth, and his servant slept before it, a woollen blanket covering his mid-section.

It was a cold night, and so the man rose to cover the youth on the floor.

Then he noticed the blurred view of everything around him.

Ah. Of course.

He turned to see himself sleeping peacefully on his bed, his long beard hanging off of the edge, the hilt of a dagger jutting out from beneath his pillow.

The blankets would have to wait.

He moved through the oak door until he was outside beneath a starry sky. Mist clung to the ground about him, and steam rose from the damp thatch of his home. The waters surrounding him were full of night life, of hooting and twitching, mating and fighting.

He walked three paces and then stopped when he spotted the warrior standing at the water's edge.

The man's long hair ran thick over his broad shoulders, partially hiding the great boar that covered his back.

The old man covered his mouth, and the warrior turned to him, beaming.

"Greetings, Father," the Boar said.

The old man walked over to him, fighting the feelings inside.

"The Morrigan has taken you?" he asked.

"Yes, Father. It was a good death." He smiled again and, as if still vibrant with life, breathed deeply of the cold night air.

The father looked at the son he had not seen for three years, and wondered at the magnificence of him.

"Was it the Romans?"

"Yes. No. The Votadini prince and I fought. I was chained at the hands."

"I see. The harm you had done them finally came back."

"Yes," he answered, his smile fading. "It could have been worse. I was helped."

"By whom? How?" The old man looked up at his son.

"A Roman. The Dragon. It was he who captured me and my men. We spoke."

"Of what?"

"Of living, and fighting. Of a good death. If not for him, I would have been sent to Rome in chains, alive and ashamed."

"I dreamed of you fighting a dragon." He hung his head. "I'd no idea it was real this time."

"It was, Father. But I am well."

"You received the rites, then? But not from the Romans, I think."

“No. The Dragon and his men took my body back to our people.”

“Why would he do that?”

This time, the warrior shrugged. “I believe he is a good man, a great warrior.”

“Who fights for Rome.”

“Everyone fights for someone. The Dragon’s loyalty lies not only with Rome.”

“Good men,” the old man muttered, shaking his head.

“Send him some help,” the Boar said. “If not for him, I would be torn to pieces and thrown to the crows.”

The father was silent.

“Father, he and his horse warriors fly the dragon banner.”

The old man looked up. He had seen such a banner in his dreams. A thunder of hooves and scales followed by Epona herself.

“I can’t see the reason here.”

“Father, please. The Dragon speaks to the Gods. They have blessed him. He must have a part to play.”

“We all do, Cathbad, my son.”

The Boar smiled when he heard his given name.

“And my part is finished.”

“Yes.”

“Thank you for teaching me, Father.” The Boar turned to the lake which reflected the night sky and stars. “The Gods call me. I go to Annwn now, I think. I’ve always wanted to join the Wild Hunt…”

Before the old man could speak again, his son was gone.

Farewell, my son.

He made his way back into the round house and re-entered his body. When his body awoke, his face was soaked with tears, his body shuddering with cries.

"My son," he murmured. He looked about, at the smoking fire, the drying herbs hanging in bunches everywhere from the rafters that met at the peak of the roof. This was his reality again.

"Huh? Wa?" The sleepy youth by the fire stirred, wiping spittle from the side of his mouth. When he saw his master's state, he came and knelt before him. "What is it, Master?" he asked in his garbled words.

"Forgive me, Morvran. I did not mean to wake you." He took a breath and dried his eyes. "My son is dead."

"Oh." The youth hung his head.

"Let us eat. Then, I want you to get the boat ready. We must go to Ynis Wytrin today."

The ride through the morning mists worked its magic on the old man.

When he had come out of the round house wearing his thick grey cloak and carrying his yew staff, Morvran was lifting the boat and placing it in the black waters.

The servant was, in a way, the only family he had left. He was of much help, and the deformity of his face and back did not detract from his immense strength, nor the kindness of his heart.

"Ready, Master," Morvran said, holding out his hand to help him into the boat.

When they were out into the mist, the old man settled in to watch the tall marsh grasses flow by as he gathered his thoughts. His son was dead, and there was a dragon in the isles who would need his help.

Of course, he knew of the new Roman invasion of the North. In the South, people spoke of those far-off events casually over their wine and oysters. He supposed that over a hundred years of Pax Romana would lead to complacency. People in the South thought more of how they could profit from the war and influx of thousands of legionaries and camp followers, not to mention the imperial court.

He had enjoyed the peace of the South in his own way, living among the people of the lake villages about Ynis Wytrin. No one knew he was a Druid of the Selgovae. No one cared. He had been helping and healing people during the peace times. He counted Romans, Christians, and others among his friends, priests and priestesses, all in their own ways. But it seemed his world was due to change.

Life moves ever on, he thought and smiled to himself. Then the old man sighed as Morvran rowed them through the secret depths. *My son is dead...*

A heron stood watching them from among the grass, and a fox pounced on a field mouse in the early dawn mist.

Before he knew it, the boat had slowed, and he spread his arms and spoke the incantation.

"Gods of Earth, Water, Air and Fire, open the gates to your sacred isle. I am your servant..."

Morvran waited until his master nodded his cloaked head, and then rowed them directly into the wall of mist. They felt the air dampen their faces and hair as they passed through with only the gentle sound of oars in the still water. They broke through to see the green hills of the isle laying peacefully about the foot of the Tor and the Gates of Annwn.

The soft morning sun lit the mist and the water sparkled beneath it. Songbirds flit back and forth among the rushes and a thin haze of smoke from the morning fire and offerings hung low in the air. The soft chiming of a bell sounded from the Christian temple where he knew Father Gilmore had begun his prayers to his god and lady.

"There is the mooring, Morvran," the old man said. "You may tie the boat and come with me this time. We may be a while today."

"Yes, Master. Thank you." Morvran smiled. He loved the place.

Once the boat was secured, they both climbed the steep hill to the ridge. The old man touched an old hawthorn tree where it was silhouetted against the sky. Then they made their way along the ridge to the sacred precincts.

As he walked, his staff tapping on the hollow hills, the old man wondered if his son had already passed there on his way to the Otherworld.

Father Gilmore knelt in his usual spot beside the well he revered so much. It was located just beside the small timber structure that he had dedicated to the one he called 'Lady'. The well itself, he believed, was used by one of his Christian forebears, a man named Joseph, who had come all the way from Palestine well over a hundred years before.

It soothed the old man to see his friend again - the familiar brown, homespun robes, the long, wild locks of brown hair tied back to reveal a bushy beard.

Father Gilmore was some years younger than the old man, but that was of no consequence. They looked forward to each other's company and conversation, and had never shared an angry word, despite the differences in their beliefs.

When the head rose from its praying, the old man spoke.

"I was drawn to you by the sound of your Christian bells. The morning is glorious without."

Father Gilmore crossed himself, stood up, and turned with a smile.

"Weylyn, my dear friend. You've been on my mind this morning."

"And you on mine," Weylyn answered, taking a step forward. "I wanted to speak with you, and Lady Etain, if I may."

"Ba, you know you need never ask!" The smile suddenly left Father Gilmore's face when he spied the red in his friend's aged eyes. "What's happened?"

Weylyn looked about the dark temple and then to the door and sunlight beyond.

"Can we speak outside? I need some air."

"Of course. I believe Etain is sitting beneath the large oak on the way to the Well of the Chalice."

"Good. Let us join her there. What I have to say needs both your counsels."

"Come." Father Gilmore lent his arm and together they walked across a small pasture where sheep grazed around fenced crops and priests and priestesses tended to their work.

"Morvran," Weylyn called to his helper who was playing a game with some young boys and girls beneath an apple tree. "I am going with Father Gilmore to see the Lady Etain. Stay here and help where you can please."

"Yes, Master." Morvran smiled and returned to playing.

Weylyn and Father Gilmore walked along the footpath at a slow pace, enjoying the peace. It had been a while since the three of them had been together, but Father Gilmore did not press his old friend. He knew that Weylyn always spoke when he was ready, and that whatever he said was worth listening to.

The Priestess of Ynis Wytrin, Etain, sat beneath the strong limbs of an oak tree overlooking the watery levels surrounding the isle. She had been there for two hours already, eyes closed, but open to all around her.

She knew Weylyn would come that morning.

A cool breeze rustled Etain's red hair, and pressed her white priestess' robes to her body. When she felt her two friends approach, her green eyes opened slowly and she stood.

"Etain," Father Gilmore called. "Look who has come."

The priestess smiled and touched the crescent moon about her neck. She strode forward with both hands outstretched, to greet the priest and the old druid.

Weylyn felt his heart lighten at the sight of her, and grasped her hands tightly.

"I've been expecting you," she said.

The druid smiled. He was humbled and awed by Etain's skill in all things, the Sight among them.

"Then you know?" he asked.

"Yes. I'm sorry." She breathed deeply, calmly. "I saw Cathbad pass here early this morning on his way to Annwn."

"What?" Father Gilmore jumped in.

Weylyn sighed and sat on one of the three stumps where they usually met. The others waited for him to speak. He looked at both of them for strength, and smiled at their history in that place.

Etain and Gilmore had both grown up in Ynis Wytrin, one dedicated to the Goddess, the other to the Christian god. They had played as children, but when they were older, they did not know how to reconcile their beliefs, and so they had quarrelled.

When Gilmore had caught a sickness one day, the fever had almost taken him. Etain, whose healing knowledge went beyond all that of the other novices or elders, had gone to him. She had looked upon her childhood friend who was near death.

No one knew what she did with her herbs, medicines, and prayers. She had sat with Gilmore for three days and nights, and finally emerged with the young man at her arm to walk in the sunlight.

Father Gilmore had been her greatest friend, and staunchest supporter ever since. As a result, the bond between everyone on the isle had become stronger than ever, their faiths co-existing in peace.

Weylyn remembered when he had come to Ynis Wytrin from the North. He had been sick of war, and slaughter, and hate, and had only wanted to live peacefully. Etain and Gilmore had welcomed him openly, seeking the great wisdom of ages he had to offer on the history of Britannia as it was now known.

They had not been offended when he had wanted to live outside of Ynis Wytrin, for they knew his desire to help people who needed it most. Etain believed he did not want to live too close to the Gates of Annwn, unready as he was to leave the physical world.

Father Gilmore hoped that Weylyn wanted to atone for the deaths and sacrifices of his long-ago days under Roman oppression, that the aged Druid believed doing good would make amends with the world.

The three of them had become a close unit that seemed to tie the isle together. When Weylyn looked up, prepared to speak, the other two leaned forward.

"My son came to me this morning. He is dead."

"Oh, my friend," Father Gilmore said. "I'm so sorry."

"How did it happen?" Etain asked. "Did he receive the rites? He must have, for when he passed this way, he glowed with strength and joy as he headed toward the Tor."

"He did receive the rites."

"But how did he die?" Gilmore pressed. "Your son was a great warrior, no?"

"He was. One of the greatest of our people." The old man shook his head and pressed the end of his staff into the soft grass. "He lost in battle to a Roman dragon in the North."

"The scaled warriors followed by Epona herself?"

"You've seen them?" Weylyn asked Etain.

"Yes," she answered, her green eyes staring into the distance.

Father Gilmore was quiet, but listened intently as Weylyn continued.

"The Dragon captured him, but my son said he treated him honourably. He helped Cathbad to die in battle against his Votadini enemy rather than be taken in chains to Rome like Caractacus."

"Why would a Roman do that?" Gilmore asked. "For sport?"

"No. My son said the Roman was a good man, with loyalty elsewhere than Rome. He…he wanted me to send help to the Dragon for some reason."

"Why?" Etain asked now, surprised that she did not suspect the answer.

Weylyn shrugged. "That is what I cannot reason through."

"It is peace here in the South," Gilmore said after a minute. "Is it a good idea to intervene when the drums of war are pounding in Caledonia?"

"Perhaps not."

"And yet," Etain began, "all is for a reason. Cathbad was warlike, and sometimes cruel. But he was intelligent and gifted with the Morrigan's attention."

"Yes?" Weylyn looked up.

"Perhaps a more subtle intervention is needed to help this dragon. We do not know the purpose, but if someone we trust could be sent to help, or find out how to help… I don't know for certain. Usually, I am more attuned, but now, for some reason, this eludes me. Perhaps because we all have a role to play, and must make our own choices?"

They fell silent, each working over their thoughts on the matter. The wind whistled in the tree branches above them.

Weylyn turned his staff around, and Etain's eyes searched beyond the veil. It was Father Gilmore who expressed doubt.

"The Romans can't be trusted. We know this!" His eyes were shut tight against memory and persecution as he spoke. "No matter how long the Pax Romana has lasted here in the South, peace will always be shattered if we are not vigilant."

"And hope shall never die, my friend, if we trust one another from time to time." Etain put her hand on Gilmore's shoulder and he opened his eyes.

"What of my sacred charges?" he asked. "I'm sworn to keep them safe, hidden."

"We need not invite the Dragon to Ynis Wytrin. Only send him help," Weylyn said.

"The children will remain safe behind the mists," Etain reassured. "Besides, not all Romans hate Christians. Have not many Christians come from Rome itself where they live beneath the city?"

"Yes, but…a dragon-"

"Is a symbol of power and prophecy in this land, Gilmore."

"None of us has friends in the imperial court anymore," Gilmore added. "There is no one to trust."

"The emperor believes in his dreams, and the movement of the stars," Etain said. "What if I sent him a dream?"

"It's worth a try, but the dream would be open to the interpretation of his astrologer whom, I hear, he listens to closely." Weylyn stood up. "I feel it should be something more tangible. These are men of the world, and no one is safe at war, man, woman, or child."

Etain stood too and walked a few paces until she looked up at the terraced slopes of the Tor. "We will send the twins, Einion and Briana."

Both men looked up at her, then at each other.

"That's it!" Weylyn said.

"Are the Dumnonians ready?" Gilmore asked as they moved beside Etain.

"They are tested in battle against the Hibernian sea raiders, and have kept up their training all these years. They know Roman customs and the language." She turned to face them, her eyes wild with decision. "They're perfect!"

"But, fighting sea pirates is different than fighting Roman legions," Weylyn said, having known all too well.

"They won't need to fight," Etain continued. "They need to-"

"Blend in!" Gilmore finished.

"Exactly." She smiled. "They need to get close to the Dragon, into his confidence and service. That way, they can ascertain his worth, and perhaps his role in all of this. If it comes to nothing, they can disappear."

"And if it's meant to be, they can give the Dragon the help my son believed he needs."

"Yes."

"How will we keep in touch with the twins?" Gilmore asked. "The Roman couriers are corrupt and will hand anything over for a few denarii."

"I have been training Briana to hear me from afar. I believe she is ready for this."

Gilmore looked doubtful, but he saw no other option. So long as his own charges were safe in Ynis Wytrin. Besides, he had known Briana and Einion for some years. They were both strong and dedicated.

Together, the three of them looked up at the silhouetted shapes of the brother and sister atop the sacred hill. The girl waved to the three of them, then leaned to speak to her brother. A moment later, they were gone, following the winding path down to the bottom.

"Good," Etain said. "She heard me."

Etain trusted that the Goddess was guiding her thoughts on the matter. She had never failed her before. As she watched Einion and Briana come down the path to meet them beneath the oak tree, she remembered when they had come to Ynis Wytrin.

Their village in the harsh Cornish moors had been attacked by a local chieftain who had a blood feud with their father. There was a great battle, but in the end, their father was slain, and their mother, brothers and sisters too. The whole of their village had been put to the sword and it was only by the Gods' grace that the twins had managed to hack their way free, the only survivors.

When the twins had shown up at the headquarters of the garrison at Isca, they were told to leave. The local Roman administrator had been a patron of the attacking chieftain.

Einion and Briana's story wrenched Etain's heart whenever she thought of it, but it also served as a reminder of the Goddess' will. How they had managed to make it to Ynis Wytrin, she could not imagine. Wounded and hungry, they had walked all the way into the centre of the sacred isle.

No one was ever able to do that. What could it have been but the Goddess' will?

But Einion and Briana, now roughly thirty-six summers into their lives, still held a deeply-nursed anger, a thirst for vengeance. Their pain was lessened in Ynis Wytrin, but Etain did worry about sending them away to war among the Romans.

The time is now, she thought as the twins sat on the ground before her, Weylyn, and Father Gilmore.

"You wanted to see us, Lady?" Briana asked, observing the serious faces of the three elders with her bright blue-grey eyes.

Beside her, Einion sat, legs crossed, back straight with his heavy shoulders slumping forward slightly. He nodded to Father Gilmore and Weylyn.

"We have some news to tell you...and a quest of sorts," Etain began.

The twins looked at each other, and then back to Etain who began with Weylyn's dream. They listened intently to all, but when it came to the task of going north into the war, Einion stood quickly and paced, his long brown hair whipping round.

"Our war is not in the North, my lady. It's in Dumnonia where that petty chief warms our father's ancestral seat and holds court on the bones of our family!"

Briana stood up and went to her brother's side. She was slightly taller than him, quick, strong and lithe beside his powerful bulk. The length of her long, thick, blond hair flapped about her as she whispered to him.

Einion calmed visibly, and turned back to the others.

"Forgive me. I must apologize. You have always been so kind to us and-"

"There is nothing to apologize for," Weylyn cut in. The old druid walked over to Einion and pat his muscled arm.

"We are deeply sorry for the death of your son, Weylyn," Briana said.

"Thank you. I'm sure he is happy in Annwn now. But he did leave me with this troubling task."

"But to help the man who defeated and captured your son?" Einion said.

"A man who helped Cathbad to enter Annwn," Etain pointed out.

"Both of you know what other Romans would have done," Gilmore added.

"Aye," Einion agreed.

"What if he will not have us in his service?" Briana asked. "Why should he trust us?"

"As ever, the Gods will guide us, and him," Weylyn said.

"Just as they guided you both to us all those years ago," Etain said, smiling at them.

"But to leave Ynis Wytrin… What of Aaron and Rachel?" Briana looked at Father Gilmore. "Einion and I are the strongest fighters in the sacred isle."

"The children will remain safe," Gilmore said. "I trust Etain's judgement."

"We cannot demand this of you, nor would we consider doing so," Weylyn added. "You must make your own free choice in this, as in all things."

The twins looked at the three people who had saved them, the people who were now their family.

To leave Ynis Wytrin… they thought.

"What do you think, Einion?" Briana said. "Is it time to go?"

Einion smiled, knowing the truth and the will of the Gods when he heard it.

"My sword and spear are ready if yours are, Sister."

"Thank you, both," Weylyn said and bowed to them. *For you, my son...* he thought as he looked back to the Tor rising into the sky.

Inside their small stone dwelling near the Well of the Chalice, Einion and Briana set about gathering their things. The fire had been built up and cast an orange glow over the brother and sister, their sleeping mats, and the wall where a variety of herbs and weapons hung together.

They had not spoken since accepting the task Etain had given them, but now, Einion turned to Briana and stopped folding a thick wool blanket.

"Is this madness? Are we to go in among the Romans and just hope for the best? When they see us, they'll clap us in irons."

"I've never known you to run from an adventure, Brother."

"We have a debt to pay to that old bastard, Caradoc." Einion threw the blanket into a corner and reached for the sword that had been his father's where it hung on the wall.

"We have many debts to pay," Briana said to him. "But the Gods led us to Ynis Wytrin for a reason - perhaps to heal, to grow in strength, perhaps even to help this dragon... Surely you see that?"

"I do," he conceded. "I just feel that by going north, we'll never be able to avenge our family's dead."

"Trust in the Gods, Einion. Trust that they direct us to a higher purpose."

"Which gods are you referring to? The Goddess? The spirits of oak and stream? Or the Christus that Father Gilmore prays to?"

"All of them together, as they are in this place." Briana put her hand on her heart and closed her eyes.

"We aren't staying in this place, Briana. We're leaving the goodness of Ynis Wytrin for war among the Romans and the tribes of the North."

"I pray to the Morrigan too, then, and to Epona who loves horses." Briana opened her eyes and strode to the wall above her sleeping mat to take down her long sword and bow. "The Gods will guide us."

Einion smiled at her. "As they always have." Then his smile faded. "We'll need to dress as plain Romans, and hide our swords if we are to get north of the Wall."

"Yes. And I'll need to dirty myself and tie my hair up."

"Of course. I don't want to have to fight every Roman who takes a fancy to you."

"Ha. I can take care of myself," she answered.

The next second, Einion leapt across the floor brandishing his sword straight at her.

Briana parried the thrust, unsheathed her own blade and slapped his wrist with the flat so that his sword dropped. His fist came round toward her head. She ducked and kicked a long leg into his gut sending him sprawling beside the fire.

"Why did you do that?" she yelled at him.

"To see if your skills are still sharp," he moaned and rolled onto his knees before rising. "I'm glad they are."

Briana helped him stand. When Einion faced her, the tears rimming her eyes grabbed at his heart.

"I'm sorry," he said, holding her close.

No matter how good a fighter she was, Briana always despised violence. Einion wondered if it was the violence of the day their family had been murdered that had done that to her.

She had taken many enemy lives that day, but not enough.

When her muffled sobs stopped, Briana held her twin at arm's length.

"I would die for you, Einion."

"And I would die to protect you."

They spent the rest of the night packing their things, checking all of their weapons, and poring over a map of the Roman roads north.

In the morning, they were to leave Ynis Wytrin.

When the sun rose beyond the mists of the sacred isle, Einion and Briana descended the terraced slopes of the Tor. In the soft light of early morning, they had made offerings to the Gods prior to their journey. They then found Etain, Father Gilmore, and Weylyn waiting for them with two young children, and Morvran, the latter holding the bridles of two white, strong and sturdy moorland ponies where they stood on the dewy grass.

Briana smiled and went to kneel before the young olive-skinned boy and girl.

"Rachel. Aaron. Einion and I must go away for a while."

"We know. Father Gilmore told us last night," said the girl. Her dark brown eyes looked directly at Briana, who could tell she was holding back tears.

"When will you be back?" the boy asked Einion. His dark eyes were wide and bright in the early light that now began to pool around them as it peered over the top of the Tor.

"We don't know," Einion answered. "But we *will* be back, never fear."

One of the horses whinnied, and Morvran shook the reins to quiet it before slipping them each an apple.

Rachel reached out to hug Briana, and the boy placed his hands on Einion's head.

"We will pray for you both to return," Aaron said.

Einion smiled awkwardly and stood while the girl whispered in Briana's ear.

"Epona will guide your horses where you need to go," Weylyn said to Einion and Briana as they stood up, Briana still holding Rachel's hand.

"Speak to me every night, my dear," Etain stepped forward and kissed Briana on the forehead.

Weylyn looked to the sky, eyes closed, and then held aloft a bough of oak leaves, touching it to their hands, hearts, and faces.

"The Gods will watch over you wherever you go," he said.

Father Gilmore stood behind Rachel and Aaron with a protective hand on each. He nodded to both Briana and Einion. No more words were needed.

"We packed food and some Roman coin in the saddle bags for you," Weylyn said, standing beside the horses. "And there is this." The old druid held up a small vellum scroll. "I was worried about whether this Roman dragon would accept or trust you. So, I wrote a letter that you are to hand to him, and only him. In it, I explain what my son said to me."

"What if he doesn't believe it?" Einion asked.

"Then do not waste your time or risk your lives," Etain said. "Come back to Ynis Wytrin if that happens."

They all stood silent on the green grass of the isle, a company about to break apart. The wind picked up, and leaves danced across the ground at their feet. As the sun faded away behind a bank of cloud, Etain spoke.

"The time is now. The barge is ready to take you to the other side." She hugged each of them one more time, and held out a skin of water to them. "This is from the Well of the Chalice. If you are ever wounded very badly, use it. Keep it safe."

Briana took the gift. "We will," she said.

Brother and sister then gathered their satchels, daggers, swords, spears and bows, and fastened them to the ponies.

Einion smiled at his mount, and rubbed his mane before leading it to the docks. The others followed as they went.

Briana could not help one more backward glance at what had been their home and refuge for the past ten or more years.

They arrived at a small quay that jutted out into the reeds and rushes. At the end, a barge large enough for them and the two ponies waited. The water was calm, and bugs skittered across the surface.

The four rowers, novices of Etain and Father Gilmore, stood to help secure the horses.

Einion and Briana settled in the prow and turned to the priestess, the priest, and the druid.

"Thank you for everything," Briana said, staring at Etain who raised a hand in farewell.

Einion bowed his head.

"God go with you," Father Gilmore said in his low voice.

Weylyn said nothing, but stood staring at the brother and sister he was responsible for sending out into the world beyond Ynis Wytrin. He clutched his staff, his lips moving as he recited the incantations of protection.

When Einion and Briana disappeared into the mists, Weylyn closed his eyes and stood there alone for a while after Etain, Gilmore, and the others had gone.

Thank you, Father...

Weylyn looked up, but all he could see were the wind's ripples on the water.

VI

AGNI INTER LUPORUM

'Lambs among Wolves'

It was raining again. For weeks it had poured, and the only place one could avoid being splashed with filth was indoors, or in the private garden of the peristylium.

Adara Metella sat beneath the covered arcade looking out at the garden. She inhaled the ever-so-slight fragrance of sage and thyme where they grew in the muddy border of the garden, six feet away.

Her thick blue, woollen cloak was wrapped tightly about her, as it had been from the day she and the children had arrived in Britannia weeks before. She had known Britannia would be colder than Rome, of course, but not so wet, with a dampness that seemed to seep into every part of one's bones.

At least they don't seem bothered, she thought as she looked at Phoebus and Calliope playing with some wooden blocks and animals on the stone floor beside her. She loved watching them play together, Phoebus narrating to his sister all that he did, and Calliope humming all the while.

The children asked about their father and when they would get to see him, but Adara felt that the forced distance from Lucius was much harder on her. She was alone with her thoughts most of the time, and given the climate, prone to contemplating the minutiae of their situation.

Adara did not know how long it would be until she saw Lucius who was fighting in the North. She did not have any help, but avoided purchasing a slave for fear of not finding one she could trust with the children. Nor did she know how long she would be confined to Eburacum.

The town proved surprisingly large when the river barge had approached. The red-lined walls of the legionary fortress dominated the soft, smoky surroundings, foreign and out of place, like a muscled Hercules, stubborn and unyielding. The size of the settlement clinging to the fortress' walls was an even bigger surprise. Red roof tiles radiated out on all sides, and the streets played host to shops, markets, fora, tabernae, and brothels. It was all to serve the men of the Legions and their families.

With the imperial family in residence at the palace on the other side of the river, south-west of the base, there seemed to be a greater influx of tradesmen and those currying favour. Litters were carried through the crowded streets at all times, and groups of women strode through the masses in their scented finery, hired bodyguards following them closely.

Eburacum was Rome in miniature, but that did not give comfort to Adara. People stared at her and the children whenever they ventured out. She had felt exposed ever since they had left Gaul.

The relief Adara felt when the barge had docked and she found Alerio Cornelius Kasen waiting with some men to greet her, was her high point thus far. Alerio, Lucius' closest friend, had greeted her and the children warmly, but formally, in front of his Praetorian troops.

"Lady Metella," he had said. "Welcome to Eburacum. I'm relieved to see you here safe."

"Centurion Cornelius," Adara said, patting the children. "It's good to see you."

He smiled and bent to see Phoebus and Calliope eye-to-eye. "You've both grown! Come, the empress has arranged for the use of a small domus for the three of you, and a kitchen slave, while we wait for the orders to move north."

"Thank you, Alerio. But…where is Lucius?"

"He's fighting beyond the Wall."

"Will we see him soon?" she asked.

His face told her instantly. "No, but I can make sure a letter gets to him at Trimontium."

"Yes please," Adara had said.

She had only seen Alerio twice since that first day, once to tell her about the town and where to go to obtain warmer clothes, second to invite her to an audience with the empress at the imperial residence. That was two weeks ago.

Alerio had come to accompany her and the children, by litter, to the palace up the street. It was just past midday and the rain had abated.

Adara was happy they had brought fine clothes for all of them, but they froze for wearing them. Luckily, the palace corridors were warmed by intermittent bronze braziers, and heating from the hypocausts beneath the floors, which allowed them to remove their wool cloaks for the audience with Julia Domna.

"Lady Metella, and her children," the steward announced as they were shown into the room.

Adara approached the empress where she sat on one of several couches surrounded by a few other women. Holding Phoebus and Calliope's hands, she and the children bowed as she had instructed them, smiling at the woman who had helped save their family in Rome when Plautianus had fallen.

"Metella," Julia Domna rose in a rustle of silks and held her hands out to Adara. "After so long, we meet again at the edge of the Empire."

"Empress, we thank you for your hospitality here in Eburacum, as well as your past kindnesses."

"Oh, dear," the empress waved a hand and smiled. "No need to be so formal in this far-flung province. Though you are most welcome. I see the children have grown. The time passes so quickly." The empress paused a moment, looking at Phoebus and Calliope who, at five years of age, were yet very shy.

Adara was relieved to see the empress smile, though she did notice more grey in her tightly-bound hair, and age-lines about her brown eyes.

"Forgive me, Metella," the empress suddenly said. "I don't believe you know my other guests. My sister, Julia Maesa." She motioned toward a woman reclining on a couch reading a scroll by herself. She had the usual aloof look Adara remembered seeing at a distance in Rome. Julia Maesa nodded and smiled, politely enough. "And these two ladies are Perdita Narbonensa, and Diana Firma."

The two ladies beamed at Adara.

"Perdita and Diana have lived here in the North for many years, and are acquainting us with the workings of Britannia. Aren't you, ladies?"

"However we can help, Empress," the one named Diana said.

"You can help by making this atrocious rain stop," Julia Maesa said.

"Oh!" squealed the lady Perdita. "At least we've had no flooding. I once knew a woman whose litter was swept away on the river for nearly a mile before the troops finally caught her."

"Really?" Adara asked.

"Yes. And that was a year of moderate rains."

"Gods help us!" Julia Maesa said, clearly unhappy with her lot.

The empress turned back to Adara and pat the couch beside her. "Come. Sit with me so that we might talk. Children," she turned to Phoebus and Calliope who had stood very still and very quiet since they had arrived. "You may help yourselves to some honeyed sweets on that table over there." She smiled.

"Thank you, Empress," they said in unison, before going to the table where a slave girl helped them.

"They're lovely, Metella," Julia Domna said.

"Adorable!" Diana added. "If you like, I can introduce them to my own children. I have a son who is eight, and a daughter who is six."

"How are your children enjoying Eburacum, Metella?" Perdita asked.

"They enjoy the new sights well enough, and I have been teaching them their letters."

"You?" Julia Maesa said. "Surely you have a slave to help with that."

"I am waiting until I see my husband before purchasing one. I want to be sure about who we bring into our familia."

There was silence.

Adara felt her neck growing hot under the scrutiny. Then the empress spoke.

"It is always good to be sure of those under your roof, Metella. You are quite right to be cautious."

"True." Perdita nodded. "I once had a Selgovan slave make off with all my silver platters in the night. Just up and vanished!"

"I fear more for my children," Adara said. "I left our valuables in Etruria, since it seemed we would be moving about with the army."

"You make us sound like camp followers," Julia Maesa retorted.

"No, no!" Adara said quickly. "I just mean, well, we were told we'd be able to join my husband at some point."

"We have heard much of Praefectus Metellus' deeds since we arrived," the empress added.

"Yes, Empress. Against the Selgovae, I take it?"

"Oh! Brutes, they are!" Perdita burst out after a sip of wine. "And thieves."

Adara could see Julia Maesa roll her eyes and the empress suppress a smile.

"Well, at any rate," Julia Domna ignored the uncouth interruption. "With Praefectus Metellus sweeping away the rebels ahead of the main army, we shall be dining at the edge of the world in no time."

"We're there already," Julia Maesa sighed and stood. "I feel drawn to the caldarium," she said as she smoothed the fabric of her yellow stola. "Ladies," she nodded to Diana, Perdita, and lastly Adara, to whom she whispered, "You must come to dine with me at some point so we can get better acquainted."

Adara nodded politely as Julia Maesa bowed to her sister, the empress, before leaving the room.

"Forgive my sister's coolness, ladies," the empress said. "She is far more accustomed to Syrian heat, than to British damp."

"Not to worry, Empress," Perdita said, leaning in conspiratorially. "When my late husband brought me here from Narbo to live in Corinium on the Wall, I wouldn't let him touch me for two years, his hands were so cold!"

"Ah, Perdita!" Diana laughed out loud.

Adara chuckled. It did not escape her that behind the empress' own laughter, she was keenly observing the other two ladies. *Some things remain the same no matter where you find yourself in the Empire.*

Adara sipped her wine and cast a look across the room to Phoebus and Calliope who were onto their third helping of pastries. They waved to her, and she smiled back.

Adara had to admit to herself that the afternoon audience with the empress had alleviated her feelings of loneliness. She also had a duty to the empress for her care and protection.

Being beholden to anyone annoyed her, but she thought it a wise course - whatever ensured the safety of her family. Truthfully, she had been grateful for the chance to meet new people.

Diana, whose husband was a centurion on the Wall, was kind and honest, and her high opinion of Phoebus and Calliope only served to solidify Adara's kind regard of her.

When a slave brought Diana's children into the room, Adara was struck by their height. Like their mother, both the son and daughter were tall and big-boned, with yellow hair. They were dressed as Romans, but it was obvious they were Britons. The boy, Cassius, was kind to Phoebus, and the girl, Julia, wished to play with Calliope at the soonest possible moment.

"We'll arrange a meeting," Diana said to Adara, smiling at the four children.

Lady Narbonensa had no children by her late husband. She did, however, have a vast fortune from his olive oil import business in Northern Britannia.

"He didn't leave me offspring," she laughed, "but he left me well-clothed and fed!"

Indeed, Adara noticed that even by Roman standards, Perdita Narbonensa was extremely well-dressed, her short lovely frame draped in a silk stola, a fur-lined cloak, and enough gold and jewels to pay for passage back to Narbo and a luxurious villa there.

"Why don't you go back to Narbo?" Adara asked out of curiosity. She could not conceive of anyone preferring the grey rains of Britannia to the sun and warmth of the Middle Sea.

"All I know is here now," Perdita answered. "Here, I'm respected. Back home, I would only be told I'd failed to have any children."

Adara let it lie there, as it was the only time she had seen Perdita's permanently jovial mood fade, her dark brown eyes seeking the floor mosaic behind the tendrils of her black hair.

Diana and Perdita became frequent visitors after that day. They often rescued Adara from herself, bringing her out into the world where she had less chance to brood. Both ladies had homes in Eburacum and extended intermittent invitations to Adara and the children.

One thing for which Adara was grateful was the fact that she had not yet seen Caesar Caracalla about the town. She remembered, with an inkling of dread now, that piercing stare and frown from her days in Rome.

Since the fall of the Praetorian Prefect, Gaius Fulvius Plautianus, Caracalla and Geta had run wild. The gossips whispered that the whole of the Britannia campaign had been devised by the emperor as a means of keeping his sons out of trouble in Rome.

Whatever the reason for the war, Alerio told Adara that Caracalla was always training with the men of VIth Legion within the base, or out patrolling along the Wall, meeting the British legions and auxiliary cohorts. If she did not see Caracalla, Lucius certainly would.

One day, the sun made an unexpected appearance over Eburacum, and within half an hour, Perdita and Diana showed up at Adara's door.

"You and the children must come out, Metella," Perdita said, as Diana waited in the litter with her children. "The day is too glorious to be shut up within plaster walls, no matter how prettily-painted they are."

"To be honest, we would love to, Perdita. Just give us a few minutes."

"Splendid!" Perdita returned to the litter to wait with Diana.

Adara hurried the children into some warm clothes and boots, and wrapped them in their matching grey cloaks.

"Are Cassius and Julia coming too, Mama?" Phoebus asked.

"Yes! They're outside. Now gather your things and let's go while Helios still shines bright in the sky."

The marketplace was full of people, and the vendors smiled as their stocks seemed to evaporate along with the myriad puddles dotting the paving stones. The air still felt cool to Adara, but Perdita and Diana seemed warm enough in their light cloaks as they walked among the stalls.

"Stay close, children," Adara called to Phoebus and Calliope as they ran with Cassius and Julia to the central fountain in the square.

"You really must purchase a slave to help you, Metella," Diana said as they browsed through a display of red Samian ware. "You can't expect to do it all on your own."

It was not an unkind comment. Rather, Diana sought to be helpful. She knew how tiring it was to have two young children tearing about the domus.

For the moment, Adara was content to feel the sun on her face. She closed her eyes and breathed deeply as Diana stopped at a fabric merchant's stall. She imagined herself back in the agora of Athenae, the home she had left behind so very long ago.

"Who is that speaking to the children?" Perdita suddenly asked.

Adara looked ahead and caught a glimpse of a crested helmet at the fountain. Her heart leapt and she pressed through the crowd.

Gods...please let it be Lucius!

"Mama?" Phoebus called to her when he spotted her. He was clutching Calliope's hand, his eyes darting about.

"Phoebus, Calliope?" Adara called and reached out to them just as the red cloak turned.

"Ah," the soldier said. "I believe these must be your children, lady..."

"Metella. Yes. Thank you." Adara held out her hands and each child took one.

The stranger turned to face Adara with the fountain at his back.

She noticed several other soldiers waiting for him.

"They weren't bothering you, I take it? Ah... Tribune..."

"Claudius. Marcus Claudius Picus. No, they were not." He smiled, but the children held tight to their mother. "They saw my helmet and it seems they thought I was their father."

"Do you know my husband?"

The man's smile hardened slightly, his cold eyes sliding over Adara.

"Yes. Actually, I just met him at Trimontium."

"Is he well? Do you know when he might come to Eburacum?" Adara asked, desperate for any information.

"Well, I don't think he'll be coming back here any time soon, Lady Metella. Your husband is at the front, and has recently been ordered to press north at all speed, into Caledonia."

"Already?" Adara could not hide her disappointment.

"Yes. In fact, the fighting is very bad."

"Mama, he said Baba was in trouble for allowing a prisoner to nearly escape," Phoebus said, his voice cracking with worry.

"He said Baba could already be dead," Calliope said quietly, then more forcefully, "I don't believe him!" The young girl stared at the tribune, unafraid.

Adara felt dizzy for a moment, and struggled to keep calm, her grip on the children's hands tightening.

"That's always a risk in war, children," Claudius said in a low voice, while still smiling. Then he looked at Adara. "I think your husband must have been mad to leave you alone in Britannia," he said evenly. "This is a wild frontier, and anything can happen."

"Lady Metella!"

The voice came from beyond Claudius.

"There you are!" Alerio came walking up with a century of Praetorians behind him, nearly filling the square. "Tribune," Alerio nodded to Claudius.

"Centurion. I see you know this fair lady." Claudius stood taller than Alerio, but the latter was not cowed.

"Yes. We're old friends." Alerio's eyes swept over the children's faces and he stepped closer to the tribune. "Caesar Caracalla asked for you, Tribune. He's at the palace."

"And you've come to fetch me, Centurion? How obedient of you."

"I owe my duty to Caesar," Alerio replied, his thumbs hooked on the chest harness carrying all his decorations. "I wouldn't keep him waiting."

"Thanks for the warning, Centurion," Claudius said before turning to Adara. "Metella, I'm sure I'll be seeing you again." Claudius spun and, followed by his centurions and optios, went in the direction of the royal residence.

Alerio watched them go and then turned to his own optio. "Take the men ahead, Silvius. I'll see you at the barracks."

"Yes, sir!" The man saluted and the century tramped off.

Adara could see Diana and Perdita beside her, but she was unable to speak. *Lucius... Lucius... Gods please make it not true... not dead.* She gripped the children's hands tightly, her face white.

"Adara?" Alerio said, and Calliope tugged on her mother's cloak. "Adara, are you all right?" He spoke quietly so as not to create a scene. "Did he hurt you?"

Finally, her eyes locked onto his. "He... he said that Lucius was in trouble... that he was sent to the front and could be..." Her hands were shaking now and she felt like vomiting.

"Adara, listen to me. Lucius is fine. I just got word of another victory. He's not hurt."

"What?"

Alerio nodded, his eyes retaining a memory of past kindness. "Yes, he's safe."

"The tribune said he was in trouble."

"There was an incident, but all is well. Don't worry. The emperor and empress know his value."

"And Caracalla?" she asked.

Alerio looked around. "He's fine with Lucius." Alerio saw her relax. "But you need to stay away from Tribune Claudius. He's not to be trusted."

"The children thought he was Lucius. I didn't know who he was."

"He was involved in the incident at Trimontium, and bears Lucius a grudge now. I'm going to warn Lucius about it."

"Don't tell him about this, Alerio. If Lucius knew, he would come after Claudius."

"Well, I'll try at least to keep a watch, but you need to get away. Do you know anyone you can visit?"

"She knows us, Centurion," Perdita came up to them with Diana and her children. "I have a villa near Coria. We were thinking of moving there soon." She turned to Adara. "Why don't you and the children come to stay?"

"That's a good idea," Alerio said. "I'll work it out with the empress and see if I can give you an escort."

"We'll have a wonderful time," Diana reassured, patting Adara's back.

"Thank you, Alerio. If you could arrange it, I'd be grateful. That way, we'll be that much closer to Lucius."

"Mama?" Phoebus asked, fighting his worry. "So, is Baba all right? He's not dead?"

Alerio knelt down in front of the boy. "He's more than all right, little man. Your father is the hero of this war." He stood, holding Phoebus' hand. "I can tell you about it while I walk you home through the market." Alerio glanced at Adara who smiled her thanks.

As they all walked, she tried to calm her nerves. She shuddered to think what would have happened had Alerio not been there.

That night, Adara was grateful for some familiar company for her and the children.

After Alerio had seen them home from the market, Adara asked him if he would like to come dine that evening.

He happened to be off duty that night and accepted, if not a little reluctantly.

Adara hoped she had not offended him in some way. The fact was that time with an old friend was a welcome change for her and the children. They had been quite shaken by the afternoon's events, and if she was honest, Adara felt that by speaking with Alerio, she was that much closer to Lucius. She also did not want Alerio to forget his bond of friendship with Lucius.

"Renia," Adara called for the kitchen slave the empress had hired for her. "Please bring the wine and figs when you are able."

"Yes, mistress," the girl answered, walking back to the kitchens. A few minutes later, she returned with clay pitchers of wine and water, a plate of figs, and two more pastries which she handed to Phoebus and Calliope with a kind smile.

"That'll be all. Thank you," Adara said.

"You seem to have settled into British life well enough," Alerio said as he sipped his wine, spilling a little on his tunic. "Sorry. Long day today."

"It's just good to see a friend," Adara said.

"Lady Diana and Lady Perdita seemed nice enough."

"Oh, they are. But I've only just met them. They don't know Lucius or anything from before. You know."

"Yes. I know." Alerio stared into the bottom of his quickly emptying cup.

"How is life in the Praetorian Guard, then? Everything you imagined?"

"I don't know what I imagined, if anything. I get paid more, and people move out of the way more easily. I think I was just happy to be given a position after being dismissed from the II Augustan. I just want to keep busy."

"Numidia seems a lifetime ago." Adara looked at the children whose heads were beginning to bob above their sweets. They had been born at the base in Numidia, and the joy had been infinite for a while.

Alerio did not speak. His gaze was far away.

"Do you ever think about her? I mean about-"

"Every day of my life," he said before looking up.

"Me too." *I miss Alene more than I can say,* she thought, but could not voice the words. She knew Alerio's pain may have been greater than any at Alene's murder. Every time Adara saw her own children, she thanked the Gods for Alene. She had saved them that day in the desert.

Alerio poured himself more wine, unwatered this time.

"Every day," he repeated.

Adara did not speak more of it. They each sat in silence with their memories, and the shadow cast by the dead.

Two weeks later, as the sun rose to its zenith, Adara, Phoebus, and Calliope found themselves in a covered wagon heading north on the road to Coria with the lady Perdita, lady Diana, and the latter's children.

Birds were singing in the hedgerows and were it not for the tramp of their military escort, Adara might have felt a sense of peace wash over her. As it was, the face of Mars was always peeking above the horizon.

They were heading north just a few days ahead of the emperor, Caracalla, and the larger part of the army.

Adara knew that should have been a comfort on a frontier that was at war, but it was not. All it meant was that Lucius, Dagon, and the men were pressing farther north into Caledonia.

While Phoebus and Calliope dozed fitfully in her lap as the wagon rumbled along, Adara gazed out at the green landscape, her eyes picking out two distant riders whom she followed until her own eyes closed.

Part II

CALEDONIA

A.D. 209

VII

EXCUBIAE

'Vanguard'

The world was deathly still. It was unnatural.

It seemed that the frost, a remnant from the previous night's plunging temperature, had frozen the entirety of Caledonia's fields and forest ferns. The grass and bracken cracked softly beneath the men's feet and the horses' hooves. Water trickled in the river to the left, the occasional reed twitching where it plumbed the cold black depths.

As he rode, his sword drawn, Lucius Metellus Anguis thought for a moment that even as he shivered beneath his wolf-pelt cloak, he would have liked to pause and take in the still beauty about him. It had been days since his last offering to Apollo, Venus, and Epona. However, he knew that a moment's lapse could get them all killed, the horsemen and legionaries who followed him into the face of the Caledonian highlands. The bulbous mountains ever loomed above and before the Romans as they marched. The hues of brown, deep green, and yellow would have been beautiful if it were not for the constant threat of ambush.

After being ordered to leave Trimontium two weeks after the incident with the Boar, Lucius and his Sarmatians had set out to meet the Votadini and a detachment from VIth Legion at Camelon, near the eastern end of Antoninus' old turf wall. The order had come directly from the emperor and Caracalla, who was to play a large part in the campaign.

You are to proceed north with speed to Camelon to join with the Votadini and a detachment from Eburacum. They will report to you, Praefectus. From there you are to engage the enemy to the north and north-east, along the old line of Rome's frontier. Secure what positions you can. Make treaty with the Venicones in whose lands Rome will establish a major supply base for the larger campaign. Do this in all haste, for the good of the Empire.

L. Septimius Severus, Imperator

The emperor had signed the letter, but Lucius wondered if the tone was not Caracalla's. Besides, the emperor was said to be in poor health again.

Before leaving Trimontium, Lucius and the Sarmatians dedicated an altar to Epona, the goddess who watched over them. The mason had not much time, but still, it was something to honour the goddess, something to show that they had warred in that place.

They arrived at the temporary camp at Camelon to meet up with the Votadini. Three centuries from VIth Legion arrived under the command of a centurion by the name of Arius Torens, an Iberian grunt with a neck the size of a wild boar's. He had also brought two engineers, named Fulvius and Orontus, who were to direct any building works required to keep things moving ahead of the imperial army.

Coilus and Afallach had been pleased to meet with Lucius and Dagon again, but Torens had no time for niceties, or orders from others for that matter, until Lucius produced his own orders. Torens gritted his teeth and took his frustration out on his subordinate centurions, Porax and Ulpens.

When their forces were fully mustered, Lucius ordered the march from Camelon into Caledonia, leaving a small group behind.

That had been three days before, and it had been blood ever since with the Caledonii springing an ambush on them immediately from the West after their crossing.

The warriors themselves were not so dangerous to the heavy cataphracts as the surprise with which they assaulted, and the bogs and fens into which they tried to lure the Roman cavalry. In that first attack, they had lost two Votadini, and one Sarmatian. They had charged ahead to override the Caledonian leader in his small war chariot pulled by shaggy ponies, but what these three riders had not seen was the deep line of a burn that stood between them and the Caledonian chief.

Their horses plunged into the ditch, their legs snapping, and before the riders could raise their shields or get unstuck from beneath their writhing mounts, several Caledonians who had been hiding beneath bunches of gorse jumped out, speared them, and were on their way before the men's comrades could come to their aid.

The march was much slower after that.

There had been several other such guerrilla attacks since then, but Lucius was determined not to lose any more men to the enemy in such a way.

They pressed on in a narrow formation, following the line of the river as it showed on the aged map Lucius had procured. It showed a line of forts and temporary camps that he hoped to use. The positions were always good, and from the look of the map, it would create a sort of curtain wall between the lands of the Venicones and their mutual enemies, the Caledonii, who clung to their highlands.

The sun was angling brightly now onto the frosty, crystalline grass beside the river as Lucius rode with Dagon and Coilus at the front where the one century of Torens' men went ahead to check the ground.

"I don't like this, Praefectus," Dagon muttered. "They should have shown themselves by now."

"Not one of their attacks has been identical, Princeps," Lucius answered, feeling the comforting weight of his sword in his hand. "But you're right. Normally, they'd have jumped out by now. We're almost at the site of the old camp." Lucius looked back to see Coilus' stern face, the banners of their cohorts, and beyond them, the cavalry and infantry stretching into the distance.

The wind picked up then, and the draconaria standards began to howl, their windsocks whipping violently.

"Looks like your dragons smell blood, Praefectus," Coilus said.

Lucius smiled, about to joke when he heard a man's gravelly voice.

"Morrigan!"

The word sounded more like a curse.

"Morrigan!!!"

"Hold!" Lucius ordered, and the column stopped.

"Praefectus!" Torens called from the front of the line as the man continued to yell.

"Morrigan!!!!!"

"What is it, Centurion?"

"Seems like a Caledonian, sir. Bastard's calling out the name of their war goddess." Torens pointed to where a muscled tribesman stood atop a mound, holding a short spear and a small round shield.

"MORRIGAN!!!!!" he said again, pointing his spear at the Romans.

"It's a trap," Dagon said as he and Barta rode up beside Lucius.

The Caledonian's torso was bare, his body tattooed with blue crescent and z-rod designs.

"Centurion," Lucius turned to Torens. "I think we should spring this trap. I'm tired of surprises. I want you and your century on me and my princeps. Coilus, you, Afallach, and Brencis will charge any attack from the other directions."

"Yes, Praefectus!" The Votadini chief saluted and turned to his son.

"Ready, Centurion?" Lucius asked Torens as he lowered his face mask.

"Oh, aye. I'm ready, sir!" he smiled. If there was one thing Lucius did like about the gruff centurion, it was his willingness to get stuck into a fight.

"Morrigan!!!!" the Caledonian chanted.

As they followed the river's edge to the ground where the enemy stood, Lucius realized he was standing on the ditches of the old fort. Several sheep grazed about them, seemingly unaware of the approaching force.

"Morrigan!!!! he yelled one last time before driving his spear into the nearest sheep's skull.

Torens approached with his century. "Oi, you!" He pointed his vinerod at the Caledonian who just stared at him. "Shut your fucking face or you'll have two feet of Roman steel in your guts!"

They were now just ten feet away.

"Morrigan! Morrigan! Morrigan!"

"Sir, look out!" Torens' optio yelled as the earth about the centurion began to bubble and shift. Three Caledonians sprang out of the ground, painted blue, and black with mud, their axes swinging for the centurion.

Torens cried with rage as one axe buried itself in the back layers of his lorica. The centurion's scutum slammed into the attacker on his left. Then his men arrived to drive them back and surround the remaining three.

Lucius rode up, but before he could speak, the air whistled with arrows from the trees on the other side of the river.

"Form up!" Lucius called down the line.

The infantry formed a shield wall facing the river and the cavalry searched in vain for a crossing.

"There he is, Praefectus!" Coilus rode up beside Lucius. "Argentocoxus!"

Lucius looked across the river to see the lean, feline form of the Caledonian leader speeding back and forth on his war chariot.

"Are the scorpions ready?" Lucius asked the centurion, Porax.

"Yes, sir!"

"Then fire!" Lucius yelled.

The winches of three scorpions clicked into place.

"Iacite!" The bolts soared over the river into the milling Caledonians amid painful cries and guttural curses.

At the far end of the line, Brencis had his cavalry turmae searching for a ford. When Lucius saw his dragons finally begin to cross, he rode back to Dagon and Coilus.

"Coilus! Send half your men to help Brencis on the other side."

Coilus nodded to Afallach who rode off with his cavalry, their hooves pounding the mud.

An arrow whizzed by Lucius, and then three more shredded through his cloak as the enemy took aim at the Dragon.

On the riverbank, Barta spotted a Caledonian pointing Lucius out to his archers. A second later, the big Sarmatian's horse was bounding in front of Lucius and it went down with four arrows in its side, beneath the scale armour. Barta rolled away, the Dragon vexillum still gripped in his hand. As he got to his knees, the first big Caledonian burst from the infantry grouping, his spear pointed at Barta's face.

A flash of red, black and grey saw Lucius there first, his sword planted in the Caledonian's skull before he could hack down on Barta. Lucius tossed Barta his second spatha and turned to look down the river where chaos reigned. The arrows had ceased from the other side of the river as Brencis and Afallach's cavalry rode down and pursued the Caledonians, trying to cut their way to Argentocoxus whose troupe of war chariots sped toward the hills.

"Ahh!" One of the infantry manning a scorpion cried out as a dagger drove down into his neck. Suddenly, out of the ground on the other side of their line, Caledonians sprang from the undergrowth.

"On me!" Without waiting, Lucius charged down the back of the line as fast as Lunaris could carry him.

The fifty or so Caledonians began to run when the heavy Sarmatian horses began bearing down on them, but this time, there was no escape to the hills. They ran north, and without the river to impede the horses, they were hacked to pieces.

After being harassed and bloodied for days, the Sarmatian and Votadini cavalry took their vengeance on the tribesmen.

Lucius stabbed and swung to either side, and the long kontos lances of his men impaled the enemy two at a time as they stumbled over each other to get away. Lucius did not think or feel as he rode and killed among the Caledonii, like a lion among a herd of sheep.

It was over as fast as it had begun. The surviving Caledonians, including their chieftain, had melted away into the hills and bogs.

When Lucius stopped, he was breathless, as was Dagon beside him. They watched as some of the men took the heads of their fallen enemies, as was the Sarmatian way.

"Do you want me to stop them?" Dagon asked.

"No. Let them," Lucius answered.

Across the river, they could hear Brencis howling into the wind after Argentocoxus.

"Coward! Coward!"

The aftermath of the engagement was the same as always - a chorus of groans, coupled with the cawing of carrion birds waiting in the trees for their chance to swoop down and devour some bloody flesh, a bit of sinew, or the eyes of dead men.

Details were arranged to help the wounded, which were many, and line up the Roman dead. The latter, Lucius thanked Epona, numbered only five, all of them infantry.

Those troops who were fit enough were set to dig ditches and pile the earth for ramparts, atop which rows of stakes were planted. The old camp would give them a secure spot, but the watch would be tripled through the night. Turmae of riders went out in several directions too, to scout for more signs of enemy activity, but no traces were found.

"They're like ghosts," Dagon said to Lucius as he bound a gash on his praefectus' arm.

"Not ghosts, Princeps," said Torens as he approached, blood on his face. "Dead men and cowards. When we find them, we're going to put them back in the bloody ground, by Mithras!"

"Centurion," Lucius stood. "Are you wounded?"

"No, sir. Just a cramp in my shoulder. Lorica needs fixing is all."

Lucius smiled at him. "You and your men fought well. I'm glad you're with us."

"Sir!" Torens saluted, and went back to helping get the camp set up.

"I think he likes you," Dagon laughed.

"We need all the good men we can get," Lucius answered. "Speaking of good men. How are ours?"

"They've calmed down, now that enemy's blood, has been spilled." Dagon was thoughtful for a moment. "This terrain,

Anguis," he addressed Lucius in the familiar now that they were alone. "It's not suited to cavalry charges."

"No. I agree. The Caledonii hug the hills and rivers too much. We're going to have to lure them out into the open. Barta!" Lucius called.

"Yes, Praefectus!" Barta came over and stood to attention.

"Thank you for coming to my aid," Lucius looked up at the Sarmatian's dark, weary face. "I know your mount meant a great deal to you. We can perform the rites to Epona together if you like."

"Thank you, Praefectus. I have ridden Melia for many years. She was my friend, and if it is all right with you, I will perform the rites alone." Barta looked down, but Lucius put a hand on his shoulder.

"I understand. Do as you need to, and ask her spirit which horse should replace her. You shall have it."

"Sir." Barta saluted and went back to where he was piling wood and bracken about his horse's body.

"Here come Coilus and Afallach," Dagon stepped forward to greet the Votadini who had just returned from patrol.

"Anything?" Lucius asked.

"No sign of the enemy, Praefectus." Afallach dismounted and saluted. "But we did find some allies."

"The Venicones are coming," Coilus said. "They'll be here tomorrow."

"Good," Lucius said. "We'll need their men."

"Well, erm... Maybe we should not expect much of them, Praefectus," Coilus added.

Lucius' face darkened. "Why?"

"They're reluctant to ally with the same side as the Votadini," Coilus' mouth was tight. "I told them they should say that to you, Praefectus."

"Let them tell me, then." Lucius worked his jaw. "I'll give them a choice."

"What choice is that, Praefectus?" Afallach smiled.

"An easy one," Lucius answered. He knew they needed the Venicones. Their lands were flatter, fertile, and had access to the sea. *I'll be damned if I'm going to let them dictate terms.* Lucius walked to where his command tent was now raised in the middle of camp. "Have Hippogriff see to the slaughter of the sheep we took," Lucius said over his shoulder to Dagon who followed. "I want all the men to eat well tonight."

"I'm hungry already," Dagon answered.

When darkness fell, the camp was on full alert. Torches had been lit every six feet around the ramparts and in the larger perimeter around the camp where cavalry and infantry were set to the watch.

There was no drinking or gambling. In shifts, men slept, and ate, and kept the watch. Despite the grumbling about the lack of wine, every man had been happy with a belly full of hot meat and hard bread.

In the command tent, Lucius sat with Dagon, Barta, Brencis, Coilus, Afallach, Torens and his two centurions. Lamps hung form the tent poles to light the central campaign table where Lucius had spread the hide map of the region.

The officers, each still armed, sipped their water and chewed their rations while Lucius ran his finger along the route they had taken, and the direction he wanted to go.

"Considering the number of days we've travelled and fought, it doesn't feel like we've taken much ground," Afallach said as he leaned over the map with Lucius.

"No. And the imperial army will be past the wall any day now," Lucius tried not to show worry, but he knew he needed to be further along. "I hope the Venicones will have some useful information for us."

"Ha!" Afallach stood and paced, his father taking his place beside Lucius.

"Praefectus, I've had dealings with their chieftain before. He's called Conn Venico."

"What sort of man is he?" Dagon asked. "Can he be trusted?"

Coilus shook his head. "He can, and he can't."

"Explain," Lucius said.

"Conn Venico looks out only for himself, and his people. Mostly himself. He'll side with whomever offers him the best deal. He's a slippery one, Praefectus. You'll want to be careful what you say or promise."

"Does he have many warriors?" Torens asked. "Why don't we just take their lands and have done with it?" The centurion cracked his knuckles and wiped his mouth.

"He does, though they are more like peltasts. They don't have cavalry like ours. They're hill fighters," Coilus said.

"Which is something we lack," Brencis added.

Dagon walked over beside Lucius to look at the map. "If we can secure these lands between the Bodotria and the Tava, up the line of forts we're on now, it will give the emperor a large swathe of land from which to strike out and resupply."

"My thinking too, Dagon." Lucius smiled. "If we can do so peacefully, by treaty, all the better. We don't want to worry about a knife in the back as we attack inland."

Everyone agreed, but there was still the question of what terms the Venicones would require.

After making his rounds of the camp, and checking on the fortifications, Lucius returned to his tent for some rest.

At the small altar beside his cot, he lit a chunk of myrrh in the flame of a small lamp. It began to smoulder and smoke, and he placed it before the images of Epona, Venus, and Olympian Apollo. He knelt and raised his hands, palms up.

Gods... Accept my offering to you this night, and all the nights of my life. Please watch over my Adara, Calliope and Phoebus, wherever they are. Keep them safe until they reach me, and ever after that. Guide me through this time of death, and battle, and blood. Help me, as ever, to lead with honour, and to do justice to the lives that have been sacrificed.

He paused, a shuddering breath escaping his mouth.

Lastly, whisper to my sister, Alene, wherever she is in Elysium, that she is ever in my thoughts, and that I miss her.

With that last thought, Lucius passed his hand over the flame of the lamp, and swirled the sacred smoke of his offering about his face. He stared at the face of each god before him, and remembered them on that high peak at Trimontium.

There will be help... Epona had said.

The words echoed in his mind, welcome and hopeful, like the sun in that rain-soaked land.

Lucius lay down on his cot, uncomfortable because of his cuirass and cingulum. "Better uncomfortable than dead," he mumbled as he leaned his sword against his cot, close to hand.

The smoke from his offering began to cloud the tent, softening the light of the lamps that hung above him. He crossed his hands over his armoured chest and felt the image of the dragon there, its outspread wings stretching across the surface of hardened bull's hide.

Anguis... he heard in his mind, as though a voice called out in a thick fog. *Anguissssss....*

It was the screams that woke him. His face hurt, and his eyes rolled in his lolling head.

The screams again.

"Adara!"

Then laughter, and more screaming, followed by a thunder of hooves.

"Adara!"

His hands and legs were bound to a chair, and heat radiated from all sides. Then, a roar. A terrible sound of fire and breaking trees.

Fire surrounded him in a giant ring, and he felt the flame licking at his bubbling flesh.

"Ahhh!!!" he cried out.

Another roar to drown out the cries and then...

Lucius rolled off his cot into the corner of his tent with his sword in hand. Sweat stung his eyes, and the room swam before him. He crouched like a cornered animal, breathless and panting before he spotted Barta and Dagon kneeling before him, their hands gripping him tightly to avoid being slashed.

"Anguis! Anguis! It's us!" Dagon pleaded, his arms shaking against Lucius' strength. "The Gods have sent you a dream. All is well, here and now. We're friends, Anguis."

Lucius recognized Dagon's red-brown hair and beard, and the dark form of Barta beside him. Then he remembered fire and cries of pain and despair, and he struggled more until his strength leached from his limbs and he collapsed, his weapon falling beside him.

"Help me get him up," Dagon said to Barta as the two of them hooked their commander's arms and pulled him to the cot to lay him down. "Get water."

Barta rushed to a basin he had just filled with fresh river water, and filled a clay cup. "My lord," he said, handing the cup to Dagon.

"Drink, Anguis. Drink and be well, my friend." Dagon looked up at Barta. "Go and see if anyone heard. Tell them he is well. All is well."

"Will they believe that?"

"Our men will. Luckily, the Votadini, and infantry are too far to hear."

Barta swept from the tent, leaving Dagon with Lucius, whose eyes gazed absently about the tent walls.

"The Dragon came to me," Lucius said to Dagon, who was sitting on a stool beside him, head in hands.

"Anguis," the Sarmatian whispered. "Thank the Gods, you're all right."

Lucius looked at his friend, the unease visible on his face. Their people took dreams very seriously. Dreams mattered, and always bore portents.

"I'm fine now," Lucius assured. "Just a little tired."

"I thought it best to let you rest." Dagon helped Lucius sit up. "Besides, it's not too late. Fourth hour of daylight, I'd say."

"Have the Venicones shown themselves?" Lucius asked as he stretched and walked to the wash basin to splash his face.

"Not yet. Though Lenya just returned with his turmae. Conn Venico is coming. He'll be here in about one hour."

"Help me get ready, then." Lucius dried his face. "I need to look powerful for this meeting."

"You've no need to try, Anguis."

Lucius paused, his back to Dagon.

"That bad?" Dagon asked.

"Yes. That bad." Lucius turned. "But when Apollo speaks to me, it's usually for my own good."

"Let's hope so." Dagon began polishing the cuirass Lucius was already wearing. "Seems the Gods have been speaking to you a lot more in this land."

Lucius did not say anything. All he could hear at that moment was screaming at the back of his consciousness.

The day turned cloudy within the hour, and gusts of wind rushed out of the distant glens as the Venicones approached from the East.

Lucius sat atop Lunaris, with Dagon and Coilus on either side. The vexilla were held high behind them by Barta and Afallach who seemed to have developed a mutual trust and respect.

"That's Conn Venico," Coilus said to Lucius as they looked to the approaching force. "On the white, lowland pony."

Beyond the chief of the Venicones rode about one hundred men on similar ponies, and close to five hundred foot soldiers armed with round shields and spears.

The Venicones' long hair bounced and swayed as they approached the Roman camp, all except Conn Venico, who was bald, and still on his horse. He stared directly at Lucius until he came to a sudden stop before the Roman banners.

"Hail, Praefectus Lucius Metellus Anguis. I bring you greetings and friendship."

Lucius nudged Lunaris forward so that he looked down on the chieftain. "Salve, Conn Venico!" Lucius' voice had to compete with the wind. "Rome thanks you, and Emperor Septimius Severus extends his friendship to you and your people."

Conn Venico inclined his head. "We've been waiting for you to come into our lands, Praefectus."

"Seems the Caledonii were also waiting," Lucius said as he scanned the ranks of Venicones. *And where were all of you?* he thought. "Argentocoxus has been harrying us all the way from Antoninus' wall, but never giving battle. He was boldest when we arrived here." Lucius indicated the fort and the river.

"Argentocoxus is a fox, Praefectus, and not easily cornered."

"A wonder you did not know he was in your lands, Conn Venico," Coilus said, looking with evident dislike at the chieftain.

Conn Venico answered without looking at Coilus. "The Caledonii are always crossing into our lands to raid, Praefectus. Much as the Selgovae to the south are always in the lands of the Votadini."

"Were in our lands," Coilus corrected. "My son killed the Boar."

"I heard," Conn Venico answered quickly, his pale eyes passing from Coilus to Afallach. "Very brave, I'm sure. A good thing the Dragon had captured him first."

The sound of Coilus' slithering blade was immediate, but Lucius' hand shot sideways to stop him, while keeping his eyes on Conn Venico, who smirked just a little too much.

"Well, the Venicones are here now, and that is what matters," Lucius said. "Come!" he called out. "Let's go to my command tent to discuss your expected role in the campaign. The emperor has great expectations of the Venicones, and will reimburse you accordingly."

"Let's talk then," Conn Venico answered. "Rodric!" he called to his second in command, a short, burly clansman with woad markings across his bare chest and arms. "Take my horse and settle the men on the plain."

"Yes. I'll do that," the man grumbled.

Lucius turned Lunaris and went back into the fort with Barta, Coilus, Dagon, Brencis, Afallach, and Conn Venico following. Centurion Torens fell in with them.

Inside the tent, water was poured for each man, including Conn's man, Rodric, who came in last after seeing to his lord's orders.

Lucius made sure the Sarmatians were standing between the Venicones and the Votadini. He leaned over the map, and pointed to their position.

"We're here, and will leave two turmae and a century of Torens' men here when we press on." He looked at Conn Venico. "What is the terrain like from our position to the old fort at Alauna?"

Conn Venico leaned on the table. "First off, your map is inaccurate. There are two burns in your way which will hamper your cavalry. Other than that, the land is flat, and suited to heavy horse. Many trees were cleared by your predecessors and our farmers."

"What about the old camps?" Lucius pressed.

"There are many along the ridge, but most are moss-covered, and require rebuilding. Alauna is in good repair, as is Bertha, which can be supplied by water."

"What about this one?" Dagon pointed to a spot on the map.

"Fendoch? Ha!" Conn Venico shook his head. "Fendoch is at the foot of the highlands, and overrun with Caledonii. Even if you were to take it, and build up the defences, you'd be food for crows before the end of the first night."

Lucius scanned the map silently, the others' eyes on him. "We need to re-establish a strong line of defence along this ridge," he said. "If we have that secured, the rest of the army can move in to establish the main settlement near the sea."

Conn Venico's eyes shot up. "Settlement?"

Lucius smiled. "Yes. Did you think the emperor was simply coming to parley? He means to establish a permanent Roman presence in Caledonia now. That means agriculture, trade with the legions, citizens, and merchants from all corners of the Empire."

Coilus watched Conn Venico carefully. Slowly, the latter smiled and nodded his agreement.

"If you'll permit me, Praefectus, a perfect spot to establish a base is near my own settlement on the south bank of the Tava, which leads directly to the sea, as well as to the fort of Bertha. It's perfect."

Lucius wondered why he was being so amenable to having Rome take almost all his land from him.

"Good," Lucius smiled. "But first we must pave the way for the emperor. I want to lure Argentocoxus out into the open, but I need a good open area in which to do that."

"He'll never come out, Praefectus," Conn Venico insisted. "Besides, how would you do it? Argentocoxus is no fool."

Lucius smiled, but did not offer up his plan. "He's bold right now, and feels he's bloodied us."

"But he has, hasn't he?" Conn Venico looked about the tent.

"If that's what counts for bloodied in Caledonia," Torens' deep voice rumbled, "then I've no doubt we'll win this war."

Lucius stared at the centurion, but said nothing. Torens' men had been the unlucky ones.

"Before we go any further, Conn Venico, and make you a part of our plans, you and your men must take the Sacramentum, and swear to fight for Rome and the emperor."

"Of course. Romans love ceremony, and I had expected as much." The chieftain nodded once. "It will be no issue for us all to swear."

"We are, all of us, sworn to serve and protect Rome and the emperor. I trust you know the weight of the Sacramentum?"

"Of course, Praefectus." Conn Venico scratched his bald head.

"Good," Lucius answered. "I'm glad to hear it. For the Gods would send Furies to harass anyone who did not keep their word under it."

Everyone was silent, some staring at Conn Venico and his man, Rodric.

"We are here to serve Rome and the emperor, Praefectus."

"Excellent. We'll hold the ceremony tomorrow morning, before setting out for Alauna."

"I'll tell my men to set up camp for the night." Conn Venico turned to leave with Rodric, not waiting for another word from Lucius.

When they were gone, Coilus came up to Lucius and whispered. "See what I mean, Praefectus? A slippery one."

Lucius dismissed everyone to go about their rounds and patrols, while he remained with Dagon to look over the map.

"Going to be a slog, I think," Dagon said, rubbing his bearded chin as he watched Lucius run his finger along the string of marching camps and forts.

"Yes. And we need to get the Caledonii to come out and play."

The night passed with only one incident between the Venicones and the Votadini - a fight over a passing comment.

When the perpetrators were brought before Lucius, prior to the Sacramentum of the Venicones, it could not be surmised which man had been at fault. So, both were tied to one of the transport wagons, and given ten lashes each for breach of discipline.

Coilus had been adamant that the task be performed, while Conn Venico had pushed back to no avail.

It was not how Lucius had wanted to begin the march to Alauna, or indeed the Sacramentum, but discipline was paramount, and no favourites could be shown among the allies. They needed the Venicones.

So, it was with sullen faces that the Venicones lined up before the altar that had been erected for the sacrifice, to take their oath of loyalty in the face of the howling wind rushing them from out of the hills.

Within an hour after that, the main part of the force had packed up their tents, and kit, and lined up on the grass along the river, ready to move out.

Lucius had given orders to his two decurions, Lenya and Hipolit, as well as the centurion, Ulpens, to hold the position at all cost so that the rest of them were not cut off.

"If any attack comes," Lucius said to the two Sarmatians he was leaving in charge of two turmae, "send one rider south and another to find me. Be sure to light your signal fire. Understood?"

"Yes, Praefectus," they answered. "We won't let you down, sir."

"I know. And hopefully you'll be able to rejoin us soon."

Now Lucius watched the two men who stood behind the camp's palisade. All remaining horses and baggage had been moved inside the fort, and a patrol sent out.

"Sound the cornu!" Lucius yelled, and Torens' voice barked the order. "Move out!"

The long file of Sarmatians, Votadini, legionaries, and Venicones began to head north toward Alauna.

VIII

LINEA DEFENSIONIS

'The Line of Defence'

They marched with ghosts.

The long file of men, horses, and wagons plodded over the hill-bound fields, searching for signs of road, camp, tower, or fort, built by their comrades over a hundred years before. The sky darkened with menace, and howls could be heard in the distance, coming from the land of the Caledonii.

Every few miles, the marching Romans and their allies passed moss-covered stone markers. They passed what appeared to be a marching camp, and a derelict signal tower where now, owls nested.

Dagon, where he rode beside Lucius at the head of the column, began to despair of finding any strong position that was worth refortifying. Truthfully, he had begun to lose some faith in Lucius' plans. The Venicones were not trustworthy, and they were marching against their neighbours, their cousins, the Caledonii.

He shifted in his saddle, pulling the lined wolf fur cloak over his scale armour so as to cover it from the mist that had been falling since they had departed.

Anguis, keep your wits... he thought, looking at Lucius.

"What's that, Dagon?" Lucius turned suddenly to him.

"What, Praefectus?" Dagon asked, shocked.

"Nothing. I thought you spoke. Sorry I'm so quiet. This land makes me uneasy. I have to wonder if I'll ever see the sun again."

They did not speak again for some minutes. Dagon watched Lucius out of the corner of his eye. He was used to Lucius' dreams, the images the Gods sent him, but this time the dream seemed to strike at some deep fear. Dagon reminded himself of what his uncle, Mar, had said of Lucius before he passed to the great grassy plains of the Afterlife.

Trust in Lucius Metellus Anguis, my nephew. Trust in the Dragon. The Gods love him, and he will never lead you astray.

Dagon knew his uncle had been wiser than any other man, and so he held the ghostly words close, just as he kept his uncle's sword ever to hand. Dagon reached down to touch the hilt. Something nagged at the back of his mind as his grey eyes scanned the landscape.

Lucius' demeanour was growing darker the farther north they went. For all his people's warlike characteristics, Dagon knew that without joy, there was little worth fighting for. He did not want Lucius, their men, or himself to be numbered among the battle-butchered slaves of Rome's armies.

Are we not all slaves to Rome? Dagon wondered, his thoughts drifting to the Votadini, the Venicones, the common troops, and his own Sarmatian countrymen. *I never thought I would grow war-weary...but I want more...*

Yet he knew the days when his people, men and women, would unsheathe their sacred swords and ride to battle on thunder clouds with the dragons howling at their backs were long gone. Such was the price of weakness.

Dagon looked again at Lucius, his war-brother, his captain, and knew that his path was true. Lucius' family had also become his family, and he wanted to help him find the peace that only came from being in their presence.

"Look!" Lucius said, pointing to a turmae of Sarmatians where their draco standard fluttered wildly toward them. "Hippogriff's patrol!" He kicked and Lunaris shot forward.

"Praefectus!" Hippogriff saluted as his warhorse reared. The decurion turned sideways, handling his mount expertly, his long kontus spear pointed downward. "We've found the camp!"

"Alauna?"

"I believe so, Praefectus. It's as Conn Venico described - a great square beside a river, with five ditches of intact defences."

"Any sign of the enemy?"

"No, sir."

Lucius watched as Hippogriff's riders reigned in behind their decurion.

"We need to establish ourselves at Alauna as soon as possible." Lucius turned to Dagon. "I'll take seven turmae and go ahead to secure the camp. You follow with the rest at a double."

"Why not take more men?" Dagon suggested. "In case it's an ambush."

Lucius nodded. He had wanted to move fast, but saw the right of it and cantered along the Sarmatian horse column. "Xylon, Badru, Pekka, Magar, Vaclar, Dima, Ferda, and Oles... On me! We ride now!"

Lucius wheeled back to the front of the column with Barta following, and the draconaria of each turmae falling in behind.

Dagon watched Lucius' red cloak plunge into the mists with his countrymen at his back.

"You heard the praefectus! Double-time! To Alauna!"

The column lurched into motion again with Torens' cornicen sounding a long note on the horn.

"Will the infantry be able to keep up with us?" Afallach asked Dagon.

"They should," Dagon said as they heard the crack of the centurion's vinerod on one of his men. He laughed. "They will. Coilus," Dagon began, "we should fan out. Send some of your men wide on our left flank."

"Right away!" The Votadini chieftain spun his horse, and went back to his men to give the order. A minute later, Votadini horsemen swept in an arc to the West.

Alauna lay quiet beside the river, its embankments long since deserted. A doe stood grazing in the middle of the camp, comfortable in the still mist. The river trickled nearby, and the branches of young trees at the riverbank swayed in the wind.

When the ground began to shake, the doe looked up, her nose pointed and flaring into the mist. She turned and bounded away, but only just as the barbed arrow took her in the neck, and she tumbled into the ditch of the first vallum. Her bulging eyes gleamed as she saw the dragon head appear above her, and the man came down to her with something in his hand.

"Looks like we have something more than rations tonight, sir!" Magar called up to Lucius who sat astride Lunaris at the top of the defences.

"Good shot, Magar," Lucius said. "But hurry. We need to secure this place."

Magar called for two of his men to come and carry the beast up before slinging his bow back over his shoulder and returning to the top where the horsemen were swarming about the camp like hornets.

In the middle, Lucius was looking around, checking the sight lines, state of defences, and their proximity to the highlands to the West.

"Good. This will do nicely," he said to Hippogriff.

"Area secure, Praefectus!" Xylon reported.

"Good!" Lucius shielded his eyes and stared to the North where he spotted what looked like a herd of deer staring at the horsemen. "Magar!"

"Yes, Praefectus!"

"One deer won't feed the cohort, or our friends." Lucius pointed. "See if you can take a few more for a proper feast."

"Yes, sir!" Magar jumped into the saddle, strung his bow, and thundered after the quarry with his men.

When Dagon and the rest of their force arrived two hours later, Alauna had already been turned into a real camp once again.

The venison had been good, and outside, beyond the defences, the bones and fat still smouldered in offering to the Gods.

Conn Venico and his man, Rodric, walked silently along the tent rows and horse lines. The chieftain had business to take care of. He was restless.

"I don't like being held hostage like this, Rodric. Not one bit."

"I agree. The Roman isn't even using us to hunt the Caledonii."

Conn Venico looked sideways at his burly servant. "I'm surprised to hear you speak of hunting your own people."

"I serve you, Conn Venico."

"And I now serve Rome."

"Yes."

"And?"

"And what?"

"You would know for how long I would serve Rome. Correct?"

"That is your affair."

"Hmm." Conn Venico stopped and ran his hand over his bald head. "You think these Romans and Sarmatians are weak. But let me tell you, they are not. They are fierce." He stopped to look up at the darkening sky. "When the Boar sent word to me that I should join the rebellion against Rome and the Votadini, I declined. The key, Rodric, is survival, and striking at the opportune moment." Conn Venico continued to walk, his voice low, his eyes wary of the troops who warmed their hands by the fires before their tents.

"Then there is the emperor, Septimius Severus himself. A man who killed his every opponent, even Clodius Albinus who ruled for Rome in Britannia, and who would have dealt with us in a way that would have been more to our advantage. No, Rodric. We must be Rome's ally for now. And if they settle my lands, and establish a city, trade will come from around the world to our doorstep. There is as much power in trade and money as there is in military might. What is it? Why do you frown?"

"You would invite the world to take away your freedoms. You invite Rome to fuck you and your people."

"Careful." Conn Venico towered above him. "I have my limits."

"Yes, my lord. But mind where this so-called dragon sets himself up."

"Oh, I do mind it. Let him do the work for now. The emperor will be here soon anyway. Besides, he defeated the Boar of the Selgovae, and he was a much greater foe than Argentocoxus who hides in the hills like a coward. The Caledonii will bow to Rome soon enough, and the Venicones will be on the right side of the conflict." Conn Venico continued walking, but Rodric remained standing where he was among the horses, his fists clenched, and cursing the man he served.

For two days, Lucius drilled the cavalry and infantry with help from Afallach and Torens. He knew the various forces needed to work in concert if it came to an open battle. There was no way they could ride up those mountains, or into the bogs without being decimated.

Patience, however futile, was needed until they could draw the Caledonii out onto the plains.

Lucius rode as hard and fast as any of his men. He trained with kontos, sword, and javelin, until the Sarmatian and Votadini cavalry moved as one entity, like a great writhing school of silver fish in the sea.

The infantry had a harder time melding with the Venicones foot soldiers, so much so that Lucius and Torens decided the

Venicones would be used as hill scouts to perhaps draw out the enemy.

One thing bothered Lucius and the commanders, however, and it came to light on their third night at Alauna, days after any sightings of the enemy.

"We've had no word from the legions for a while," Dagon said, leaning on his fists on the map. "Conn Venico, have your people reported anything?"

"Nothing, Princeps." He looked then at Lucius. "They should have crossed Antoninus' wall by now, no?"

"Perhaps. An imperial army moves slower than one legion."

"How many troops is the emperor bringing?" Rodric blurted out, his gravelly voice annoying Lucius.

"More than one legion," Lucius responded, staring at the man.

Rodric stared absently at the map, his jaw working.

"We should send riders south to check on Lenya and Hipolit, and see if they've had word."

"My thinking exactly, Brencis. Can you take two turmae tomorrow?"

"Yes, Praefectus." Brencis smiled. "I can take Shura and Dima with me."

"Perfect. And we'll leave Alauna tomorrow for this position." Lucius pointed at the map. "The old camp called Strageath, by the river."

"We'll need to leave men to hold Alauna, Praefectus," Coilus said.

"Let's leave two of your own turmae, Coilus. Are you amenable to that?"

"Of course," the Votadini chief nodded.

"We should leave some infantry here too, Praefectus," Torens said. "Alauna's too valuable a position. What say I leave three contubernia here with one of my optios?"

"That should be enough. Then, from Strageath we should be able to patrol north toward Fendoch."

"I told you before, Praefectus," Conn Venico began, "Fendoch is overrun with Caledonii. You don't have enough men."

Lucius smiled. "If the cowards won't come to us, we'll go to them, and drag them into battle." Lucius turned to Brencis. "As soon as you have word of the imperial army, I want you and your men to come back and join us with all speed."

"Yes, sir. What shall I tell the legates if we find them?"

"Tell them we are securing a foothold in Caledonia, and that if they want to keep it, they should come as quickly as possible." Lucius looked at the map again and pointed. "Conn Venico, is this the position you propose for settlement? Here beside the Tava?"

"Yes, Praefectus. Just east of my own capital."

"Brencis, take note. The emperor's fleet can sail up the Tava to here and begin building, according to the chief of the Venicones."

"But, Praefectus, I really should be there when-"

"You will be, Conn Venico," Lucius cut him off. "Centurion Torens will take command of your troops, apart from your personal guard to escort you back home."

The chieftain looked thoroughly displeased, but held his tongue. "Very well, but I will leave Rodric with you for his knowledge of the hills, and the men's fear of him."

"Good," Lucius agreed. "Gentlemen, tomorrow we march."

It was past midnight when Dagon appeared at the entrance to the command tent with Hippogriff. Both of them were cloaked in black and had come quietly as commanded by Lucius.

Their praefectus was awake when they appeared, and poring over his old map of the region. "Good. You're here," Lucius greeted them and invited them to sit at the table with him. Wine was waiting, and all three tipped a bit to the Gods before sipping.

"Ahh. My Greek side appreciates the vintage, Praefectus." Hippogriff bowed his head. "Hand me a scroll and I'd be in Elysium," he sighed.

"And what does the Sarmatian in you appreciate, my friend?" Lucius smiled and laid his pugio on the table, pushing it aside.

"To ride like the wind beneath the dragon banner and slay our enemies, Praefectus. Nothing more."

Dagon rubbed his jaw, looked to Lucius, and nodded. Hippogriff was one of their best decurions, a thinker and a fighter.

"I have a special patrol for you, Hippogriff," Lucius said in all seriousness.

"I'm happy to serve the Dragon, sir."

"I don't trust the Venicones. I wonder if they won't send warning of our movements to the Caledonii. We can't trust their information fully."

"What can I do, Praefectus?" the veteran Sarmatian said.

"I want you to take your turmae ahead before first light, and go directly north to scout out Fendoch fort. Search for the enemy, but don't engage them unless you have no choice. It may well be overrun with barbarians." Lucius ran his finger along the map from Alauna to Fendoch. "According to this, the hills are relatively low, the terrain open."

"But be mindful of the bogs,' Dagon added. "They could be anywhere."

"It may be that our maps are inaccurate" Lucius said. "Go easy and quietly at first. Once you see the state Fendoch is in, ride immediately to this position here." Lucius put his finger on a spot up the Tava river.

"Bertha?" Hippogriff squinted in the lamplight at the small mark and letters on the map. "That is still some distance from where we are now, Praefectus."

"Yes," Lucius stood up, arms crossed. "But we've been moving too slowly. We'll leave men at some of the old watch towers and marching camps along the ridge as we go."

"You'll be stretching our forces very thin, Praefectus," Dagon said formally.

Lucius looked at him. "The army should be coming soon."

Dagon and Hippogriff were silent as Lucius drained his cup and stared at the map.

"I'll go and prepare my men then, Praefectus." Hippogriff stood tall beside Dagon. The tattoos of griffins and horses ran up his neck from his torso.

Lucius forced a smile. He knew the Sarmatian could handle the mission, but as with any decision concerning his men, a shard of doubt worked its way into his confidence.

"Go, my friend. May Epona give you speed," Lucius said, as the red-haired goddess burst into his thoughts.

"And may the God of War's sacred blade cut down any opponent you meet," Dagon said, reaching out and pressing his hand on Hippogriff's scale-armoured chest.

"My lord. Praefectus." Hippogriff bowed to both of them and went out of the tent where the rain had started to fall, causing the torches to sputter throughout the camp.

"I wonder how Adara and the children are?" Lucius said suddenly. He sat down on a stool, and poured another cup of wine for both of them.

Dagon watched Lucius as the hard shell of war cracked momentarily. "I'm sure they are well, Anguis."

"Are they?" Lucius looked up, his eyes terrified. "I haven't heard from them. The Gods are telling me nothing."

"Careful, my friend," Dagon urged.

"I don't... I just..." Lucius shook his head, his lengthening hair hiding his eyes. He sighed, removed his leather arm guards, and rubbed his forearms where the images of twin dragons coiled about him.

"Anguis," Dagon spoke softly, "You can't conquer Caledonia on your own. Not even with our cavalry."

"I can try. We can keep moving."

"At what cost? It won't bring your family to you any faster."

"What do you know, Dagon?" Lucius was suddenly on his feet. "Your family is all here among the men."

"Yes. And you are my brother too, and what I would not give to have what you do, Anguis." Dagon calmed himself. He rarely felt angry with Lucius, but now he was dangerously close. "What good will you be to Adara, Pheobus and Calliope if you are dead? We're at the edge of the world here, and they are just as vulnerable as we are. The only difference is that they are at court, and you are fighting the Caledonii. Both are battlefields. You should have realized that the moment you plunged your blade into Plautianus."

Lucius lunged at Dagon then, his hands taking hold of the younger man's cloak at the shoulders. The dragons on his arms flexed and writhed.

But the Sarmatian did not move or raise his hands. Dagon stood still and tall, and stared into his friend's wild eyes.

Lucius released his grip and spun around, his back to Dagon. "Leave me," he said, his voice hoarse and low. "Go."

"As my praefectus commands." Only then did Dagon's head hang, and he went out into the night to make his own preparations for the march.

The line of the old Roman defensive ridge consisted mostly of run-down watch towers, signal stations, small fortlets, and marching camps.

The rain had not stopped since they left Alauna three hours after Hippogriff's turmae had cut north to go straight to Fendoch. The clouds hung low, and Lucius held a hand up to shield his eyes as he and Coilus watched Conn Venico and his bodyguard head east to the chieftain's capital.

"I hope the legions arrive soon, Praefectus," Coilus said to Lucius, his face creased with concern.

"Me too," Lucius answered. "He's not my choice for someone to watch our backs."

Coilus said nothing, but rejoined the moving column, leaving Lucius alone.

Lucius watched the men and horses filing past, the vexilla and draconaria hanging limp and sodden in the rain. Their faces were grim, each one of them. As the last horse passed, Lucius stayed where he was. He closed his eyes and remembered days long ago when he had watched another column of his men marching over the hot sands of Africa Proconsularis and into Numidia. He had lost the faith of those men in the end. Death had walked too closely to Lucius for the average fighting man.

Only Dagon and the Sarmatians had kept their faith in him, been eager to serve and follow him. Those horsemen were family to him as well.

Apollo, help me to inspire these men as I once did. They've given me much...

He reached down and pat Lunaris' thick neck. "And so have you, my friend."

The stallion neighed as he watched the other horses disappear along the forested ridge.

"You're right. Let's go. I have an apology to make."

Lunaris reared and splashed along the road.

When Lucius came even with the first of the Sarmatian horsemen, he greeted them. "Eiki, Boas, brothers, stay warm with your love of war!"

The men looked up and after a moment smiled and cheered back at him. "Praefectus!" a few others called out.

Lucius saluted and continued up the line. "Oles, Pekka," he called the next decurions. "Soon we'll charge our enemies and you'll take as many scalps and Caledonian beards as you can make a cloak of!"

"Salve, Praefectus!" they called back.

All the way, the Sarmatians began to cheer, and chant, and roar their ancient battle songs from the lands north of the Black Sea.

"And our Votadini brothers! We're happy to ride with you to war!"

The Votadini, led by Afallach, roared their approval, and the horse banner waved proudly beside the dragon.

"Men of sixth legion! Are you with us?" Lucius asked, Lunaris prancing proudly alongside the legionaries.

"They'd better be!" Torens bellowed, extolling good-natured laughter from the men. The centurion even smiled, though very briefly.

"And our Venicones allies?" Lucius said, looking at Rodric where he strode at the head of Conn Venico's men.

They said nothing, but began a rhythmic battering of their short spears on their round shields, faces forward, determined.

"Then let's ride to bloody battle, and feed the gods of war and the Underworld with enemy dead!"

Lucius drew the sword from his back and charged to the front where Barta held the Dragon vexillum high with one arm. Lucius then slowed beside his princeps.

"Welcome back, Anguis," Dagon said, a big smile on his face.

Lucius reached out and pat his friend's shoulder.

"Forgive my despair, Dagon."

"We, all of us, have despair, Anguis. Especially the great among us. There is nothing to forgive."

Lucius nodded his thanks. "Race to that next watch tower?"

"Perhaps-" Dagon was off like a ballista bolt, and Lucius spurred after him, the men cheering from behind.

IX

ORDINATIO IMPERIALIS

'Imperial Order'

To Lucius Metellus Anguis,
Praefectus, Cohors III Britannorum
Quingenaria Sarmatiana

From his loving wife, Adara Metella
Greetings.

My beloved Lucius,

I do not know if this letter will even reach you. I have sent others, but have had no replies from you. Venus showed you to me in a dream last night, and you seemed well enough. I cling to the hope that you are safe, wherever you are in the Caledonian wilds.

I know I should be strong, Lucius, for you, for Phoebus and Calliope, but I cannot help my fear. I feel adrift. We have left Eburacum and have been in Coria for two weeks now, guests of a new friend, Perdita Narbonensa.

The legions passed through the town a few days ago, with the emperor and Caracalla leading them.

I have been invited to a banquet with the empress tonight before she moves on to join the emperor. I wish I could join you in the North, no matter the climate or the danger. I don't feel complete, and neither do the children. Phoebus got into his first fight with the son of another friend, Diana Firma, whose husband is stationed on the Wall. Phoebus is not hurt, though the boy was older than him. Calliope was the one who stopped the argument, She has a way with people it seems.

I have heard much talk of your deeds, in the marketplace. People speak in whispers of 'the Dragon'. I hope you are keeping Dagon and Barta close at all times.

I am at a loss as to what more to say. Apart from my deep love of you and the children, I feel only fear and uncertainty much of the time. But I believe in you, always. I believe in the Gods' gifts to you, and their protection of our family. That must count for something on the edge of the world, no?

I've decided to try and travel north, and somehow, some way, I will get to you. Then life will seem real again. For now, I shall continue to pray to the Gods, and hope that you do indeed hear my voice in the dark hours of the long nights.

Courage, my truest love. May Venus, Apollo, and Epona watch over you.

Your Adara.

Adara rolled the papyrus up and held it, staring at the small flame of lamplight coming from a clay griffin head. She was grateful to be in Perdita's villa outside of the actual town. It was peaceful.

The streets of Coria were noisy, even in the more residential east annex of the settlement. When the soldiers were on leave, they came from all the closest outposts to buy things and spend their wages in the taverns and brothels that catered to the men of the legions. It was the same across the Empire.

Perdita Narbonensa's villa was small but beautifully furnished, and it had a protective wall guarded by a small army of well-oiled slaves.

Adara had come to discover that widowhood suited Perdita just fine, and that her slaves offered her more than solid protection. Thankfully, Perdita was discreet with her guests around. Adara and the children occupied a room on the opposite side of the villa from Perdita's personal rooms, with a view to the South.

The rooms were painted with scenes from what might have been Sicily, or even Greece - green hills, olive groves, and Doric temples dotted the landscape between shuttered windows. The work was not as fine as Adara's mother's, but they still wrung some bit of nostalgia from her heart. She imagined Perdita using this room to sit and gaze out the window while imagining herself back in her distant home on the shores of the Mare Internum.

Perdita said she did not care to go back to her native Narbo, but Adara wondered whether she was being entirely truthful about that. Did one ever truly stop caring about where one was from?

Adara closed her eyes and thought of Athenae and her parents' home on the slopes of Hymetos, the buzzing of the bees, the scent of wild thyme drying beneath the hot sun, and the olive groves where Apollo and Venus had appeared to her.

Dreamlike days, long past, but ever haunting and lingering.

She also missed riding Phoenix around her childhood home, but knew he was better off in Etruria. A part of her regretted not riding more since the children were born.

"What are we doing here?" Adara whispered to herself, putting her head in her hands, the dark curling strands of her hair obscuring the light.

"Mama? Are you sad again?" Calliope turned over on her bed beside Phoebus to look up at her mother.

Adara turned to smile at her daughter. "Are you still awake?"

"Yes, Mama. I didn't want to sleep until you left for your party. I like your blue stola the best."

"Thank you, my girl." Adara leaned over and kissed her cheek.

"Will there be important people at the party?"

"The empress, and her sister will be there. So, yes." Adara felt a tightness in her chest as she looked at Calliope, and Phoebus dozing beyond her.

Then Calliope reached out and placed her hand on Adara's heart. "We will be fine, Mama. Lady Perdita's girl slave is very nice to us. She will watch us while you are gone. Besides, if we are sleeping, Phoebus will not be able to fight."

Adara laughed softly. "You are right." She thought for a moment. "It really upset you, seeing him fight, didn't it?"

Calliope nodded. "I didn't like it. It scared me."

"We should probably not wake him up then."

"No, Mama." That loving, knowing smile.

Adara bent to tuck Calliope more tightly beneath her covers.

"Is that a letter to Baba?" Calliope asked, pointing to the small table where Adara had been sitting.

"Yes. I'll take it to the headquarters building tonight, on the way to the party."

"I hope he gets this one. He must be very lonely without us."

Adara's green eyes glossed over, but she fought back the tears with yet another smile. "Yes. He must be."

"I'm sure Dagon will help him. And the big dragon, um..."

"Barta."

"Yes. Big Barta. I like him. He watches over Baba like Baba watches over us when we are together."

"Yes, he does, my girl. But now, I want you to sleep."

"Yes, Mama. But first, I shall pray to the horse goddess to help Baba to come back to us soon."

"You do that." Adara kissed Calliope and Phoebus once on their foreheads before standing and gathering up her thick cloak and the roll of parchment. "Good night, my girl."

Adara went out of the room and found the slave, Celia, waiting.

"Don't worry, lady," the slave said. "I will sleep behind the door until you return. My mistress has given me strict instructions."

"Good. I'll thank your mistress. And you shall have something when I return and all is well with them."

"Do not worry," the slave repeated, her head bowed.

Adara watched the girl go in and close the door before she went down the corridor to the courtyard where Perdita was waiting with her litter and eight of her bodyguards.

"Time to go!" Perdita clapped as Adara slid into the litter beside her. "Are you well, my dear?"

"I'm well. It's just-"

"After a few cups of wine, you'll be smiling," Perdita interrupted. "Walk on!"

It was not the phrase Adara was looking for. Then again, she was leaving her comfort behind with a slave.

The litter cut through the dusk light, and Adara listened as Perdita talked of some of the wild parties that used to be thrown at Coria.

"We had such fun!" Her pupils seemed to dilate at the memories. "But now, I don't think we'll enjoy such times. The empress is very conservative, you know. So into the whole ideal of Roman virtue."

"Aren't you?" Adara asked, though she knew the answer.

"Gods, no! It gets lonely living alone." Perdita elbowed Adara playfully. "Even when my husband was alive!" She winked and cackled.

"I need to stop at the headquarters building before we go in," Adara said abruptly.

"Another letter?" Perdita shook her head. "He's fighting, my girl. He's not of a mood to write letters. Men forget all about us when they go off to war."

You don't know Lucius, Adara thought, more aggravated with Perdita as the evening and her drunkenness wore on.

The torch-lined streets of Coria were thronging with people. Contubernia of legionaries on duty tramped through the town, pushing their way through merchants, shoppers, Britons, and foreigners from everywhere. The bulk of the army had already passed through, but the residual trade showed no signs of slowing.

Adara peered through the curtains of the litter at the passing faces, most eyes trying to see the ladies carried within. They passed through the east gate and came to a stop on the main east-west thoroughfare, just outside the headquarters building.

"I'll wait here, my dear. You go give your letter and come back." Perdita reclined again, huddled in her fur cloak.

Adara pulled her hood over her head and approached the guarded double-doors. "I need to go to the headquarters to have this sent to my husband," she said to the guard.

The man nodded, recognizing her again, and waved her through.

The courtyard was dotted with groups of soldiers talking, but most stopped when they saw her walk past.

Adara realized she was gripping the papyrus too tightly, and pressed on. Inside she came to a table where a weary-looking optio sat poring over despatches. "Erm." She stood before the man who looked up.

"Oh, Lady Metella. You're back. I told you yesterday, there are no letters from the praefectus."

"Thank you. That's not why I'm here. I wanted to send this." She held out the scroll, and he accepted it reluctantly.

"I'll see what I can do, but it may not reach him. Depends on where he is and how the fighting is going."

"I know. I thank you for your diligence."

The optio sighed, and forced a smile. "If only everyone were as polite as you, lady. I'll get this onto the next delivery."

Adara inclined her head and turned. She got two feet before she stopped suddenly.

"Lady Metella. The Dragon's wife." Marcus Claudius Picus barred her way out of the building, a sly grin on his face. "I did not expect to see you."

"Let me pass," Adara said, holding her head high, rage in her emerald eyes. "The empress is expecting me."

"Why then, we must be going to the same party. Shall we sit together?" Claudius moved a little closer, but Adara stepped back.

"I think not, Tribune. Shouldn't you be on the march?"

"First cohort leaves tomorrow as escort to the empress and her sister."

"How nice for you to avoid the fighting," she said stepping quickly around him.

He grabbed her wrist.

"How dare you touch me!" she fumed, her heart pounding.

"Is there a problem, my lady?" the optio asked. "Sir, perhaps you should unhand the praefectus' wife?" he tried.

Claudius let go.

Adara gave the optio a grateful look, and slipped out the door.

Claudius strode over to the optio and punched him so hard the man stumbled back against the wall, his nose a bloody mass of pulp. "Next time, Optio, I'll have you crucified," he hissed. Before leaving, Claudius grabbed the papyrus scroll Adara had left, and slid it up his sleeve.

The optio did not see a thing.

When Adara stepped back onto the street, she saw Perdita standing beside the litter with an older soldier. They spoke in whispers, and laughed together as they held hands.

"Ah, there she is!" Perdita waved Adara over. "Adara Metella, this is Caius Brevia. He's quarter master for the wall forts. Used to do business with my dearly departed," Perdita actually chuckled, almost choked on the last two words.

"Lady Metella," Brevia bowed slightly, his eyes taking her in quickly. "I'm enjoying the stories going round of your husband's exploits."

Adara smiled politely. "Have you news of his whereabouts?"

"No, lady. Last I heard, he was giving Hades to the Caledonians."

"Shall we all go to the party?" Perdita said suddenly.

"Yes, let's." Brevia gave Perdita his arm and led her across the street to another lane beside the Temple of Jupiter Dolichenus.

Adara followed, watching for signs of Marcus Claudius Picus. Now that she knew Claudius was at the party, she thought seriously about returning to the villa, but decided against it for fear of offending the empress and her sister. Before she could fully make up her mind, Adara was walking through red doors into an atrium filled with people.

There were many ladies present, no doubt the wives of various officers and local men of importance. Mixed in among the latter were merchants, and other officers of varying ranks.

Adara walked around the impluvium in the middle of the atrium floor and felt the cool air from the roof coming down through the hole in the ceiling. A slave came to remove her cloak for her. This caused her to feel vulnerable, and she crossed her arms, the serpent bangle Lucius had given her in Numidia jingling as she did so.

She walked slowly among the other guests, searching the room for the empress, or even Julia Maesa, her sister, but she could see neither. She followed the steady flow of visitors down a corridor lit by braziers, accepting a cup of wine from a passing slave. At the end of the corridor, she came to a room that was bright with lamp light. There, at the other end, Empress Julia Domna reclined with her sister.

There were several men about, seeking to be a part of the discussion. They were not military men, but rather had a manner of philosophers about them. One man, however, looked familiar, but Adara could not place him.

She peered at him between heads and saw him glance her way as he spoke with the empress.

"Metella, there you are."

The voice startled Adara, and caused her to spill some wine on the mosaic floor.

"Will you share a couch with me?" Marcus Claudius Picus asked, though it was more of a demand from a man who was used to getting what he wanted.

"I think not," Adara answered, moving away. She could see the man with the empress rise and come toward her.

"You must be lonely out here on the frontier," Claudius whispered. "You must feel adrift..."

The word made Adara turn.

"Does your husband not care to write to you?"

"I..."

"I too am lonely, Metella. Especially with all the British trollops floating around."

"How dare you!" Adara felt an unfamiliar anger boil beneath her skin. "Stay away from me, Tribune. Or by the Gods, I'll -"

"Ha, ha!" Claudius laughed and was about to retort when the other man came up to them.

"Lady Metella?" the newcomer said.

Adara turned to see the kind face and striped toga of a senator. Her wide eyes betrayed her state, but the man put her at ease.

"Senator Dio," he reminded her. "I know you husband well." He nodded to the tribune who simply stared at Dio and Adara as they moved away toward the empress.

"Of course! Senator Dio! It has been a few years, has it not?" Adara asked, gaining control again.

"Yes. I was back in Bythinia, and then Athenae for a while."

She nodded. "My father wrote that he met with you in Athenae."

Dio smiled. "A long way from Britannia, isn't it?" Dio glanced at Tribune Claudius who had moved off into the crowd.

"Quite," Adara answered, her hand wiping a rivulet of sweat form her brow.

Dio took her hand. "You are among friends now."

She took a breath. "Thank you, Senator."

"Senator Dio," came Julia Domna's commanding voice from a few steps away. "Do bring Lady Metella here so that I may greet her."

"Yes, Augusta," Dio said, bowing to the empress. He led Adara forward so that she stood before Julia Domna and her sister.

Adara bowed as the empress rose from her couch, her silk saffron stola rustling audibly.

"Welcome," the empress said, reaching out to hold Adara's shoulders and kiss her on both cheeks as everyone looked on. "Come, sit with us, my dear." The empress sat back down indicating Adara should take the couch to her left. "I believe you've been in Coria for a few weeks now," Julia Domna said, her big brown eyes never leaving Adara's face.

"Yes, my lady. At the invitation of Lady Perdita."

"Hmm. Yes. Lady Perdita." The empress looked a little disappointed.

"I hear that you are leaving tomorrow," Adara said, "to join the army?"

The empress nodded. "Yes. We are heading into the wilds in search of strange beasts, painted men, and mountains of gold."

There were chuckles from those within earshot.

Adara flushed, but caught on. "I've heard of the painted men, but surely not the talk of strange beasts and mountains of gold."

"Quite right, Metella. Senator Dio and I were just talking about the ridiculous rumours that always spread about unknown lands."

"I dare say, my lady," Dio began, "that we should only find great deer and bears among the Caledonii."

"The truth is," the empress said, "that Caledonia has been a thorn in Rome's side for too long, just as the Parthians used to be. The emperor believes it should become a fully-fledged province."

"From what I know," Adara dared, "the lands north of the Wall have never been easily subdued. Once Rome leaves, will not the Caledonii rebel again?"

"You should have more faith in our legions, lady Metella. Both our husbands are seeking to settle matters and extend the Pax Romana.

"Oh, I do, Augusta. I was only thinking of the rumours of an entire legion being lost in the North."

"You mean the Ninth? Under Agricola?" Dio asked.

"Yes," Adara answered. "If a whole legion could be wiped out..."

"And how would you stabilize that savage land?" the empress asked. Her eyes sparkled, and Adara remembered how she thrived on discussion, even in military affairs.

"After subduing them, would it not be better to establish settlements for trade? Perhaps if they saw civilization?"

"I suspect they would reject it," Dio interjected. "Civilization means different things to different peoples."

"How so, Senator?" the empress asked.

"What we view as civilization in Athenae or Rome, would feel foreign to the Caledonii. For the latter, civilization might be to run among their forested hills and carved standing stones. They have writing, but much of their knowledge is committed to memory. They roam freely across their glens, and drink of fresh mountain streams."

"They sound like beastly savages to me, Senator," Julia Maesa said, sipping her wine.

"They might think the same of us, lady. In Rome, there are few trees, the water is not always clean, and the streets in some areas are overflowing with human waste."

"The Caledonii don't have temples, do they?" Adara asked. "Surely a civilization honours their gods properly, and without human sacrifice."

"I don't know about human sacrifice, but I do know that their temples are the sacred groves, and the rings of stones beneath the stars."

"I might add, Senator," the empress said, "that Rome's ancestors had men fight to the death at funeral games. Is that not also human sacrifice, Metella? Are we uncivilized when we go to the Colosseum?"

"Rome's ancestors had their solid beliefs, Augusta. I do know from my reading that in Athenae the philosophers were creating ideas while men died in funeral games in Rome." Adara bowed her head. *Why did I say that?* she chided herself.

The empress smiled at her. "Not just a pretty face." She paused, looking at Dio and Adara. "I would like both of you to accompany me north tomorrow. We shall see Caledonia and the Caledonii together, and decide on their level of civilization. Will you come?"

"It was my intention to follow and chronicle the events, Augusta," Dio said.

"Good. Metella?"

"I have my children, Augusta. May I bring them?"

"Of course. Even I came here with my children." The empress smiled, though not broadly. The tension between Caracalla and Geta still irked her. That had been why she had convinced the emperor to leave Geta in charge at Eburacum, while Caracalla journeyed with the army to the front. "Besides, I think you have been absent from your husband long enough, Metella. They too need us women, don't they?"

"Thank you, Augusta," Adara said, bowing her head.

"Think nothing of it. I like your company. But I think you should notify your hostess that I am removing you to the North."

Adara got the hint, and stood from the couch.

"I will send a wagon to gather you and your belongings tomorrow morning."

"Augusta," Adara bowed and made her way back through the crowd. The couch she had been occupying was filled instantly by another person.

Adara's heart lightened considerably at the thought of moving closer to Lucius. Surely she and the children would be safe with the empress, surrounded by Praetorians and legions of Rome's finest.

Not even the thought of that viper, Claudius, dampened her elation. Soon, she and Lucius would be together, and all would be well. *Surely it will!*

She accepted another cup of wine from one of the slaves, and smiled to herself as she sipped.

"Adara? There you are!"

Adara turned to see the tall form of Lady Diana who stood by while her husband talked with a group of soldiers.

"I heard the empress had you sit with her just now." Her tired eyes were wide with an awe that made Adara pity her a little. Things were different so far from Rome.

"Yes. We talked for a bit. She has asked me to go north with her tomorrow."

"Oh, Perdita will be perfectly distraught," Diana said, anticipating the sadness Adara's absence would cause her friend.

"I know. I must find her and tell her. Have you seen her?"

Diana looked over people's heads toward the garden. "I think I saw her with Brevia beneath the peristylium earlier."

"Good. I'll go find her. I'll be back." Adara began cutting through the crowd, past a pair of flute players near a table groaning with food.

"Wait! I'll come too," Diana said. "If I hear any more talk of killing I'll be bored to death." She glanced at her husband and pointed to where she was going. He nodded, and went back to his conversation.

The crowd thinned out and Adara was able to breathe more easily.

"Do you see her?" Diana asked, as she caught up.

They looked about the garden, around shrubs and herb beds. Toward the centre was a fountain. They heard a faint laughter above the gentle trickle of water. The two women walked along the curving path until it opened onto a circular area with stone benches around a fountain in the shape of a satyr.

"Good gods!" Diana blurted out.

They blundered onto Perdita, bent over one of the benches. Her rich stola was hoisted about her waist, and behind her Brevia pumped in and out of her like an aged stallion in rut.

"Perdita?" Adara said, incredulity upon her face. "The empress is in the domus."

Brevia laughed, and pumped, and grunted faster, his hands on Perdita's shoulders as he continued.

"Not...now...Metella," Perdita said, gripping the bench and biting her lip.

There was more laughter beyond, from the other side of the fountain where a few men chuckled and drank as they watched.

"Come, Adara," Diana said. "Let's go from here."

"What's your rush, Metella?" Claudius broke away from the group of men, and came toward her. "Why don't you and I get a bench and show them how it's done?"

Adara's hand shot out and caught Claudius' face full-force, before Diana forcefully pulled her quickly away to disappear into the crowd that was edging its way into the peristylium.

Claudius Picus' face contorted with rage as he watched them go, his cruel mind turning over the hurt he wanted to cause her. The laughing behind him ceased when he wheeled around.

He stalked over to Brevia, who was nearing his climax, and shoved the man into the shrubbery. "Make way for your superior, ingrate." Claudius pushed Perdita down so hard that she cried out, hoisted his toga, and began to ram.

Brevia stood by and said nothing, afraid, like the others, to challenge the Patrician tribune.

Inside the domus, Adara found Senator Dio at the table laid out with food.

"Metella?" He stopped serving himself right away. "What is it?"

"Lady Perdita, and Brevia... Tribune Claudius."

At the latter's name, Dio's eyes darkened. "Has he harmed you?"

"I..."

"He tried, Senator," Diana spoke up. "We need to get Lady Metella away from here."

"Where is your husband, Lady Diana?" Dio asked. "Do you have slaves to escort you?"

"Two. And our cart."

"Can you ask your husband to take Lady Metella home?"

"Yes." Diana went in search of her husband. Soon she was back.

"Sir," Diana's husband, Tertius, addressed Dio. "I can escort Lady Metella home. Some of the lads will help me."

"Good man," Dio said. Then he turned to Adara. "Do not worry. I shall travel with you tomorrow, and the empress shall know of this."

"Thank you," Adara said, her green eyes meeting his briefly.

"I'll see that Lady Perdita gets to her litter and her slaves safely," Dio reassured. Knowing Claudius Picus, it was not difficult to decipher what had happened. "Just you go now."

"Come dear," Diana said, a protective arm around Adara as they left the room, and made their way outside.

"Thank you for your help," Adara said to both Diana and Tertius.

"Think nothing of it, lady," Tertius said, fingering the dagger he had hidden beneath his tunic. "These Patrician bastards think they can do anything..."

Soon, they were in Tertius' covered wagon on the road to Perdita's villa.

When they arrived at the villa gates without Perdita, the slaves were reluctant to allow them entry until Diana, whom they knew well, told them that Perdita was coming and that she would need care when she arrived.

"Go inside and see to your packing, Metella," Tertius said. "I'll wait here in the courtyard for Perdita's litter."

"Come. Let's go." Diana led Adara inside while her husband took a cudgel from the gate house, and stood against the wall with the few friends he had brought. Together, they stared at the dark fields beyond, waiting, familiar work for men who had stood watch on the great Wall.

Adara swept past the slaves, down the dimly-lit, painted corridor to the south room where the children were sleeping. She had regained her senses, and now raged at herself inwardly for being made to feel weak and afraid.

"Bring Lady Metella's trunks to her cubiculum," Diana said to the steward as they walked. "She needs to pack."

"But why? So soon?" the man asked. "The domina said nothing of this."

"The empress has asked that Lady Metella be ready to go north with her tomorrow."

The slave's eyes popped wide. "I'll send them right up."

Adara opened the door to the room to see the slave, Celia, sleeping on the floor beside the door.

"Get out, girl!" Diana nudged her as Adara went past and fell to her knees beside the sleeping children.

Thank you, Apollo and Diana, for watching over them. She wanted to cry for all the relief she felt then, but held back the tears. She had work to do.

Celia set about lighting the lamps in the cubiculum, while Diana watched Adara.

Diana understood her fear. She too had children, and had reared them in her husband's absence for long stretches of time. It could fray the nerves to madness.

"Celia," Diana said. "Have a platter of food and some water brought up."

"Yes, my lady. Right away." Celia went out just as the steward and four slaves arrived carrying two large trunks into the room.

Shall we pack for your, Lady Metella?"

"No," Adara answered, standing from beside the beds. "I'll do it myself."

The slaves bowed and left, leaving Adara, Diana, and the children alone in the room.

When Adara awoke, it was to find the small round faces of Phoebus and Calliope staring at her.

"Mama? Why are all of our things packed?" asked Phoebus. "Are we leaving?"

Adara rubbed her eyes and looked out the window to see sunlight filtering in through the panes. The faint screeching of a magpie could be heard, as well as hurried footsteps in the corridor outside. Adara stood and turned to her children.

"Yes. We are leaving. The empress has asked that we go north with her to join the army."

"So we'll see Baba?" Calliope sat upon her knees on the bed.

"Yes." Adara realized the empress might send for her soon, and panic set in. "We must get ready. Put on the travel clothes I've set aside for you, while I change as well."

Adara had finished packing during the night, but as soon as she had finished, she had collapsed exhausted beside the twins.

Diana had gone out to see her husband then.

Phoebus and Calliope helped each other with their woollen tunics and breeches, while Adara changed from her blue stola to a more sedate, dark green one with a thick grey cloak. The calfskin boots were hardly fashionable, but since she had arrived in Britannia, wearing light, brilliant fabrics and thin shoes seemed ridiculous. When she finished, she washed her face and helped the children.

"Was it a nice party, Mama?" Calliope asked.

"Ah, it was fine. So many people." Adara tried to shake the images of Perdita from her mind, but without success. *I need to see if she is all right before leaving,* she thought.

"Did you see your friends?" Phoebus asked.

"I saw Senator Dio, a friend of your father's."

"And the empress?" Calliope pressed.

Adara stopped. In her frantic state, she was forgetting the two people who meant more to her than anyone, apart from Lucius. She knelt down before both children.

"I'm sorry. Yes." She smiled. "The empress was there, and Perdita, and Diana, and so many ladies dressed in fine stolas, and men in shiny uniforms and white togas."

"Ooo..." the children smiled.

"But now, my loves, we need to go down and wait for the empress' people to come for us." Adara opened the door and led them out into the corridor. "We'll break our fast while we wait."

"I'm so hungry," Phoebus said as they went.

"Oh, Celia!" Adara called the slave girl as she passed. "Is your domina back?"

"She's locked in her cubiculum, Lady Metella. Won't see anyone."

"Please take the children to get some food in the triclinium while I go to see her. And tell the steward that our trunks are ready to be taken to the courtyard."

"Yes, lady." Celia bowed and smiled to the children. "Come on then. Let's get you fed."

Adara nodded to the children, and they followed the slave girl while she went in the opposite direction to Perdita's cubiculum.

"How is she?" Adara said as she came up to Diana, who stood outside the locked door.

Diana looked exhausted. Dark circles rimmed her eyes, and her hair sprouted in tangles, a contrast to the precision with which it had been made up the night before.

"She's not well at all. Something happened after we left, but she won't speak of it." Diana now whispered. "When her litter came back last night, I was standing with Tertius in the courtyard. I could hear her sobbing from afar. She demanded we turn around so she could enter her own domus without us seeing her. Of course, her slaves won't tell me a thing, on her orders."

"Gods, what more did Brevia do to her?" Adara put her hand on the blue and gold door just as it swung open.

"Perdita stood there, a shade of her former, confident, smiling, lustful self. The person who stood in her place was bruised to black and blue, her eyes swallowed up in swelling. She limped, unable to walk with ease as she approached Adara and Diana, her eyes never leaving the former.

"Oh, Perdita...what did he do to you?" Adara felt her stomach lurch.

"What did *he* do? HE? I was enjoying Brevia until you came along."

"Perdita!" Diana said, shocked.

"Why don't you ask me what the tribune did to me?" Drool spilled out of Perdita's swollen lips, but she carried on. "Do you want to know how he fucked me so hard I thought I would die? How he tore my clothes, and bit at my breasts in a filthy rage, all because you hit him?" Perdita ripped open her tunica to reveal a bruised and bloodied torso. Her breasts revealed teeth marks and dried blood. She began to sob again, and Adara reached out to her with a shaking hand.

"No!" Perdita's fury came back. "Because of you, you cold bitch, I'm humiliated in front of half the people of Coria who saw me carried out of there!"

"I couldn't let that viper near me, Perdita," Adara protested.

"Maybe you should have? Your husband is off, probably raping his way through Caledonia while you sit here with your brats pretending all is perfect. What you need, Metella, is a good fuck to straighten you out!"

"That's enough, Perdita!" Diana pushed her back gently into the room. "She doesn't mean that, Adara."

Adara stood there shaking with sadness, but now more so with rage and fury. She had pitied Perdita, but her vitriolic words regarding her family made her want to slap the woman. However, she held herself back.

"I understand that you were wronged, Perdita, and I feel awful for you. The tribune should be killed for what he did." Adara paused to catch her breath. "I'm sorry you feel the way you do about me, especially as I thought we'd become friends, and you've shown me such kindness beneath your roof."

Now Adara's face darkened.

"My children and I are leaving within the hour, and we thank you for your hospitality." She wanted to tell Perdita it was her own fault for degrading herself so, for putting herself out like a common whore for the first aged has-been that showed interest. Instead, before turning to leave, she said, "But gods help you if you ever speak so of my family again."

Perdita limped up to Adara, and spat in her face.

"Get out," she muttered.

Adara wiped her face, and with her head held high, turned and went back down the corridor to get the children.

A half hour later, Adara, Phoebus, and Calliope stood in the courtyard of Perdita's villa, watching the trunks being loaded into the covered wagon that the empress had sent with Senator Dio, and a contubernium of her personal Syrian guard.

Dio dismounted from his horse to speak with Tertius who told him in hushed tones what had happened.

Adara recognized some of the Syrians who had ridden with the cart from the time the empress had kept her and

Lucius safe at her private villa along the Tiber, in the days before Plautianus had been killed.

"It is good to see you again," Adara said to the leader, unable to remember his name.

The man smiled and bowed his head. "We are honoured to be your escort, Lady Metella," he said before seeing to the rest of the luggage.

"I'm sorry you are leaving like this," Diana said as she came up beside Adara.

"Me too." Adara meant it. She had felt close to Diana, even Perdita for a time, but it was all soured now, and she could not wait to be away. Adara turned and sighed. "Thank you for helping me."

"I think it'll be Perdita who needs the help now," Diana said, shaking her head.

"Yes."

"We're ready to go," Senator Dio said.

"Good," Adara turned to Diana and hugged her. "Take care."

"You too, Metella. I... I know she didn't mean all that...the things she said."

Adara's smile faded. "Goodbye, Diana." She turned and helped the children climb into the wagon, then accepted Tertius' hand as she climbed up.

"Thank you, Tertius. You're a man of honour."

"Shh. Don't let the wife hear you. She'll think I've gone soft." He winked and Adara smiled.

"Forward!" Dio called out, and the wagon creaked into motion.

Adara watched the villa disappear behind them as they rolled away, the sound of the horses' hooves clipping on the cobbles of the Roman road. The sun was finally shining brightly, and by midday, Adara, Phoebus, and Calliope were part of the imperial wagon train guarded by a legion of men.

As they crossed through the gates of the Wall, just north of Coria, the world opened up before them, wild, and green, and unknown.

Adara gazed out the opening, the children dozing in her lap. Across from her, Julia Domna, and Julia Maesa spoke idly about various people while Adara half-listened, lost in thought.

"Senator Dio tells me there was some trouble last night."

Adara looked up to see the empress staring at her, her dark eyes studying her intently. "Ah, yes, Augusta. Lady Perdita was badly assaulted at the party."

"Really?" Julia Maesa lifted her head. "I heard nothing. So strange." She popped another grape into her mouth and closed her eyes as she settled into her pile of furs.

"Lady Perdita was bound to get into trouble," Julia Domna said. "I meant you, Metella. What happened?"

Adara wondered whether she should say anything. If Tribune Claudius was a favourite of the emperor and empress, she could put her family in danger.

Julia Domna, astute as ever, could see the doubt and fear plain on Adara's face. "Have I not protected your family in the past, Metella?" the empress added. "What happened?"

"Tribune Claudius and some other men, I didn't know them, were watching Perdita and Brevia...in coitus...in the gardens. I had gone to tell her that I would be leaving her villa and stumbled on the scene with Lady Diana." Adara stopped, embarrassed and angry all over again. But the empress nodded, wanting to know more.

"Tribune Claudius approached me, not for the first time, and said we should...that he and I should...do the same."

"What did you say?" Julia Maesa's eyes opened wide.

Adara could see her pupils were dilated, curious for some details to break her ever-present boredom.

"Nothing. I slapped him hard across the face, and fled the scene with Diana. Senator Dio ensured I got home, escorted by Diana and her husband."

"And after that," the empress began, "Claudius beat and raped *Lady* Perdita before the others."

"You knew, Augusta?" Adara asked.

"Of course. I know everything that happens. That is how I keep the emperor alive. I wanted to hear it from you, Metella."

"But, are you not angry, Augusta?"

"Not with you. Tribune Claudius is a vile creature, but he is wealthy. He was a supporter of Plautianus, and would have died in the proscriptions after Plautianus' timely slaying by your husband if he were not a friend of Caracalla."

Adara's eyes widened in horror, but she knew she had to be careful when it came to the empress' sons.

"Yes. My son interceded on Claudius' behalf, and the emperor agreed to spare him."

"He is handsome, but *such* a wretch," Julia Maesa said, laying herself back down.

"At any rate, Metella, I am loathe to think such a thing went on beneath the roof of a domus where I was holding what I thought was a civilized gathering."

Adara glanced out the window at the marching troops, row upon row of crimson, and iron, and brass clanging as they went.

"Do not fret," the empress said. "I ordered Claudius to march last night and replaced him as my escort. He is nowhere near us."

Adara breathed deeply and relaxed as Calliope shifted in her lap and began to sing softly in her sleep.

"By Apollo," the empress said, looking in wonder at the little girl. "She sings in her sleep?"

"Yes, often." Adara smiled.

Julia Domna stared at her a moment longer. She recognized a shadow of her former self, when her own children had been born, what seemed ages ago. It was another lifetime when last her sons curled up trustingly in her arms, amid the silken folds of her stola. The young woman before her was caring and naive, she knew, but she was also intelligent, and so, the empress decided to pass the time in the philosophical converse she so enjoyed.

"Tell me, Metella. What do you think of the role of women in Athenae versus Rome, or even here, in Britannia?"

Adara looked up from stroking Calliope's soft blonde hair, and went quickly over what the most powerful woman in the Empire was likely to think on such a subject.

It was going to be a long journey.

X

MACHINA BELLICA

'War Machine'

The emperor drove his legions on at a relentless pace. Three legions, the Praetorian Guard, and thousands of auxiliary troops from across the Empire tramped across the landscape of northern Britannia.

In the wake of this invasion army, near to a legion of supply wagons, merchants, and camp followers clung to the great lumbering beast like parasites or symbionts, depending on their need or role.

From distant rocky crags, in faraway eyries, rebel britons of the Selgovae, Maeatae, and the Caledonii watched and waited as the men of Rome repaired their overgrown roads, chopped down Britannia's forests, levelled her heights, bridged rivers, and filled her swamps.

The emperor wanted this victory, and he threw tens of thousands of men into the campaign. At the front of this war machine, Septimius Severus put his son, Caracalla, in command. It was time the young Caesar proved his worth, now that he was apart from the brother he seemed to hate with fury.

The army never stopped in one place for more than a night or two, and parties of troops and engineers were constantly scouting ahead to re-establish strategic positions, fords, and signal stations. Rome was re-establishing the blueprint of her former glory in that northern land.

Caracalla was given his chance to shine. He slept, and ate, and marched with the men of the legions, striving to become one of them, brothers in blood, dried beef, and back-breaking work. He joked with the men, learned their marching songs, and drilled with scutum, pilum, and gladius. The young Caesar seemed to be thriving on the march, but the enemy remained elusive, and Caracalla was untested where it truly mattered.

At the centre of the marching column, the emperor's great wagon rolled, a mobile command centre girt with iron, and topped with soaring purple and gold vexilla and aquilaea.

Because of his illness, Septimius Severus rode in the titanic wagon amid pillows, tables, stools, and scrolls. Here he met with his advisors to discuss the campaign, the unimaginable logistics, treaties, troop movements and dispositions. It was nowhere near the size of the force he had taken into Parthia. That had consisted of over thirty legions. The conquering of Caledonia, it had been decided, was a much lesser challenge than the defeat of the Parthian Empire. Severus, though he remained inside his mobile metropolis, knew everything that went on in the crimson ranks of his army.

By night, from the sprawling command tent at the centre of his city, the emperor consulted with his seers and astrologer, with his loyal chamberlain, Castor, ever by his side.

For the last day, as rain and sleet lashed the army, Severus waited as the engineers checked the ford of the Bodotria river. He was growing impatient, and his cough worsened as the weather did likewise. What weighed on Septimius Severus' mind was the lack of communication from the Sarmatian and Votadini cavalry cohorts led by Lucius Metellus Anguis.

For months there had been reports of victories and the capture of enemy contingents. Now, silence. It was as though hundreds of cataphracts and legionaries had been swallowed up in the black bogs of Caledonia.

"Do you remember the Ninth Legion?" the emperor said to the Praetorian Prefect as they waited in the wagon, the sound of rain near-deafening.

Aemilius Papinianus, Prefect of the Praetorian Guard since the fall of Plautianus, finished writing something and handed it to his second, Domitius Ulpianus, who took it and filed the paper.

"Yes, sire," Papinian answered. "I have heard of the disappearance of that legion, but I believe it is only hearsay, stories put out by the Caledonians, or others."

"Perhaps," the emperor said, shifting in his chair covered with cushions. His eyes drifted to the ceiling of the elaborate wagon which had been painted with constellations. Severus eyed Papinian for a few moments. The man was an apt administrator, and his knowledge of Roman law was unequaled. He was brilliant, and his Questiones were a testament to that.

However, the emperor knew that Papinian was not an able soldier. He was not fit to lead the Guard against the Caledonii in the field.

"Castor," Severus gestured for his chamberlain. "More of that foul-smelling tea. I feel a cough coming on again." The tea was brought and Severus took a sip, and cleared his throat. "If we don't hear something soon, Papinian, I want you to send three cavalry cohorts to look for them."

"Yes, sire," Papinian answered.

The praetorian prefect, a Syrian and kinsman of the empress, was close to the same age as the emperor. His dark hair was short and curling, the hairline retreating from his creased brow.

When the emperor looked at Papinian, he was reminded of his wife's father, a tall, severe man with a long narrow nose, more of an academic or priest than a man of war. Those were important traits in a civilized man, he knew, but the emperor also knew they had come to fight in Caledonia.

Septimius Severus closed his eyes for a few minutes and tried to imagine heat and sunlight, days in his youth when he rode gladly to battle, even so recently as in Parthia when he marched more than thirty legions across the deserts of Mesopotamia to Ctesiphon. Now his legs pained him, and the British weather had made his cough twenty times worse.

"The stars," the emperor muttered.

Papinianus and Ulpianus both looked up from their papers at Severus.

Castor brought an extra blanket, and laid it over the emperor.

Severus' eyes shot open suddenly, and he seemed his old alert self again. "This is too slow! Papinianus, have one of your men go and tell my son I wish to see him."

"Yes, sire." Papinian rose from his stool and stepped out onto the back platform of the colossal wagon where several Praetorians waited with horses below. "Centurion Cornelius!" he called, pulling the cowl of his robe over his head.

"Yes, sir!" Alerio snapped to attention.

"The emperor wishes to see Caesar Caracalla. Take a horse and ride to the waterfront."

"Sir!" Alerio saluted again, mounted one of the horses, and rode down the rows of men and wagons, through the squelching mud, until he reached the spot where the engineers were gathered.

Through the downpour, Alerio could see Caracalla discussing the fording of the river and overlooking the repairs to the bridge.

"Sire, it won't handle all these men, horses, and wagons," one of the engineers pleaded. "It's too old."

"Then work faster on the new bridge!" Caracalla rubbed his jaw roughly. "We've already wasted enough time here. The emperor is waiting...I'm waiting! We're all waiting when we should be fighting." Caracalla glanced sideways at Alerio in his Praetorian uniform, and nodded. "These Caledonian bastards swim across this water, man! Should we do the same?"

"No, sire." The engineer calmed himself. They were all getting used to taking orders from the young caesar. "We'll continue."

"What about pontoon bridges?" Alerio ventured suddenly.

Caracalla turned quickly to look at him.

"Sire, I remember crossing the Tigris on your father's Parthian campaign. Several pontoon bridges got the army across and into the fight."

"You see?" Caracalla spat at the engineers. "Now that's a thought! Staring you right in the face. Just because there was a timber bridge here before doesn't mean you have to build the same thing again."

"But the current..." another engineer began but cut himself short.

"It could work, sire," said another. "We would need to begin immediately."

"Then start cutting trees," Caracalla said, finally turning to Alerio. "What is it, Centurion?"

"The emperor wishes to see you, Caesar." Alerio saluted.

"Ah, my father is more impatient the sicker he gets."

Alerio looked at the ground.

"Very well, Centurion. Let's go back to him. I need something to eat anyway." Caracalla snapped his fingers and his horse was brought to him. He mounted, as did Alerio, and they trotted back to the emperor.

"Father!" Caracalla said as he entered the wagon with Alerio behind him. "You wanted to see me?"

Both Papinianus and Ulpianus stood and bowed slightly to Caracalla. "Sire," they said in unison.

Caracalla ignored them, and sat across from the emperor. A slave filled his cup immediately and handed him a silver plate of bread, cheese, and cold meat.

Alerio remained at attention by the door.

"Why is the fording taking so long?" the emperor demanded of his son.

"Your engineers, Father, leave much to be desired. They've no guts for the fucking task."

Papinianus and Ulpianus looked up from their writing.

"I would remind you that you are not a common soldier. You are a caesar, and should behave like one." Severus' long beard twitched as he spoke, low and level.

Caracalla said nothing.

"What is being done? We can't sit here like this."

"Father, I've ordered them to move faster on construction of a pontoon bridge."

"Very good. I did that same thing in Parthia," the emperor looked pleased.

Caracalla looked at Alerio and then back to his father. Alerio said nothing.

"The first pontoon bridge should be ready by tomorrow morning," Caracalla said. "I would like to take three centuries of the Guard, and some cavalry across to scout."

Septimius Severus coughed several times, using the hem of his gold-embroidered tunic to wipe the spittle from the corner of his mouth. *I should test my son,* he thought. *But is this the way?* "Very well," Severus agreed. "As soon as the temporary pontoon bridge is complete, ride across and check for signs of our men, allies, or the enemy. Then return to report."

"I'll do that." Caracalla smiled.

"Take Centurion Cornelius with you."

They all looked at Alerio who saluted and stood to attention.

"Yes, Father," Caracalla answered, running his hand over his thick, wet hair.

"Now go, and ensure they finish," the emperor said. "I need to go over these petitions with Ulpianus. Even at war, on the edge of the Empire, it seems there are still many with the audacity to ask for things."

"It must be allowed, sire, if we are to have the citizens feel they all have an equal share in Rome's glory. It can only support your cause in Britannia if you conduct business as usual." Papinianus, hands pressed together over his work, looked at everyone expecting them to agree wholeheartedly.

Ulpianus continued writing, and Caracalla rolled his eyes.

"Yes, yes," the emperor said. "I have read your Questiones, my friend. I am aware of your admirable stance on the matter. Now, Ulpianus, what's next?"

"Sire..." Ulpianus stood with a papyrus scroll in hand and began to read.

Caracalla stood, grabbed his long black cloak from Alerio, and they both stepped outside. Caracalla put on his cloak and stared silently at the ranks of legionaries.

The men were cold, and wet, and eager for a fight, but they would have to wait longer.

"Go gather three centuries of the Guard, and a turmae of horsemen from the Scythian auxilia."

"Yes, Caesar!" Alerio saluted.

"I'm going to go threaten the engineers." Caracalla's hand fastened tightly on a beam of the wagon's railing. "I need to get away from here."

With that, the young caesar was tramping through the mud toward a contingent of sixth legion troops that had just arrived.

Alerio watched as Caracalla greeted tribune Claudius. The sight gave him an ill-feeling, but he had no time for it. He had work to do.

Lucius, I hope you're out there somewhere...

Alerio had been in the Praetorian Guard for a few years now, ever since his role in the downfall and prosecution of the former prefect, Gaius Fulvius Plautianus.

Before the emperor and witnesses, Alerio had testified against Plautianus with proof, however false, that the prefect had plotted against the emperor.

True, it had been Lucius' sword that had cut down Plautianus when he tried to attack the emperor and Caracalla, but Alerio's testimony had been completely damning. He had wanted revenge on Plautianus for hiring the assassins who had inadvertently killed Alene, Lucius' sister and the only woman he had ever loved.

Alerio thought about her every day, and tortured himself with thoughts of the life they might have had together.

Argus, Lucius' bastard half-brother, and a Praetorian spy, had taken that away.

Alene's face floated before Alerio every night, and every night he reached out to her shade to find that he was ever alone. He was surrounded by thousands of troops and camp followers, and he had never felt so alone.

Being around Caracalla was never an uplifting experience either. The young caesar had been grateful to Alerio for his help, but not so much that he should think to promote him beyond the rank of centurion.

Alerio watched as his century and the other two lined up on the riverbank, waiting for the final pontoons of the first bridge to be affixed to the north shore of the Bodotria.

A turmae of Scythian cavalry rode up to wait beside them. On the near end of the temporary bridge, Caracalla sat atop a fidgety horse, waiting for the engineers to finish their work.

When one of them waved from the other end of the bridge, Caracalla spurred his horse onto the fresh-cut boards of the bridge and charged across to the other side.

"Forward!" Alerio called out, and all three centuries began to march as a cornu sounded, and the black Praetorian vexilla were hoisted high.

The Scythians brought up the rear, and once all had crossed the bridge, they fanned out on either side of the marching column.

Ahead of the small force, more clouds seemed to be forming, with the highlands for a menacing backdrop.

Caracalla was reckless, eager to get stuck into the fight, but Alerio knew the enemy was too smart for that. The Caledonii and Maeatae knew their own lands, and they would use that advantage. Alerio hoped they would find Lucius' cohorts soon.

They followed the wreck of a Roman road that led north until it became too dark to go farther.

Caracalla ordered the building of a marching camp when night approached.

"I hope Praefectus Metellus hasn't gone and got himself killed," Caracalla said to Alerio and the other three centurions as they gathered around a small fire inside the campaign tent.

"It would take more than a few Caledonii to do that, sire," Alerio said.

"He's supposed to have made a treaty with the Venicones," Caracalla went on. "But where are they? We've crossed into their lands and yet they're nowhere to be seen."

"I suspect we're closer to the Caledonii where we are now, sire," said one of the other centurions. "Might be they've overrun the Sarmatians and the Venicones."

Caracalla looked alarmed for a fraction of a second, but regained his composure. "Then where are the Caledonii?

Cowering in their fucking hills, no doubt." He stood up and shouted into the tent roof. "That's right, you sheep-fucking barbarians! Rome is here!"

There were bursts of nervous laughter from some of the men outside the tent, and Caracalla looked amused.

Alerio finished chewing on a hunk of bread and spoke. "Oh, the Caledonii are out there, sire. They're watching us, our every move."

"Why don't they attack?"

Alerio shrugged. "Maybe they're waiting for the right moment." They were all silent, the only sound coming from the third centurion who was running a sharpening stone along the blade of his black-handled gladius. "I should make the rounds, sire, with your permission." Alerio said as he stood.

"Yes. Good. Go. Make sure no one on guard duty is sleeping."

"Yes, sire." Alerio saluted and stepped outside into the misty night.

Two thirds of the men were now asleep in their tents. The rest kept a close watch around the camp perimeter atop the dirt embankments where stakes had been driven in at intervals.

Alerio smiled to himself at the difficulty, and length of time it took for the Praetorians to erect a marching camp. They were tough as nails, and could certainly fight, but their camp techniques were sorely lacking compared with those of regular army legionaries who could dig defensive ditches, erect a stockade, and put up their tents three times faster. *And that after having marched twenty miles!*

These men are good enough, Alerio thought as he walked along the lines. He pulled his black cloak closely about himself to ward off the chill air that seemed to be coming out of the hills like an icy river. He felt for the pommel of his gladius, his other hand gripping his vinerod. His eyes searched the plains before the mountains whose outlines he could just make out.

Hundreds of thousands of Caledonii and other tribes lay beyond the teeth of those mountains, no doubt aware that Rome had returned, no doubt confident that they could chase Her away once more.

Mars, God of War, Alerio prayed. *Stand with us in the battle lines when the time comes. Help us to defeat our foes and offer their blood to the rich earth in your honour...* Alerio opened his eyes, found the curve of the moon in the distance, and turned to go back to his tent to try vainly for some sleep.

Caracalla took a long while to rouse himself the following morning, and so the force did not set out again until the fifth hour of daylight.

The misty rain that had been coming down earlier had stopped now, but the air was colder.

Caracalla ordered the Scythians to ride west and east to scout for any sign of the enemy, or their own troops, while the three centuries of Praetorians continued up Dere Street, the old Roman road.

It was while the Scythians were away that the Praetorians spotted what appeared to be three shaggy cattle with long horns grazing a mile ahead beside the road.

"Looks like a good meal, sire," one of the other centurions said.

Caracalla reigned in his horse and peered into the distance. "Centurion Cornelius."

"Yes, sire?" Alerio answered.

"The men are hungry. Move in with your century and see if you can kill the beasts. We can dine on beef tonight!"

"What if it's a trap, sire?" Alerio ventured, his gut alerting him.

"Nonsense! There's no one for miles around. The cattle must have drifted away from their herd. Go, before they get away."

"Yes, sire." Alerio turned to his optio, Silvius, and nodded. "Quick and quiet. Pila at the ready."

The century followed Alerio's lead and went into a jog on the grass beside the road so as not to make any noise on the cobbles. As they moved in, Alerio's eyes swept the area. All he could see was a landscape of windswept tufts of wet grass and yellow gorse.

At the approach of the troops and their jingling armour, the cows turned and began to walk in the opposite direction.

"Pila, iacite!" Alerio called out, and the first two ranks of men launched their pila. Most missed, but one grazed one of the beasts and it started to run. A second went down, dead with a pilum shaft embedded in the back of its head.

As the Romans neared the carcass, a wind picked up and the grass all about them began to rustle.

"Shields up!" Alerio yelled, raising his scutum as an axe crashed into it.

"Attack!" Silvius called back.

"Forward!" Caracalla yelled from down the road, goading his horse into a run as the other two centuries followed.

"Testudo!" Alerio was yelling as more axes and spears came whistling from the hands of Caledonii warriors who had been hiding beneath pieces of cut turf. It was as if the entire plain had come alive. Two hundred warriors came from every direction, their bloodlust urging them on to extinguish Roman lives.

"Centurion!" Silvius yelled beneath the battered shield formation. "Chariots coming from the West!"

"Damn!" Alerio looked about at his men. Four had gone down in the initial attack and if they did not do something soon, more would die. The humid air within the testudo became suffocating, tinged with the iron tang of blood from the wounded, and stinking of piss and shit as men felt the terror of meeting the Caledonii for the first time. "Testudo march! Move south toward the others!" We'll be safer in one mass. Go!"

The men hoisted their shields and began a crouched march toward Caracalla and the other two centuries.

"Enemy chariots closing in, sir!" Silvius called.

The clang of a sword could be heard where Caracalla was charging back and forth at a group of ten Caledonii. The testudo was surrounded now, sword and spear points seeking to puncture the shell while enemy warriors sprang onto the top to weigh down the roof of the testudo.

Alerio could hear his men grunting with exhaustion, their arms and shoulders on fire.

"Try and stab at them!" Alerio ordered. "Thin them out and we'll break for the others." A loud battle cry from the approaching chariots was heard now. "Prepare for chariots!" Alerio yelled, planting his feet and preparing for the impact.

A crack of thunder sounded close by, and then a loud pounding of hooves blanketed by a great roar. Then one of the chariots flipped and crushed a group of Caledonii in front of Alerio. He peeked out to see the field writhing with horses and battered men falling.

"Ala Sarmatiana!!!" came the cry as the testudo roof caved in and three dead Caledonii fell into the Praetorian century.

"It's our cavalry!" Alerio said. "Break testudo and make for Caesar's side!"

Alerio and his men broke and ran for Caracalla who had been unhorsed and was now fighting two opponents. Alerio's pilum impaled one of them, while the young caesar's spatha severed the neck of the second.

It was now chaos.

The Sarmatian turmae slashed, and stabbed, and cut, and trampled the Caledonii who were thrown into flight as quickly as they had come. The enemy now ran headlong into the returning Scythian cavalry who rode into them like howling gorgons.

The remaining Caledonii now fled toward the hills.

"After them!" Caracalla screamed.

The Scythians charged in pursuit with half of the Sarmatians, as the others formed a perimeter around Caracalla.

The Praetorians set about killing surviving Caledonii who died spitting blood and curses at the Romans. When the last of the death cries ceased, the Sarmatian decurion rode up to Caracalla and Alerio, dismounted, and saluted.

"Good timing, Decurion," Caracalla said, his eyes still wild with the thrill of battle and his brush with death.

"Sire. Decurion Brencis of Ala III Britannorum, Quingenaria Sarmatiana." Brencis bowed. "Praefectus Lucius

Metellus Anguis sent me to find you and the emperor with a message."

"What message?" Caracalla asked, handing his sword to Alerio to be cleaned.

Brencis stood still in his scale armour, spattered with blood. "We have retaken the Gask frontier, sire. Most of it. The treaty with the Venicones is finalized, and a site assigned for a fortress on the south bank of the Tava estuary."

"Can our ships get there?" Caracalla asked, his mind still reeling.

"Conn Venico, the chieftain of the Venicones assures us, yes. His capital is also there."

"And what of Praefectus Metellus, Decurion? What is he doing?"

Alerio looked at Brencis too, as Caracalla asked the question, his eyes intent.

"Praefectus Metellus has retaken forts and signal stations along the frontier, and is moving toward the Tava river. He asks that reinforcements be sent with all speed."

"How long can he hold out?" Alerio asked.

Brencis shook his head. "Not long, Centurion. Our forces are spread thin along the frontier, and there are war bands like this one coming out of every crack and crevice of this gods-forsaken land." Brencis kicked the body at his feet. They had been delayed by many such bands on their way south to find the army.

"Ride back to him, Decurion," Caracalla commanded. "Tell him the army is now in Caledonia, and on the way."

Brencis saluted. "Sire!" He turned to tell his men that they were turning north again right away. He was tired, and they could have used some rest, but the situation did not allow for it. *Anguis needs us.*

Alerio went to speak with Brencis while Caracalla knelt down to observe the body tattoos of the Caledonian he had killed.

"Decurion," Alerio put a hand upon Brencis' shoulder. The blood-spattered Sarmatian turned to look down at the shorter Roman. Alerio realized that he was younger than he looked, the beard and blood masking his youth.

"Centurion?" Brencis answered.

"How is the praefectus?"

"He's fighting. Has been for many months. We all have."

Alerio could forgive the Sarmatian his tone. He did not know him, and he was right. The army had taken too long to muster and march. Lucius had held the van for too long.

"I'm his friend, Decurion. I only wanted to ask after him and send a personal message."

Brencis' face softened slightly. "Yes, I can take your message."

"Tell him his wife and children are coming north with the empress' entourage in the wake of the army."

"He will be glad of it."

"I'm sure," Alerio said. "Tell him they are well."

Without another word, Brencis went to his saddlebag and removed a sealed letter. He returned to Alerio. "For Lady Metella, from the praefectus. Can you give it to her, Centurion?"

"Of course." Alerio accepted the letter and put it in his leather scrip. "Tell Lucius that I'm trying to keep this moving quickly, and that I'm looking out for his family."

Brencis nodded and swung up into his saddle, his scale armour clinking heavily as he did so.

These men have always been tough, Alerio thought. *But they are tired.* As Alerio stepped back, the rest of the Sarmatians returned with the Scythian horsemen.

Several Caledonii heads dangled from Sarmatian saddle horns, and Alerio tried to hide his disgust at their brutality. Then he remembered when he had removed Argus' head and desecrated the body so that he would feel eternal torment in Hades.

We're all animals... he thought.

"There are no trees near enough for a pyre," Caracalla said to the centurions as Alerio walked up. "Have the men dig a pit so we can at least bury their bones. We don't want their bodies making the enemy think killing Romans is easy."

Alerio went to give the orders.

As the sound of shovels plunging into the sodden ground broke the silence, Silvius took a note on his wax tablet of the names of the dead Praetorians.

Alerio turned to see the Sarmatians charging north again beneath the howling draco standard. The sky was darkening to iron once more, and Jupiter lashed the distant hills with lighting and thunder.

XI

DUCTI AB DEI

'Guided by the Gods'

They had been travelling for months, it seemed. Time no longer had any meaning for Einion and Briana.

The brother and sister had set out from Ynis Wytrin long before, their path taking them farther and farther away from the vengeance they sought in Dumnonia, in the southwest of Britannia. There had in fact been times when they considered turning back, no matter what the druid had said.

"What care do I have for the Boar of the Selgovae and the wishes of Weylyn's dead son?" Einion said one night from the other side of the fire where they camped in a midland forest.

"We've sworn to do this, Brother." Briana insisted. She felt the right of what they were doing more than her brother, whose heart was weighed down more by the pressures of revenge.

That night, Etain had spoken to Briana as they had practiced, her voice cutting unmistakably through Briana's dream haze.

You must keep going, Briana. Be strong and move quickly. Epona will guide your horses. But watch for the Morrigan's messengers. Be wary.

Etain's voice wavered near the end, leaving Briana fearful. But it had been enough for her to impress the urgency upon her twin brother.

As the last embers of their fire died in the cold of a dewy morning, Briana leant over Einion, her voice soft as she woke him. She had heard him weeping again in his sleep; something he never did in his waking life. "Einion, we must ride. The Gods are watching us."

Einion rubbed his eyes, rolled onto his knees, and looked around, his eyes sweeping the forest all around them.

Briana had already saddled the horses and packed their things, apart from her brother's blanket and some small amount of food for him to eat before they set out.

Einion closed his eyes and took his sister's hand, pressing it to his forehead for comfort. He nodded, not speaking just yet, and she kissed his cheek and let him come into himself again after what had obviously been a night of torment.

They both missed Ynis Wytrin, but Briana felt more certain of their course and Epona's will now.

Within the hour, the two of them were riding north again, devising a way in which they could cross the Roman wall without attracting too much attention.

Einion and Briana had travelled without issue for most of the journey thus far. Britannia, south of the Wall, was peaceful for the most part, comprised of small Romano-British settlements and villa lands.

Burst riverbanks in a few places had forced them to take detours that cut into their travel time, but no one had waylaid them. The only rough interacting they had experienced was when they had stopped to resupply in Lindum and a couple of civilians had approached Briana with unwanted attention in the marketplace.

Einion, who had been haggling with one of the butchers, watched in dismay as one of the brutes grabbed his sister's wrist and pulled. Within moments, two of the man's fingers were broken, and his friend's nose crushed sideways.

Some troops from the local garrison showed up to investigate the ruckus. They were British levies from a local tribe and had had trouble with the two men before. When they saw what Briana did, they smiled and told her and Einion to leave town quickly.

"We're going to have to dull your looks if we're to get past all those troops along the Wall," Einion said to Briana as they galloped across the field, away from the main road.

"I shouldn't have done that," she said, upset that she had nearly put an end to their progress with one rash action.

Einion looked sideways at her, one eyebrow raised. "Oh, yes you should have!" he insisted. "We can't let the likes of them, or anyone else, treat us like lowly slaves to be fondled and spat at. Ever!"

"I know," she agreed. "I was lucky they were weak. The fingers were easily snapped."

"Ha, ha!" Einion smiled and tore a hunk of bread from one of the loaves he had purchased.

There were fewer civilians and more troops the farther north they got. One day, as they crested a hill, the Wall suddenly stretched before them, from east to west, like a giant stone serpent.

"What if this praefectus and his family are no better than those bastards back in Lindum?" Einion asked as they stared at the Wall in the distance.

"I don't know. The Gods will tell us."

"Look." Einion pointed toward the line of Dere Street passing through Coria and beyond the Wall. "So many people, and not just the legions!"

In the red wake of the vexillaria of Rome's centuries, a huge train of merchants and camp followers clogged the roadway at the city gates.

"That's how we'll get through," Briana said.

"I can't pose as a merchant. We've got nothing to sell," Einion pointed out.

"You can tell them you're a bounty hunter trying to track down runaway slaves."

"That could work... What about you?"

Briana sighed, dismounted and put her hand into some mud. Then she began wiping in on her face to look more dirty. She tousled her hair, and then looked at her brother with doe-like, blinking eyes.

"That'll be fifty sestercii an hour, soldier."

"Please," Einion waved his hands. "I don't think I could handle any more ingrates grabbing you. Besides, even with mud on your face, you're still beautiful. They won't buy it. If you had a couple of missing teeth and some bruises, maybe..."

"Men who bed with whores don't see the actual person. They think only of the act."

Einion fidgeted. The idea did not sit well with him.

"Brother, this is the best way for me to blend in. There are probably a thousand whores down there, trying to reach the men of the legions who have nothing else to do with their money except whore and gamble."

"Life certainly is different now that we've left Ynis Wytrin."

"Yes," she answered, kneeing her mount down the trail to the plain before Coria.

Toward midday, Einion and Briana rode into Coria amid the hysteria of undisciplined civilians eager to catch up to the larger army.

Einion asked a few discreet questions of some non-Roman merchants in the marketplace. They needed to know who they were following and where the 'dragon praefectus' was.

"I asked one of the soldiers passing through yesterday how the campaign was going," said an Iberian spice merchant who leaned in close to Einion's ear.

"What did he say?" Einion asked, holding his breath against the smell of garlic wafting out of the man's mouth.

"He said the dragon praefectus is in Caledonia. Some say he is lost to the savages. Others say he is winning the war on his own."

"What do you think?"

The merchant shrugged. "I hear all sorts of things. All I know is that for many months, we heard about the Dragon's victories north of the Wall. Then he joined with the Votadini and marched into Caledonia."

"My thanks." Einion began walking away.

"Hey, hey! You not going to buy something?"

Einion turned back, picked up the smallest bag of salt there was, and flipped a coin to the merchant.

"Cheap Briton!" the merchant spat.

Einion went to Briana who stood with the horses near a fountain by the granaries. "Any trouble?" he asked her.

"No. The town is emptying out quickly."

"Like flies on the back of a moor cow." Einion watched as bedraggled remnants of civilians scrambled to gather their belongings and join the exodus.

"It's time we joined the swarm, Brother," Briana said, throwing back her cloak and lowering the hem of her tunic to reveal more of her breasts.

Einion did not think the mud on her skin would hide enough, but followed her anyway. Their horses' hooves clipped on the large cobbles as they passed between the red-tiled buildings of Coria.

The Wall was not far and they came to a stop in the line of people waiting before the massive double, oak gates that gaped onto the green plains of the war zone beyond.

Briana tried not to look too much at those about them, but it was difficult not to. True, she had seen some of the world - she had trained, and fought, and killed enemies, just as her brother had, but the evident misery and desperation of the creatures about her was something she had not seen in the Dumnonia of her youth, or in Ynis Wytrin. They were surrounded by whores with torn clothing and missing teeth, beggars who eyed their horses and saddle bags, and other scavengers and slavers. They were parasites of humanity.

Goddess, guide us... Briana whispered as she and Einion approached the contubernium of men manning the gates.

"What are you, then?" asked an optio, his eyes focussed on Briana's chest.

"What do you think?" she answered firmly, her head still down. "Soldiers need a little relief at the end of a march, don't they?"

The optio smiled and looked at his men. "I could use some now, my little lupa. What say you join me in the gatehouse?" He reached for her, but she slapped his hand playfully and looked up, smiling without showing her white teeth.

"Come find me in the camp at the end of the day. My name's Circe."

"Oh, I'll bet it is. I'll find you, lovely. Just make sure you wash. You've got mud all over yourself." The optio slapped her behind, and Briana moved with her horse through the gate.

"Who are you, Briton?" Briana heard them ask Einion after she passed. She looked back to see the optio and another trooper holding her brother back, each with a hand on his chest. *Don't fight! Don't fight!* she thought.

Einion held his head high and looked the two men in the eyes. There were others behind him now too.

"I asked you who you are!" the optio repeated, louder this time.

"I'm a slave hunter," he said confidently. "Been hired to travel north to find a slave family that ran away."

"Who hired you?"

"Some fat bastard merchant back in Lindum, named Titus. Said his male slave, a woman, and two brats run off to the North. You know the type. Old Titus was probably diddling the man's wife every night and when they saw a chance to run, they took it. That's where I come in, isn't it?"

The optio eyed Einion closely and looked at his men.

"You haven't seen any dirty runaways, have you?" Einion asked, his heart pounding now beneath his calm exterior. He wondered if he could make a run for it.

"Are you kidding?" There's hundreds of them," the optio laughed. "Good luck finding the ones you want. Be like finding a hair in a pile of cow shit. Go on! Get a move on!"

Einion nodded and passed through the gates, aware of the pila in the hands of the troops looking down on him. Once he was mounted again, he trotted up the line of travellers to Briana's side.

"I thought you would do something foolish," she said, the relief thick in her voice as she pulled her cloak closer about her head and body.

"I wouldn't be riding beside you if I had done something."

They rode in silence for a while, moving past those who were walking until the red, black, and brown of legionary and Praetorian troops became visible.

"We need to move faster," Einion said. "At this rate, we'll never get there. What are you three looking at?" Einion looked down on three men carrying swords and satchels who had been staring at Briana and her saddlebags.

"Bugger off and mind your own business. We'll do as we please, not as some fucking Briton tell us," a short, stalky man replied.

Einion drew his blade and the three men's hands went to their own swords.

"Let's go!" Briana suddenly manoeuvred her horse off the left side of the road and began trotting north-westward over the grassy plain.

Einion pointed his sword at the three men and kicked his mount into a canter after her with the men cursing them as they rode away.

"They were eyeing you pretty closely," he answered.

"I can take care of myself."

Einion felt himself more on edge, especially since arriving in Coria. The crowds made him feel uneasy, and now that they were north of the Wall, the possibility of violence seemed more palpable. He took a few deep breaths, felt the wind whipping the brown braids of his hair. "Forgive me," he finally said. "I feel exposed away from the sacred isle."

"Me too," Briana said. Her smile always made him feel happy. "But this is part of our journey."

Einion nodded and looked at the three-mile-long procession they had just left. In the centre of the march they could see a massive wagon surrounded by troops.

"Must be someone important in there," Einion said.

"I heard someone in the market say the empress and her sister were leaving today."

"That would explain all the troops."

"Come, let's give our horses their legs for a bit, while the land is open." Before Einion could answer, Briana's blue-grey eyes flashed and her horse was speeding away, her blond hair streaming wildly behind her.

Einion kicked his horse after her, and the two of them overtook the marching troops' van in no time.

Briana had glanced back at the wagon before moving on, her eyes drawn to it by three white birds that seemed to be winging in circles above it.

On that vast, green plain, between the veils, Epona watched as the two riders from Ynis Wytrin went north, away from the dragon's wife and children.

The white stallion reared as the goddess cast her heavenly eyes about. Three hounds began to howl then, their red-tipped ears perked up, their snouts pointed aloft to the black carrion birds of the Otherworld that flocked in untold numbers toward the north as well.

Those are not the birds of my god-cousin, Apollo.

Epona's red hair blazed in the dying sunlight as she whirled in a confusion that was foreign to her.

How many gods are here in the land now, behind the veil of this war? A screeching sound made the goddess cry out then, and she searched the black north for the source of those pained cries. *My warriors!*

Her stallion plunged forward cutting whorls in the ethereal air as Epona sped north, her eyes ablaze with anger and fear.

The moon hung high and full in the sky. The forest was lit with white light, and in the branches of a gnarled copse of trees, owls hooted, their eyes taking in every movement on the forest floor far below.

Einion and Briana's small fire sputtered in the bowl of the forest floor where they now slept, far from the line of the Roman road. They lay beside it, huddled beneath their cloaks. Both slept soundly.

Einion grasped his sword in his hand where he was propped up against a tree. The quiet had lulled him away from his watch and his eyes closed as exhaustion set in. They had ridden long and hard once they left Coria and the Wall, and now they camped on the north side of the Bodotria.

On the ground, Briana lay curled and shaking, soft whimpers blowing past her lips. In the mists of her mind, she saw a man lying still, silent in exhausted sleep. He had a lonely, pained expression on his face that made her want to cry.

She tried asking him if he was all right, how she could help. But all he did was convulse, his muscles flexing extremely taught, then lax, over and over again.

A shadow crept up to him then, a deadly blade searching for a spot to stab.

Stop! Her voice made no sound. *Wake up!*

Briana! came a voice from beyond her vision.

"Etain?"

No! No!

A sound of gasping hissed in her ears, and the knife came down.

Briana woke quickly. She sweat beneath her cloak, and her breathing was quick, panicked. Einion? she looked quickly around to see her brother dozing. "Good watch, brother," she said, smiling, before standing and making her way to a fallen tree to relieve herself.

It was cold, and her breath frosted in the pale light. Myriad stars still peeked down at her from the indigo sky.

Briana undid her leather riding breeches and squatted. It was peaceful, and she thought how good the hunting must be in that place. The owls hooting reminded her of places she and Einion had explored as children back home in Dumnonia when the moon was full.

There was a sudden flutter of wings, and the hooting stopped. A pained grunt made Briana's stomach clench and her heart race.

"Einion!" she called standing and jumping over the log as she pulled her breeches up.

She did not have time to react before the cudgel caught her awkwardly on the side of her head. The taste of blood and mud filled her mouth then, and she felt her legs being pulled.

Briana!!! a watery voice yelled out.

Briana's eyes spun and she shook her head to regain her vision. She was on her stomach, and turned just enough to see a warrior glaring down at her, a smile beneath his long moustache.

The man was naked, his body painted in blue whorls that turned nightmarish as she felt a stab of pain between her legs.

No!!! she wanted to cry out, but could not.

A clang of metal and cries roused her more, and Briana threw her head back, feeling a crack of bone, and hearing a grunt of pain from her attacker. She turned, kicked up, and grabbed for the dagger at her breast band. She slashed low, into the man's groin, and then up as he doubled over, his face plunging into her blade.

Beside the fire, she saw her brother limping around, his sword bloodied and pointing at two more painted warriors.

There was no speech, only animals circling each other.

Briana ran as Einion went down again from a fresh wound. She threw herself over the flames of the fire and slammed into the two men, knocking them over.

Einion leapt from his good leg, pinning the head of one to the ground with his sword.

The other, Briana hit with one of the rocks from the fire pit, burning her hands as she did so.

The warrior groaned, and while he was dazed, she grabbed for his dagger and sliced sloppily into his neck as blood gushed onto her from his severed artery.

"Einion?" she said, half asking after him, half crying out to him, the shock, fear, and anger threatening to overwhelm her.

"Sister," he answered, struggling to his feet just before her body collapsed, shaking into his arms. "Are you hurt?"

Briana tried to say no, but she could not. Only tears came down her face as the pain between her legs burned. Her eyes went to where she had been attacked.

A muffled groan came from the dark.

Einion looked at the side of her face where red blotches showed the cudgel marks. He held her head in his hands and spoke. "Briana. There might be more of them."

"What about you?" She looked at his thigh where it was damp with blood. "We need to treat that."

But Einion was looking from his sister to the fallen tree where the sound came from. He bent over, picked up her sword, and gave it to her. "Come," he said, his face dark.

They both limped up the slope and around the fallen tree to find the warrior bleeding from his groin and eye where Briana had planted her dagger.

The warrior said something they did not understand, and then laughed feebly as he heard their footfalls approaching on the forest floor.

"Your friends are dead," Einion said as he dug his blade into the man's bicep.

The warrior screamed, and Einion slapped the side of his face with the flat of his blade. "Where are the Romans?"

The man spat gobs of blood.

"Where is the dragon praefectus?"

The warrior stopped laughing, and muttered something.

"What?" Einion pressed.

"Dead soon..."

"Where?" Einion pushed his blade through the other bicep this time.

"Bertha!" the man cringed. "Bertha!"

"Where is that?" Briana said, speaking for the first time.

The warrior turned to her voice and groaned mockingly, his one eye looking at her even as he lay dying.

Briana spat on him, and walked up with her sword. She set the tip of the blade at the base of his neck, upon a blue crescent moon, then gripped the handle tightly with her burnt hands. She forced herself to look at him as she pressed down, turning the blade slowly in circles as he choked on his own blood.

"We curse you," Einion muttered as Briana drew her sword out and dropped it from her burnt hands.

Her brother held her close as she wept into his shoulder.

"I'm sorry," he said, the guilt heavy upon him.

She did not speak, but she could see Etain by her fireside in Ynis Wytrin, weeping for her.

It was fortunate that no more of the Maeatae or Caledonii came that night, for there was no way Einion and Briana could have left. They needed to clean, cauterize, and bind their wounds first, which they did beside a shallow spring nearby. While Einion saw to the horses, Briana washed herself in the cold forest water.

She raged inwardly at herself for what she perceived as her weakness, though she knew it could have been worse. Einion could have been dead, and she close to, used by others.

That will never happen again, she swore. *By the Great Goddess and Epona... Never!*

When she was dressed again, Einion walked up, his sword and spear in hand. "Are you able to ride?" he asked with difficulty.

"I'll manage. Where are we going? He said 'Bertha', but we don't know where that is."

"He also said the Dragon would be dead soon."

"We need to hurry and find out where Bertha is."

"Let's go then." Einion made to mount up, but Briana held his arm.

"Wait. We should offer something."

A moment later, brother and sister stood over the last flames of their fire, each with a fistful of grain from their food stores.

"Oh Goddess Epona, lover of horses, thank you for...watching over us. Please speed us to the Dragon. Guide us, benevolent goddess."

Briana dropped the grain from her bandaged hand into the flames, and Einion did likewise.

The fire sizzled and the smoke wafted into the breeze that weaved its way north through the trees.

They did not see the goddess standing beside them as they made their offerings. They did not feel Epona's gentle touch of blessing upon their brows as she had reached out to them before they set off again.

XII

ARBOR MORTIS

'The Tree of Death'

At the top of a snowy, wind-lashed peak, they looked down through the glens, and along the freezing rivers. Their sight weaved through forest trees and over boggy levels to see the line of horse warriors led by the Dragon.

Apollo, Far-Shooter, leaned on his great silver bow, his eyes angry and intent, the stars in them fiery and vengeful as at the beginning of all things.

Beside him, Venus stood still, her whirling blue eyes worried, uneasy. Her blond locks hovered slowly in the space about her divine person. "How could this happen?" Love said.

"We've seen wars before," Apollo answered. "We will see them again."

"But to desecrate our Lord's sacred oak in such a way…it is unthinkable." Love wrapped her white himation tightly about her, though she felt no cold.

"There are others involved here."

"The dark one…Morrigan?"

"Perhaps."

"The Dragon will need us, our help. His wife, his children…they are coming."

"It is not them I worry about." Apollo stepped to the very edge of the precipice, his eyes searching. "Why can I not see?"

Love placed her hand on his shoulder. "Perhaps he is meant to face it alone? The Sun does not see all in this land."

"If we stop helping our heroes, we stop being needed. Offerings will no longer scent our altars and temples."

"You underestimate our young Dragon." She smiled, though an inkling of fear crept into her when she thought of his family.

"I sense his thoughts. He is not himself. I worry he will forget who he is."

"I've not known you to be so caring," she said.

Apollo looked at Venus. "It has been a long road for him, and it is not finished."

"But a moment to us." Love stared down at the world, her heart feeling a hurt for those whose lives were so fleeting.

"Yes." Apollo raised his head, eyes closed now. Stars seemed to gather about them on their peak.

"Our cousin, you forget, is down there with them. Epona has more power in this land. She said she would help."

"I remember," Apollo opened his eyes again. "She is on her way."

"And she has sent help," Love added. "The two mortals."

"Yes."

They were silent as they caught another glimpse of the mounted warriors moving along the river between hills and gnarled trees.

"Careful, Anguis." Apollo took one of his long-shafted arrows and nocked it on the string of his great bow.

"What are you doing?" Love asked.

He stared down the shaft, his star-whirling eyes sighting an approaching enemy. The muscles of his divine arm were taut, powerful, and calm. "Sometimes, I still see." He loosed to light up the dark sky.

Lucius could see less through the eye holes of his cavalry mask as their horses trotted along the rushing river, amid the moss-covered boulders and fern undergrowth, but it was a necessary precaution.

The ambushes they had experienced lately had seen several of his men's faces explode from sling stones and small javelins. The Caledonii had never shown themselves outright, nor been seen in any battle formation. They preferred to move like armed wraiths in that crooked landscape at the foot of their wretched highlands.

Where are they? Epona, guide us... Lucius' prayer went up.

It had been too long since Hippogriff's turmae had left Alauna for remote Fendoch. Lucius had waited at Bertha, where they had re-established the old fort as his ala's base along the river.

Seven days had passed without word or rider from his decurion. Lucius cursed himself for not having sent more men, for not having gone himself. They had re-taken the Gask ridge for Rome, the troops of the legion now arriving to properly garrison the forts and watch towers.

But at what cost?

On the eighth day at Bertha, Lucius rode out with six turmae of Sarmatians, leaving Coilus and Afallach in command at Bertha. He also took the Venicones foot soldiers, led by Rodric as a guide.

"If you don't hear from me in five days, send help," Lucius told Coilus.

"Let me come with you, Praefectus," Afallach had asked, despite the wound to his shoulder he had received in their last battle.

"Stay here with your father. Rest. I need you healthy again," Lucius had said before mounting up and heading through the gate of Bertha's fortifications.

Dagon followed, with Barta holding the dragon vexillum.

It was a cold day when they set out, and it seemed to get colder with every mile between Bertha and Fendoch, their destination, frozen, as if a thousand shades of the dead chilled the air about them.

"Light torches!" Lucius commanded on their third day out.

"But the Caledonii will see us," Dagon said.

"I prefer a fight to having our horses tumble down some rocky height."

Along the line, torches were lit and they continued in the unnatural, pre-dusk darkness, swallowed by the close air about them.

"Praefectus!" called Shura from the van.

Lucius, Dagon, and Barta rode to the front and dismounted where the decurion was kneeling in the mud.

"It's one of ours, sir."

"Ambush." Dagon walked further along the river. "There is more," he said. "Fan out, he called to the men. "Swords at the ready."

"Rodric," Lucius said, turning to the scout. "Have your Venicones head into the trees. I don't want any unexpected visitors."

The Celt stared at Lucius a moment and then nodded, but barely. Lucius watched the Venicones disappear into the dark beyond the reach of the torches. Then he drew his sword from his back and walked farther along the river, his eyes scanning the ground and the trees.

Lunaris was agitated. More and more bits of bloody armour and tunic appeared, leading them on. "Easy, boy..." Lucius soothed. "Easy now." *Gods, what's happened here?* he thought, the feeling in his gut growing ever darker.

With the point of his sword, Lucius lifted a piece of red wool, standard issue for military tunicae.

"I don't see any bodies," Dagon said as he stood beside Lucius and Barta.

"Praefectus!" one of the Venicones came running out of the dark from along the river bank.

"What is it?"

"Half a mile along..." the man took deep, gulping breaths, "...you must come."

"What? Why?" Lucius did not feel any great trust of the Venicones, but the man did look scared. "Mount up!" Lucius called out and moved forward with the others.

All their mounts started and sidled, clearly upset the farther they went. Lucius had seen many battlefields in his years as a soldier, from the sack of Ctesiphon, in Parthia, to the battle against the nomad armies in Numidia. He had lost friends in horrible ways, and so too had he killed his own enemies.

Carnage had become commonplace in his life, but nothing had prepared him for the sight that met his eyes when they came to the remains of the fort at Fendoch.

A short distance from the ditches and embankments of Fendoch's remains, a great oak tree sprouted up from the earth, its limbs wide, gnarled, and menacing.

Lucius swallowed and struggled to hold back the vomit that burned at the back of his throat. He hung his head when Lunaris stopped, his ears closed to the cries of rage from his men all about him. *Why, Gods? Why?* he asked. He felt someone gently touch his leg, and he looked down.

Epona's wide, wet eyes looked up at him, her fiery hair flat and damp. *Look what they've done!* the goddess said in Lucius' mind. He could hear her as she touched him. He could feel her sadness, and rage, and thirst for vengeance on the desecrators. *Look!* she repeated.

Lucius looked up slowly to take in the sight of the tree now, his senses numb to the scent of death filling his nostrils, the bloated and rotting, crow-pecked flesh of men and horses. He dismounted and left Lunaris where he stood, the goddess stroking the stallion's mane and neck.

Lucius looked up at the tree where all thirty-two of the men of his turmae dangled from nooses above the bodies of the slaughtered horses. As he walked, he knew that it was not mud beneath his feet. Every body bled, the eyes gouged out, the tattoos of beasts that covered each Sarmatian - serpents, griffins, pegasuses, dragons, eagles, all of them - stabbed and severed to offer no protection as they wandered blind through the Underworld.

The Sarmatians' braided hair and beards had been cut off, and now lay in heaps about the base of the tree, along with their genitals.

Lucius could feel their blood dripping on him as he walked beneath, but he did not care. He saw only the tree's trunk now.

Splayed across the trunk, Hippogriff's muscular, tattooed body shuddered where it was nailed into the coarse bark.

"He's alive!" Lucius yelled to Barta and Dagon, as he stumbled to stand beneath the dying decurion. Something, a scroll, protruded from Hippogriff's mouth, and Lucius removed it to see the world 'Arrian' on the papyrus. He clutched it tightly in his hand; it was the copy he had loaned Hippogriff from his own collection. The Sarmatian had been carrying it everywhere.

"Hippogriff, can you hear me?" Lucius was unsure what to do. If he moved him, he would surely die.

"Hippogriff! Warrior!" Dagon said in their shared tongue.

"My Lord?" Hippogriff said, blood pouring from his mouth and empty eye sockets.

"We are here," Dagon said.

The warrior shook his head slightly. "Death…has come… I… Anguis?"

"I'm here, Hippogriff," Lucius said, his hand on the man's bloody side.

"Anguis… I'm sorry. I…ambush…"

"I know."

Hippogriff's body shuddered on its iron spikes, taken from the nearby fort.

"It's…been my honour to…serve the Dragon." More blood spilled from his mouth, more shuddering as his collapsed lungs refused him any more air. "Burn me…us…to our gods…please…" Hippogriff cocked his head suddenly as if he could see something. "Goddess?"

Lucius turned to see Epona standing among the dead horses, her eyes running with tears as she looked up at Hippogriff and her other warriors.

"Anguis... I go...to see Alexander now...and Bucephalas..." he spasmed. "My Lord Dagon..." before his head fell forward and he breathed his last bloody breath.

Beside Lucius, Dagon wept, his forehead leaning on his friend and fellow warrior.

Lucius felt his limbs shaking as he looked up at all the men hanging above. He had never struggled so much to contain his rage as he did at that moment. "Barta."

"Yes, Praefectus," the big Sarmatian said, even his voice shaken.

"We'll get them all down and perform the rites at dawn."

"Yes, sir."

Lucius turned to the goddess who yet lingered among the dead. I'll find who did this, he told her, his eyes meeting hers before she nodded and disappeared.

Torches burned violently in the gusting wind around the tree where Lucius and the Sarmatians toiled through the night. The Venicones were set to watch the perimeter, staring into the darkness to the hills beyond, in case the enemy took advantage of the situation.

Rodric, Conn Venico's man, watched the dark keenly, removed from the praefectus whose rage, he could tell, simmered uncontrollably beneath his officious surface.

"Don't some of your countrymen prefer burial, Dagon?" Lucius asked as they laid Hippogriff on the cold ground.

Dagon stared at the face of one of his best warriors. "It no longer looks like him…" he thought out loud.

Lucius looked and shook his head. "No, it doesn't."

"When we are near our homes, on the plains and among the hills of our homeland, yes, we prefer burial." Dagon looked on as the last Sarmatian bodies were laid upon the bier they had made. "But we shall burn them since we are far from our country. That way, their spirits, and those of their horses, shall get there much sooner."

"Very well." Lucius pat him on the shoulder and went to hoist another log. He saw Dagon kneel beside Hippogriff and each of the others in turn, praying in the language of their ancestors, a prince, now a king mourning his dead subjects, his people.

The Caledonii did not appear as the Sarmatians worked.

Soon, the sun broke from its nightly bonds in the East. Several biers had been created for the Sarmatian warriors, and the horse corpses dragged together with great difficulty, fern and what dry brush they could find stuffed between the bodies.

Lucius and his men stood facing the rising sun, tired, dirty, and hungry, but they wanted to honour their brothers. As the light of a red-orange sun touched the biers, three riders holding draconaria charged along the field, their standards howling as the torches were lit. Lucius, sitting atop Lunaris, his dirty crimson cloak limp about him, looked at the men all around.

"I am not Sarmatian like you, warriors. I'm Roman. But I would gladly die alongside any of you, my brothers. For you are the greatest warriors I have ever known!" His voice pitched high, racked with emotion. "I swear to you, and to Epona, goddess of our camp, that I will avenge the deaths of our men and their slaughtered mounts, or I will die trying! May they ride evermore in the green plains beyond the black river to their own Elysium."

The men cheered, and their horses neighed and reared to a rattle of scales and the howl of draconaria.

Lucius nodded to Dagon who rode up and accepted a firebrand from Barta.

"Oh Gods of our ancestors, of war, and of the sacred sword… Accept these riders into your realm, and heap honours upon them. For they have earned it, each one of them."

Dagon looked at all the deathly faces lying in neat, pale, and bloody rows. He recognized each man, remembered their deeds and skills. The young Sarmatian lord, heir to his uncle's sword, held the torch toward the sun and thrust it into the midst of the logs and brush beneath Hippogriff's body.

At every bier, men set their torches to their work, and after several minutes, thick smoke began to rise, and slowly flames began to take hold, lapping at sizzling resin and death-white skin upon which the dead's desecrated tattoos writhed and shrivelled.

"Farewell, my brothers," Dagon said to himself.

For some time, they watched, and the Venicones waited, not daring to say anything.

Lucius did not even care for the fort nearby. The place was cursed, and shades would haunt it for a long while. As he stood there, stone-faced and sad at the sight of his burning men, he spotted a fiery ball of light skidding across the sky from the mountains to the northwest.

A pang of dread crept up Lucius' spine as the ball came faster, and closer, and became bigger. It seemed to shake the ground the closer it came. It sped past them, a blinding light, and slammed into a distant field on the other side of the river. Everyone shielded his eyes and prayed to his gods when the object slammed into the earth.

It was the distant screaming that brought them to their senses, a sound of hundreds of men, some horses too.

Lucius shielded his eyes and peered into the distance where the fiery ball had landed. He saw men scrambling and running in all directions. "Caledonii!" he yelled, and every man turned to look.

The Sarmatians pointed their kontos spears in the direction of the enemy.

"Should we leave them be?" Dagon asked Lucius, an edge of reluctance in his voice.

Lucius turned to him, drawing the sword from his back, and lowering his mask. "Not today, Dagon. Not after this." Lucius turned to the riders. "It's time to avenge our brothers!" he yelled, the anger spilling out easily. "Kill them! Ride them down and leave none alive!" He kicked and Lunaris carried him forward as the Sarmatians roared and charged after their dragon across the shallow river, up the opposite bank, and on across the plain toward the fleeing Caledonii who looked back over their shoulders as they ran in terror.

Lucius looked up to see three white birds flying above him and then, to his left, Epona charging upon her white stallion, her battle cry up, spurring every Sarmatian horse on the field. About her, her three hounds strode and slavered as at the hunt.

Death was what they wanted now, and somehow the Caledonii knew that even the heavens were against them that day.

The Sarmatian arrowhead formed, barbed and deadly, the sound of scale armour, of both men and horses, like crashing waves. The dragon standards howled, and above, more fiery balls preceded them to slam into the mountainsides, blocking off the Caledonii's escape to their hills.

Lucius found himself yelling at the top of his voice, the incoherent sound of battle cries.

They caught up to the first Caledonii and both sword and spear tasted blood in the ensuing chaos of slaughter. The Sarmatians became the beasts tattooed upon their bodies, their mounts carrying them to the very gates of Hades where they crammed Caledonian dead past the threshold, one after another.

Lucius hacked at life and limb, uncaring for all the rage he now unleashed. Heads fell, gape-mouthed and wide-eyed as he passed with Barta and Dagon close behind him.

Epona rode on, her horse's mane flashing in the dark, lit by fire from the heavens. She did not kill, but charged to one single spot on the slope of a hill, just behind the Caledonian war chariots.

Lucius looked ahead and saw Argentocoxus in his chariot, surrounded by huge warriors. They all wheeled suddenly, and Lucius spotted the source of their urging, the spot to which Epona raced with divine fury.

Behind the Caledonii, a tall woman stood upon a boulder. Her hair was long and raven-black, her eyes, even from a distance, were fiery and full of wrath. The Caledonii began to charge the oncoming Sarmatians, their voices crushing the air before them.

"Morrigan!!!" they all yelled wildly, like it was a curse. Above them, clouds of black birds darted out, levelled at the oncoming Sarmatians.

Epona charged ahead, her hounds and birds darting into the darkness, screaming. "Come, my warriors!"

All horses jumped to, and her white hounds harried the enemy horses so that they reared fearfully at the ethereal threat about them.

Apollo, help us, Lucius prayed in a moment of clarity before plunging back into bloodlust.

The dark clouds descended, nearly upon them, when one last ball of fiery rock careened out of the sky to burn through the cawing blackness.

The Morrigan screamed and every man there felt his ears bleed at the sound. They slammed into the Caledonii, and a new symphony of blood-curdling cries choked men's throats as casualties littered the field.

Lucius drove for Argentocoxus, wrenching a spear out of the bloody ground as he passed, and hurled it to slam into one of the chariot's ponies. The beast howled and fell, taking the other with him and throwing the chieftain and his driver through the air. But Lucius charged on heedless of Epona at his side as she yelled warning.

No!

The Morrigan crouched upon her rock, black robes hanging off her like primordial filth.

When Lucius, Barta, and Dagon were no more than a hundred feet away the Morrigan rose to her full, terrifying height, and screamed so loudly that it shook the earth. Lucius felt Lunaris rear and himself pried away from his saddle to fly back through the air to land on the blood-soaked ground beside Barta and Dagon. Their horses fled, and they lay prostrate, dizzy, and confused as groups of Caledonii raced toward the fallen dragon and his men.

How dare you raise your sword against me! The voice in Lucius' head was horrifying and painful, and he cried out. *Now you will die, Roman!*

Lucius opened his eyes to see the Morrigan coming down from her rock, her eyes burning with hate.

A flash of brilliant white passed before the Morrigan then, and she spun, holding her arm where flame and blood now seeped out.

Epona wheeled her mount, returning for another strike with her hounds.

The Morrigan's eyes flashed and then glanced to the sky where a great fire came toward her. She bent low, and then a huge wolf stood there. She jumped just as the fire slammed into the place where she had been standing, and bits of rock scattered all over the field.

Get up! Epona yelled to Lucius who was struggling to his feet, his hands groping for his sword. Something slammed into him and he felt the point of a dagger digging at his ribs. Then the cracking of a neck could be heard, and Barta was raising Lucius to his feet.

The clash of swords was loud then, and anger took over once more. The two men fought off the enemy as they milled about Dagon's body. Lucius cut, and slashed, and stabbed. He pressed his enemies' eyes with his thumbs, and bit at their arms and faces when they got too close.

It was all blood, the taste, the smell, the colour of the world around them. The risen sun did nothing to dampen it.

Lucius realized that Dagon was up and fighting beside him.

The Caledonii were fleeing again, as many of their number screamed even as the Sarmatians cut away their scalps, and beards, and hacked at their tattooed heads.

Lucius picked out Argentocoxus' bodyguard, a huge man who charged, howling, when their eyes met.

Lucius spun, driving his pugio into the man's sternum with a loud thump, and then turning back at him with his sword, he swung at his stomach so that the guts poured out in a stinking heap.

Confusion nestled on the man's face as he looked down, unable to move his legs.

Lucius, breathing rapidly, shaking and full of blood, reached up and grabbed the man's hair, forcing him to his knees as he stared into his clouding eyes. With his other arm, Lucius brought back his sword and sawed into the thick neck, screaming as he did so. When he held the head up to his warriors, the cry went up in the valley and Lucius hurled the head to the last burning spot where he had seen the Morrigan.

At a far peak, Apollo rolled his powerful shoulders and lowered his silver bow, having unleashed enough fire from heaven.

Lucius found Epona along the river with the three horses he had been searching for.

The goddess stood, still brilliant, stroking Lunaris' neck and muzzle, giving attention in turn to Barta and Dagon's mounts. All three of them had bolted from the killing field – a first for each.

Lucius walked past the white hounds who sniffed him as he passed the goddess' white stallion.

"They are full of fear and terror," she said without having to look at him. "The Morrigan's evil has burned their spirits, but I shall heal them." Epona put her forehead to Lunaris'.

The dapple-grey stallion's breathing calmed, his eyes blinking slowly.

"My child," she said.

The whole time, Lucius did not speak. He stood there, seeking the comfort that her presence provided.

She turned to him when she finished comforting the horses. "I cannot heal you, my Dragon." Her eyes looked sadly upon the bloody visage of Lucius Metellus Anguis. His body shook as the anger leeched from his veins, and the Morrigan's curses ate at him. "You fought bravely. I have never seen the like." Her face darkened, and she closed her eyes. "There is much more fighting to come."

In the distance, they could hear the Sarmatian warriors screaming and cursing as they cut the heads from their fallen foes, and hung them from their saddle horns to carry back to base, or offer in the still-smouldering fires of their own fallen brothers at Fendoch.

"Goddess…" Lucius reached out, but he could not touch Epona.

Her eyes burned with compassion, and the goddess pitied the mortal before her. Epona's beauty warmed the chill in Lucius' veins. Her strength gave him strength, and though he could have lain with her, knew she would have allowed it, he stopped himself, flashes of Venus at the back of his mind.

"Thank you, my goddess…" he managed to say.

"I am here for you, Anguis," she whispered. "Things will change now. The legions have arrived, and your family too."

Lucius looked up suddenly, hope flashing in his eyes.

"Yes. But you have been too near to the Morrigan. You must be strong in the time to come." Her hand went to the side of his face, and he closed his eyes. "Take your horses and return to base. Rest. Then you must slaughter the Caledonii."

She was gone.

Lucius looked around and all he saw were the three horses, staring at him. He went to Lunaris first and the stallion leaned into him, his powerful neck on Lucius' shoulder.

"We're alive still," he whispered before taking the reins of all three, and returning to his men.

Blood, and shit, and offal polluted the field, and only now, after the fury of battle had run its course, did men bend over and puke as their senses returned to them.

Lucius found Dagon and Barta sitting on a boulder. "Are either of you wounded?"

It took a moment for the question to register, but Dagon finally looked up, his face cut, muddy, and scared.

"I…Anguis? Was that Epona riding with us? I thought I saw…" He shook his head "Am I mad?"

Lucius shook his head. "You're not mad, my friend."

Barta looked up, haggard and wary. "And the other? The…dark one? Did we charge against a god?"

Lucius did not know what to say. The terror had been unlike anything else. The Morrigan had nearly destroyed them. *Gods, give us strength.*

"Yes, Dagon…Barta. The goddess rode with us. And yes, we did threaten another goddess."

"It was the first time he had seen either of the men before him truly afraid. Lucius handed them each the reins of their own horses and grabbed each man's forearm, pulling them up. "Gather the men," he said. "We must reach the Dragon's Lair by sundown."

None of the Caledonii challenged them on their journey back to the Dragon's Lair, the name they had given to the fort at Bertha which Lucius had adopted as his own.

When they arrived outside the torch-lit palisade, it was to find three cohorts waiting for them, encamped about the fort and along the river.

The legions had arrived in Caledonia.

From the banners flying outside the walls of Bertha, Lucius could see that the cohorts were a detachment from the sixth legion, the Victrix from Eburacum, Torens' legion.

Bertha's gates were open and a cornu sounded from the gatehouse as they approached. A detachment of legionaries stood guard, forming an avenue down which Lucius, the Sarmatians, and the Venicones foot soldiers marched. The legionaries eyed Lucius and his men with dismay, many making signs against evil as they passed.

Blood and gore still caked the horsemen's scale armour, their helmets, cloaks, and faces. A sickly array of trophies hung from their saddle horns – blank, staring heads, bloody beards, and blood-stained torcs from the necks of fallen Caledonian warriors.

The men of the legion were silent, and all that could be heard was the rushing of the river beyond, the clink of mail armour and horse harness.

Before the gates, sitting atop their horses, were Coilus and Afallach, along with Brencis and another officer Lucius thought he recognized. Centurion Torens also stood there nodding grimly at Lucius as he approached.

"Hail, Praefectus!" Torens said.

Lucius looked at all the faces about him and forced himself, with great difficulty, to slide back into the role of Praefectus. "Salve, Torens!" he answered. "Looks like our reinforcements have finally come to Caledonia."

Torens smiled. "You could say that. Six legions have arrived – the II Augusta, IX Hispana, XX Valeria Victrix, II and III Parthica, your old outfit I understand, and the rest of my own VI Victrix." Torens nodded to the men about him. "Close to the whole Praetorian Guard is also here with the emperor. They're with Conn Venico now."

"All right, Centurion," said the broad striped tribune behind him. "I'll do the updating now."

"Sir," Torens stood back, his face a mask that did not hide his annoyance well.

"Praefectus Metellus," the tribune said. "I haven't seen you since Trimontium."

Lucius realized who the man was. "Ah, Tribune Claudius."

"Yes." Claudius straightened his cloak and looked over Lucius, "Caesar Caracalla has sent me along the Gask Ridge. The horsemen you stationed along the way are back here now," he nodded to the walls of Bertha, "and I have dispersed legionaries along the same frontier to begin building works, and the proper manning of the frontier."

"Good," Lucius answered. "It's better to have my men together. Especially since we've just lost a whole turmae to the Caledonii, plus several more casualties."

"I can see you are filthy from battle," Claudius said.

"When did you arrive?" Lucius asked.

"Just four hours ago. Camp is set and I was just about to see to my accommodation."

"Well, Tribune," Lucius began. "I'm afraid that Bertha is full. I'm sure you have a sturdy campaign tent. For myself, after actual fighting, I'm in need of a good night's sleep in my quarters." Without waiting, Lucius nudged Lunaris past the tribune.

Claudius stared with fury after him as the rest of the Sarmatian horses walked around him, all smelling of death.

"Coilus. Afallach," Lucius greeted the Votadini as he passed and they followed, eager to hear of the battle.

"Brencis!" Dagon called to his cousin as he and Lucius stopped.

"Looks like you got our message through," Lucius said.

"Yes," Brencis answered without smiling. "But did I hear that we lost a turmae? Thirty-two of our brothers are gone?"

"More," Lucius said. "We will talk of it later. For now, tell the tribune, Torens, and Rodric that they should come to my quarters tonight for a debriefing."

"Praefectus!" Brencis saluted and stepped back to allow Lucius and the rest to flow into Bertha beneath the dragon vexillum which now fluttered above the gatehouse.

As Lucius passed some of the barrack blocks, he noticed a wooden cell where a man and a woman were being held. Their eyes met his as he passed, but his sole thought was of being alone, and getting clean in his quarters.

The gathering was tense.

Lucius, Dagon, Brencis, Barta, Coilus, Afallach, Rodric, Torens, and Tribune Claudius stood around the table sipping their wine and trying to assess the situation.

For so long, the Ala III Britannorum Sarmatiana had been alone with the Votadini and detachments of sixth legion in Caledonia. Now, however, several other legions and auxiliary units were on the scene, each eager to get stuck into the fighting and crush the Caledonii and their allies.

"I'm telling you, Tribune," Lucius said, fed up with Claudius' air of superiority and incessant smirking, as if he were party to an inside joke or other information. "You won't lure the Caledonii out into a full-scale battle. Argentocoxus is too smart for that."

"Yet you engaged him just a few days ago, Praefectus. Why not again, since you missed getting him last time?"

Lucius held his tongue, eager to just reach across the table and pommel the man. "We came upon the Caledonii by surprise, and caught them unawares. Argentocoxus was one of the only ones to get away."

"Convenient."

"I think, with respect, Tribune, that what the praefectus says bears listening to." Coilus stood beside Claudius, his leather cuirass brilliantly polished, and a red cloak pinned at his shoulder with a golden brooch.

"It may be," Claudius forgot Coilus' name and shook his head, annoyed, "that your tribal warfare works thus on a small scale, but when the armies of Rome march out, the sight of Her legions are often enough to press the enemy into peaceful submission."

The other men around the table looked doubtful. The idea was ludicrous at best.

"Where have you served, Tribune? If you don't mind my asking," Lucius could not resist.

"I spent some time along the Danuvius, at Vindobona, and then in Iberia." Claudius crossed his muscled arms, perfectly shaped in the gymnasium, not on the battlefield. Lucius noticed the distinct lack of scars on his arms.

"Britannia is different. The rules are different. The terrain, the enemy, the weapons we face, the tactics they employ. Why do you think Hadrianus built the bloody wall? Consolidation of victories and the consideration of an acceptable loss. Caledonia isn't worth it."

They all looked at Lucius, shock on their faces. All except Claudius who smirked again.

"I'm sure the emperor and Caesar Caracalla would be interested in your opinion of their goals for the Empire, Metellus." Claudius laid his cup on the table." Now, I must get back to my tent. Tomorrow morning I return to the emperor. I expect you will be called to report soon, Praefectus, so don't get too comfortable here."

"I am ever at the emperor's bidding," Lucius answered.

Claudius turned to leave, then snapped his fingers at Rodric. "You, Veniconi."

"Rodric," the man grunted.

"Yes. Come with me. I want to ask you about the best possible route for me and my men."

Claudius went out of the building, his crimson cloak brushing the door frame as he went. The others were silent a moment.

"What an arrogant bastard!" Brencis blurted. "Oh, sorry, Torens. I know he's your commanding officer."

Torens' face was stony as he looked at Lucius. "He is a bastard, true. But he's a dangerous man, Praefectus. Watch out for that one. He may be ignorant of warcraft and strategy, but he's in with Caracalla. And he has an evil streak in'im."

"He's not the only one with friends in high places," Lucius replied, though he could sense the truth of Torens' warning. "I'll take your words to heart, Torens."

The centurion nodded and then left.

"So, what are the orders for now?" Dagon asked.

"I suspect Claudius was right that the emperor will call for me soon, so that meeting will tell us more. For now, patrols along the defensive ridge facing the highlands. I want rotating detachments of three turmae to go out intermittently. The Caledonii aren't going to meet the legions on the open field, but they will continue to harry our forces and attack the fortlets and watchtowers."

They all stared at the map on the table, each nodding in turn. Rodric came back into the room as Lucius spoke.

"I don't care if it takes years," Lucius continued. "For what they did, I'm going to hunt down every last Caledonian warrior until none are left."

Rodric stared at Lucius from across the table, just behind Coilus and Afallach.

"What is it, Rodric?"

"Nothing, Praefectus," the man replied in his deep gravelly voice. "Just that the tribune thought I should return with him to report to Conn Venico, who is now with the emperor."

"You and your men have helped us well enough, Rodric. You deserve a rest. Go back to Conn Venico and tell him that many of his enemies have died on the tips of our lances and swords."

Rodric nodded slowly and then after a glance about the room, left. His tattooed, bare torso headed out into the night.

Lucius rubbed his temples and remembered what he had seen on his way into the fort. "Brencis, who are those two prisoners in the cage outside?"

"Ah, yes. I was waiting until the tribune was gone before I brought it up."

"And?"

Everyone looked at Brencis. They knew Lucius was not keen on keeping female prisoners.

"After I gave the dispatches to Caracalla, when we found him –"

"And saved him, from what I hear!" Dagon interrupted.

Brencis inclined his head. "They fell for the cow bait the Caledonii use." Everyone nodded, understanding. "Anyway, as we were riding north, we spotted two horsemen. They looked different than the Caledonii and Venicones, so we chased them down to ask after their business." Brencis took a swig of his wine and continued. "They told me, in Latin, that they had an urgent message for the 'Dragon Praefectus'."

Lucius looked up from the map. "For me?"

"Yes. So I told them I'm one of your men and that they can give me your message. They refused."

"Who are they?" Dagon asked.

"A brother and sister from the South, sent to give a message to the praefectus. That's all they would say."

"Did you hurt them?" Lucius asked.

"Well," Brencis paused. "They wouldn't give us the message, or agree to come with us, so we used a little force." Brencis began to laugh. "It took six of us to subdue the man!"

"And the woman?" Lucius' face darkened. "I hope you didn't harm her." The woman's caged eyes popped into Lucius' mind then.

"No. But she hurt us! Fast, she was. Kicked one of my men down below and swept the legs from beneath two more before I finished blinking."

Lucius raised an eyebrow. "The woman took down three of my Sarmatians?"

"Like I said, she was fast. They've obviously been trained somewhere. That's why I locked'em up."

"I want you to feed them, and give them a room in the barrack block. Guarded, mind you. Bring them to me in three hours. I really need to sleep. Orpheus is creeping into my veins every second after these past few days."

"One more thing, Praefectus," Brencis said, holding up a hand. "A message from Centurion Alerio."

"What?"

"He was with Caracalla. He says your wife and children are coming north with the empress."

Lucius nodded absently, and turned as if in silent dismissal.

The men all left to give Lucius his due rest. He ordered all of those who had returned with him, including Barta, to get some sleep as well.

Leaving two lamps burning in his room in the small praetorium of the fort, Lucius laid down without his armour on for the first time in days. The smoke from the incense he had lit on the small altar wafted throughout the room. As he lay back he thought of Adara, and the children. *Thank you, Gods,* he prayed. *May I see them soon and hold them close.*

His eyes rolling, Lucius gave in to comatose sleep.

Lucius had been dreaming and hoping, praying for word of his family for so long. But when his eyes closed, all he could see were his dead men hanging from that deathly tree, their burning, savaged bodies, and the blood of the battle afterward.

The sound of the Morrigan tore at his senses as he slept, and sweat poured from his pores. He was outside himself, beyond the newly white-washed walls of his praetorium with the leaking roof. The whinny of horses was far away.

He was walking across a field toward the tree where he found his men still hanging. This time, their eyes opened and their mouths gaped as they tried to yell, to scream, to give warning even as the Morrigan's crows pecked out their eyes.

Lucius, barefoot and wearing only a pair of crimson bracae, fell to his knees, unable to breathe. A pressure about his neck built and built, and his legs began to shake, his eyes blurring.

The Morrigan was before him, her eyes boring into his.

Lucius felt his head crushed by ghostly blows. Then a light appeared before his vision.

Not now. Wake! Wake, beloved!

Goddess Venus? Lucius wondered as she faded away and was replaced by another visage.

A round grimacing face stood over him with a long moustache drooping down to the hands that were wrapped around his throat.

Lucius' eyes opened wide to see Rodric on top of him while two others pinned his legs.

"You fucking Roman!" the man growled. "You're finished killing my people. I'm going to piss on your corpse."

Lucius felt his consciousness leaving him.

Not now! the voice had said.

His arm reached for the dagger he had laid on the floor in the dark. He felt the handle and swung it up to slam into Rodric's head. The air immediately rushed into his lungs as he gasped but he did not have control of the dagger which now pointed at him. "Ahh!" Lucius yelled as the blade plunged into his ribs. *Apollo, give me strength. Epona!*

There was a loud cry and then one of Lucius' legs was free, then the other. Several shapes danced and cried in the background, but Lucius was focussed on Rodric, whose muscly bulk tried to wrap an arm about his neck.

Lucius slammed his head into Rodric's face. He grabbed the dagger and plunged it into the man's ear.

Rodric screamed and leapt at Lucius even as his eyes rolled and blood poured from his head.

Lucius stumbled to the side and Rodric flew head first into the wall with a crunch, leaving a red smear on the white wall. Lucius fell to his knees, gasping, and looked up to see a man and a woman, the brother and sister, each standing over a dead Veniconi warrior.

By the door, Brencis stood in disbelief. “You see? Fast!” he said before rushing to Lucius’ aid. “Dagon, Barta, get in here!”

XIII

AUXILIUM

'Help'

Lucius realized that he must have passed out, for when he awoke he was back on his cot with a thick bandage about his torso. He tried to speak, but it hurt.

Dagon was beside him. "Easy, Anguis," the Sarmatian said. "We almost lost you."

Lucius looked about and tried to sit.

"We had to cauterize your wound. You're lucky it was shallow and sloppy."

"What…" Lucius cleaned his throat and sipped some water from the cup on the table beside his cot. "What happened?"

Dagon sighed. "Rodric and two of his men tried to kill you. They killed the guards I had placed at your door while Barta slept, and then snuck in here."

"Who died?" Lucius closed his eyes.

"Blenna and Kordo."

"There were three? I…I only remember Rodric."

"He had two other warriors with him. If it hadn't been for the two Britons, you'd be dead, or at least very badly injured."

"I've had worse."

"I dare say. But how long will the Gods shield you, Anguis? We can't let our vigilance lessen in this place."

"Seems not. Where are the man and woman?"

"Eating with Barta and Brencis. I didn't think we should lock them up anymore after that."

"No. Here," Lucius stood and tried to find his legs again. "Help me get dressed. I want to meet them."

Dagon took a blue tunic from a chair and helped Lucius get it over his head. The latter cringed as he raised his arms, stretching the wound.

Lucius cinched a cingulum about his waist, his pugio attached, and waited while Dagon laced up his boots.

"I'll go and get them." Dagon left.

Lucius went over to the altar and closed his eyes. "Gods – Apollo, Venus, and Epona…Thank you for protecting me. Please do not desert my family and me. We honour you –"

"Erm," Dagon cleared his throat as he and Barta came in, leading the two Britons.

Lucius rose slowly and turned toward them. The man had a badly bruised and swollen eye, but still managed an air of strength and pride. His long hair was tied back with a leather thong and he held the girl's hand protectively.

The woman was not young, but of Lucius own age, tall and beautiful with blond hair that was braided back to allow her to fight. She appeared quick and slender, and Lucius could see by the way she held herself how she could have given his men a good fight. She had a bad bruise on the side of her head.

Lucius walked to stand before them, trying not to let his pain be too apparent. "You don't need to be afraid among us," he began. "I'm Lucius Metellus Anguis, Praefectus of the Ala III Britannorum Sarmatiana. I believe you were looking for me?"

The brother and sister looked at each other, then the man spoke.

"I am Einion, son of Conmore of Dumnonia. This is my sister, Briana."

The girl looked at Lucius, her eyes lingering on the dragons coiling about his forearms.

"We've come a long way to see you, Praefectus," Einion said.

"I'm sorry you were hurt," Lucius said, looking at Briana's head. "As you've seen, we have reason to be cautious."

"I gave fight to your men," Einion continued. "It is understandable."

"We also had trouble with some of the Caledonii," Briana added, trying to curtail the tremble in her voice. She hated feeling weakness. "Three more you need not worry about."

"You are warriors of your people?" Lucius asked.

"We fought to protect our family in Dumnonia…until an enemy massacred everyone, including our family. We are the only survivors." Einion's jaw worked rigidly.

Lucius looked at him and held out his hand. Einion reached out reluctantly to grasp it.

"I cannot thank you enough for last night," Lucius said, gripping Einion's forearm before taking Briana's hand. "Thank you," he said, turning to sit and motioning for the others to sit as well. He poured some wine and looked at them. "Now. This message. It must have been difficult for you to bring to me when your family's enemy still lives far in the southwest?" Lucius looked from one to the other. For some reason, he felt a great affinity toward both of them. Even Barta, he noticed, was relatively calm with them in the room.

"It is an important message," Briana said.

"Tell me," Lucius said.

Einion and Briana looked at Dagon and Barta.

"Don't worry about them. They are my brothers. I would gladly lay down my life for them, as they would for me. Tell me."

Einion leaned back and waited for his sister to speak. Briana took a vellum scroll from her satchel, which had been returned to her, and handed it to Lucius.

"This is from a wise and kind man in the South," she said as she pushed the scroll across the table.

Lucius picked it up and opened it. "Who is he?"

"His name is Weylyn, and he is the father of the Boar of the Selgovae."

Lucius felt the blood pumping in his ears, only just hearing Barta's blade slither out of his scabbard. "Barta, stop." Lucius held up his hand, and looked at Briana and Einion. "We had a long battle with the Boar. Forgive us," Lucius said, wiping the sweat from his brow, his wound throbbing. "What does the Boar's father want of me?"

"To offer you help," Briana said. Lucius looked up. "His son told him of your kindness, and he wanted to repay you."

Barta and Dagon made a sign against evil when the girl spoke, but Lucius' eyes went from Briana to the letter. He began to read…

I write to you, ile Anguis, at the request of my son, Cathbad, the Boar of the Selgovae, as you knew him.

Before going into Annwn, my son came to me to tell me of his death.

I too, in my youth, had fought against Rome's legions. I am a Druid, as you call us. That information could mean my death, but I hope you take it as a sign of my good will that I trust you with that knowledge.

I hope you also take it as a sign that I trust the two who carry this letter to you, implicitly. My son spoke of you as a great warrior, and an honourable Roman whom the Gods favour.

I loved my son, and though we had often quarrelled, I believe the words he gave me on his way to the Otherworld. I know he would not have gone into Annwn, or joined the Wild Hunt, if you had not countered your own people and allowed him a warrior's death. The fact that you ensured his body was returned to our people for the rites only confirms what I have seen in my dreams: That you, a powerful dragon, were meant to come to Britannia and that you have a role to play in this land of ours.

The Gods do not lie. They have no need to.

Before he went through the ghostly gates, my son asked that I send help to you and your family.

Yes, he mentioned you have a family. I do not ask you to betray your emperor, for I know you are far too honourable for that. You know your heart, and your loyalties. All I ask is that you accept my help, for the sake of my son's wishes, if anything.

The man and woman before you, Einion and Briana, are also touched by the Gods, and have an unknown role to play. They will tell you their story when they see fit. Take them into your service. Keep them close, for they will be mighty defenders of your family. By the Gods I serve, I swear you can trust them with your lives.

If you read this in disbelief, the pained memories of bloody battle with my son too much for you to overcome, send Einion and Briana back to me. But I hope that will not be the case.

May your gods and ours protect us all.

Weylyn

Lucius stared at the scroll, not yet looking up at Barta, Dagon, or the two Britons. His head spun. Is it possible? Could the Boar have gone to his father?

He looked at Einion and Briana for a moment before speaking. He remembered the dead of his own family all too vividly. *Die parentes...*

"It's true? This Weylyn is the father of the Boar of the Selgovae?"

"Yes," Einion answered.

"He asked me to take you into my service."

Briana nodded, though Einion was still.

"Wait a moment," Dagon stepped around the table to Lucius' side. "After what happened tonight?"

Lucius handed him the scroll to read. "I'm short on trusted allies outside my cavalry brothers," Lucius said gravely. "How do I know I can trust you?"

"That is an answer only you can give yourself, Praefectus." Einion sat forward "We are here at the request of a friend to whom we owe a debt."

"I have never wanted slaves nor had any on campaign. Why would I want any now?"

"We are not slaves," Einion said evenly.

Briana put out a hand to calm her brother. "We were sent to you in good will, Praefectus. No, we are not slaves, but we will serve as you see fit." Briana paused. "There will always be help..."

Lucius jumped up. "What did you say?"

Briana looked confused, as did the others.

Lucius stared at the girl with her brother beside her. Epona's face floated behind them. The room suddenly felt very small, and Lucius wanted for fresh air. "I'll give you my answer tonight," he said. "Then you will either stay and serve me, or return to the South."

Barta opened the door leading into the courtyard, and the two Britons went out, glancing confusedly at Lucius as they went.

"What do you make of that letter, Dagon?" Lucius asked when they were alone.

"I think you should be cautious. Then again, if he is a Druid, we could report him and troops would apprehend him in no time. We know what Rome thinks of their kind."

"Yes. He did risk much sending this letter. But...I don't know."

"What, Anguis?"

"Something the woman said... There will always be help."

"Yes?"

"I've heard that before."

Dagon rubbed his beard and looked at Lucius.

"How's your wound?"

"It burns, but I'll be fine." He could not help thinking of his men hanging from that tree. "I'm fine."

"Good. Let's go for a ride. You'll think more clearly."

Lucius, Dagon, and Barta rode slowly along the river a short distance from the camp. They looked at the odd mixture of thatch and tile roofs within the fort walls, and the small vicus of camp followers who had come with the legions and decided to open for business.

"Tell the men to mind which whores they visit in the vicus," Lucius said. "I don't want anyone unable to ride."

"I've already instructed them," Dagon answered. "Though some of the men are indeed longing for a woman."

Not that Lucius worried much about the Sarmatians. They knew when it was time for fighting and fucking, and if it ever came to a choice, fighting would always win out. But every man needs a release, and as disciplined as they were, they were only mortal men.

"What about the letter, Anguis?" Dagon cut to the quick of the matter.

Lucius looked down at the rushing river, Epona's words at Trimontium a constant whisper in his head.

There will always be help...

Dagon continued, "Anguis, I know you have a connection with your gods that even I don't understand. Few men do. But from the time I met you in that taverna in Carthage, I knew that you were touched by them. The Dragon...*ile Anguis*...it is power, and prophecy, and it has never led you astray."

Lucius turned his arm over where the tails of his tattoos came out from beneath his arm guards. He felt the cold wind on his face and closed his eyes.

"This Druid, he also seems to believe in the dragon. The girl, Briana, her eyes kept going to your forearms as if for reassurance."

"So you're saying I should take them into my service?" Lucius asked. "What about my family? I hope to be with them soon. What of their safety?"

"I know your fears," Dagon said. "We've lived by the sword for long now, and you can't help but think danger lurks in the shadows to take your family away, the same as -" Dagon stopped.

"As what?"

"The same as happened to Alene."

Lucius' eyes turned on Dagon, but the young princeps stood his ground. "I'm only saying that perhaps this is a gift. Einion and Briana may bring some relief, some aid, rather than the pain you are constantly expecting. Perhaps they are the help you need?"

Lucius could see the sincerity in Dagon's eyes. He wanted to believe it, that there were more allies, that the Gods were proffering help.

"I do not speak with our war god, he of the Sacred Sword, but I know he is pleased because he allows me to live a victorious life of battle." Here Dagon reached out to Lucius. "You, Anguis, your gods speak with you. It would not be wise to shun their gifts."

Lucius nodded. "Barta," he called the big Sarmatian over.

Barta approached on his huge horse from where he had been looking at the river a short distance from the two men. "Yes, Praefectus?"

"You have always been a good judge of men. That is why you are such a good personal guard. What do you think of the two Britons?"

Barta rubbed his great black beard, the muscles of his thick forearms pulsing as he did so. "I think they could have let the Venicones kill you if they wanted you dead, sir. You can trust them."

"What role? Personal guard? House servants? They are warriors, it seems."

"Make the man your personal guard," Dagon said. "That way, Barta can keep an eye on him. More eyes watching your back is a good thing," Dagon suggested.

"And the woman? I doubt she wants to do laundry."

"I don't know. Another bodyguard?" Dagon said.

"Or someone to watch over my family should she be trustworthy…" Lucius thought out loud, not sure where the idea came from.

"Could be." Dagon smiled.

Lucius found Briana and Einion sitting in one of the rooms of the principia when he arrived. They were binding each other's wounds with fresh linens when Lucius and Dagon walked in.

"Forgive me," Lucius said, as Briana covered her shoulder where Einion had been looking at a bruise. "I can come back."

"No, Praefectus. Please. We were just seeing to our wounds," Briana said, pulling her long hair over her left shoulder.

"We're finished," Einion said, stretching and standing up.

Lucius swept his crimson cloak back over his shoulders and crossed his arms. "I've decided to accept your offer...Weylyn's offer of help."

"You can trust us," Einion said.

"I know," Lucius answered. "You will both serve as my personal guards and assistants for now. Dagon and Barta will also be your superiors." Lucius held a hand up to stop their protestations. "We are in the service of Rome, and appearances must be upheld. I don't want to pretend you're my slaves, so you can be in my personal employ. Whatever you need – food, clothing, weapons – I shall get for you."

"We don't need charity," Einion said.

Lucius smiled. "Not charity. Payment for services rendered. In return, I want your eyes and ears open at all times. You can track well?"

They nodded.

"Good. That will help too. And hunting. I...I also have a family," Lucius paused. "I don't know when I will see them again, but when I do, you will help me to keep them safe." Lucius looked away, suddenly very tired.

"Praefectus?" Briana said, stepping forward with a glance at Dagon. "Our parents and younger siblings were taken from us by our enemies. I swear I will not -"

"We, sister!" Einion inserted.

"We, will not allow harm to come to your family."

"You lost family also?" Lucius asked.

"Yes."

"Then that is something we have in common."

The following day, Einion and Briana were slowly introduced to the men as Lucius' new aides.

The Sarmatians seemed unbothered by the newcomers, giving the man a quick assessment, and the woman a lingering look. They returned to their drills quickly enough.

Coilus and Afallach, on the other hand, were suspicious of the two Britons.

Lucius had decided he could not tell the Votadini who had sent them because of their history with the Boar's father.

"I sent for them," was Lucius' only answer. "They came highly recommended."

Coilus and Afallach said nothing, but continued with the training of their own men.

"I'm sorry I caged you," Brencis said to Einion as they walked. "Had to play it safe." He smiled.

"It's fine. You fed us," Einion answered curtly. "Just make sure it doesn't happen again."

Brencis, as was always his manner, slapped Einion on the back and laughed loudly.

"Centurion Torens!" Lucius called as the veteran came down the via Decumana.

"Praefectus!" Torens saluted.

"I want you to meet my new aides, Einion and Briana. They'll be working closely with me now."

Torens looked them up and down, and sniffed. "Aye. Well, we can always use more help. What's the woman going to do?"

"A personal assistant and bodyguard," Lucius said.

"Bodyguard?" he snorted and began to turn away before his vinerod came whisking sideways through the air at Briana.

The girl slid quickly out of range, her right leg kicking Torens' wrist to knock his vinerod onto the street.

Einion's dagger was already at his throat.

Torens' grizzled face cracked into a semi-smile. "I see you're as fast as I've heard."

Einion lowered his knife.

"Good!" the centurion bellowed, then turned to Lucius. "Sir, a Praetorian messenger awaits you in the Principia."

"Very well." Lucius walked past Torens with Dagon, Barta, Briana, and Einion.

"Didn't I tell you, Centurion?" Brencis said to Torens after they had left.

"Aye, you did. Best keep her away from the men though." He watched her go. "She's a Venus in our midst. Better than any of the toothless whores outside the walls, anyway!"

Part III

DARKNESS AND LIGHT

A.D. 209

XIV

ARX

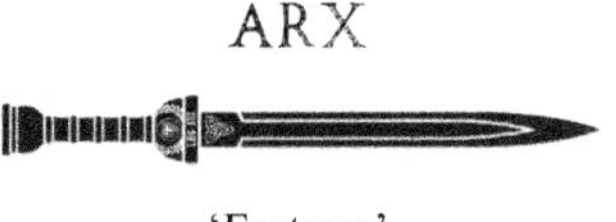

'Fortress'

"Salve, Optio!" Lucius saluted the Praetorian messenger who paced the broken courtyard of the Principia.

"Praefectus!" The man saluted back and held out a wax tablet for Lucius to read. "Sir, the emperor commands you and your captains to report to him at Horea Classis tomorrow by the fifth hour."

"Tomorrow? Horea Classis?" The name was not familiar to Lucius.

"That is what they are calling the place known by the locals as Carpow."

"Is it suitable for the emperor yet?" Lucius asked.

"Three legions have been building day and night, sir, and the coastal praefectus has brought ships into port with materials and supplies. It is ready."

"Very well. Tell the emperor I'll be there with two turmae tomorrow."

The man nodded, took back his tablet and made to leave. "One more thing, sir!" he added.

"Yes?"

"You are to bring the body of Conn Venico's man, Rodric."

Lucius' face darkened. "The man who tried to kill me. Yes. I'll bring it." *The spies have arrived in force then…*

When the messenger was gone, Lucius turned to Dagon and Barta. "I want two turmae polished and ready to go early tomorrow."

They nodded.

"See if you can strap Rodric's body to a cart or something so that it doesn't spook the horses."

"I will," said Dagon. "I believe he's still mostly intact."

"Box him if you have to," Lucius said before turning to Einion and Briana. "I guess you two are going to meet the emperor."

Lucius' force followed the river southeast from the Dragon's Lair. They rode with a turmae of Sarmatians, and a turmae of Votadini, the dragon and horse vexilli fluttering at their head, above the draco standard which hummed in the wind.

Lucius reined in when they approached the Tava estuary to take in the sight before him. Dagon and Barta were with him, as were Coilus and Afallach, Einion and Briana.

The siblings had been quiet for the journey, their eyes searching every patch of scrub, and every copse of trees for an ambush. Neither of them knew what to expect. Their shock at being told they were going to meet the emperor of Rome had been great.

"Just stay close to me and Barta," Dagon had reassured them. "Remember, I'm not Roman either. Nor is Barta. Lucius is the only one."

Dagon joined Lucius at the front where he was looking out from a slight ridge over the plain. It seemed as though an entire city had sprung up out of the mud. The fort at Horea Classis covered over eleven hectares. The engineers had certainly earned their pay, for the fort was complete with masonry walls surrounding a tile-roofed praetorium and principia, barrack blocks, granaries, storehouses, and, judging from the smoke rising into the air along the river, a bath house as well. Four gates allowed traffic in and out of the heavily guarded gatehouses onto the via Decumana and via Principalis.

The navy had also arrived, and supply ships were moored at newly built quays to be unloaded. Other ships waited at anchor out in the estuary about a small island.

"Gods," Coilus said to himself. "None of this was here before."

"How many men are there, Praefectus?" Einion asked.

"Oh, looks like about twenty-five thousand," Lucius said. Of course he had seen many more on the Parthian campaign, over thirty legions, but somehow, where they now stood, the numbers seemed massive, compared with the vast, open plains of Parthia.

"I think there are more than that. Look!" Dagon pointed to the areas around the fort where each of the legions were erecting their own camps.

"Make that about forty-five thousand in all," Lucius corrected. "Plus camp followers and tradesmen." He dared not hope that his family was down there somewhere.

"Here comes another patrol, Praefectus!" Afallach said as a century of legionaries came marching toward them.

Lucius advanced and returned the centurion's salute.

"Salve, Centurion!"

"Praefectus Metellus?"

"Yes."

"We've been told to watch for you. You're to proceed to the principia with your captains as soon as you arrive at the east gate of the fortress."

"Understood," Lucius said. "Which legion are you with?"

"Caius Valerius, Centurion, second century, fourth cohort of III Parthica." The man snapped a salute.

"That was my first legion," Lucius said, smiling at the man. "Good to have you with us in Caledonia, soldier."

"Is the fighting as bad as they say, Praefectus?"

Lucius could see his men were young, green, not unlike Lucius and his friends the first time they had marched into Parthia. Each one of them had their ears cocked to hear what he had to say.

"It's heavy. When we can engage the enemy," Lucius said. "They like to surprise us with ambushes," he said truthfully. "Just keep your wits about you, men, and you'll teach the bastards a thing or two!"

There was a cheer, and the centurion smiled, saluted again, and stepped aside for the turmae of hardened horse warriors to pass them and go down to the fortress on the deep green plain.

The air smelled of the salt sea, mixed with the pungent scent of fresh plaster, cement, and the sweetness of freshly-cut timber. The turmae approached the looming walls of Horea Classis where thousands of heads turned to follow the group of horsemen as they came to a stop outside the east gate.

Lucius realized most of the troops looking at them had not yet engaged the Caledonii, whereas his ala had been fighting the enemy constantly in one way or another since before most of them had arrived in Britannia.

"Second and sixth legions have outdone themselves," Dagon said in a low voice to Lucius as they dismounted.

Lucius looked up at the fortifications and deep ditches before them. "Quick work indeed," he said.

The fortress walls were lined with helmeted legionaries gazing down at them or looking tentatively out at the hills to the West. There was a lot of activity between the camps of the various legions, much back and forth from each fort to the main fortress where orders were dispatched from the principia.

Berths had been set up on the banks of the river and a steady train of troops flowed from the ships to the newly-built granaries. The men carried sack upon sack of grain and other provisions. The legionaries had to eat.

Lucius dismounted, his nose detecting a rotting scent. He turned to see the wagon carrying Rodric's mangled body. "Put it over there!" he ordered the trooper driving it. "I'll not pollute the emperor's fortress with it." He turned to his officers as two of the men unloaded the box with the body, and laid it on the ground.

Lucius knew there would be questions about Rodric's death, and he was ready for them.

"Dismount and stay in formation!" Lucius ordered the Sarmatian and Votadini horsemen. He wanted their discipline to shine through with all those eyes upon them. "Dagon, Barta, Coilus, Afallach, Einion and Briana, come with me." He leaned in to whisper to Einion and Briana. "Remember, you're my servants."

They nodded, their eyes taking in the sight of so many Romans in one place.

Lucius cast a last look at his troops, then made his way to the gatehouse across the deep fossa.

"Praefectus Lucius Metellus Anguis, III Ala Quingenaria Sarmatiana, here to report to the emperor," Lucius informed the centurion at the gate.

"It's about time!" came a familiar voice from inside the fort.

Lucius looked to see Alerio striding toward him, wearing his Praetorian regalia. Lucius smiled and strode directly to his old friend. He noticed Alerio looked much older, and world-weary, but his smile was indeed genuine.

"Centurion!" Lucius laughed. "It's good to see you." They clasped forearms. "Been here long?"

"A couple of weeks now," Alerio looked about. "Had a little trouble on the way." He remembered the Caledonian attack.

"This is a land of trouble," Lucius said.

"Well, let's not talk of that yet." Alerio's face grew serious. "The emperor is in there with Conn Venico."

"I see."

"What happened?"

"What happened is his man tried to kill me while I was sleeping!"

"Hmm…"

"The body's with my men. In a nice box."

Alerio peered around Lucius and out the gate. He noticed those with Lucius.

"Salve, Dagon. Barta," Alerio nodded to the two Sarmatians.

"Centurion Cornelius," Lucius began. "May I introduce Coilus, Chief of the Votadini, our staunch allies, and his son, Prince Afallach."

Alerio shook Coilus' hand, and turned to Afallach. "You killed the Boar of the Selgovae, I hear."

"Yes, Centurion," Afallach said, gazing straight ahead. He had not spoken of the event much since then.

"Come!" Alerio said, seeing his discomfort. "They're waiting." He began to lead Lucius along the road. "Who are the two Britons?" he asked.

"My Dumnonian servants."

"Really? I thought you didn't want slaves?" Alerio stopped before the doors to the principia.

"They saved my life."

"From who?"

"From Conn Venico's man, Rodric, and the two men he brought with him."

Alerio looked them over quickly before nodding to the two guards who unbarred their pila to let them into the principia courtyard.

Lucius cast his eyes about quickly for any sign of the empress and, more importantly, Adara but he could only see tribunes, centurions and other officers of the various legions milling about in small groups.

They walked across the courtyard to the large, guarded meeting room at the far end. All conversation died down at their approach, and Alerio stood at the entrance to announce the new arrivals.

"Sire." He bowed. "Praefectus Lucius Metellus Anguis, and Coilus, Chieftain of the Votadini, and their captains."

Alerio turned and waved Lucius and Coilus forward into the room followed by the rest.

It took Lucius' eyes a moment to adjust to the dimly-lit room where incense wafted thickly, but he eventually focussed on the emperor and Caracalla who sat on a small dais thirty feet away. Lucius stepped forward, his crested helmet beneath his left arm, snapping a salute with his right.

"Ave, my Imperator, Lucius Septimius Severus!" he said, bowing deeply to the emperor.

Septimius Severus looked weaker than Lucius had ever seen him. His skin was mottled beneath his patchy beard, and his wheezing breath was audible above the hushed whispers of those lining the walls.

The emperor's eyes fixed suddenly on Lucius and then…clapping.

The emperor began to clap, and was followed by others, including Caracalla who rose from his seat and stepped down to come toward Lucius.

"Praefectus Metellus!" the emperor coughed. "We are happy to see you alive and well."

"Thank you, sire!" Lucius bowed again.

"You have done great service to your emperor, and to Rome. Thanks to you, our campaign in Caledonia is off to a good start."

Lucius nodded, and cast his eyes about to see some familiar faces – Papinian and Ulpian, a smiling senator Dio, Nearchus Chioticus, the coastal praefectus, and various other tribunes and legates of the other legions whom he had only seen in passing. Then his eyes fell on Conn Venico to the emperor's left.

The man stared coldly at Lucius who returned his gaze.

Caracalla came up to Lucius and took his forearm in friendship. "I too am happy to see you, Metellus," he said for all to hear.

"Caesar, I'm glad to have you and the legions here," Lucius answered, bringing a smile to Caracalla's usually hard face.

"And Coilus, Chieftain of the Votadini," the emperor continued. "Rome salutes you and your warriors, and I thank you for your friendship." A great coughing fit seized the emperor then, and Papinian stepped up to give him a cup of hot wine.

Coilus waited to respond.

"Most gracious, Imperator," Coilus said. "My people and I are ever loyal to Rome, and we are ready to serve as you see fit."

"Very good!" Severus said, a smile upon his spittle-wet lips.

Caracalla looked past Dagon and Barta to Einion and Briana, his gaze raking over the latter.

Both kept their heads down, distinctly uncomfortable in the gathering, especially Briana who was the only woman in attendance.

"So, Praefectus," Papinian spoke up next. "Do tell us what you have to report."

Lucius nodded, handed his helmet to Dagon, and stepped forward to address everyone. He felt his nerves then, unused as he was to addressing such gatherings.

"As you know, after subduing the Selgovae, my Sarmatian cavalry and I, along with our Votadini allies, crossed the

Bodotria river into Caledonia. We have had many small engagements every step of the way as we sought to secure the forts and watchtowers along the Gask Frontier, which faces the highlands."

Lucius walked over to the emperor's right where a large leather map was stretched between two posts.

"The forts of Doune, Alauna, and Strageath, I left heavily manned, while my own ala units have been based at Bertha here." Lucius pointed. "Between each of these are a chain of thinly manned fortlets and watchtowers which have now been reinforced by the incoming legions."

"What of this fort?" Caracalla said, pointing to Fendoch where it lay isolated at the foot of the highlands.

"I did send a turmae of my best men to scout as far as Fendoch, sire. When they did not return, I rode out myself and found them…" Lucius felt his throat tighten at the memory of the tree and fought back the anger that rose in him, the feeling of failure.

No weakness! he chided himself. "The Caledonii had ambushed them and hung their naked and savaged bodies from a tree, above their slaughtered horses."

The emperor's face darkened, and Caracalla stepped forward.

"What happened then?"

Lucius looked at Caracalla and back at the map. "The Caledonii refuse to come out into the open for battle. They prefer guerrilla tactics of ambush and surprise. And they are good at that."

There were murmurs about the room.

"But we found them!" Lucius said, louder. "A battle took place and we slaughtered the Caledonian force that attacked our men."

"And what of their leader, Praefectus?" came a voice from the doorway.

Lucius looked to see Tribune Claudius standing there with his arms crossed.

"What of the Caledonian chief, Argentocoxus?"

The room was silent but for the creaking of leather armour and the emperor's raspy breathing.

Lucius stared at the tribune evenly, and turned to the emperor.

"Sire, Argentocoxus was the only one to escape."

"A great pity!" Claudius said as he moved into the centre of the room near Caracalla. "You might have ended this war already."

Lucius stepped closer, eyeing the cold, tall, carefully manicured tribune.

"Sire," Coilus spoke up. "If I may…" he cleared his throat, bowed to the emperor. "It is well known that Argentocoxus has many sons who are trained warriors. If the chief dies, there will always be another to take his place." Coilus backed up, and Lucius gave him a nod of thanks before he continued.

"Sire," Lucius said. "The only way to take this land, I believe, is to hammer the enemy into submission until they are so weak that they have no will to fight. They will never accept Rome willingly. One can see it in the fanatical way in which they fight."

There were more murmurs around the room, mostly of disagreement.

"We could waste years in Caledonia if we use that strategy," Caracalla said, turning to the emperor.

"Sire," Lucius continued. "It is true that this will be no easy conquest. The Parthians met us on the open field, but the Caledonii never will. They'll lure us into their bogs, and defiles, and pick our troops off one by one."

"What of buying them off?" Papinian asked, causing some disgruntled comments among the hardened veterans present.

"I believe that no matter what sum we were to give the Caledonii, the moment Rome leaves, they will betray any trust we may give them."

"You speak of trust!" Conn Venico burst out, stepping into the space to face Lucius. "How can you speak of trust when you kill your own allies?"

Lucius turned to the Veniconi chieftain, his anger up. *Stay calm,* he told himself.

"Conn Venico, you should be more careful of the men you trust so closely with your affairs. Your man, Rodric, attempted to assassinate me as I slept. He brought two more of your men to do it."

"Why was I not told of this?" the emperor turned to Papinian.

"Sire," the Praetorian Prefect said. "I wanted to confirm the facts first."

"The fact is, sir," Lucius addressed Papinian, "That if it were not for my two servants there," he pointed to Einion and Briana, "I would have been dead and no longer able to serve."

"Then I am glad they were there to serve you, Metellus," Septimius Severus nodded toward the Britons who kept their eyes down.

"What if the praefectus is lying?" Conn Venico said.

"Careful," Lucius growled, striding toward the chieftain. He could hear the faint movement of Barta's armour flexing. Lucius said out loud, "Rodric was not Veniconi, Conn Venico. He was a Caledonian, no?"

"Praefectus, stand down," the emperor said. "Conn Venico, is this truc?"

All eyes were on the Veniconi chieftain who looked about for support. Sweat began to bead on his bald head.

"I must admit, sire, it is true. He was a Caledonian. But he was ever loyal to me."

"Sometimes, those we believe to be allies are nothing more than vipers in the sand," Lucius said low and evenly.

"I am loyal, sire!" Conn Venico said decisively. "I am merely upset at the betrayal of my trust by Rodric. The praefectus had every right to kill him and his accomplices."

"Very well," the emperor said. "Let that be an end to it."

"Yes, sire," Conn Venico said, backing away. "Praefectus, you may dispose of his remains as you see fit," he offered.

Lucius shook his head. "As requested, I have brought Rodric's remains here, for you."

"Where, may I ask?" Conn Venico said.

"With my men outside the walls. You can dispose of the traitor as you wish, away from here."

"Sire, what about the escape of Argentocoxus?" Claudius piped up suddenly as Conn Venico merged back into the crowd.

"This is not a trial, Tribune!" Papinian said.

"Indeed. Enough!" the emperor coughed. "Praefectus Metellus and the Votadini deserve our thanks, not our accusations." Septimius Severus' hands gripped the arms of his chair tightly as he stared at the gathering. "By all reports, there was fire from heaven the day his forces engaged the Caledonii. Am I correct, Metellus?"

Lucius felt awkward, but answered. How did they know about that?

"Ye…yes, sire. There was, as you say, fire from the sky."

"Yes," Severus nodded emphatically. "Many of us saw it in the distance, though we did not know where it struck."

Men about the room nodded, some making the sign against ill omen.

"The Gods favour Metellus' actions in Caledonia," the emperor insisted, "and I will have words with any man who says otherwise, for that man will bring grief to my legions with his sacrilege."

"It seems our praefectus has become a god in Caledonia then!" Caracalla laughed.

Lucius backed away to be nearer to Dagon as the emperor stared at his son.

"I only jest, Father!" Caracalla said. "Yes, as always, we must see the signs the Gods give us. So, no treaty or bribes. What then is our strategy for this war?" he asked the larger gathering.

A great round of opinion drowned out Lucius' thoughts then as all the commanders in the room clustered around to ask questions and look at the map.

Dagon, Barta, Einion, and Briana stepped back with Afallach as the discussion raged on with Lucius and Coilus trying to temper the commanders' naïve enthusiasm about the war.

In the end, the emperor ordered a co-ordinated campaign to strike at the Caledonii from all points of the defensive ridge that Lucius' forces had begun re-establishing. The legates of the various legions were given orders to send garrisons out, and when all forces were in position, there would be a co-ordinated assault inland, up the glens and into the lower highlands to try and engage the enemy and bring them to battle.

Lucius had hoped, in part at least, to dissuade the emperor from his plans, but Severus was set on conquest and he wanted Caracalla at the head. Lucius emerged from the principia with Alerio to find Barta, Dagon, and the others waiting for him. He finally had a chance to ask Alerio the question that had been gnawing at his insides the entire day.

"Is my family here yet?" he asked as his hand fidgeted with the pommel of his gladius.

Alerio smiled. "Yes. They arrived two days ago, and are in the praetorium with the empress."

"They're here?" Lucius suddenly felt nervous. *They're here...*

"Come. I'll take you to them." Alerio led the way onto the Via Principalis.

Lucius turned to Barta, Coilus and Afallach. "Return to the men. Tell them we ride for the Dragon's Lair at first light."

"Are you well, Praefectus?" Coilus said, putting a hand on Lucius' shoulder. "You seem pale all of a sudden."

"My family is here at last, Coilus."

The old chieftain smiled. "Ah, yes. I'm happy for you. Go to them."

Lucius nodded and went out.

Alerio, Dagon, Einion, and Briana followed.

As they walked, Briana leaned in to speak with her brother. “The praefectus should be careful.”

“Yes,” Einion agreed.

“Few in that room were friendly toward him.”

“The Gods have shown us our purpose,” Einion whispered.

Evening saw a lapis sky, deep and dark, slashed here and there with veins of white, wind-blown clouds.

Lucius looked up from the street outside the courtyard of the new praetorium. “It’s going to be a cold night,” he said as they waited.

“Many stars, but no moon,” Briana added.

“Should we worry about that?” Dagon asked.

“Perhaps,” she answered.

They heard raised voices coming from inside the praetorium, and Lucius and Dagon rushed in to see a group of people, including several ladies.

Lucius did not notice the emperor, Castor, Papinian, and Caracalla coming behind him as he strode over to the small crowd.

“Baba!” cried two little voices.

Lucius looked down to see his children’s frightened faces, and reached out for their hands.

“Phoebus, Calliope, what are – ”

Lucius stopped short when he saw Adara. Her face was red and angry as she stood before him. The Tribune Claudius was gripping her arm tightly, and she was trying to pull away.

"Lucius!" Alerio's voice came from out of one of the doorways, but he did not hear him.

Claudius smiled mockingly at him, challenging him. "Praefectus, your wife and I are old friends. I was just telling her about your –"

Before anyone could speak, Lucius had rushed in and slammed his fist into Claudius' face.

Blood exploded from his shattered nose, and Claudius fell back into the stone wall.

"Praefectus!" Papinian's voice yelled. "Guards!"

Lucius was deaf to it all. His fists grabbed Claudius's cuirass and he hauled him back up. Claudius' knee came up into Lucius' torso where he had been stabbed by Rodric, but he did not feel the pain. Lucius raged, his elbow slamming into the side of Claudius' head. "You ever lay a hand upon my family again, I'll kill you!"

"I already have," Claudius laughed, and spat blood onto Lucius' chest.

Lucius slammed him against the wall and brought an arm back to hit him again, but he was restrained by Alerio and three other Praetorians who came running.

"What is the meaning of this outrage?" the emperor yelled, just as Julia Domna and Julia Maesa came into the courtyard.

Lucius' eyes found Adara's where she hugged the children close. She shook her head, willing him to stop.

"Metellus!" the emperor yelled. "Have you become a barbarian tavern brawler? I command you to stop!"

Lucius shrugged off the Praetorians, Alerio keeping a hand on his shoulder as he knelt before Severus.

"Sire," Lucius began, "I…I…" He could not think, blinded by rage, the pain in his side which he was now feeling, and the happy reunion with Adara and the children which he had been robbed of by Claudius.

"He attacked me, sire!" Claudius said to the emperor and Caracalla who stood staring at the two men. "I demand justice for this slight! Officers should be held accountable, sire!"

Julia Domna stood with her sister, staring at Claudius, her eyes dark, her lips pursed.

Adara caught the empress' eye for a moment, pleading.

Julia Domna stepped to her husband's side, her long fur cloak brushing the droplets of blood that had spattered the ground. She leaned over and whispered into her husband's ear.

The emperor's face registered shock and dismay, an anger they had all seen but on rare occasions. His eyes flitted to Adara, Phoebus, and Calliope briefly before looking at Lucius, and finally settling on Claudius.

"Tribune," the emperor said loudly. "You were once a supporter of Plautianus the traitor. But, owing to the wishes of my son, I spared your life. But it seems to me that you have been behaving in ways that are unacceptable for a Roman tribune, despite the clemency I have shown you."

"But, sire!"

"Do NOT make me speak of events at Coria, for which I have witnesses." Severus coughed violently and a chair was set behind him. He sat down and continued. "You are lucky not to be paying with your life."

Claudius hung his head, his eyes sweeping over the empress and Adara.

"You are removed from duty as senior tribune of VIth Legion."

"Father, really?" Caracalla said.

"Enough!" Severus barked, fire in his aged eyes. "Claudius is demoted to the rank of centurion to replace some of the deaths at the ridge fortresses." He turned to Claudius. "Your legate will see to the details. Either you accept, or you live in a cell for the rest of the campaign."

"Sire," Claudius muttered.

"Take him away!" Papinian ordered the guards. "Back to VIth Legion's camp!"

Claudius was marched away, his eyes fixed on Lucius with hatred as he left. When they were gone, the emperor turned to Lucius who still knelt before him.

"Metellus, though it pains me to cut your family reunion short, you will spend this night in a cell – the price of your aggression against a fellow Roman, however much provoked."

Lucius hung his head, unable to speak but for "sire…"

"Tomorrow, you and your men will return to the fort at Bertha to await orders for the continuation of the campaign. You may take your family with you if you desire."

"Yes, sire. Thank you, sire," Lucius said, his eyes looking up at Severus and the empress.

"As I said before, Metellus, you deserve our thanks for all that you have done. But even the highest ranks must honour Disciplina in my legions. Understood?"

"Yes, sire." Lucius stood and saluted.

"Good. Take him away to the principia cells."

Alerio and the three Praetorians who had subdued Lucius nudged him forward, out of the principia and away from Adara and his children, the former shushing Phoebus and Calliope when they began to protest.

Dagon went with Einion and Briana back to the men to let them know what had happened, and that they would all be setting out on the morrow with Lucius' family.

"Purify and clean the wagon," Dagon said. "Make it suitable for a lady and children. It stinks of death."

As darkness covered the world and the watch fires flickered to life about Horea Classis, Lucius sat in his cell, picking absentmindedly at a plate of food.

It had taken him a long time to calm the rage inside him. He remembered a similar humiliation in Parthia when he was tied to a stake and lashed, even though he had saved an officer's life. He was angry at everyone.

I only defended my family!

He knew he had gone too far, that he should have spoken first, but the look on Adara's face had upset him so much. He knew Claudius' type – arrogant, self-important, superior to everyone else. He hated his type, and the fact that the tribune had obviously upset Adara drove Lucius to act.

As small as his own punishment was, he felt humiliated.

"Can I get you more food?" Alerio said as he came around a corner to sit on a bench opposite Lucius' cell.

Lucius looked up and sighed.

"How are Adara and the children?" he asked, getting to his feet, the throbbing in his wound adding to his silent anger.

"They're upset," Alerio said. "It took Adara a while to stop the children from crying. They were quite scared by the fight."

"I lost my head." Lucius leaned on the bars, his hands gripping the iron where the torchlight caught the dragon ring around his finger. "Is Adara…is she all right?"

Alerio stood, approaching the bars. "She's upset too. It hasn't been easy for her, you know."

"I know. It was a long journey."

"More than that. She's had few friends, and less help. And…"

"And what?"

Alerio wondered whether he should tell Lucius about Claudius' constant harassment of Adara, or his incessant bad-mouthing of Lucius. *He'll kill Claudius if I tell him.*

"A beautiful woman travelling alone in Britannia, well, it's been difficult on her. I've kept my eye on her though," he added.

"Thank you, my friend. It's been too long since we talked." Lucius paused then looked up. "What happened in Coria? The emperor said something about Coria to Claudius."

"There was a banquet held by the empress the night before she went north. Adara was there, and several other ladies. There were also several officers of the wall and legions. Anyway, Claudius apparently raped some poor woman, a rich widow, in the garden in front of guests while the empress and her sister were not far off."

"The man's a fucking animal!" Lucius spat, then his stomach lurched. "You said Adara was there?"

Alerio sighed. "The woman was a friend of Adara's, her host at Coria. Adara got out safely with help from another friend and Senator Dio."

"So, she's all right?" Lucius needed the reassurance. It felt better to know before he had a chance to speak with her.

"Yes. But it shook her. The woman was badly beaten."

Lucius' mind reeled. He wondered after all if he should have left Adara in Etruria where they would have been safe with his mother and younger brother, Caecilius.

Gods...Apollo, Venus and Epona...thank you for keeping them safe, for watching over them...

"Anyway," Alerio continued. "You had best be careful of Claudius now," Alerio dropped his voice to a whisper. "He's close to Caracalla, and, well…the emperor –"

"Is not well," Lucius finished. "I've never seen him so ill."

"No. He's not well at all. Castor and Papinian do all they can for him, but he insists on doing things by himself."

Lucius was silent then. Caracalla would probably be emperor someday and he was very different from his father. Where Geta ended up in all this remained to be seen.

"You'd better get some sleep," Alerio said. "I'm on duty in the praetorium tonight, so I'll be able to watch over Adara and the children. I've also got men I trust watching your cell block."

"Alerio," Lucius said to his old friend. "Thank you again for watching over them." He reached his hand through the bars, and Alerio clasped it tightly.

"I know they are precious to you. And…"

"And?"

"And Alene…died to protect them."

Lucius felt his throat tighten as Alerio's eyes glossed.

"How could I do anything less?" he said before walking away.

Lucius sat back down against the cold stone wall to try and sleep, and not give into the fearful demons that lurked in his dreams.

Adara slept little that last night in the praetorium, beneath the roof of the emperor and empress. After an hour of soothing words and songs, Phoebus and Calliope had finally drifted off to sleep, whimpering slightly as they lay curled in the crux of Adara's arms among the furs.

For herself, she was afraid for Lucius. She had not recognized him right away, and he had struck out so quickly, he would not have had time to realize that she was the one who had called Claudius over to rail at him for what he had done to Perdita in Coria. It was then that Claudius had grabbed her wrist and Lucius arrived.

She was grateful that Lucius had arrived, but the confrontation had intensified so quickly. She knew the children were a little afraid of their father now, how his face had looked, and how he had bloodied the other man, but Adara had explained that their father was only protecting them, and that he always would...*like a dragon,* she had said.

When Lucius was taken away by the Praetorians, Adara had bowed before the empress to thank her, but rather than displaying her usual warmth, the empress had been quiet, cold, and told Adara to return to her quarters as she walked away to join Caracalla and the emperor.

Julia Maesa had come up to Adara and whispered, "It's all right. He got what he deserved."

Adara was not sure if she was speaking about Claudius, or Lucius.

Now she did not know what the morrow would bring, but she thanked the Gods she would finally be with Lucius again.

When the dim morning light began to filter into the small guest cubiculum from the single, high window, Adara was already awake and preparing to leave. She checked every corner of the room to make sure she had found all of the children's play things. When she was finished, she knelt before her small statue of Venus, able to hear Phoebus and Calliope's gentle breathing as she closed her eyes.

"Goddess, I thank you for bringing us to Lucius safely. It has been a long road, and much has happened… Please make it so that he still loves us…and desires me. I'm afraid, I hope without cause. Goddess, I honour you and thank you for your protection and guidance."

Adara bowed her head, and took the statue in her hands to wrap it and place it safely in one of the trunks that contained their things.

"Mama?" Phoebus woke, rubbing his eyes. "Is it time to leave? Where is Baba?"

The boy sat up, swaying sleepily, and Adara smiled despite her apprehension of the day ahead.

"I don't know when we're leaving, my boy," she answered, holding his little head to her stomach, and caressing his ruffled brown hair. "But I want us to be ready as soon as he arrives. I don't know how far we'll need to travel, but I do know your father likes to leave early."

There was a yawning sound as Calliope emerged from under the fur coverings behind her brother.

"Do you think Baba will remember us, Mama?"

"Good morning, Calliope," Adara smiled and kissed her daughter on the head. "Yes, of course he'll remember us." Adara sat down and put her arms around both of them. "Listen to me," she began. "Your father has been fighting a war. He has probably lost friends in battle. I know he seemed different when you saw him yesterday, but I want you both to remember that he loves you more than anything in this world. Just be on your best behaviour, and try to help out as best you can. Can you do that for me?"

"Yes, Mama," they both said.

"Good. Now, let's eat and get dressed in our travel clothes, and then we'll be ready when your father arrives."

Both children began to dress while Adara fed them bits of bread, cheese, and dried dates which they ate absentmindedly as they completed their tasks.

At the third hour of daylight, there was a knock on the cubiculum door. Adara slid the latch and opened to see Alerio in his Praetorian uniform, waiting with four other men.

"Good morning," he said.

"Good morning. Are we leaving now? Is Lucius…"

Alerio smiled and stepped aside.

In the middle of the praetorium courtyard, Lucius stood alone, in full armour, his weapons returned to him.

Adara put her hand to her mouth and stepped out, the children both clinging to her.

Lucius smiled and walked toward them, the previous day forgotten for the moment. "Am I dreaming?" he said as he reached out for Adara's hand which shook as he took it in his.

"I ask myself the same thing," she answered. Her green eyes stared up at Lucius who looked from her to the children with a mixture of happiness, relief, and sadness.

Lucius realized he felt nervous, embarrassed even, after what had happened yesterday. "I'm sorry," he said.

"Just take us away from this place," Adara answered in a low voice.

Lucius' eyes raked the courtyard which was beginning to fill with favour-seekers and clients of the emperor's. He knelt down, his greave scraping on the ground as he reached out for his children. "You've grown." He smiled as Calliope ran her little hand through his longer hair.

"Mama is making us eat lentils every chance she gets," Phoebus said.

Lucius chuckled. "Well, they're working." He wanted to hug them, to kiss his wife' lips, but the Praetorians were lurking everywhere and the emperor's offices were already active with his staff.

"Lucius,"Alerio said. "You should get going. Your men are ready with a wagon outside the walls."

"Yes. Let's go."

Lucius took Calliope's hand, Phoebus took Adara's, and they went out onto the Via Principalis in the direction of the east gate. Alerio and the Praetorians followed, carrying the two heavy trunks.

Outside the walls, arrayed in orderly rows on the damp ground, the two turmae of Sarmatians and Votadini awaited Lucius and his family. Beneath the draco and vexilli stood Dagon, Barta, Coilus, Afallach, Briana, and Einion.

Adara smiled when she saw Dagon's familiar face, and the children ran toward him as he swung down from his saddle to receive them.

"Phoebus! Calliope! It's good to see you! And you, lady Metella," he bowed to Adara.

"It's good to see you and be among friends again," Adara answered, not seeing Lucius' quick glance at the Praetorians carrying their trunks.

"In the wagon," Alerio ordered his men to secure the trunks. "I'll meet you back at the praetorium," he said, before the four guards made their way back inside the fortress.

"Alerio, thank you for helping us these past months," Adara said. "Will we be seeing you anymore?"

"I don't know. It may be a while. I must go where the emperor goes." He looked to Lucius. There was still much to talk about, but it seemed time was ever against them.

"Who's going to look after you?" Lucius asked.

Alerio smiled thinly. "I'll be fine." He pat the gladius which hung at his hip. "I'll probably see you when things get going. Caracalla won't sit still for long."

"Erm. Praefectus," Barta interrupted in a low voice. "Up on the wall."

Lucius and Alerio turned to see Caracalla staring down at them, frowning. The young Caesar saluted and Lucius saluted back.

"We'd better go," Lucius said, taking Alerio's forearm. "Send word if you need us," he offered.

Alerio looked over at the tattooed and battle-hardened horsemen who would all have given their lives for Lucius. He smiled at Adara and the children, and then turned to go back as

Caracalla stared on. "Gods keep you all safe," he wished over his shoulder.

"He's been such a big help and comfort to us," Adara said as she took Lucius' arm. "But I do not know some of your companions." She turned to the Votadini, Einion and Briana.

"Adara Metella, may I present Coilus, Chieftain of the Votadini, and his son, Prince Afallach."

The two men bowed to Adara from atop their horses.

"Gentlemen. It is an honour," Adara said as she put her hands on the children's shoulders.

"And these two are Briana and Einion. They serve me now."

"And we shall serve the lady Metella and her children too," Briana said, smiling.

"Oh?" Adara looked at Lucius in surprise. She knew his dislike of slaves.

"I'll explain later," he said. "Just know that Einion and Briana have my complete trust."

Adara looked at both of them and said, "I'm grateful for your help, and loyalty to my husband." She smiled and Lucius noticed Einion blush and lower his head, while Briana stared kindly back at Adara and the children.

"Barta," Lucius suddenly said. "Would you mind hoisting my two little imps into the wagon?"

Phoebus and Calliope, who had met Barta before, stared up with wide eyes as the big Sarmatian reached out for them to climb onto his arms as though climbing a tree. He actually smiled as the children climbed into the wagon.

"You're the biggest man I've ever seen," Phoebus said.

Barta looked at them, still smiling. "Then you haven't seen the men your father has fought."

"Were they big?" Calliope asked, her voice tremulous.

"Giants," Barta answered as he turned to help Adara up, the children staring at one another. "My lady," he bowed his head to Adara.

Lucius and the others mounted up as Adara and the children settled in among the furs and trunks in the wagon.

"Baba?" Phoebus called. "Where are we going?"

"To the Dragon's Lair!" Lucius said loudly as all the horses neighed and stamped the ground. "Forward!"

Lucius led the way with Dagon and Barta, Coilus and Afallach, while the two turmae spread out around the wagon, beside which rode Einion and Briana.

Adara held the children tightly as they rolled on, following the river on their right. She had barely been able to speak to Lucius, and it frustrated her. But she also knew he was on duty, and at war - something to keep in mind as they went away from the imperial fortress to the edge of the war zone. She had no illusions as to how much their lives were about to change.

But we are together now. Thank you, Venus and Apollo. Thank you...

XV

SANGUIS ET FAMILIA

'Blood and Family'

The journey from Horea Classis to the Dragon's Lair was slower on the way back. This was due, in large part, to the presence of Adara and the children.

Lucius ordered a slower pace so as not to jostle them too much. On the way to Horea Classis, the only cargo in the wagon had been Rodric's corpse.

Lucius had much on his mind as he rode in silence beside Dagon and the others. He was aware of a stillness in the grey air around them. Apart from the gurgling of the river's rush, all he heard was horse harness, creaking leather and mail, and mumbled conversation. There was no wind now, nor the squawk of birds. The world was brown and grey, lifeless. He thought he should be elated to have his family with him at last, but he felt numb instead.

Is there a forward base camp safe or suitable for them? he wondered, doubting more and more his decision to bring them to Caledonia. Lucius knew that he could trust every man in his ala, and the Votadini, to keep his family from harm. The same could not be said of the imperial camp.

It still rankled that he had been put behind bars for the night. He had replayed the meeting with his family over and over again in his mind, but it had been ruined. He imagined running Claudius through, and knew he had not seen the last of him. He had dealt with traitors before, but Claudius was a very different kind of opponent, and not one to give up easily.

A cornu sounded in the distance and the fort finally came into view. Muddy ditches stretched out around the partial stone and wooden stake palisades beyond which rose smoke from the evening cook-fires.

"Dagon, have Vaclar ride ahead to have the men fall in," Lucius ordered.

"I'll do it myself, Anguis," Dagon cantered up ahead until he reached the large gates.

The cornu sounded three more times, and Lucius could hear the familiar chink of armour and harness as the Sarmatians and Votadini assembled. Those who were off duty mounted the walls to look down on the procession.

Adara peeked out the window of the wagon to see the fort and all the faces looking her way.

"Don't worry, Metella," Briana said as she rode beside the wagon. "From what I've seen, they are all good men, despite their rough appearances."

Adara smiled and nodded, but her smile quickly faded when the wagon pulled onto the Via Decumana and she got a close look at the fortifications. Her stomach lurched, and she turned quickly to see that the children were still asleep.

Decorating the palisade walls of the fort were numerous grisly mementos of the battles Lucius and his men had fought. Rotting heads with long moustaches that covered lolling tongues dotted the pointed stakes of the fortifications, and severed arms, legs, and blue-tattooed torsos were nailed to the walls where they served as either warnings to attacking

Caledonii, or talismans against other forces in that land of darkness.

As the wagon passed through the gate and up the road to the principia, Adara tried to rally herself. The scent of stables was welcome after the stench of death rot outside the walls.

"Adara, are you all right?"

She looked up to see Lucius in his crested helmet, his face mask up, looking at her.

"I'm sorry about the walls. I… I didn't think –"

"It's fine," she said quickly. "We're here. We're together." She held his eyes a moment. "It's good to actually look at you."

Lucius smiled a little, then his eyes looked aside. "I'll introduce you and the children to the men, then I'll show you to our quarters."

Adara nudged the children who woke suddenly. They poked their heads out to see the street lined with scale covered warriors with long braided hair and beards, standing stalk-still.

"Come. Meet my warriors," Lucius said as he took Calliope in his arms. Adara stepped down with Einion's help, and Phoebus hopped down to walk beside his mother until they stood beside Lucius.

"This is my family!" he said in a loud voice. "They are dear to me, and I ask all of you to do your utmost to keep them safe." As they walked along the rows of men, Lucius introduced all his decurions.

The children asked several questions about the animals tattooed on the men's arms or necks, and the Sarmatians were happy and proud to speak of them. The two children seemed to shed a light on the camp that had been missing, and everyone felt it.

For Adara, it would take time to become accustomed to the situation. Being among men at war was different to being among them in the city, but she trusted Lucius.

There were no tribunes' wives with whom to socialize as there had been in Numidia. Adara was happy for the presence of Briana, though she needed to get to know her. However, initially, the woman made her feel comfortable, not because of her smile or rough beauty. It was something more intangible.

The Dragon's Lair looked rough and unkept after the splendour of the imperial camp and the empress' propensity for colourful eastern silks about her quarters, the place where Adara had spent much time. However, even Adara could tell that the fort, her new home, had solid defences. The roads were muddy and unpaved, but they were clear of all debris.

"You've done much to the defences?" she asked Lucius as they walked into the principia courtyard with Dagon, Barta, Coilus, Afallach, Briana, and Einion.

"It needs more, but it will hold in case of an attack." He stopped to look at her and the children as the others went to the individual cubicula about the courtyard. Lucius reached up and stroked Adara's cheek. "I can't believe you're here..." he whispered, his eyes softening for the first time.

She looked up at him, his longer hair, and the dark circles beneath his eyes. It seemed that with every separation, Lucius changed. Part of her fretted over what she would find beneath all the armour, wool, and fur.

"How would you like a bath?" he said.

Adara's eyes widened. "You have baths here?" She had given up on the idea upon seeing the fort.

Lucius laughed. "Of course! The river is just beyond the walls. Once we cleared the channels, the water began to flow again."

"What of the men? Will they not need it?"

"We have our own, Adara. I saw to that." Lucius smiled and picked up Calliope again. "Right through there." He pointed to a door nearby. "The hypocausts are partially caved in, so the heat is not that even, but it works well enough to wash these little ones!" Lucius rubbed Phoebus' hair roughly and the boy looked up smiling.

"Baba, when will you take me around the base?"

"Tomorrow," Lucius answered.

"Not now?"

"I'm hungry," Calliope said.

Adara smiled and looked at her husband. "How are the food stores?"

"Recently stocked with grains, game, and a bit of cheese. There should be fresh bread from the ovens this morning."

"I've prepared the baths for lady Metella and the children, Praefectus," Briana said as she came up to meet them.

"Oh. Thank you, Briana," Lucius said. "We'll eat and then a bath?" he looked to Adara. "You can do that while I'm on my rounds."

"It's late. Yes. First, where are we all sleeping, Lucius?"

"I'm sorry. Right. Come. Let me show you." Lucius led the way to his rooms. "I'll have Xylon fashion beds for the children tomorrow. He's skilled with wood. Tonight, they can sleep in the furs on the ground."

Lucius pushed open the door to his rooms where he found the food Briana had laid out for the four Metelli.

"Thank you, Briana!" Calliope ran to the table and reached up for a piece of bread.

The Briton smiled. "My brother and I are here to help in whatever way we can," she said.

"Where did Lucius buy you?" Adara asked, her eyes going to the long sword at the girl's waist. Slaves did not usually go armed in private quarters.

"Oh, erm, sorry," Lucius said to Briana. "I've not had a chance to speak to Adara about you." He turned back to his wife. "Briana and Einion are not slaves. That was pretence in front of everyone else."

"Oh. I'm sorry!" Adara said, thoroughly embarrassed.

Lucius continued. "They are brother and sister from Dumnonia, in the South."

"The beds are set," Einion said as he joined them from the other room.

"Beds?" Lucius asked.

"I gathered some ferns from along the river to soften the ground for the children." Einion smiled at them where they sat with their mouths full of bread and dates.

"You are not slaves. I see that," Adara said. "So, what are you?"

"Friends, lady Metella," Briana answered. She understood Adara's confusion. "I'll let the praefectus tell you. Just know that my brother and I are here to help. It's the Gods' will that we do so, for your husband helped another."

Adara looked at Lucius and back at the Britons.

"Well, I'm grateful to have you here, Briana and Einion."

"Me too," Lucius said. "They saved my life a few days ago."

Adara's eyes widened and Briana inclined her head.

"The Gods' will, lady. We'll leave you now. Praefectus?"

"Thank you, both," Lucius said as he unhooked his cloak and pat Einion on the shoulder. "See you tomorrow."

They exited where Barta once more stood guard.

Out in the courtyard, they could hear Dagon's voice as he told Brencis what had happened at Horea Classis. Then the door closed again.

Lucius looked at the table set with a small meal where he usually went over maps with his captains.

"Let's eat," he said awkwardly. He sat down across from Adara with the two children close together on one side. Reclining would have been more suitable for a family meal, he knew. "I'll make some changes around here so you can be more comfortable."

Adara looked at him as though he said the strangest thing in the world. "I've had enough of comfort, Lucius. All I care about is that we're together again." She reached across and squeezed his dirty, calloused hand.

"Us too, Baba!" Calliope said, smiling.

"Will you show me the stables tomorrow, Baba?" Phoebus tapped the table excitedly, his body almost bouncing off the stool. "I want to see the horses. Please?"

"In time," Lucius answered. "There is one thing you need to remember. This is not a safe place to play and run around in. We are at war and could be attacked at any time. You have to stay within the principia most of the time."

"We can't play outside?" asked Phoebus, the disappointment clearly etched on his young face.

"Not always. I'm sorry, but the Caledonii could attack at any time, and I've seen what they can do."

Lucius sipped his wine from a Samian cup and it tasted like blood for a moment. He could see the tree where his men's lifeless bodies hung, savaged and grotesque, swaying in the dark. He wanted to yell, but –

"Lucius?" Adara's voice. "Lucius!" She spoke loudly making him jump.

"Sorry. What was I speaking about?"

Adara tried to hide her own confusion from the children who both stared at their father. "Are we to be shut up in here like prisoners, Lucius?" Adara asked. "The children need to play. They need to run."

"It's for your own safety." Lucius' eyes strayed to the map on the wall, his eyes darting about his quarters as if scanning the shadows.

Adara stared at him, but he would not meet her gaze. She saw that the children's faces had lost their smiles, and Calliope's lower lip jutted while Phoebus sulked in silence.

"Are you all right after last night?" she asked her husband. "I was worried for you."

"That was the emperor slapping my hand and sending me to bed. That's all."

"Yes, but in front of all the commanders? They're your peers, Lucius. It must have upset you."

"Yes, it did," he said. "But it's done, and you're all here." Lucius downed the rest of his wine and stood. "I need to give the watchword and do my rounds. The baths are two doors away in the courtyard. You can clean up while I'm gone." Lucius grabbed his cloak, and left Adara and the children alone.

"Mama, why is Baba acting strange?" Calliope asked.

Adara looked from the door back to her two children, and smiled. They were dirty, and tired, but still managed to do their utmost to help.

"Your father has had a very difficult time without us. He's also angry he could not speak with us yesterday."

"But we've only just arrived and already…"

"He has much to do." Adara sighed, thinking of the baths. "Come, finish your food and we'll go take a nice warm bath to clean you both."

"Yes, Mama," they muttered in unison.

Outside the door, Lucius stood in the muddy courtyard staring up at the night sky. He sighed heavily, and turned to Barta. "I'm going to do my rounds."

"Yes, Praefectus," Barta answered, falling into step with Lucius as he went to Briana and Einion's cubiculum door and knocked.

"Praefectus?" Einion answered. "Are we needed?"

Lucius looked beyond him to see Briana sharpening her long sword by the light of an oil lamp.

She looked up and came over.

"Yes. Can I trust you both?" he asked, his eyes intense.

"We've already sworn so," Einion said.

Lucius grabbed the Briton and held him tightly by the tunic. "Can – I – trust – you?"

Einion stared back. He saw the confused look on Barta's face behind Lucius.

"Yes, by the Gods, Praefectus, you can trust us."

Briana reached out and put a hand on Lucius' forearm. She spoke softly. "You can trust us with your life," she said with certainty.

"Not mine," Lucius said, releasing Einion. "My family."

"Of course. Yes," she answered.

"I shouldn't have brought them here. It's too dangerous, but the die is cast." Lucius leaned on the door frame. He was tired, his wound sore, and his mind battered. "Serve me by protecting my wife and children, both of you. Wherever they go, you go. I want you to be their constant friends and shadows. I can't fight this war if I'm always worrying about them. Do you understand?"

Einion and Briana, having lost the whole of their own family, stood before Lucius in full comprehension of the fears that then raged behind his eyes.

Even dragons have fears... Briana heard Etain's voice whisper at the reaches of her consciousness.

"We will be their protectors, Lucius Metellus Anguis, until our dying breaths," Einion said, gripping his sister's hand as well as Lucius'. "You won't lose your family."

Lucius felt a tightness in his throat as he nodded, unable to speak. He nodded and turned as Adara and the children were going to the small baths on the other side of the courtyard.

Adara paused, looked at Lucius and the others, and shuffled the exhausted children through the bathhouse door.

Briana sheathed her sword and went to stand outside the door.

Lucius could hear her tell Adara she would be outside if they needed anything.

"Thank you," Lucius said to Einion.

The Briton smiled, nodded, and went to join his sister.

The world was dark beyond the walls of the Dragon's Lair. Dark, distant trees hummed and swayed in the wind coming down out of the highlands as if they were the wraiths of a massing army. The river nearby gurgled in the darkness, and the torches of the sentries flickered and whipped in the breeze.

Lucius walked along the battlements, greeting the Sarmatians and Votadini who were on duty that night. Behind him, heavy footfalls reassured him of Barta's presence. That was good, for his thoughts were too scattered to be ready for any surprises.

Control yourself! he chided. Ahead, he saw Dagon walking toward him.

The Sarmatian saluted. "Praefectus, may I speak with you?"

The two men stepped to a corner of the roof of the gatehouse.

"Anguis," Dagon said. "What are you doing here? I was to have this watch. You should be with your family."

Lucius crossed his arms and stared out at the dark. "I wanted to make sure all is well," he said.

"The Caledonii are not yet ready to come at us, my friend. We can handle the watch without you."

"I know."

"I know I'm young, and unmarried. I've not had time for women," Dagon admitted. "But I can plainly see that you are a fortunate man. I can also see that Adara, despite her fear, is here to be by your side."

"Has she said anything to you?" Lucius asked.

"No, Anguis. But from what Centurion Alerio told me, she has had a long, difficult journey to get to you. She has cared for your children like a lioness, and kept them safe. Do not avoid her."

"I'm not avoiding her," Lucius said, a little angry at the truth in Dagon's words.

"Then why are you out here? You should be with her, Anguis. She was sent by the Gods to be with you. She is the mother of your children whom I have known since birth, and she is the one who presented you with that sacred sword you wear constantly at your back."

Lucius' hand went up to feel the pommel jutting from behind his shoulder. He remembered Apollo showing it to him in a dream long ago, and then receiving it from the hands of his wife after their marriage.

"Such gifts are never to be ignored or forgotten among my people, Anguis," Dagon said. "Nor, I suspect, among your own ancestors."

Lucius looked at Dagon and knew he was no longer looking at a boy, but rather a king among his people, wise, just, brave, and honest.

"Thank you, Dagon," Lucius said. "I don't know what I would do without your sage advice and counsel."

Dagon smiled. "The Gods protect you and yours, Anguis. You have little need of me, though I am happy to provide my friend with some small measure of support whenever I can."

"More than that, Dagon. More than that." Lucius took his friend's forearm and squeezed. Then he turned to go back to the principia, and Dagon turned back to the palisade wall to stare out into the night, resuming his thoughts of having a family of his own one day.

When Lucius returned to the principia, he found Einion outside the door of his quarters. "Where's Briana?"

"She's inside with the lady Adara. She helped put the children to sleep."

Lucius opened the door quietly, but it creaked on its hinges.

The two women looked up from where they sat beside a brazier, sipping wine.

"Lucius," Adara said. "Briana and I were talking. She's been so much help with the children. A song she sang had them asleep in moments!"

Lucius smiled as he looked at the two women sitting companionably.

"We were telling each other of our family homes," Briana said. "The land of Greece sounds magnificent, but so hot!"

"Ha! Yes, it is," Lucius laughed. "Much warmer than this wet and frozen land."

"Briana was telling me of Ynis Wytrin, the Isle of the Blessed, where she and her brother have been living," Adara said excitedly. "It sounds so beautiful, and full of magic."

Lucius had forgotten how Adara's eyes sparkled when she was happy and smiling. "I'm glad you're getting acquainted."

"Adara asked how I came to be here with Einion," Briana said. "I told her it was your tale to tell." The Briton got up from her stool, tendrils of her long blond hair coming apart as she placed her cup on the table and took up her sword. "I'll leave you now. It sounds like you've been too long apart."

"Thank you, Briana," Adara said.

Briana inclined her head, smiled, and went out.

"You seem to have taken a liking to her very quickly," Lucius said as he unclasped his crimson cloak and hung it on a wall peg.

"You said you trust her and Einion. That's enough for me. Besides," Adara approached her husband and kissed his cheek before beginning to undo the buckles of his cuirass. "These long months I've grown adept at reading people." She unhooked the swords from his back and waist and set them aside. Then she ran her hand over the dragon with outspread wings on the chest of Lucius' armour before undoing the final buckle.

As she leaned close, he inhaled the clean scent of the woman he had missed, and then shrugged out of his armour. He realized he stank of sweat and horse, and was oddly self-conscious of it. "I should wash," he said as she leaned into him.

She was wearing his favourite blue stola with a wool cloak hanging over her shoulders.

"I don't mind. I haven't seen you in ages. I want to sit and drink some wine with you. I want to speak with my husband." Her hand traced through his long hair, more wild than any image of Alexander. "Lucius?"

"I promise, we'll have time. Just let me get clean." He backed away, picked up a clean tunic and breeches from a nearby bench, and went out again.

"Venus, help us," Adara said as she sat down and gazed into the flames of the brazier. She had never seen Lucius so distraught and distracted. Life in the fort would be restrictive, necessarily so, but she was happy that Briana was there. The woman, only slightly older than herself, was kind and good with the children. Something had compelled Adara to befriend her instantly.

Apollo and Venus, as ever we will be guided by you, she thought as she sipped her watered wine and yawned.

Outside, the watch called the hour and the tramp of hobnails indicated a change of guard.

Adara remembered Lambaesis, the triclinium of the tribune's house where she and Lucius had sat with their newborn children…and Alene.

Could we have such times again in this place? she asked herself.

She knew the answer was no, of course not. Alene was gone, they had all lost a piece of themselves when she had been slain outside the walls of the Numidian fortress. Adara looked over at Phoebus and Calliope whom Alene had saved that day by sacrificing herself, and melancholy swept through her then. Adara dabbed her eyes and took a deep breath as Lucius came back in carrying his dirty clothes and pugio, which he set aside. He wore a stained thin-striped tunic and matching breeches.

"Here," she said, holding out a cup of wine.

Lucius accepted it and poured a little on the floor in thanks to the Gods for bringing them together again. He then walked over to the children and knelt beside their fern beds to get a better look at them. "They've grown so much," he said as he reached out to stroke Calliope's cheek.

The girl smiled in her sleep, puckered her little lips, and turned over to face her brother whose hand she grasped.

Lucius laid his hand then on his son's chest and felt the soft rise and fall of his breathing. He smiled.

"They look like you," Lucius said as he rose from the floor.

"They're a good mix of us both, I think," Adara answered, motioning for him to sit beside her.

"Do they still get on well?"

"Yes. They're inseparable."

"Have they given you a difficult time?"

"Travelling? No. They don't always want to do their lessons, but that's expected. I figured that since they were unlikely to have any Greek tutors in Caledonia, I should begin teaching them something on my own."

"How come you didn't write often?" Lucius asked unexpectedly.

"I did!" she protested.

"You did?" Lucius shook his head. "I didn't receive many letters."

"The last letter I wrote was from Coria. I told you we were coming, and also that Phoebus had been in a fight?"

"He's fighting?"

"Yes, though not often. It was a misunderstanding with Diana's son."

"Diana?"

"Oh, just a woman I was introduced to in Coria."

"Alerio told me what happened with Claudius."

"I'd rather not talk about that filthy man. But that was another lady, my host, Perdita Narbonensa. Yes. He brutalized her." Adara became quiet.

Lucius went down on his knees before her and gripped her hands tightly. "I'm sorry I wasn't there, my love. I'm so sorry." He looked up at her and she reached down to hold his head and stare into those tired, brown eyes she had gazed at so often before.

"We're together now. We'll make a new home in this place." She looked about the plain, whitewashed walls.

"I can get some paints and other materials. Perhaps you can add some colour to this place?" He smiled.

"I think I could."

Lucius lowered his head into her lap and let her run her hand over his head, his still-damp hair. It was soothing. They had so much to talk about, and yet words did not come easily.

"Tell me what's happened, Lucius. Everything. I want to know." She pulled him up and he sat again opposite her.

There was so much. He did not know where to begin. He sighed and poured more wine.

"Only if you tell me everything that's happened to you in Britannia."

"Try stopping me," she joked, even though she dreaded the retelling.

"Very well," he began. "It started, I guess with killing…"

Into the small hours of the morning, as rain began to patter on the roof tiles of the principia, Lucius told Adara of the bloody battles he and his men had fought since arriving in Britannia. He told her of the Boar of the Selgovae, and what he had said to Lucius, of how Afallach had killed the abductor of his sister, and slayer of his people, while the Boar had received the death he wanted. Lucius mentioned his first encounter with Claudius Picus, and the march north into more battles and blood.

Adara was shocked as Lucius broke down when he relayed the savage death of Hippogriff's turmae at the hands of the Caledonii. She understood his grief, for the Sarmatians had become his family too, a family whose patron goddess walked and fought among them. Adara resolved to make offerings to Epona as well, in thanks for her protection.

When Lucius described the assassination attempt of only a few days ago, Adara stared at the bed where he had been stabbed by the Caledonian killer just a few feet away, and it sent a shiver down her spine.

"And what of Einion and Briana?"

"They were sent here by, well, by the shade of my former enemy."

"What?"

"The Boar of the Selgovae. His father is the Druid Weylyn who welcomed Einion and Briana at the place they call Ynis Wytrin."

"Briana mentioned him and two others there – a priestess, and a Christian priest." Adara nodded. "Weylyn was the Boar's father?"

"Yes. When the Boar was with us, we spoke, as I've told you, and he spoke of family, and of my loyalty to Rome."

Adara stared at her husband, trying to decipher his thoughts. "You're still loyal to Rome, Lucius…aren't you?"

He did not answer right away. He remembered sitting in a cell just the night before, after all he had done and risked. "I'm loyal to you, and to our children. I'm loyal to my men."

Adara reached across and put a hand on his knee. She noticed the far-off look in his eyes as he continued.

"The Boar was an honourable warrior, and even though he had done despicable things, I didn't want to see him a slave in Rome, or spat on by the likes of Claudius Picus. I allowed the Boar to break free and fight for his life, and I knew Afallach would succeed in killing him."

"Why? Why did you do it? If you'd been caught…"

"I did what I thought was right," Lucius shrugged. "Afterward, I made sure the Boar's body was taken to his people for their proper rites."

"And his shade told his father?" Adara felt her spine and neck prickle.

"It would seem." Lucius rose and went to a table beside his bed where he picked up Weylyn's letter. He handed it to Adara who read it and looked from Lucius to the door and back.

"That is why Einion and Briana are here?"

"Yes. They owed Weylyn and the others a debt, and the Boar felt he owed me. But there's more." Lucius sat back down and leaned close to Adara. "When I was alone on the mountain at Trimontium, Epona came to me."

Adara's eyes widened.

Lucius continued, "She said 'There will always be help.' And those were the exact words Briana said to me when they arrived here. In a voice that seemed not entirely her own."

Adara shook her head. “Ever since we met, I’ve known the Gods favour you, us, and our family. And I make offerings every day to them.”

Lucius nodded. He did as well.

“But…”

“But what?” he asked.

“I just hope their favour doesn’t run out. Gods forgive my doubts, but these past months have been –” She stopped talking, and Lucius went to his knees before her.

“What is it, my love? What’s happened?”

She fought to control herself. She was tired, exhausted, but it felt an age since they had last spoken and she knew he could ride out to meet the enemy at any moment. These were not the halcyon days of the Middle Sea. This was Caledonia, the edge of the world, and her husband was at war.

“I’ve been trying to be the best mother for our children, Lucius. They’re so good and caring. Don’t let their youth fool you. They’re brilliant and attuned to the world about them. But they haven’t had my full attention. I’ve been overwhelmed trying to keep them safe, fed, and clothed as we went from town to town, as I sat with the empress and her sister, and other ladies of the court.” Adara shook her head.

“I knew the others looked down on me for not wanting slaves to look after Phoebus and Calliope, for teaching them myself. I know they thought I should leave them with a slave while I sat and gossiped with them and bore their snobbery with a smile.”

“Were they cruel to you?” Lucius asked, feeling heat rise up his neck as his anger built.

"Never outwardly. Such things are always conveyed by a pathetic look, a whisper to someone else, or the laughter behind the closed door of a room I've just left."

"It seems you've been fighting too, my love," Lucius said.

"I hate them," Adara answered hoarsely, trying not to cry for all the pent-up emotion of months. "Then there was Claudius."

"What did he do to you?" Lucius stood. "Did he hurt you?"

"No. It was more comments he made, things he said about you being in grave trouble, or even dead. He relished saying such things."

"Did he touch you in Coria?"

The question took Adara by surprise, but she shook her head.

"No. But he would have done had I not left the banquet quickly." She shook her head and shut her eyes. "Poor Perdita… That's why he was grabbing my wrist when you saw us. I had just slapped him for what he did to her.

Lucius breathed deeply and nodded, a little relieved. "Alerio told me what he did in Coria. I was hoping Claudius would be sent back to Rome, or imprisoned, but he's too close to Caracalla." Lucius took her hands as she rose and kissed them.

The gold, intertwined dragons on each of their fingers glinted in the firelight. It felt surreal to be so close, to be touching.

Lucius pulled her close so her head rested on his shoulders.

"Lucius, my moon blood is flowing now. I…I can't."

"The goddess' will - I'll just hold you in my arms. I've missed you." Lucius breathed her scent in, and it brought back a thousand happy memories.

"It's late," Adara said. "You have your early duties to attend to." She moved to the bed and got under the blankets in her tunica. Part of her was grateful she could not make love to Lucius now. Her mind was polluted with fear, and thoughts of Claudius and Perdita. They had ruined their reunion, she would not let them ruin their lovemaking.

Lucius went around the room putting out some of the lamps, then lit a small piece of incense on the altar to Apollo, Venus, and Epona. With his sword leaning beside the bed as always, Lucius began to remove his tunica and breeches.

As Adara watched, sorrow seeped into her veins.

Not only had Lucius' gentle demeanour been pushed into the shadows, but his body had also changed under the weight of war. He was no longer smooth and supple, graceful as a willow branch and strong as an oak. Now, Lucius' person was hard and angry, forged in the crucible of war. There was a tenseness and speed in every chiseled muscle and bow-taut tendon that made Adara ill-at-ease.

Oddly enough, the dragon tattoos were the main source of comfort and familiarity about his appearance.

In her mind, Adara knew that he was still the man she loved, that these changes were brought about by living at death's door each day, by being constantly on the lookout for enemies.

Despite this, her heart cracked not a little as she watched the dark mists of her dreams begin to envelop her truest love. *And now he has us to worry about...* she thought.

Lucius could feel his wife's eyes on him in the semi-darkness, could hear her muffled gasp.

"I know I must look different to you." He stood, covered only by knee-length breeches. "My hair is long, there's been no time for barbering. And the tattoos are symbols of power and protection. All of the men have them. It was fitting that I should too."

"I don't mind either of those things," she said, pulling back the covers for Lucius to get in beside her.

When he lay down, Lucius kissed her on the mouth, his lips hard and unfamiliar to her.

It would take time.

She felt him harden with desire, but he did not ask anything of her.

"Good night, my love," he said before turning over and going to sleep.

It took Adara several minutes to nod off, her mind awash with worry for Lucius and the soundly-sleeping children at the foot of their bed.

The next morning, when the cornu sounded over the walls of the Dragon's Lair, Adara awoke alone and cold in bed. Her hand went to where Lucius had slept, but he and his armour had already been gone for three hours by then. She had forgotten the rhythm of life in an army base.

"Good morning, Lady," Briana's voice cut through the morning fog of Adara's sleepy mind.

Adara turned to see Briana at the table, feeding Phoebus and Calliope bread with honey and milk.

"Good morning, Mama!" Phoebus said through a mouthful.

"I overslept," Adara muttered.

"You needed it," Briana said. She saw Adara reach for a rectangular bunch of linen and look around. "I've hung a curtain in the corner for you, Metella," Briana pointed and Adara nodded, going across the room to the closed space. "The Praefectus rode out with the princeps, Dagon, and the others early this morning."

"Yes. They do that," Adara said.

"My brother is guarding the door here." Briana nodded toward it.

"Do you think this war will last long, Briana?" Adara asked as she kissed the children.

"The Caledonii are savages, and not easily swayed, my lady."

"Please, call me Adara. You're not a slave."

Briana smiled kindly at Adara and noticed the worry floating all about her. At Ynis Wytrin, she had learned how to read such things on people. She put a comforting hand on Adara's shoulder.

"Don't worry. From what I hear, and have seen, the Praefectus is a match for any Caledonian."

Adara put a hand out to touch her children. "I know," she said. "It's not necessarily the Caledonii I'm afraid of."

You should be, Briana thought, but did not utter the words.

Adara saw the hard look in the Briton's eyes, but said nothing as she tied her hair back and sat to eat with Phoebus and Calliope.

Weeks passed and routines set in for Adara and the children, Briana and Einion, who all adjusted to a new life.

The days lengthened and warmed after nights of cool mist, and all the while, Lucius' family remained within the walls of the principia. Their world had shrunk. It was muddy and grey, and saw the constant comings and goings of army messengers carrying orders to Lucius and his cavalry.

The Roman offensive had begun in earnest after a week in the Dragon's Lair, and now the nights rang not only with the howl of wolves in the distant pine forests, but also with the cries of wounded men as they were brought back to the base medicus after a day of fighting.

As the necropolis of the Dragon's Lair grew, Adara and the children saw less and less of Lucius who was gone for days at a time with his Sarmatians and the Votadini.

Adara had had little time to acquaint herself with Lucius' allied commanders. Apart from one hurried meal in the principia in which they were all present, most returned to base to wash, sleep, re-group, re-supply, and ride out again to try and pinion the Caledonii against the walls of the wretched highlands.

For Adara and the children, Einion and Briana proved to be welcome distractions. They had grown used to the Britons' presence and personalities.

Einion was always there when needed, and involved Phoebus in any tasks that were suitable to a young boy, such as carrying wood or sharpening smaller weapons.

Briana became a source of feminine companionship and comfort for Adara that neither of them had expected.

Not since Alene had been alive had Adara felt close friendship with another woman. Of course, Briana could never have replaced Adara's sister-in-law; Gods knew that was impossible, but Adara did find herself drawn to this beautiful stranger who understood her and was skilled in matters both spiritual and martial.

Adara could see great pain behind Briana's eyes, and she felt for her.

Briana had wanted to tell Adara many things for reasons she did not know. She could see strength in Adara, a strength she had not seen in any Roman lady in the South. Briana tried to teach Adara and Calliope about the herbs and healing plants of Britannia. She told them of Ynis Wytrin and all she had learned there, and the mother and daughter were fascinated by the place that seemed to be hidden from the rest of the world.

"Can we go there, Mama?" Calliope asked at one point, her eyes excited.

"Maybe. Someday," Adara said. "But I suspect you need to be invited?" She turned to Briana.

"Most are invited, yes," Briana told them. "But some, like Einion and I, are guided there by the Gods."

"Which gods?" Calliope asked.

"I'm not sure, little one. Our horses seemed to know the way. Perhaps it was Epona?"

"We have lands in the South," Adara said, "but I doubt we'll ever see them with this war raging."

"One never knows the Gods' will," Briana said, smiling.

Calliope began showing the rows of herbs to her doll then, now in a world of her own.

Adara turned to Briana. "Will you teach me to fight?"

"To fight?" Briana looked at Calliope quickly and then back to Adara. "Why? Surely it's not fitting for a Roman lady to think of such things?"

"I'm no Roman lady. The goddesses of my land fought in wars against the Titans and Giants, and beneath the wall of Troy ages ago. The Amazons are some of the fiercest warriors in the world…" Adara hung her head, her hands shaking a little.

Briana now saw that the woman before her hated feeling helpless. She could see the strong mind behind the beautiful face, and knew there was a will for more.

"Just think on it," Adara said. "You may not always be here to protect us, and Lucius is always at war. These past months, I… Some things happened that… I just don't want to be taken by surprise." Adara's voice had risen and her green eyes stared into Briana's. "I know you've had bad things happen to you."

Briana looked away, her fists clenching and unclenching.

"Forgive me. But I know you've been hurt," Adara said. "I can see it whenever I'm near you. I can also see that whoever hurt you would not have survived."

Briana looked up and shook her head silently.

"Teach me, Briana," Adara pleaded. "I want to be able to raise my own sword in defence of my family. I don't want to be a victim."

For a moment, it seemed Alene's face appeared in place of Briana's, and Adara shook her head, her eyes tearing up.

Briana took her hand and squeezed. They understood each other then.

"The Dragon's wife is strong. I will teach you, Adara Metella. All that I know if I can, and if the Gods grant it."

"Thank you," Adara said.

That night, as the torches were set alight around the defences of the Dragon's Lair, the horns sounded as a thunder of hooves approached the western gate of the via Principalis.

"Open the gates!" the legionaries from sixth legion yelled.

Beneath the tangle of corpses, beards, and scalps nailed to the grisly palisade, rode Lucius, Dagon, Barta, Coilus, Afallach and their combined forces.

Einion came out of the principia courtyard to the street to see the horsemen arrive splattered with mud and blood. He noticed many of the Sarmatians had heads hanging from their saddle horns or from the long shafts of their kontos lances.

"Tend to the horses!" Dagon ordered some of the Sarmatians who had remained at base.

"Yes, lord!" answered Magar, one of the decurions. "Praefectus!" the man saluted when Lucius dismounted and handed him Lunaris' reins.

"Check his left hindquarters," Lucius said. "Close call with a battle axe."

"What happened?" Einion asked Lucius whose face mask was still down beneath the blood-soaked crest of his helmet.

"We met some of their chariots and engaged them."

"Survivors?" the Briton asked.

"None."

"Let me fight with you, Praefectus. I can ride, and swing a sword," Einion pleaded.

"No, Einion. I need you here to keep my family safe. That's your charge!"

Einion bit his tongue and said nothing. He knew the right of that, knew he lacked understanding of the concerted cavalry tactics Lucius and his men employed.

"Forgive me," he said to Lucius. "It's just these walls are feeling smaller by the day."

"I know." Lucius slapped him on the shoulder. "But having you here is my greatest need." Lucius walked past him into the principia where Phoebus sat on a bench, his mouth open as he took in the sight of his father.

Lucius raised his cavalry mask. "Phoebus, what are you doing out alone?"

"I was with Einion, Baba."

Lucius turned to Einion. "I thought I said to stay with him!"

"I was, Praefectus. I only came out when I heard you approach. He was perfectly safe."

Lucius grabbed the Briton and pinned him against the wall. "Never alone! What if an assassin got in, or some Roman messenger?"

Einion shrugged Lucius' hands off violently. "Are you telling me your family is in danger from your own people as well as the enemy?" He stared Lucius in the eyes.

"What do you think?" Lucius asked evenly before taking a deep breath. "Forgive me. I'm weary from battle. I just wish…I… Just please stay with them. By the Gods, don't let them out of your sight."

"Very well," Einion said. "I understand."

Lucius turned to go with Barta and Dagon when Phoebus pulled on his cloak.

"Baba! You still haven't shown me the horses."

"Not now, Phoebus!" Lucius barked as he went to wash the blood and offal from himself.

Phoebus stood there in the torchlight, his lip quivering.

Einion noticed the boy fought very hard not to cry. He admired his spirit, and realized Phoebus reminded him of himself when he was young. *I just hope the Dragon is a better father than mine ever was,* he thought. "Come," he said to Phoebus. "It's nearly time to sleep." Einion put a hand on Phoebus' shoulder and led him to the door beyond which his mother and sister sat with Briana.

By the third hour of darkness, Lucius entered his rooms wearing a clean tunic and breeches, along with his sword. He found Adara laying between the children as they slept bundled in furs.

Briana sat at the table, humming and sharpening her sword by lamplight. She put a finger to her lips and looked at the sleeping forms. "It took some time for her to get Phoebus to sleep," she whispered.

Lucius approached his family, rubbed his tired eyes, and crossed his arms.

"May I offer some advice?" Briana asked.

"Yes." Lucius turned to the woman standing close to him, her eyes on a level with his, earnest and strong.

"Protection is not all you have to offer. Sometimes, the greatest gift a man can give to his wife and children is time, and a measure of tenderness."

She did not wait for his dismissal, nor for him to say anything. She inclined her head, and went out into the courtyard.

The words stung Lucius, for he knew he was failing the people he most sought to protect, the people he loved more than anything.

Damn this war!

As if jarred by his thoughts, Adara sat up abruptly, her deep green eyes alert and fastened on his.

Lucius held out a hand and helped her up from the low, wide, wooden bed frame that Xylon had fashioned for them.

"I feel like I haven't seen you in weeks," Adara said as she stood up, adjusting the furs over the children who curled up side by side as if to fill the void she had just left. "Are you all right?" Adara looked over Lucius for blood and bandages, but her eyes avoided his.

"You don't look at me as much anymore," he said sadly.

"I don't see you, and when I do, you're usually hurrying out to fight." Now her eyes did meet his, and he reached for her, pulling her close to his chest. She could feel the muscles of his hardened chest against her, and leaned into his warmth as he hugged her.

"I'm sorry," Lucius said. "I'm fighting this war so as to end it quickly. If we could only get Argentocoxus -"

"You're fighting because if you don't, our family is doomed," Adara cut in. "Don't lie to yourself or to me, my love. I see the anger in you. I see that your heart is not in it."

Lucius pulled away and went to the table where a pitcher of wine and two cups were set out. Beside them lay Briana's sharpening stone which Lucius touched with his finger. A measure of tenderness, he thought of the words as he ran his finger along the stone. He poured the wine and turned to hold a cup out to her.

"Do we need to talk about war? I'm sick of fighting," he said.

"What would you talk about?" she asked, feeling the unwatered wine warm her throat as it went down. "Rome? Etruria? Horses?" Now she smiled. Things started to feel familiar again.

"Talk is not always needed." Lucius put his cup down and lifted his hands to Adara's neck and hair so that his fingers traced the line of her face and twirled her long black curls.

She stood and kissed him.

Neither of them could remember the last time they had kissed in such away. It was soft, and wet, and warm. Slowly at first, their lips pressed to each other, and then their tongues darting in and out, testing each other's will for more.

Eventually, all resistance faded, and Lucius swept Adara up in his arms and carried her across the room to their bed. He laid her down and she reached up to pull his tunic over his head.

In turn, he pulled her tunica and woolen breeches off, leaving her naked in the lamplight, her skin and her nipples reacting to his touch and the cold air.

"You're so beautiful," he whispered as his hand ran slowly all over her body as if he were re-familiarizing himself with every inch.

Adara's legs pulled him down as his hand massaged her breasts. He had forgotten the pleasures that Venus could offer, the joys of pleasing his wife.

Lucius kissed her everywhere until he reached her most intimate places and he was rewarded with deep sighs that rumbled in her breast after a time.

Adara pulled Lucius up, her hands clasping his tattooed forearms tightly. "I want you inside me, my love. It's been too long."

Lucius stood and removed his own breeches as she lay back and opened her legs to him. When they joined, waves of heat and pleasure pulsed between them as if they were one.

"Slower," she whispered.

Lucius realized he had been rushing, like he did in all things of late, and he slowed, kissing her neck, her eyelids, inhaling the smell of her hair. He felt his wife's body stiffen and relax, her hands tighten on the muscles of his back as her hips pressed more urgently into his until eventually, their eyes locked on each other, and they reached that breathless moment that they had been longing for.

Husband and wife lay together then, peaceful and warm beneath the furs of their bed. Only the light from one lamp remained as Lucius lay behind Adara who clutched his arm to her breast so that he could feel the intimate rise and fall of her chest as she slept.

For Lucius, sleep did not come as it should have. Holding his wife, he stared at the wall from the tangle of her curls. Worry had begun to wash over him again, its poison leaching into his veins even then.

It was only by the grace of Venus that his lids closed. For the goddess stood there, in that room, with the lovers she had blessed long ago.

When Venus leaned over Lucius and blew softly, the warmth of her breath soothed his racing mind to allow him just one peaceful night.

Enjoy peace while you can, my children, Love thought. *Remember this, and hold it close in your hearts...*

The next morning, as rain bore down heavily from an iron-grey sky, Lucius woke early to give Dagon the orders that the men were to remain within the fort for the day, apart from the usual perimeter patrols and messengers.

They had fought hard the day before, and Lucius knew they would welcome a day of rest and repair. He felt the fighting would get worse soon. Something in his bones told him so.

"I'll handle things, Anguis," Dagon said. "Go to your family."

Lucius thanked him and strode across the courtyard to see Briana emerging from his quarters, with Einion in position by the door. Lucius smiled at them and went in. As he closed the door he could hear Dagon addressing the two Britons. His waxed cloak dripped water on the threshold as he removed it and hung it on a peg beside the door.

Briana had lit all the braziers and lamps and the room was now warm and bright compared to when Lucius had left earlier that morning.

Adara was sitting on the small couch near the children's bed as Phoebus and Calliope rolled and giggled among the furs like young wildcats at play.

"You're back?" Adara said.

"Yes. We're staying here to regroup today. Dagon is taking care of things."

"And you?" she asked.

"I'm yours for at least this morning." Lucius sat on the edge of the bed and was immediately wearing two happy children about his neck. He laughed as their elbows and knees pommeled him accidentally as they crawled all over him.

"Time to eat, children," Adara said, laughing as she shooed them off their father.

Lucius rose and gave Adara a long kiss before going to the altar where he lit a piece of incense in the oil lamp's flame.

Smoke swirled about the statues of Apollo, Venus and Epona as Adara watched Lucius kneel in silent prayer before the images of their household gods. She rarely saw him so calm and quiet. The sight was soothing.

The family broke their fast together and spoke of the children's grandparents far away in Athenae and Etruria. Phoebus and Calliope never asked about Lucius' father, for they knew he had been cruel. Adara had taught them early on not to speak of it, at least for Antonia's sake when they were with her in Etruria.

"Is grandmother a fine painter, Mama?" Calliope suddenly asked.

"One of the best," Lucius put in.

Calliope's eyes widened and Adara knew what was to come.

"Can I draw and paint, Mama?"

Adara smiled. "The paints are finished, my girl, but you can use some charcoal on papyrus, or a piece of slate if we can find one." Adara brought a piece of papyrus for each of the children from their trunk and the two children sat there, following their mother's lead as she showed them some of the techniques she had learned from her own mother, Delphina.

Lucius watched them with great pride and not a little regret. He realized he had grown unused to family life since the campaign had begun. He finally noticed the changes in everyone.

Calliope sat at the table learning painting with Adara, her pictures reflecting reality rather than the childish scribbles he remembered; a bird, then a tree, true in shape and colour. His daughter conversed with Adara as she sketched, a running commentary on the world about them.

Adara praised her and turned to Phoebus, who was attempting to draw a horse running.

Lucius smiled at the concentrated look on his son's face.

Phoebus was a young boy springing into youth, and Lucius had missed a large portion of that time.

He remembered seeing Phoebus carrying wood across the courtyard of the principia, intent on helping Einion add to the growing wood pile. If Phoebus were to be given an axe, he would definitely have a go, believing he could do anything.

Lucius remembered reading about the boy Alexander among the scrolls his old tutor, Diodorus, had left him. Alexander had been determined to ride a horse no other man had been able to ride. When King Philip told his son he was welcome to try, Alexander shocked the court by turning the stallion to face the sun so as not to be afraid of his own shadow. He then rode the horse which he named Bucephalus.

Lucius wondered if Phoebus wanted to see the horses because of that very story which, he felt sure, he had told him at some point. *Children don't forget...* he reminded himself, remembering how he had never forgotten his own father's actions, the threats, the harsh words, or the beatings.

As Lucius watched Phoebus carry wood with Einion, he had noticed his son's muscles forming, realized he should be teaching him with rudus and shield soon, to build strength and skill.

The children had grown, matured, and he had missed so much, like a man asleep for too many seasons.

Then there was Adara. To Lucius, now that he really looked, she had grown even more beautiful with the passage of time. He looked at her then and liked the way her hair was tied back in a braided leather thong, how she wore woolen breeches and a short tunica; she looked more like an Amazon or British warrior maiden, than a Roman lady.

She had explained to him that the climate was far too cold and damp for a silk stola, and that she wished to wear warmer clothes when formal dress was not required.

Lucius agreed. They were approaching summer and it was still cold. It hurt Lucius that he had been apart from her, like too many years away from the sun, and he resolved to touch her more, to kiss those full lips he had loved from the first moment he had seen her at the imperial banquet in Rome, all those years ago.

Lucius went to the table to peer over Adara's shoulder at the children's work. "Very good!" he said, bringing smiles to their little faces.

"Thank you, Baba!" Calliope said, holding out her picture of the birds and tree. "This is for you!"

"Thank you, my girl! Listen, all of you. I have an idea. If this rain stops, how about I give you a full tour of the fort, beginning with the stables?" He looked at Phoebus whose head whipped around.

"Really? Can we?" the boy asked, his face alight.

"Yes. You can help me inspect the horses and care for Lunaris. He's a little hurt, and I think seeing you will help him."

"And I'll sing to him!" Calliope said.

Both children's eyes blazed with joy, and Adara took Lucius' face in her hands and smiled, her head tilted in that way he remembered from long ago.

"Thank you," Adara mouthed, as the children danced around the room.

After another hour of heavy rain, the downpour finally stopped. Shortly after that, Lucius and his family emerged from their rooms.

Phoebus chatted excitedly to Lucius as they walked across the courtyard to where Coilus and Afallach stood speaking with Dagon.

Before a word could be spoken, however, Brencis came marching into the courtyard from the street outside. "Praefectus!" he stopped suddenly and saluted.

"What is it?" Lucius asked.

"Caesar Caracalla, sir. He's here!"

"What?" Lucius felt anger begin to prickle beneath his armour.

"He's outside with a force of Praetorians, more men from sixth legion, and the Scythian cavalry."

Lucius, Dagon, and Coilus exchanged looks. Something had definitely happened.

"Baba, are we going?" Phoebus' childish voice harried the edges of Lucius' working thoughts.

"Not now, love," Adara said to her son as she held Phoebus back.

"What does Caesar say?" Lucius asked, just as a cornu sounded and the sound of shouted orders and tramping feet echoed in the street. Lucius and his captains turned to see Caracalla come into the courtyard flanked by four Praetorians, one of which was Alerio.

Caracalla wore black armour and his long black military cloak. He was splattered with mud and soaking wet, but he seemed to be revelling in it, that is, until he set eyes on Lucius. "Praefectus!" he roared.

"Caesar!" Lucius saluted, as did Dagon and the others.

"What in Hades are you doing here? We're on the march!"

"What's happened, sire?" Lucius asked. "We haven't received any communications."

"What's happened? Did you not receive word here at your Dragon's Lair? Argentocoxus and his men have been cornered near the fort of Fendoch. The men of III Legion have him. They managed to send some riders out, but so did the enemy. We have to get there, now!"

Lucius could not speak a moment. His eyes drifted painfully to his son and the disappointment he saw there was acute and heart-wrenching.

"Praefectus!" Caracalla screamed. "While you're here playing happy family, our men are doing their part and dying for Rome! Shall I leave you here?"

Caracalla was now in Lucius' face and it took much for the latter to hold his anger. He had given nothing but blood for months – years! – while Caracalla had fattened himself in the imperial camp.

"My men are at the ready, as always, Caesar," Lucius said in a low voice.

"They are not your men," Caracalla growled.

"We are all Rome's men, sire. And we are ready to meet the Caledonii." Lucius turned to Dagon, Brencis, Coilus, and Afallach. "Everybody mount up! We ride in fifteen minutes!" Lucius roared.

"Yes, sir!" they shouted, and dispersed to muster the men, and spread the world among the decurions.

"I'll see you outside the walls," Caracalla said, turning and going out, followed by his Praetorians.

Lucius walked to Adara and the children who were now flanked by Einion and Briana. He knelt down in front of Phoebus. "I'm sorry. I have to go."

Phoebus looked away at first, then back again. "Can you show me the horses when you return?"

Lucius smiled. "Of course." He ruffled the boy's hair and stood in front of Adara.

"Gods protect you, my love," she said as Barta arrived with Lucius' crested war helmet.

"I'll be back soon. They'll probably be gone by the time we get there."

Behind Lucius, Dagon, Brencis, Coilus, Afallach, and the decurions had all assembled in rows.

Calliope came up to her father and handed him a small sheaf of dry wheat. "For your horse goddess, Baba."

Lucius smiled and took the offering to the stone altar at the centre of the courtyard, he laid the wheat across its blackened bowl, and looked up to see three white birds perched on the roofline of the principia.

"Goddess Epona, mother of our camp… Guard us as we ride to battle and desert us not in the fray. We honour you." Lucius turned then to all his men.

"Let's ride out and bring Argentocoxus to his knees for what he's done to our brothers!"

The men roared approval, and turned to go to their mounts which were being held in the street. Lucius glanced back at Adara and the children one more time before lowering his face mask and going out.

The now familiar way to Fendoch sped by as Lucius led Caracalla, the cavalry, and infantry across the bogs, fields, and bulbous hills to the area where the messenger had said the fighting was hard.

The draco standards howled as they rode. The dragons of ten turmae thundered ahead of the Votadini and Scythians, with infantry forces falling farther and farther behind.

Caracalla kept pace with Lucius who noticed that the young Caesar's horsemanship had greatly improved beyond the driving of a chariot in the hippodrome.

Lucius did a mental check of all his weapons as Lunaris sped along; he gripped the sixteen foot kontos, felt the weight of his sword at his back, the bounce of his gladius and spatha hanging from his saddle horns. When he looked over, he saw Dagon doing his own check, and Barta, and all the rest of his warriors. Each of them could sense it, the closeness of the enemy, and the tang of blood in the air.

As their cavalry pounded across the wet, deep green landscape, their konti shivered as they rode together, a thick forest of naked saplings bristling and capped with iron leaves.

Then the screams reached their ears, the sound of dying men unmistakable.

"What is it?" Caracalla yelled from where he rode with his Praetorians, the Scythians farther back.

"Our men are retreating!" Lucius called, but Caracalla did not hear him.

The young Caesar looked around, confused and angry, as the shouts of centurions reached their ears.

The fortifications of Fendoch appeared in the distance as they passed the tree where Lucius had found his men hanging.

"Sarmatiana!!!" Lucius yelled, and their speed picked up with the Votadini matching them. "Coilus! Take the right flank! We'll go left!" Lucius added, and signalled to the old warrior.

Coilus smiled, nodded, and deftly twirled his spatha as he led his men to the side.

"Where are they going?" Caracalla cursed when he saw the Votadini vexillum veer off to the side. Suddenly, he saw it – a mass of screaming Roman legionaries, bloody, and terrified, running toward them.

Caracalla, the Praetorians, and the Scythians reigned in hard so as not to careen into their own men.

"What are you doing, cowards?" the Caesar screamed. "Turn and fight!"

When Caracalla looked, he saw the vast field swarming with massed bands of Caledonii.

"Sire! Close ranks!" Alerio yelled to the Praetorians around them as a wall of screaming barbarians slammed into them.

"Attack!" Caracalla yelled as they spurred their horses forward, the Scythians yipping above the screams, relishing a chance to bloody their blades. Caracalla looked to the left and saw the dragons of Lucius' cavalry carving a wide arc to the left, and then ten Sarmatian arrowhead formations slammed into the enemy's left flank.

The horses' lungs heaved along with their riders', but they moved as one beneath the dragons.

When the enemy was within sight, and impact imminent, the arrowheads formed at Lucius' command and the Sarmatians cried out.

"Ile Anguis!"

"Sarmatiana!"

"Epona!"

The power of battle and their gods of horse and the sacred sword were upon them now, the beasts tattooed upon their flesh writhing and lending each warrior power for the fight.

To Lucius' left, a flash of white, red, and gold told him that Epona was by his side.

As one, Lucius and Dagon lowered their konti, and the Caledonii turned to face them, hurling javelins, sling stones, and other missiles at the armoured wave rushing in upon them.

Lucius let go of his reins and gripped the kontos with both hands.

"Sarmatiana and Epona!"

A wash of blood sprayed into the sky as the lances ploughed into the enemy.

Lucius spitted three warriors on his kontos and it was ripped from his hands. He reached back for his dragon-hilted sword and slashed without hesitation as the faces of his fallen men and the warriors at his back flashed in his mind.

The Caledonii were everywhere in bursts of blue, brown, and green.

Lucius saw Dagon's horse trample a group of five and then press on, their skulls crushed beneath the stallion's hooves.

The sounds of iron and agony reverberated through the earth. There were so many Caledonii that the cavalry could not get back into formation. Each man fought for survival, and Lucius struggled to regroup as he scanned the madness of the killing field. He saw a ring about Caracalla, who had been unhorsed and was protected by Alerio and the other Praetorians.

On the other side, Coilus and Afallach hacked a bloody trail of Caledonian dead toward the enemy's centre where a tall warrior stood in a chariot, yelling orders at the sea of men about him.

"Argentocoxus!" Lucius yelled, kicking Lunaris' flanks.

Suddenly, something slammed into him and he felt hands pull him from his screaming horse.

"Anguis!" Barta's deep voice roared as he planted the vexillum and swung his long sword, taking two enemy at a time.

Lucius felt a blade, then two, bite at his scale armour, and then Barta yelled and went down, groaning, his face awash with blood.

"Barta!" Lucius reached for his blade and spun upward taking a Caledonian across the face and looking down at Barta.

In the distance, the white horse of the Votadini was rushing toward Argentocoxus and his bodyguard.

Afallach spotted Argentocoxus' chariot in the midst of the swirl of screaming and blood, and a madness seemed to overtake him. His spatha slashed left and right, his father echoing the slaughter a few feet away as the Caledonii rushed them.

The enemy tried pulling the horse banner of the Votadini from Afallach's grasp but he held onto it.

When a mass of Caledonii turned to face Lucius and the Sarmatians far to the left of the battlefield, Afallach saw his chance – a path had opened directly to Argentocoxus. The Votadini prince charged.

"Dunpendyrlaw!" he yelled as his horse shot for the gap. "On me!" he called to his riders.

"Afallach, no!" Coilus yelled as he tried desperately to hack through to follow his son.

The Votadini followed their chief and their standard where it rushed the Caledonian leader.

As Afallach rode hard and fast, trampling Caledonian warriors as he went, one of Argentocoxus' bodyguards turned to face the oncoming prince with a levelled javelin. The barbarian took three steps and launched.

The javelin slammed into Afallach's mount, cracking its breastbone. The horse flipped forward, throwing Afallach headlong into the enemy, the white horse banner of the Votadini trampled in the mud.

Afallach heard blades unsheathing and felt his ribs crack under kicks and blows. He blinked through the blood pouring over his eyes and he was pulled up by his hair.

The Caledonian who had taken out his horse spat in his face and pressed a blade to his neck.

"Morrigan!" the man growled.

Afallach looked up, ready for the blow, only to see his father, Coilus of the Votadini, soaring over the heads of their enemies, his sword slashing down into the skull of his son's attacker.

"Dunpendyrlaw!" the chieftain cried as he and his horse cut down the Caledonii.

Argentocoxus' chariot was already speeding away, but Coilus, full of rage at the hurt to his son, went after him, and the cries of the enemies whom he killed filled the battlefield.

Argentocoxus' driver lashed the chariot's ponies, but Coilus drew even, his hand free and wielding his sword and shield, his mount dancing beneath him as though they were one.

But the old warrior did not see the huge black wolf until it was ripping him from the saddle to slam into the churned earth at the base of Argentocoxus' spinning chariot wheels.

"Morrigan!" the Caledonian chieftain yelled.

The only sound Coilus could hear through the pain of his broken and torn body was the screaming of his horse as the great wolf tore into its belly. He looked up to see

Argentocoxus smiling down at him. Beside his old enemy, stood the Morrigan, tall and dark, her black hair dripping with blood.

"You chose the wrong side," Argentocoxus said as he raised a battle ax.

Coilus spat at them both.

Then, all was darkness, and the screams of battle faded to silence.

My son...

"NO!!!!"

Lucius heard Afallach's scream near where the Votadini banner had gone down. His eyes searched, and he saw Argentocoxus' chariot speed away toward the forest.

He found Lunaris, breathless and terrified, bleeding from many cuts, and mounted up. Lucius had lost his helmet, and his cloak was trampled in the mud, but he still had his sword.

Without a thought for anything else, he drove Lunaris after the enemy chieftain.

"Anguis, no!" Dagon yelled as he stood with the regrouped decurions about Barta and the dragon vexillum. "After the praefectus!"

Lucius could see Argentocoxus alone now, with only his driver as they made for the woods. He drew the pugio from his belt and threw.

The driver screamed and grabbed for his shoulder-blade where the pugio had plunged deep.

Argentocoxus tossed the body out.

Just as Lucius drew close, his sword reached out, ready to offer death to the Caledonian chieftain.

Then, Lucius was engulfed by shadow, ravens swarming him like angry bees, pecking at his eyes and ears. Behind it all, Lucius heard laughing, and a terrible screeching.

"Morrigan! I call on you!" Argentocoxus said.

Lucius hacked and three of the birds fell.

Ahead, before the trees, the Morrigan stood with outstretched arms, full of menace.

Lucius drew his last dagger and threw it at her, but the goddess raged even more at his mortal arrogance. He prepared for the impact, for death, and then the cry came amid flashing white light.

The Morrigan cursed as the three white hounds tore at her arms and legs, and then Epona, upon her brilliant white stallion, slammed into the dark goddess with unnatural speed, cracking the nearby pines like twigs in the rush of a gale.

Lucius saw Argentocoxus stop ahead, amid the trees, and get off his chariot.

The chieftain disappeared.

Lucius reined in and listened, looked. His mind spun, his heart beating as though it would explode.

The pine wood was dark. Sounds of battle beyond crept in among the naked trunks as Lucius walked forward.

"Come out, coward!" he said.

Just then, six Caledonian warriors emerged from behind the trees with the enemy chieftain behind them.

"You die now, Dragon, just like the horse lord," Argentocoxus said coldly.

Coilus? Lucius struggled for control of his rage. "I'm not the one to die today." Lucius took a step forward and it began.

The Caledonii attacked, and Lucius spun and stabbed. His blade found flesh, then bone. Then he pulled another warrior into a tree and the man fell with a crushed skull. The other three came with cudgels and daggers, but Lucius, ignoring the pain they inflicted on him, found the death he wanted to deal. He stood panting amid their bodies, their blood covering his arms and the dragon upon his cuirass.

Lucius pointed his sword at Argentocoxus. He could hear Dagon and the others rein in behind him.

"Kill him, Praefectus!" some of the men yelled, their voices uncharacteristically exhausted and panting, full of fury.

"Anguis," Dagon said beside him. "Let me fight him…for Hippogriff.

Lucius hesitated a moment. He wanted to kill the man before him. *So much pain...and death.*

"Anguis, please," Dagon continued. "Let me. I am their king."

Lucius came to, the blood lust leeching away, but not the wish to see Argentocoxus dead.

"Make it painful," Lucius said to Dagon.

Without a moment's delay, Dagon's sword lashed out and Argentocoxus stumbled back into a tree, his battle ax blocking the next blow, driving Dagon's blade into the bark.

But Dagon's hand lashed out like the tail of a vengeful chimera, slamming into the chieftain's face.

Argentocoxus, found his feet quickly.

"To Tartarus with you, barbarian coward!" Dagon wrenched his king's sword free and made for a final attack.

"A word with Caesar!" Argentocoxus suddenly yelled, his arms in the air, his face illuminated by firelight.

"Hold!" Caracalla's angry voice rang through the wood, and Dagon try as he might, could not finish the deed he wished to carry out. "Princeps!" Caesar called. "I said hold!"

Dagon's sword arm flexed and trembled as he held his blade levelled at Argentocoxus' smirking face. The pale visages of his men, his brothers, as they dangled from that tree of death cried out to him, but he held his hand as it shook.

Caesar had given an order, and his living brothers needed him.

Dagon turned abruptly, and found himself and Lucius surrounded by Caracalla and a force of blood-soaked Praetorians. He saluted, his arm heavy as lead as he raised it to Caracalla.

"Argentocoxus, sire," he said with a bow. "Chief of the Caledonii." Dagon stood beside Lucius as Caracalla dismounted with Alerio and five others who approached the Caledonian.

Argentocoxus did not run this time.

"I have heard of your greatness, Caesar, and I wish to offer you my sword, and my allegiance." Argentocoxus went down on his knee and bowed his head.

Caracalla walked forward, the point of his golden gladius above the chieftain's head.

Alerio and the other Praetorians held their blades out, ready to take action, but none was needed. The Caledonian was unmoving.

"I should kill you, Argentocoxus," Caracalla said. "Over twenty thousand Roman lives have been lost because of you."

"And I have lost over thirty thousand tribesmen," he answered. "Though I have a hundred thousand more of all the clans who would meet Rome in battle, or hold her lands here at the edge of the world.

Caracalla watched Argentocoxus closely, his mind working as his dark brow creased.

The chieftain stood up and faced Caracalla.

"On your knees, barbarian!" one of the Praetorians yelled, slamming a fist into Argentocoxus' stomach.

"Stop," Caracalla ordered casually. "Take his weapons and step back."

"But sire -"

"Now," Caracalla ordered Alerio who bent to take up the axe and sword that had been thrown down. He then backed away with the other Praetorians.

Caracalla lifted Argentocoxus' chin with the tip of his blade and met the chieftain's pale eyes.

"I have an offer for you," the young Caesar said.

"I am listening."

As Caracalla and Argentocoxus spoke beneath the black trunks of sentinel pines, Lucius came to Alerio's side.

"What are they talking about?" he asked.

"I don't know." There was frustration in Alerio's voice.

"We could have ended this here and now," Lucius pressed. "I've lost a lot of men."

"Everyone has."

Lucius breathed deeply, the frustration overwhelming. He went back to Dagon's side and stood still, his eyes scanning the forest beyond the parleying men.

Then, Argentocoxus bowed his head, saluted, and spoke aloud for the Romans to hear. "It shall be so!"

Caracalla nodded approvingly, a satisfied smile creeping up his features.

Lucius and Dagon looked at each other, then at the Praetorians with whom Caracalla now spoke in whispers. Lucius stepped forward.

"Sire. We can't let him go. More Romans will die because of him. The emperor -"

"The emperor is my father, and he gave me the command of this field army, Praefectus!" Caracalla whirled on Lucius, his hand reaching out to grip Lucius' arm and pull him aside. "Don't presume to give me orders, Metellus. You would have been dead, your whole family dead, if it hadn't been for me!"

Caracalla's face contorted, and Lucius saw the nature of the man before him. He had known it was there, but thought, perhaps, after all he had done to help Caracalla, he might have earned the right to be heard. It seemed not.

"Sire. I mean no disrespect. Indeed, you've earned many a man's respect on the battlefield today. It's just that I've seen how this barbarian thinks. He's without honour. He's false, and he'll betray us the moment our backs are turned."

"You underestimate the power of Rome, Praefectus," Caracalla answered. "He knows I can have more legions down on his head in no time. The threat of that, and a gift of silver, will buy us an ally to hold this edge of the Empire."

"A reluctant, untrustworthy ally?" Lucius pressed.

Caracalla gripped Lucius' arm tighter, and his voice was low and hard. "I don't want chaos here, Metellus. I want to leave this fucking land! We'll sign a treaty, and the Caledonii will take the Sacramentum, as Argentocoxus has just promised. They'll be our allies, and then we can all get back to Rome and ruling."

Lucius stared at Caracalla a moment before speaking. "Will the emperor agree to these terms?"

Caracalla let go of Lucius' arm. "Know your place, Praefectus." He then turned back to join his Praetorians who now stood protectively around Argentocoxus. Caracalla turned back to Lucius. "I order you to take charge of cleaning up the battlefield, Metellus. Send official loss numbers on to Horea Classis when you are finished. Then await further orders."

Lucius and Dagon watched Caracalla and the Praetorians go, surrounded by a ring of torches. Neither of them had words to describe the anger they felt at seeing their enemy go. They knew the battlefield held many horrors and so, reluctantly, they took their horses and went back with their surviving men.

Lucius turned back to the wood to see the Morrigan's wolf eyes blazing in the darkness.

The howl that she sent up rent a shiver of dread up and down Lucius' spine that he would not soon forget.

They found Afallach weeping over the headless body of his father, Coilus, Chief of the Votadini, and Friend of Rome.

The young man who had been saved by his father ignored all those about him, he ignored the blood seeping from many cuts, and the pain of his injuries. Afallach's arm and shoulder hung at awkward angles, his collar bone and arm broken in the fall from his horse, but he did not seem to care, this last son of his house. The vacant eyes of his father's severed head gazed sadly up at Afallach who shuddered violently as Lucius' hand gripped his good arm.

"Leave me!" Afallach yelled as blood seeped through his hands where he touched his father. As he bent over, his long hair became soaked with gore as he cradled the savaged body.

Lucius knelt in the churned mud and offal on the other side of Coilus, and stared at Afallach. "I grieve with you, brother. But your father's sacrifice should not be shunned. You are now the chieftain of your people, Afallach. Look at your warriors. They need you now. They need a strong leader."

Afallach looked up to see the surviving warriors of the Votadini encircling him.

One of the men held the vexillum with the rearing horse, newly affixed to a discarded kontos.

Afallach looked down again at his father. *Father, give me strength. I'm sorry if I was not good enough. I will lead our people as you would have.* Afallach looked up to see white birds circling in the sky, and a single stream of tears ebbed from each eye. *Epona, goddess, guide my father Coilus as he rides to the Afterlife. He was one of your most loyal...*

He put out his good arm, and Lucius helped him to stand. When he did, the Votadini began to slam their swords upon their shields. No words were needed to acknowledge their new chieftain, or to bid farewell to their fallen lord.

The whole of the next day, Lucius oversaw the cleanup of the battlefield, and kept a tally of the numbers of dead, dying, and seriously injured men on both sides. The Caledonii were going to be their allies now, and so he counted them as well.

Dagon raged like Lucius had never seen before. The Sarmatian princeps was overcome by their losses – near to half of their force it seemed.

Seven Sarmatian turmae had been wiped out, including the decurions whose faces would haunt Lucius and Dagon – Ferda, Eikki, Pekka, Oles, Xylon, Vanko, and Teucer. All of them brave warriors, all of them dead.

Many said they had seen a giant wolf tear into many of the Sarmatian riders and horses, and this did not surprise Lucius. He had seen the Morrigan with his own eyes. However, he had also seen the Caledonii cut the horses from beneath his riders, slaying them before the men were able to find their feet. He hated them for it.

He also hated Caracalla for letting Argentocoxus go.

By the time the field had been cleaned of bodies, and the blood washed away by the rain, Lucius was numb with anger and regret.

As the last embers of the funeral pyres burned away in the bloody dampness, there was nothing for it but to return to the Dragon's Lair. The Sarmatians and Votadini rode side by side, their mounts surrounding the wagon which carried Coilus' remains back to base.

Afallach now wounded too severely for battle, would take his father's body back to Dunpendyrlaw for burial.

As they rode beneath the dragons, Lucius looked for Epona, but he did not see her nearby. *Goddess, do not desert us…*

As the rain came down on the principia roof, Adara busied herself with any little task that might offer her mind some distraction.

There had been no word from the front for days until one of Lucius' riders arrived that morning.

"There has been a great battle, Lady Metella," the Sarmatian said, his voice deeply tired.

"Is the praefectus…is he -" The worry in the pit of her stomach was too much to bear. She could see the children listening from where they had been learning basket weaving with Briana.

Einion stood beside Adara to hear the news.

"Is the Dragon alive?" Einion asked.

The Sarmatian raised his head and nodded. "Yes, thank the Gods. He lives. As does our princeps."

Adara felt her knees weaken and reached out for the corner of the campaign table to steady herself.

"But, we have lost seven turmae of horse and riders," the messenger said.

"Seven?" Einion repeated.

The man nodded. "And Coilus of the Votadini was slain by Argentocoxus."

They were silent a moment.

"He was a kind man, Gods keep him," Adara said before reaching up and putting a hand on the weary trooper's shoulder. "Go now and rest," she said. "You have given much."

"Lady Metella," the man saluted and went out into the courtyard to return to Brencis who had been left in charge of the defences, the latter still raging at not having been there to fight alongside his people.

"Devastation seems to follow this army," Einion murmured as he contemplated the news.

"Let's hope that this is not always the case, brother," Briana said, leaving the children to go to Adara's side. "Your husband lives. That is a blessing."

Adara looked up at the Briton. "Yes. Thank the Gods. But, to have lost so many…it will be…difficult for him."

"Dagon lives as well?" Briana asked quietly.

"Yes," Adara said. "Another blessing." She turned to them again. "They'll be back tomorrow. We'll need to be ready for them."

Adara went to the door and opened it to look out at the altar in the courtyard of the principia. Puddles dotted the ground and rainwater dripped down the altar's channels where blood usually ran in warm rivulets.

"There will be many sacrifices in the days to come…" Adara said as she stared out, her arms crossed tightly against the cold.

They heard the sound of solemn horns late in the afternoon. The rain had finally stopped, but the iron grey sky above held a promise of more.

Lucius rode at the head of the long column of men beside Dagon. The dragon vexillum hung sad upon its pole, held still by Barta whose face was tightly bandaged due to the loss of his right eye in the battle. Behind them rode Afallach in a covered wagon that carried the body of his father, which was covered by the chieftain's crimson military cloak.

Adara stood on the battlements with Brencis and Einion as the force of surviving Sarmatians and Votadini approached. The oak and iron gates creaked loudly and swung fully open to allow them beneath the rows of silent cavalrymen and legionaries of the Dragon's Lair. Adara caught Lucius' eye as he rode beneath and on into the fort toward the principia.

Men who had remained behind went to help their returning brothers and discover the names of all those who rode now across the great plains of the Afterlife. Food and fire had been prepared, but none had the appetite for it, nor the will to get warm again.

As she walked along the Via Principalis with escorts, Adara could sense the mute numbness among her husband's troops who glanced kindly at her, but then turned away, embarrassed by their despair.

In the principia courtyard stood the wagon which held Coilus, his head put in its proper place with his body, the vicious wound concealed with linen.

Afallach stood before the altar silently with Lucius, Dagon, and Barta, and offered a pure sheaf of wheat to Epona.

When Adara approached, Lucius turned and walked to her. She threw her arms about his neck and squeezed, making him wince. "Thank Apollo and Epona you're safe," she whispered.

"Victory for Rome," he said sarcastically.

Barta turned then, his one eye acknowledging Adara from a bruised face.

"Dagon," Adara said as he approached them. She noticed the white pallor of his skin, the dark circles beneath his bloodshot eyes. "Are you injured?" she asked.

Beyond the doorway of Lucius' rooms, Briana stood watching.

"I'm uninjured, but for a few cuts, lady," Dagon said. "But every loss of my people has left a gash upon my heart. And the Caledonian chief is now made an ally of Rome." Dagon turned and went directly to Briana whose hand, Lucius saw, went up to caress his cheek.

"Let him be," Lucius said to Adara. "We lost so many men, his men, it will take time."

"And you?" Adara pulled back the hood of her cloak, her black hair falling about her shoulders, her face concerned.

"I feel hatred now," he whispered, his eyes hard as he stared at Afallach praying above his father's corpse. "Caracalla betrayed us and struck a deal with the Caledonian chief."

"Surely the emperor won't allow it," Adara said.

"I don't know." Lucius rubbed his temples, his headache getting worse.

"You need to rest, love. Go and bathe, then come and eat with me and the children."

"I have to see to all the men. Their morale will be low," he said.

"After then," Adara answered, as Lucius made his way to the street followed by Barta and Dagon, and leaving Afallach alone with his prayers.

Two hours later, as the torches flickered in their brackets, Lucius opened the door to his quarters to find Adara sitting with Briana while the children jumped on their straw mattress.

"Come. Sit, Praefectus," Briana said as Lucius entered.

Adara saw he was tired, but there was more. He seethed with emotion which, she expected, was normal after a battle. She hoped that now he was clean, he would feel better with wine and food, but Lucius just sat there gazing at the lamplight as though he were alone.

"I'm sorry for the loss of your men, Praefectus. They must have fought valiantly," Briana said, busying herself with tidying up.

"Yes, they did," Lucius answered.

"Dagon told me how Caesar held him back," Briana added.

Lucius looked up. "Yes. Dagon would have slain the accursed bastard, but Caracalla befriended him instead."

The two women were silent a moment, then Briana spoke again.

"He also told me of the black wolf."

Lucius looked up quickly, and Adara saw some fear there.

"You should not have attacked the Morrigan, Praefectus," Briana warned. "It's said she never forgets, that she hunts those who cross her for all time."

"She was protecting Argentocoxus."

"It's no matter. He lives anyway, doesn't he?"

"What do you want?" Lucius bellowed suddenly. "It's done now! Epona was there with me."

"And I hope she always will be," Briana answered calmly. "But the Morrigan is -"

"You can go now," Lucius interrupted. "Dagon needs you more than we do at the moment."

Briana glanced at Adara who nodded that she should go.

Phoebus and Calliope sat on the bed now, rolling over each other and laughing uproariously, ignorant of the tension their father was exhibiting.

When Briana was gone, Adara spoke. "You…you attacked a goddess on the battlefield?"

"Let it be, Adara!" Lucius snapped.

"No, I won't!" she stood before him. "You are a skilled warrior, my love. I know. But you're not an Ajax. You cannot attack a goddess on the field of battle. Even Ajax was driven mad by the Gods!"

"You're not making sense. Please stop."

"I won't stop. I'm scared, Lucius!"

Lucius looked at Adara differently then. He wanted to hug her, to escape into the smell of her hair, but her eyes were harder then, as were his. He knew he had been hardened by the brutality of battle, the deaths he had witnessed and been unable to prevent. He wondered if he was too close to his men, if being so attached, he was not a fit commander.

So many dead...

"Ever since we arrived here," Adara continued, "you've been angry and violent, displaying little tenderness for the family you claim to love with all your being. It's not enough to lie with me every few days when the mood takes you."

Adara turned, her hands covering her face as she went to the far side of the room.

"You've changed, my love, and I'm afraid it's not for the better." Her voice was sad and weak as the words left her lips.

"You don't understand," Lucius said, looking at the flagstone floor, his hands shaking.

"Oh, I do understand," she answered, her voice laced with growing anger. "Rome has betrayed you. All of us. You've lost men…friends! But if you don't look up from the blood and massacre soon, you won't see us there."

"What?"

"Lucius… We are blessed. But the Gods will take from us the things we do not appreciate. Don't you remember me? Don't you remember us?" Adara took a deep breath, unable to restrain the anger and disappointment in her voice. "You are without philotimo now…like an animal!"

"Spare me the philosophy!" Lucius remembered his friend and mentor Aelius Galenus' parting lesson on philotimo when he left Alexandria, on loving honour, and living always in a good and honourable way. He knew Adara was right. Was he fighting for the good of others anymore? What was he fighting for? Rome? Caracalla?

Adara pressed on. "You lived and breathed philotimo before, Lucius. But now, all I see these days is a savage animal, a puppet for Rome!"

Adara stood there, her chest heaving and shuddering as the words poured out. She could not help herself, even though she knew she should stop.

Lucius' eyes were unrecognizable then, devoid of love or tenderness.

Adara turned and went to the altar with a prayer to Venus on her breath.

Lucius sat there, at the table, frozen for several minutes, unable to look at her. He was also annoyed that the children seemed ignorant of the severity of their parents' conversation, continuing their play as Adara prayed.

"Keep quiet!" he shouted, and their laughter abated.

Calliope began scribbling on a wax tablet, her eyes occasionally looking up.

Phoebus, however, fidgeted excitedly, trying to decide if it was a good time to ask his father the question that had been on his mind for a long time, now that they were not vying for his attention. The boy stood up and walked over to Lucius who leaned on the table with his forehead on his hand and his eyes closed.

"Baba?" the boy said timidly.

Lucius did not answer, his mind haunted by screams, blood, and black wolves.

"Baba!" Phoebus yelled, jumping up and down.

"What?" Lucius opened his eyes. "What is it, Phoebus?"

"Can we go see the horses now? You promised that when you returned, you would take me."

"Phoebus, dear. Not now," Adara urged her son. "Your father is tired."

"Why not? I've been good. I've waited!"

"I'm busy. Maybe another time," Lucius said, feeling his head pounding.

"No! You say that every time! We've been here for a long time, and you're always tired, or busy."

"Well, I am!" Lucius said, knocking the stool back and standing over his son.

But Phoebus did not back away.

"All I want is for you to show me the horses!"

"I will!" Lucius shouted. His head was ringing with the clash of weapons, and the screech of the Morrigan's voice.

"You're lying!" Phoebus screamed. "I hate you!"

The words were like a sword thrust to Lucius' heart, but his anger had spilled over inside to drown out any other feelings.

He grabbed the boy by the tunic and shook him violently. "Do you think I've been playing at games here? I hate what I've been doing! I'm at war! Do you even know what that means?"

Now Phoebus was shaking his head, tears flowing down his cheeks.

"Lucius, stop!" Adara said, but he did not hear.

"I'll tell you what war is! It's bathing in the blood of your enemies, and of your friends. It's not knowing one second to the next if your eyes will shut forever. It's watching grown men cry, and piss and shit themselves like babies before one of these is shoved through their stomach, and their lives are ended!" Lucius drew the sword from his back and slammed it into the table-top where it bit deep, and sent the cups and wine jug to the floor to shatter into pieces.

"War is not about heroes! It's about dying, and not dying. It's about greed, and power, and killing!"

"Baba! Stop!" Calliope now yelled from where she stood on the bed, her face pleading and wet with tears. "You're scaring him!"

Lucius stopped and looked at Phoebus' terrified face as he dangled from his father's grip a foot above the floor.

"Let him go!" Adara yelled as she ran to Lucius and slapped him hard across the face.

Lucius dropped Phoebus and his hand instinctively grabbed Adara's throat.

"Let her go!" Phoebus yelled, wrenching the sword from the table top and swinging to make him let go of Adara.

Lucius' arm snapped out before the blade hit him, and he felt his hand connect with his son's face.

Phoebus went reeling to the floor, and the sword clanged on the stone.

"I'm paterfamilias!" he shouted, his entire body shaking, and his eyes wide with horror.

A hideous cry erupted from deep in Lucius' chest. He whipped around, and drove his fist into the plaster wall. A sickening crunch emanated from his hand where his ring finger broke, the dragons bent.

Without looking back, Lucius went out into the night, shoving both Einion and Briana out of the way. He stormed down the Via Principalis to the Via Decumana, and made his way out of the gate.

"Praefectus! Do you need an escort?" one of the guards called.

"Not now!" Lucius yelled, leaving the men staring after him.

XVI

VULNERES

'Wounds'

As Lucius walked along the fort's walls, his mind spun, and nausea overwhelmed him. He looked up at the palisade of the Dragon's Lair and the masses of dead enemy bodies he and his men had hammered into the wood – torsos, limbs, and bloody scalps hanging limply. Masses of Caledonian heads stared back at him, accused him, their tongues lolling out from decomposing heads as if to curse him.

The stink of rot mixed with dank mud drove Lucius toward the river where he stumbled toward the water, crawling the last few feet to the edge, and collapsed, shaking.

"What have I done?" he wept. "Gods forgive me…"

He could feel his soul crumble where he lay, wretched and helpless, for he had become his father. He could sense Quintus Metellus Pater's wicked shade laughing at him in Hades, saying *Now, you are just like me, Paterfamilias!*

Lucius shut his eyes against the vision of his father's imago, the wax mask that should have hung with the rest of their ancestors', but which Lucius had refused to have made. The face laughed at him, yelled *I'm paterfamilias!*, and laughed again before melting away in a pool of blood.

Then the Morrigan's eyes burned into Lucius' mind, causing a loud cry and ringing.

Lucius felt his body shake uncontrollably at the edge of the river. He wept as he did so, but he had not the power to stop it.

The Morrigan laughed, and he shook, and the arms of dead warriors reached out of the river to grasp at him, while on the other side, his wife and children stood huddled together, their teary faces crying out to him.

Gods, help me! Help! Lucius' soul cried out as the great black wolf appeared and began to approach, her teeth levelled at his gut.

Just as the wolf was about to lunge, a blinding flash of light hit Lucius like a bludgeon, his head snapped up from the water, and he vomited over and over.

The wolf was gone, the laughter and the voice of his father vanished.

Lucius looked at his reflection in the water of the moonlit river, and brought his trembling hands to his face, the dragons on his forearms writhing. His finger was bent at an awkward angle and, weeping, he pulled on it to get it back into place; he did not care about the crushing pain it caused. Then he stopped.

The awareness that he was not alone struck him, and he raised his head to the light across the river.

Apollo stood there, a gleaming light in the darkness, but his eyes were full of severity, the stars whirling fast within them.

At the god's side stood Venus, her eyes red with weeping, even as she shone with unimaginable beauty and tenderness.

Lucius mumbled, and tried to rise, but he was too weak. Then he felt someone lift him from under the arms, and he stood to see Epona holding him up. Behind, her three white hounds growled fiercely at the black wolf they were holding in the shadows beyond Apollo's light.

"Stand, Dragon. You cannot give up your fight now, after the sacrifices of your men and horses," Epona said, stroking the side of Lucius' head.

"Or the sacrifices of your family," Venus said, her eyes boring into him from across the river.

Lucius looked from Epona to Venus, and then to Apollo who had stepped in front of the wavering image of Adara and the children. The God of the Silver Bow stepped to the water's edge, drew an arrow from his quiver, and nocked it on the string.

Apollo's blue cloak snapped in a silent breeze as he raised the bow and aimed it at Lucius.

"For so long, we have aided you, Metellus. Your decisions have led you to this sad state."

Lucius looked down the shaft of that divinely crafted arrow and saw every mistake he had ever made in a microcosm of thought and memory. He looked at Apollo and Venus and struggled to hold their gazes, however much it burned.

"Forgive me. I have been weak. I've shunned my greatest blessings." Lucius bowed his head to Venus whose eyes softened slightly, though Apollo did not lower his bow.

"Metellus…" Apollo said. "You must be strong again!"

The bowstring snapped and reverberated, and Lucius bared his chest for the impact.

Searing pain grazed the mortal's face and then it stopped. Beyond Lucius and Epona, in the darkness, the great black wolf yelped and snarled ferociously, the sounds growing more and more distant until they could not be heard.

Epona stood to one side with her hounds, watching as Lucius opened his eyes and lowered his arms.

"Go back and honour the gifts you have been given, Metellus. Mind your true loyalty, and be prepared to fight for your life, even against yourself."

Lucius nodded. "I will, my Lord…Goddess. I will." Lucius fell to his knees again, his mind spinning, his eyes searching across the river for the Gods who were no longer there. He looked at Epona, but the goddess did not approach again. Rather, she nodded, and stepped back into the darkness of the plain, a white glow surrounding her and the hounds.

Lucius looked at the water. It began to come closer, and closer, and then he was beneath the surface.

"Praefectus!" someone was saying.

"Anguis!" yelled another voice.

Lucius felt himself pulled up out of the water, sputtering and coughing, weeping. Barta and Dagon held him up by the arms.

"I've lost my family, Dagon. I've betrayed them, and the Gods!"

"Nonsense, Anguis!" Dagon shook Lucius. "The Gods love you, and so does your family."

The horrified faces of his wife and children came into his mind again. Lucius could hear himself yelling at them, feel his body lashing out.

"I'm not my father," he mumbled. "I am not my father!"

Barta held Lucius up so that Dagon could face him. Then, the Sarmatian grasped Lucius' face and spoke closely, intently.

"No, Anguis! You are not your father. You are not! You are a man of honour - a good husband, a kind father. A great leader! Remember yourself!" Dagon spoke with an intensity he rarely showed. "Remember who you are! You are the Dragon! Loved by your men, by the Gods, and by your family," he repeated the words, as if trying to force them into Lucius' head. "Don't give in, Anguis. Don't let Rome break you."

Barta looked up with his one eye at Dagon, his chieftain, his king, and nodded. Their people had long felt the stranglehold of Rome.

Lucius focussed on his friends. The shaking stopped, and he breathed slowly again, wiping the blood and dirt from his face with the sleeve of his tunic. He put his hand to his cheek and felt the long line of the cut.

"Apollo…" he muttered, then looked at Dagon. "Forgive me. I couldn't save them, Dagon. All our men. Your countrymen."

"Nor could I, Anguis…" Dagon answered, overwhelmed by sadness. With every death of one of his Sarmatians, the memory and line of his people faded. "But we must ride on, Anguis. We must remember their shades, and honour them always when the winds howl about our dragons."

Lucius nodded. "Adara," he said, dreading the look in her eyes.

"You must go to her, Anguis. Now."

Barta and Dagon walked with Lucius back to the fort, ignoring the men who stared after them as they made their way to the principia.

The courtyard was silent. The only sound was the sputtering of torches around the body of Coilus at the centre.

Lucius stopped to look at the old man and felt sadness wash over him. Then he felt a touch on his arm and turned to see Calliope standing beside him, looking up through squinting, teary eyes. Her little hand squeezed his, and that gentle touch brought Lucius to his knees.

"I was worried about you, Baba," she said, throwing her arms about him. "I love you, Baba. Please come back to us."

Lucius struggled not to weep again, but could not help it when he held her and looked at her tiny face. "I'm sorry, my girl. I'm so sorry."

Calliope's hand touched his cheek and she nodded without saying anything. Then, "You need to see Mama and Phoebus. They are very sad."

"I know." Lucius looked at the door to his quarters where Briana and Einion stood guard, watching over Calliope very carefully, watching him.

Lucius approached them, holding Calliope's hand and leaving Barta and Dagon behind.

"Has the Dragon regained his senses?" Einion said, his arms crossed.

Lucius could tell he would try to stop him.

"Yes. I have," he answered. "The Gods have shown me my error, and my humiliation. It will never happen again. On my life."

"It better not," Einion growled before stepping away.

Briana approached Lucius and glanced down at Calliope. The little one nodded.

"You have nearly broken three beautiful hearts tonight, Praefectus. Go now. Ask them and your gods for forgiveness."

Lucius nodded, his head bowed in shame, and went through the door.

Briana and Einion remained right outside.

Adara heard the door latch from where she sat cradling her son on the children's bed. She had been worried since Lucius left, not for him so much as for what she might do. She had been looking down at Phoebus whose eyes held more sadness and pain than she had ever witnessed in them, and it made her angry, made her question the life she had chosen.

She knew she would do anything for her children. Anything.

When the door opened, Adara let go of Phoebus and stood up. "Stay there, my love," she whispered to her son.

The boy stood, but remained there while Adara went slowly to meet Lucius at the campaign table where his sword was laid across it, the sword she had given him.

He stood there a moment, looking at the floor.

"Go to your brother, Calliope," Adara said, her eyes never leaving Lucius' face.

The sight of him made her heart tighten painfully. *What's happened to you?* But she felt her children there, could hear their cries again as Lucius raged at them and struck out, and her anger rose once more.

Adara's hand reached for the blade on the table, picked it up slowly, and levelled it at Lucius' heart.

He looked up, and she met his eyes.

Neither spoke at first, instead, searching the other's eyes for some sign of what had been.

"Adara…I -"

"Don't!" She pressed the blade into his pectoral slightly. "You've betrayed us," she said.

"I know." His eyes burned as he stared at the woman he had always loved so ferociously, so deeply. "I've betrayed all of us – you, the children, the Gods…myself."

"Damn yourself!" her voice cracked. "How could you? He's just a child."

"I know. I've no words, or actions to make it better or take away the pain."

Lucius reached out a hand to his son, but Phoebus would not approach. He stared at his father from his watery eyes, sunken in a bruised face. Lucius saw himself there, as he had been many times in his youth. Thankfully, the Gods had kept a watch over him.

Please watch over my own children as you once watched over me, he pleaded.

"And what of our pain?" Adara asked, her green eyes sparking with emotion, like flint against stone, her black hair wild about her face. "We've travelled so far, been apart from you, endured so much along the way… For what? This?" She pointed to the children, and then pressed her left hand to her heart. "Have we lost you? Where is that honourable father and husband? Is he still in there?" She pressed the blade again and drew back quickly to strike.

Lucius stood still…ready.

He stared into his wife's deep green eyes and remembered how they once danced, fired by joy, and life, and youthful enthusiasm.

Now they were pleading and lonely, like two solitary jewels sinking to the bottom of a black sea.

He realized then that he was the one who had caused the pain and anguish that now clouded her countenance like an awful cataract. In his daily business of war, and the foul, clinging net of imperial, frontier politics he had forgotten what he held most dear.

Lucius Metellus Anguis had forgotten what really made him wealthy, and strong, and honourable. It was not estates, or titles, or a tally of slain enemies that made him good. It was Adara and their love, Phoebus and Calliope, their children, who raised him up to such heights as the Gods themselves would sigh at.

As Adara began to hang her head, her dammed-up tears near to breaking out, Lucius reached out to hold her chin, see her eyes. The sword lowered and he held her firmly to him, enveloped her in his strong arms and warmth, and she held him tightly back, knowing at long last that he was hers again, and would remain so.

Behind his closed lids, Lucius begged forgiveness of Venus and Apollo, for his short-sightedness and failings. *I'll never betray you or my family again…*

"Forgive me, my love," he said, the tears running down his cheeks.

Adara's body shook, and her tears flowed with his as they held each other, the children gazing in fear and a beginning of relief from their petrified state on the bed.

Lucius and Adara's hearts raced for some time, as they were unable to separate, unable to find more words. There were none.

Lucius suddenly let go of Adara and turned to their children, their faces wet, and small, and frightened. He stepped toward them and knelt.

"Before the Gods, I'm sorry for hurting you. I know you don't believe me, but by the waters of Styx, I will never harm you again. I love you both."

Calliope nodded and took her brother's hand, pulling him toward their father.

Phoebus walked slowly, reluctantly, until he stopped before his father. Without warning, his little fist swung up and slammed into the cut on Lucius' cheek, whipping his head sideways.

When Lucius looked forward again, Phoebus was weeping openly, his body racked with sobs.

"I'm sorry," Lucius said, as the boy threw himself into his father's arms and squeezed with all his might. "I'm so sorry, my boy."

Calliope stood holding Adara's hand.

Adara thanked the Gods for bringing Lucius back to them, and hoped that he would remain this time.

She had been ready to kill him for her children, she knew, but that would have been a death worse than any other. In her heart, Adara knew that Lucius Metellus Anguis was not his father.

XVII

PROMISSIONES

'Promises'

The sun had been shining and warm for days now, along the line of Roman camps from the wall of Antoninus all the way to the Dragon's Lair.

There had been no more fighting with the Caledonii, though patrols still went out at regular intervals. Time was given to the men for healing, further training, and the shoring up of defences. Troops from the legions encamped at Horea Classis repaired roads, defensive works, forts, and signal stations from the sea to the highlands.

The quiet routine felt surreal to many of the troops, especially to the Ala III Britannorum Sarmatiana and the Votadini. Their numbers had been much depleted in the fighting two weeks before, and now they were faced with treaty peace, absent many of their brothers.

The streets of the Dragon's Lair were quieter, devoid of laughter and gambling, the neighing of horses considerably less for the recent slaughter.

Lucius kept the men busy with training routines. They needed diversion. He also assigned detachments to remove corpses from the fortress walls and to bury them in a far field. They had all had enough of being surrounded by death.

Now, as the sunlight angled downward into the courtyard of the principia, Afallach stood before Lucius prior to leaving.

"I wish you could stay, my friend," Lucius said to the new chief of the Votadini.

Afallach stood before Lucius in his leather cuirass, pteruges, and greaves, his helmet tucked beneath his left arm. His shoulder was still tightly bound, but he was now able to ride and carry his father's ashes back to Dunpendyrlaw.

"I need to bring my father home, Praefectus. They will appoint me chieftain after his burial, and then I will heal."

"You'll be missed, Afallach," Lucius said, gripping the young man's arm. "I don't know what else to say, except thank you."

"The emperor said the Votadini should not attend the Sacramentum, and we must obey that. But I'm grateful to have known you, Lucius Metellus Anguis, to have fought in battle beside you."

"We'll see each other again," Lucius said, though he did not truly know that for sure.

"If your path ever leads you to Dunpendyrlaw, you'll be welcome as family."

"Thank you," Lucius answered, seeing Afallach's men waiting in the street. "You'd better go while the light is with you."

"Yes." Afallach put on his helmet. "Farewell," he said stiffly before turning toward the gate leading onto the street. There, Dagon, Brencis, and Barta bade him farewell, respect due from three warriors to another, acknowledging the trials they had shared.

Afallach mounted up beneath the green and white vexillum of the Votadini, and called to his men. "Time to go home! Move out!"

A horn rang out and they started forward, the line of horses moving out of the southern gate.

The Sarmatians and men of the sixth legion waved and saluted them as they departed with the sad remains of their dead chieftain.

Lucius did not go to the top of the ramparts with the others to see them off. He stood there, beside the altar in the middle of the courtyard, drenched in sunlight and thought. He looked at the door to his quarters. He could hear Adara and Briana laughing with the children, and smiled a little. He turned to the altar again, the sunlight reflecting in the bowl where oil and water mingled.

He pulled the eagle-headed pugio from its sheath and held his hand over the altar.

"Apollo, Venus, and Epona… My gods… Thank you for preserving me and my family. I swear to you I will not fail again." He closed his eyes and ran the blade across his palm so that his blood dripped into the offering bowl. "I will love and honour you, and my family, always. I will not shun the blessings of my life. I will not misplace my loyalties."

He tightened his fist until the blood seeped through his fingers.

"Haven't you bled and begged forgiveness enough, Dragon?"

Lucius turned to see Einion looking at him.

"I have much to be thankful for," Lucius answered.

Einion smiled and looked down, then up again. "I…ah…wanted to apologize for being so harsh on you, for challenging you. I was angry, and you reminded me of my own father at the time."

Lucius smiled sadly. It seemed they had more in common than he had thought. "You were right to challenge me. And I thank you." Lucius stepped up to Einion. "I wasn't myself then. But I've remembered."

"My sister is right."

"About what?"

"That the Dragon is great, and powerful, and wise. But the weight of all that can overwhelm."

"Hmm." Lucius put his hand on Einion's shoulder. "Perhaps that's why the Gods sent you both to us?"

"That's also what she says." Einion turned to leave, smiling. "I've long since stopped questioning her."

Lucius laughed as the Briton walked away. Then, he went to the door of his quarters from which laughter still emanated. He had been looking forward to this. He removed his helmet and stepped over the threshold.

"Baba!" Calliope yelled and ran to Lucius who picked her up and kissed her cheek.

"I want you all to put on your boots and cloaks, and come with me," Lucius said. "You too, Briana."

"Where are we going?" Phoebus asked.

"I can't tell you that. Not yet. Just come."

The children got dressed with help from Briana while Adara came over to Lucius. She looked lovely to him in a blue, wool, floor-length tunic with silver embroidery. Her hair was tied back to tame her curls, and her face seemed happier than Lucius could remember seeing it for some time.

"What are we doing?" she asked before kissing him.

"You'll have to wait too." He smiled, then looked at the door. "Afallach is away."

"I know. I said my goodbyes earlier. Will he be all right?" Adara had come to like the brusque Votadini prince, and pitied him the burden he now faced.

"It will take time," Lucius said, "but he'll heal and be a great leader."

"His people are strong," Briana added as she came up with the children and tied her long blonde hair back. She did in fact know what Lucius was planning.

"Everyone ready?" Lucius clapped his hands loudly and went out the door.

They turned left onto the Via Principalis and walked toward the east gate. Troops saluted Lucius as they went, and smiled at the children who observed them all unabashedly. Then they turned right off the main road.

"The stables!" Phoebus shouted as the smell of hay and manure filled their nostrils.

Lucius slowed to take his son's hand, and led the way. "You wanted to meet the horses. Now's the time. They've calmed enough now. The battle scared them too much before, and they missed many of their brothers and sisters," Lucius explained. "Horses are like people – they can be sad, or full of joy, calm, or violent as a storm."

They walked slowly along all the stalls, stopping to speak with many Sarmatian cavalrymen as they cared for their mounts and those whose riders had fallen in battle.

"They're all so beautiful," Adara said as they went, Calliope skipping alongside her.

"They're so much bigger than our own native mounts," Briana said as she admired a big black stallion.

They took their time walking along each row of stalls. Some of the horses were still nursing wounds, but most were fit again, eager to greet the visitors as they passed, their big heads and curious, pricked-up ears peering over the ropes and gates of their stalls.

At last they came to the final few paddocks where Lunaris was being fed by Dagon and Barta.

"Hello, boy," Lucius said as Dagon stepped aside to stand next to Briana. "Phoebus, come." Lucius picked up his son and held him up to Lunaris' cheek.

The boy reached out, his voice soft and awed by the magnificent dapple-grey stallion. "Lunaris…how are you feeling? Good, or like a storm?"

The stallion's ears twitched and he stepped in to lean against Lucius and his son.

"He likes you," Lucius smiled, and held Calliope up next.

The girl began to hum as she stroked Lunaris' forehead, his hot breath blowing the hair about her face and making her close her eyes.

There was a loud neighing from the stall across the way where a lean black gelding tossed its head and stomped a hoof.

Adara walked across to meet him. "Who's this then? Do you want some attention too?" she said, stroking his strong neck.

"His name's Hyperion, lady," Barta said. "He belonged to Oles."

Adara looked at Barta, and he lowered his head. She knew all the names of Lucius' men who had died. Oles was one of them, a decurion. She pat the horse's brow and ran her hand along his muscular flank. "He's wonderful."

"He's yours," Lucius said.

Adara turned to look at him. "Oh? No, no… I can't. He belongs to your men." She looked to Dagon.

"My men have many horses, and they want you to have Hyperion," Dagon said. "The Dragon's wife should have a mount of her own."

Adara smiled. She had missed riding, missed Phoenix, whom she had left in Etruria. "Thank you," she said, looking from Dagon to Lucius, and then to Barta.

"I wish I was big enough to ride them," Phoebus said in a disappointed voice.

"Me too," Calliope echoed.

"Come here, both of you." Lucius took each child by the hand and brought them to the very last stall.

There, they found two short, shaggy ponies, both black with white blotches all over their bodies. The children stood staring at them, and Lucius felt Adara come up beside him and squeeze his hand.

"For us?" Calliope asked, both children now turned to look up at their father.

"Yes. For you. Now you don't have to wait to ride."

"When?" Phoebus asked.

"Today."

"Really?" Phoebus leapt into Lucius' arms. "Thank you, Baba!"

Lucius had no words. He could sense the others all smiling behind him.

Dagon and Briana stepped up with two small, newly-fashioned saddles, and began putting them on the ponies.

"Where did you get them?" Adara asked.

"I found a horse trader among the Venicones. Briana and Einion know about these little beasts, so they helped look them over. They're a good age, and docile enough. But, they're also rugged, and sure-footed, with a smooth amble and trot."

"What are their names?" Calliope asked.

"They don't have any yet," Lucius said. "You have to give them names."

Calliope pet her mount's nose and neck in thought, then decided. "He looks like a 'Twilight' to me."

"Good name," said Briana. "And yours, Phoebus?"

"Hmm. I like 'Shadow' as a name." He turned to look the pony in the eye. "Do you like that?"

The pony nudged the boy playfully, and Phoebus' laughter filled the stables.

"I think he is saying 'yes'," Barta laughed, surprising everyone.

"Shadow and Twilight. Good names indeed. So? Shall we ride then?" Lucius said.

On the green field beyond the fortifications of the Dragon's Lair, laughter finally swept along the rows of Sarmatian onlookers as the Dragon's children rode their ponies for the first time. The little British beasts had been a curiosity among the cavalrymen, most of whom had never seen such ponies until they came to Caledonia.

Lucius and Dagon could hear the men laughing and placing bets on who would learn to ride sooner, Calliope of Phoebus.

It was only good-natured banter, so Lucius thought nothing of it, the smiles on his children's faces being all that he needed at that moment. As he ran beside Phoebus' pony, sweating beneath the warm sun, he glanced at Adara who clapped and cheered with the rest of the observers. An excited hue reddened her cheeks, and Lucius almost tripped as he became distracted by her, garnering more laughter from his men.

"Lady," Barta said beside Adara. "It's your turn."

Adara turned to see Barta holding out Hyperion's reins to her. "Oh, I couldn't. Not now," she said, aware that the men had seen their fallen brother ride that very horse many times.

"Show them, Metella!" Briana called over as she ran beside Calliope.

Adara had told the Briton she used to ride frequently. Now, she was being asked to prove it!

Hyperion crossed to her, his big liquid eyes seeming to ask her for attention. He seemed to need the bond a horse had with its rider, a bond he had been robbed of.

"Be gentle with me, Hyperion," she whispered, glad she had her breeches beneath her tunica. A moment later, she was putting her foot in Barta's hand and was heaved up into the saddle, her thighs snug between the four saddle horns.

Hyperion was taller than Phoenix, and Adara realized she missed the view from a rider's perspective. She gripped the reins and nudged with her knees. Hyperion walked out onto the field, smooth and calm as could be. Adara nudged with her inner left thigh and the gelding danced into a lulling canter.

Adara yelped with surprise and joy, but was drowned out by the chorus of Sarmatian warriors and Lucius cheering her on as she and Hyperion made a few circuits of the field.

"Metella! Metella!" some of the men shouted.

"Wait for us, Mama!"

Phoebus and Calliope's ponies ambled a bit behind Adara, their joy-filled voices echoing through the gathering.

Lucius stood in the middle with Dagon, Briana, Einion, and Barta. He had not felt such happiness in a long while, such lightness upon his shoulders. All he needed, all that he wanted, was there with him on that field – his children smiling, their laughter pure and bubbling, his wife, bright-eyed and lovely, her every aspect the life-source of his very heart.

Why should I want more? he thought. *Who cares for war, for empires, or any other part of it?*

Once, Lucius had thought loyalty to the Empire was at the root of his purpose in life. But there, with him, a part of him, was his purpose – loyalty to his wife, his children, his friends and warriors.

My own anima mundi.

The Gods had reminded him, and no emperor or caesar would take it from him.

Briana and Einion ran out to help the children steady the ponies and stop amid great cheers.

Their little faces beamed with excitement, especially Phoebus, who, as soon as he was back on the ground, ran to Lucius.

Lucius hoisted him into the air and spun Phoebus around. "You did it!" he praised the boy. "Woo!"

When Adara finally came to a stop before Lucius and the children, Hyperion rose onto his hind legs and came back down with a thump on the green grass.

"Good enough?" she winked at Lucius who looked over at Briana and laughed.

"Told you she'd remember," he said, going over to Adara as she deftly brought one leg over the horns and slid from the saddle to the ground. She kissed Lucius and the entire gathering hooted as the children giggled.

"I love you," he said, his grip on her hand intense and full of emotion.

"And I you, my Anguis. Thank you."

Nobody noticed the urgent sound of the cornu rising from the battlements of the fort for a few heartbeats until Barta's voice boomed over all.

"Praefectus!" He pointed to Brencis who was waving and pointing out from the east gatehouse.

Lucius followed Brencis' gesture along the river to the south-east until he spotted the column of riders approaching.

"Praetorians," Lucius muttered. "Can't they let us be?"

"Anguis," Dagon said. "We must be calm."

"I know, I know." Lucius turned to the gathering. "Back to base!" he ordered, and everyone began moving away. Lucius lifted Phoebus and Calliope back onto their ponies' backs. "Good surprise?" he asked, forcing a smile as the Praetorians got closer.

"Oh, Baba, the Gods could not have made a better surprise!" Phoebus said, his face beaming. "This must be how Alexander felt when he got Bucephalus!"

Lucius smiled and looked at the little pony. Not quite a Bucephalus, but good enough. "I love you both very much. Lucius squeezed both their hands and looked at them. "I'm glad you are happy. You're my life, both of you."

"And Mama?" Calliope asked.

"Of course," he said, kissing her cheek. "And Mama. Always. But now, I want you to go with Briana and Einion to the stables. They'll show you how to brush the ponies. All right?"

"Yes, Baba," they said together as the Britons took the reins and led them away.

Einion kept glancing backward at Lucius, but the latter waved him off.

"I'm staying," Adara said, still standing next to Lucius, her blazing eyes watching the approaching Praetorians.

"I'll be fine. Please stay with the children."

"Just be careful. I don't trust them."

"I will." He kissed her and she pulled herself up into the saddle again to go after the children.

Several of the lingering Sarmatians instinctively formed a protective barrier around Adara as she passed, seeing her safely into the fort.

"Let's go see who this is then," Lucius said to Dagon and Barta as they turned to meet the troops.

"Looks like two centuries," Dagon murmured as they walked toward the mass of purple banners and brown leather.

As the lead centurion got closer, Lucius relaxed. "It's Alerio."

"Looks like an official visit though," Dagon said.

"A summons to Horea Classis," Barta added, dabbing the sweat from around his empty eye socket.

Lucius smiled and saluted. "Salve, Centurion!"

Alerio reined in his mount and called a halt. He dismounted and strode over to Lucius. "Praefectus," he said.

"Princeps. Vexillarius," he acknowledged the other two men and glanced back at his optio and the other Praetorians.

Before Lucius could say anything, Alerio pressed on.

"I come with a summons from the emperor." He stood stiffly, his eyes, to Lucius' mind, seemed worried.

"I am ever his servant," Lucius replied loudly. "Now?"

"No. Tomorrow. You are to return with us to Horea Classis. Do you have room for my men tonight?"

"Of course. The blocks where sixth legion's men are quartered have space," Lucius said. "There is also room where our dead brothers used to be stationed."

"Thank you."

They began to walk, Alerio leading his horse by the reins. "You look like you've been picnicking," he said as they went.

"The children were riding their new ponies for the first time."

"Sounds nice," Alerio said.

"Yes." Lucius looked sidelong at his old friend. "You going to tell me what's wrong?" he whispered.

"I'll eat with you tonight, if that is acceptable."

"Of course!" Lucius turned to Dagon. "Can you show Alerio's troops to the barracks?"

"Yes, Praefectus." Dagon paused inside the gate and waited for the optio and other Praetorians as Lucius and Alerio went directly to the principia.

Alerio looked worse than Lucius had ever seen him. He had not known lack of sleep could destroy a man's countenance so, but in this case, it did.

Alerio slumped down in a folding campaign chair beside the table in Lucius' rooms.

"What's happened?" Lucius asked as he poured them some watered wine.

Alerio breathed deeply before speaking. After a sip of wine, he looked at Lucius.

"Caracalla. He's out of control."

"What's he done?"

"He keeps pushing for immediate withdrawal from Caledonia, as soon as the Caledonii swear the Sacramentum."

"Stupid," Lucius blurted. "The Caledonii will be up in arms as soon as we're gone."

"I agree. So does Papinianus. But Caracalla has his father's ear more than any."

"The emperor's love for his son clouds his judgement."

"Do you want to tell him that?" Alerio said.

"No." Lucius drank. "And the empress? What does she have to say?" Lucius remembered her past kindness fondly, but that was long ago, in sunnier times.

"Our augusta is quiet," Alerio answered. "She and Julia Maesa are holed up with their courtiers in the praetorium most of the time. I rarely see her." Alerio stood and looked at the wall map of the region. "The emperor's health is worse than ever, Lucius. I don't think he'll last much longer."

"Gods help us then. Maybe that's why no one will speak up against Caracalla?"

"I'm sure of it. Geta is still at Eburacum, and none are willing to back Papinianus beyond polite nods. Castor tries to persuade the emperor, but he cannot gainsay our young Caesar."

"What a mess," Lucius said. "Are my men and I to accompany you to the Sacramentum? I want to see Argentocoxus lie to the emperor's face."

Alerio was silent a moment, before sitting back down. "Your men are to stay here."

"What?"

"You're to come by yourself."

"But we're the ones who brought those Caledonian bastards to their knees!" Lucius looked down on Alerio. "Who decided this?"

"The emperor, persuaded by Caracalla. After the incident on the battlefield, Caesar doesn't want your men there to spoil the treaty."

"Why would my men do that?"

"I know you wouldn't, Lucius." Alerio looked very tired then. "There's more."

"What?"

"Caracalla has made Marcus Claudius Picus a Praetorian tribune for his courage in the battle with Argentocoxus."

"He wasn't even there!"

"Apparently he was."

"This is madness!" Lucius stood again, his anger beginning to rise. "The man belongs in a prison, not back among the officers!"

"I know. But he's Caracalla's man."

Lucius suddenly stopped and stared at Alerio. "Am I being led to the slaughter tomorrow? Tell me."

"No. Of that, I'm sure. The emperor wishes to thank you and…well…give you a leave for your pains."

"A furlough?" How long?"

"I don't know. Long, I suppose."

The thought did appeal, Lucius had to admit. However, he wondered what would happen to his men.

Lucius looked down at Alerio who had his head in his hands. "How are you doing, my friend?" he asked, setting aside his own worries. Lucius knew that he had Adara and the children, his Sarmatian brothers… But whom did Alerio have? A bunch of subordinates who were no doubt jockeying for higher positions, just waiting for Alerio to make a false move?

"I don't sleep well. Rarely, actually. I keep having these bad dreams about…"

"What?"

"Nothing. I'm just very tired of politics. Not sleeping doesn't help."

"Well, tonight, you can sleep. I'll have Briana cook you up some of her herbs to help you. How does a dreamless sleep sound?"

Alerio smiled weakly. "That would be great."

"Centurion!"

The door popped open and Adara and the children came into the room. "Dagon told us you were here." Adara walked over and kissed Alerio on either cheek.

"It's good to see you," Alerio made a sudden effort to be more happy. "And you, little imps!" he said, ruffling the children's hair. "I hear you are learning to ride?"

"Yes, Centurion Alerio! Baba just gave us two beautiful ponies." Phoebus still beamed, reliving the past few hours as he explained.

"Well, I know you'll be great horsemen," Alerio said.

"I'm a horse girl!" Calliope corrected.

Alerio laughed, and knelt down. "Of course you are!"

The little girl walked up to him and gave him a tight hug. "Don't be sad, Centurion," she said.

Alerio felt his throat tighten at the sudden words, and Calliope's little arms about his neck.

"I'll ask Briana if she can make up something nice we can all eat together tonight," Lucius said as Alerio stood.

"Ah, she and Einion will be eating with Dagon, Brencis, and Barta tonight." Adara turned to Alerio. "How about meat, cheese, fresh bread, and olives with Lucius and me instead?"

"I'd have it no other way," he said, relieved.

"What about us?" Phoebus said.

"You'll be sleeping!" Lucius lunged and grabbed his son playfully. "After we wash the smell of horse off you!"

That night, while the children dozed, exhausted after the day's excitement, Lucius, Adara, and Alerio sat eating, drinking, and talking by lamplight.

It seemed an age since Etruria, and Numidia before that.

Alerio had removed his heavy cuirass and greaves, and sat back in one of the three chairs, swirling his wine in his cup.

Outside, nightbirds called, interrupted by the call of the watch on the ramparts. It may have been a time of peace, but Lucius was not taking any chances. A full guard had been posted, the streets of the fort well-guarded.

"Where will you go on your leave?" Alerio asked eventually.

"I haven't thought about it yet. I'm assuming that if things go wrong here, I might be recalled?" Lucius said.

"I'm sure of it. Ala III Britannorum is an important outfit."

"Then maybe we shouldn't go too far."

"I was hoping for Athenae," Adara said longingly. "I've been dreaming of it – of swimming in the sea, feeling the sun on my face... I'd like to see my sisters and my parents. It's been so long..."

"Too long," Lucius agreed. "I wonder if Etruria is too far away also."

"Maybe," Alerio said. "Especially if you're right about the Caledonii." He turned to Adara. "Didn't your father give you both some land in Britannia?"

"Yes. In the South," she said.

Lucius got up and went to a chest of scrolls where he extracted a map attached to a deed of land. "Here it is." He unrolled the map on the table, placing empty dishes and the wine pitcher on the corners. "It's an old hill fort of the Durotriges tribe. Publius was letting Rome use it as a cavalry stopping point before, as far as I know. I didn't think we'd have a chance to see it," Lucius said, eyeing the map.

"It's not too far off the Fosse Way," Alerio pointed at one of the main Roman roads in Britannia, the line of it running from Isca Dumnoniorum in the south-west to the north-east and Lindum Colonia.

"We could ask Einion and Briana if they know it. They're from the South. Maybe they've seen it?" Adara said. "We've no idea what state it's in."

"Might be worth a look," Lucius wondered. A part of him was curious. At least it was something that was theirs, unlike the fortress in which they sat.

"It looks pretty big on the map," Alerio pointed out.

"Maybe this is the answer?" Adara said. "At least until we know the treaty is going to remain in place, and it's safe to return to Etruria or Athenae." The thought warmed her.

Lucius looked up at her, his eyes wide and bright at the prospect of an adventure with his family. "That settles it, then! We'll head south when I'm allowed to go." He leaned over and kissed Adara before sitting back down.

Alerio looked at the two of them and felt distinctly out of place.

"Sorry, Alerio," Adara said. "Here we are talking about going south while you'll be stuck here. Are things so bad?"

Alerio nodded. "Maybe. I've never had a mind for politics. All I know is that I can't sleep."

Adara stared at him a moment, remembering their conversations in Eburacum. "Alene is in your thoughts," she said.

Both men turned to her.

"What?" Adara said. "I think of her, and miss her, all the time. I can't imagine -" she broke off.

Alerio hung his head. "I dream of her every night when I do sleep," he said, his hands gripping the red Samian cup. "I see her running, in trouble, and I'm always too late to save her."

Adara reached out and placed her hand on his arm.

Lucius was silent, staring in shock at the lamplight.

"I'm sure that Alene is watching you, Alerio," Adara said. "From Elysium. She's watching you. She loved you…"

"Please stop," he said to her suddenly, before looking up at Lucius. "I don't want a dreamless sleep. Cause then, I wouldn't be able to see her. I wouldn't be able to try and help her."

The three of them were silent, each lost with a memory of ghosts, of a beloved sister and aunt, of a best friend, and of a lover.

Lucius remembered the monument carved for Alene by the sculptors Emrys and Carissa – Alene in relief, walking among wild flowers, with both Lucius and Alerio kneeling in mourning about her. It stood on the field, near the river, below the house in Etruria.

Adara sniffed, and dried her eyes. "Forgive me. I…I need to sleep." She stood, and Lucius and Alerio did too.

"I'll get some fresh air," Alerio said. "Good night, Adara." He paused at the door. "All will be well."

"Good night," she said, as he went into the courtyard.

"I'll go and see him to his quarters." Lucius kissed her.

"Do. He's felt her loss more than any of us, perhaps."

Lucius turned and went out.

When the door was closed, Adara lay on the bed next to Phoebus and Calliope, her arm stretching to hug both of them as they slept.

"Thank you for saving them, Alene," she whispered, her eyes shut tight against another wave of tears and gratitude.

Lucius found Alerio looking up at the star-pocked sky.

He swayed on his feet, and Lucius could see tiny streams of tears running down his friend's cheeks and neck as he looked up.

"We didn't mean to upset you," Lucius said.

"Don't worry." Alerio wiped his face with the sleeve of his tunic. "She is always on my mind. There's nothing for it. The Gods robbed me of my chance of happiness in this lifetime. No amount of killing or revenge will ever bring her back."

Lucius was at a loss. Of course, he knew Alerio had experienced immense sadness, but they had never talked of her in recent years. There had been no time.

"I still believe Alene would have been proud of the man you are, Alerio – proud to be your wife." Lucius wrapped his cloak about his shoulders. "She loved you, I know. I'm just sorry that…well…I haven't been the friend you deserve these last years. I'm sorry."

Alerio's eyes came down from the stars and looked at Lucius. "You're a good friend. The best I've got." He put his hands on either side of the altar. "But some damages are just irreparable."

"What will you do?" Lucius asked, his voice full of concern that surprised even him.

"I don't know," Alerio said. "Serve out my time with the Praetorians? Keep fighting? I don't much care anymore. No woman could ever compare to her, or the dreams we had together, of what might have been…"

Lucius felt his throat tighten. *Gods help him...* he thought.

"I'll be fine," Alerio said, his head up again, his soldier's demeanour back. "We should leave before the fifth hour of daylight. The emperor is expecting you to dine with them tomorrow night, and the Sacramentum is the day after."

"I'll be ready to leave. Can I bring some men for the road?"

"Orders are, just you. The Venicones and Caledonii are all arriving for the Sacramentum. Caesar doesn't want them baulking at the Sarmatian presence."

"You know that's a slap in the face, and spittle on the memory of the men I've lost."

"Yes," Alerio began to walk away, head down again, as if the shame of his orders weighed too much. The conversation had changed abruptly. "Don't worry, Lucius. I've got your back."

As Alerio's door shut, Briana and Einion emerged from the shadows.

Without turning, Lucius spoke. "What do you think, my friends?"

"It's a trap," Einion said.

"Can you trust him?" Briana asked.

"Alerio? Yes, of course. He would never betray me," he said with certainty. He knew Alerio's love of Alene would keep him on their side.

"What of the emperor and empress?" Einion asked.

"I'm less sure of their favour."

"And Caesar Caracalla?"

"I doubt it." Lucius turned to face both of the Britons. "After I leave with the Praetorians tomorrow, I want you to begin packing my family's belongings, and have a couple of wagons ready to journey south when I return."

"South?" The brother and sister looked at each other.

"Yes. We have lands near Lindinis. Adara will show you the map. You may know the place."

"I don't like this," Einion said. "What if you don't come back here? What then?"

Lucius tried to push his fear away. He felt a cold grip on his gut then. "I'll be back. But if I'm not, take my family to Ynis Wytrin, the place you told me of. Keep them safe at all cost."

Lucius, Alerio, and the rest of the Praetorians left the following morning under a sky that had gone from pale pink to iron grey in under an hour. Their pace was quick, as they tried to make Horea Classis before the inevitable downpour. It was only as they crested the last hill for a view of the fortress, docks, and surrounding camps of the legions that the first crack of thunder shook the ground, and lightning split the sky. The rain began.

Lucius was wearing his heavy red cloak and pulled it about himself to stay dry. The golden pommel of his sword stuck up at his back, the crimson horse-hair of his helmet's crest brushing it as he rode.

The main fortress was permanent and unmistakable, with the temporary camps of the legions radiating out from it to the South.

Lucius could see the vexilla of the various legions snapping in the wind, their proud red banners displaying the Capricorn, the Boar, the Bull, Winged Victory, the Centaur and various others of the auxiliaries. *The Dragon and Horse should be among them,* Lucius thought bitterly.

As they rode through, Lucius could see men beneath awnings, polishing their armour, and weapons, brushing down horses, and shining harness. Any man who had awards pulled them out to wear during the ceremonies the following day.

Alerio led them directly to the Praetorian stables where several stalls had been set aside for dignitaries and officers.

After unsaddling Lunaris and giving him to a groom, Lucius gathered his two satchels and followed Alerio within the walls of Horea Classis.

Despite the heavy rain, the area buzzed with activity. Troops stood guard everywhere on the ramparts of every fort, on guard towers, at gatehouses, and along the streets.

When Alerio, Lucius and the others approached the stone walls and tiled roof tops of the main fortress, Lucius noticed that a pontoon bridge across the Tava had been completed. He assumed this would be used to carry on the conquest in the North, if the decision was made to do so. For now, the traffic was flowing to Horea Classis, and groups of Caledonian clans hesitantly approached the Roman city that had popped up, in order to swear the oath their overlord, Argentocoxus, had promised on their behalf.

The camps of the Caledonii and Venicones could be seen to the East and South, their haphazard layouts billowing smoke from fires, and raucous noise from their rowdy clansmen travelling over the heads of the Romans.

Lucius and Alerio marched along the streets to the principia to report before they were dismissed to go to the bath house.

When Lucius finally closed the door of his guest quarters, alone at last, he sighed and checked the room for anything unusual before laying himself down for a while.

Alerio's knocking woke Lucius up. "Time to go! You've been summoned," Alerio said.

"By whom?" Lucius asked.

"The empress."

Lucius did not answer right away. He sat up on the couch, and stared at the pure white wall. His room was in the vast complex of the Praetorian barracks, just down the Via Principalis from the praetorium where the imperial family were staying.

What could she want? Lucius wondered.

Julia Domna had asked him for private audiences before to apprise him of pending dangers, but he was not so sure of her anymore.

"Lucius?" Alerio called. "Open the door."

Lucius stood and stretched, stiff from having slept in his armour. He slid the bolt and opened the door to see Alerio in full Praetorian kit.

"Sorry. I dozed off."

"The empress sent me to get you."

"Do you know why?"

"She just wants to talk before the banquet. Lots of people will be there. She wants to talk privately."

"You're being cryptic."

"No. That's just all I know. Now splash some water on your face and let's go."

Lucius followed Alerio to the praetorium where they went in a side door instead of the courtyard. A lone trooper was waiting to let them in. When they passed through, the door was barred behind them. They were in a small room, the walls of which were painted white with red borders. A bench sat against the wall, but Lucius did not sit.

"Praefectus Metellus. It's good to see you."

Lucius looked up to see the empress' cousin, one of her Syrian circle.

Lucius stepped forward. "How are you?"

"Well. I serve the empress still, as is ever my honour."

"Alerio tells me she wishes to see me?"

"Yes. Come. This way." He went through the door into a chamber filled with scrolls, tables, and couches.

As Lucius' eyes adjusted, he spotted Julia Domna reclined on a couch beside a flaming brazier. Incense smoke floated gracefully about her as she read a scroll. She wore a purple and yellow stola with a fur shawl over her shoulders. Her hair was tightly bound with the usual wavy texture that she had always favoured.

"Come closer, Praefectus," she said before looking up. "It's been far too long."

"Augusta," Lucius removed his helmet, tucked it under his arm, and went down on one knee before her. "May the Gods smile on you."

"May they smile on us all, Praefectus." She motioned to a couch opposite her, and waved her loyal cousin into a corner.

"Centurion Cornelius said you wished to see me."

"Yes. We have not spoken in some time and, well, I have heard of all you have done on the battlefield in this war. More than anyone else, I think."

"Augusta." Lucius bowed his head. "My men have fought very hard."

"And you have led them admirably." She rolled up the scroll she had been reading, a new treatise by Ulpianus, and sat up. "You've made quite a name for yourself during this campaign."

"Thank you, Augusta."

"But not all in a good way," she added, her dark eyes more stern. Suddenly, she looked her age, the pressures of her life and worries peeking out through her appearance. "My son has been complaining about you before the war council. He says you are bordering on insubordination."

Lucius stood. "Augusta I must protest -"

"Sit down, Praefectus. I know you are not, and I've convinced the emperor you are his man, through and through."

"I am," Lucius said.

"But…but…" Julia Domna's eyes glossed over, and Lucius could see her fighting some emotion. "The emperor has been ill for some time now, and the stars have had their say." She stopped a moment, rallying herself and accepting a cup of wine from her kinsman. "Caracalla is my son, and the heir to the Empire."

"And Geta?"

"Yes. Both of them are to rule jointly when the time comes. That is not secret."

"Augusta, is the emperor that ill?"

She was silent for a few beats before answering. "Only the Gods know. He still has strength of mind, as ever. But, Praefectus, you must support Caracalla."

Lucius found it hard to hide the anger in his face. He struggled, and she saw it.

"I am trying to help you. I always have," she reminded him.

Lucius had been grateful that the empress had protected his own family in the past, and his mother in the wake of his father's murder. But Lucius found it hard to forget what Adara had said about their treatment of her, or that he had spent a night behind bars not far from where they now sat.

"I only countered Caesar because I believe the Caledonii will not hold the terms of the truce."

"That is not your place."

Lucius nodded, but held her gaze.

"We all want to leave this wretched, cold island. I long for the sun, and the Middle Sea. Don't you?"

Lucius did not answer.

"The peace with the Caledonii is crucial."

"I have fought for nothing else, Augusta."

"Now, now. I know you better than that, Praefectus. You fight for your family more than anything."

Lucius looked up, caught unawares.

"And I fight for mine," she added. "Tonight, at the banquet, let there be peace between you and my son."

"Yes, Augusta."

"And Tribune Claudius Picus."

"What?"

"He is one of Caracalla's men now."

"The man is an animal," Lucius answered vehemently, catching movement in the corner of the room.

"Nevertheless, I want peace. I need it," she insisted.

"I understand." The words came reluctantly.

"Good. We will dine tonight among Romans. Tomorrow, you will attend the Sacramentum of the Caledonii and the

Venicones, our new allies, and then you will have a long furlough with your beloved family. Does that sound pleasing?"

"Yes. It does," Lucius said. "The Caledonii and Venicones will be there tonight?"

"No. We banquet with them tomorrow after the Sacramentum. You will not be there. I trust you understand?"

"Perfectly, Augusta."

"Good. I shall see you tonight," the empress said as her kinsman stepped forward to see Lucius out.

At the door, Lucius turned to Julia Domna. "Augusta," he said as he bowed and went out, leaving the empress to return to her scroll.

It was dark as Lucius made his way back to the praetorium for the banquet. As he stepped around puddles, he was careful not to splash the white, thin-striped toga he was wearing for the occasion. He had wanted to bring a pugio, but thought better of it.

Security was high within the fortress walls, as evidenced by the armed Praetorians lining the streets and surrounding the praetorium.

"Lucius Metellus Anguis, Praefectus of the Ala III Britannorum Quingenaria Sarmatiana," Lucius told the guard holding a scroll at the entrance to the courtyard.

The man nodded and pointed to a set of bronze doors flanked by flaming tripods.

Lucius went in and walked beneath the peristylium, toward the sound of people talking and laughing. As his eyes adjusted to the flickering orange glow that warmed the columns, statues, tables, and couches of the room, the faces of other guests began to come into focus – Ulpianus and the Praetorian Prefect, Papinianus, were there, as well as several tribunes and senior centurions of the legions. Julia Maesa was there, speaking with two officers, indifferent to the line of guests waiting to greet the emperor and empress.

"Praefectus Metellus," a voice said to the left.

Lucius turned and smiled as he handed his cloak to a slave. "Senator Dio," Lucius said, grasping the man's hand. "How long has it been?"

"The years fly, and the world turns," Dio said. "It's been some time."

"It has." Lucius appreciated the kind look in Dio's eyes. He had ever been a friend to Lucius and his family, as well as more respectful than most.

"How is your family?" Dio asked.

"Well enough."

The two men walked to a table where a great silver krater held rich red wine to be served in silver cups decorated with scenes of gods and goddesses. The table groaned beneath the weight of the wine, cheeses, fruit, meats, and other delicacies which Lucius had never seen in Britannia. He took an olive and ate.

"To the Gods," Dio said, tipping some wine onto the floor.

"To the Gods," Lucius echoed, his eyes closing and opening as he did so. "Senator, I must thank you for aiding my wife in Coria," Lucius said suddenly. "It was very kind of you."

"Think nothing of it, Praefectus. I was just happy to be there. It was unfortunate that…" Dio's voice trailed off, and his face hardened as he looked to the entrance of the room.

Marcus Claudius Picus had arrived, and stood there scanning the room. He was clean-shaven, freshly shorn, and wore an immaculate, broad-striped toga that shouted his Patrician lineage. The neat appearance certainly belied the monster that dwelt beneath.

Lucius had an urge to walk up to the man and pommel him, but the empress' words rang in his ears. Claudius was Caracalla's man.

"Steady, Praefectus," Dio whispered, his back to the tribune now. "Have some dates. They're all the way from Leptis Magna."

Lucius tore his eyes away from the tribune and back to Dio.

Claudius began to walk toward them with a smirk on his face, but Caracalla's voice beckoned.

"Tribune!" Caesar said. "Come have a drink with me!"

Claudius stopped and made his way to the front of the line where he saluted Caracalla, the emperor, and empress, before sitting beside the young Caesar.

"How is your mother faring, Metellus?" Dio asked.

"Ah…well, last I heard. She's enjoying Etruria, but misses her grandchildren terribly."

"I'm sure. Always a shame for a Roman, or Greek, grandmother not to be with her children's children."

"I wanted my family close, Senator. Can you blame me?" Lucius said defensively.

"Oh, I didn't mean you to take it ill," Dio added quickly. "It's just, well, I hear you will be going on extended furlough soon. And Etruria or Athenae may be more feasible then."

"We've thought of that." Lucius wondered if everyone knew he was going away. "But until it is certain the peace holds, I may remain in Britannia on our lands in the South."

"Well, as long as you keep your family close."

"What do you mean?" Before Lucius could finish, they were interrupted.

"I hope you're wrong about the peace, Metellus."

Aemilius Papinianus, Prefect of the Praetorian Guard appeared beside Lucius. He was an affable man, and Lucius had never minded him. He looked tired however, no doubt from brokering the peace treaty and seeing to security for the Sacramentum.

"Praefectus," Lucius saluted.

"At ease, Metellus. We're here to enjoy ourselves."

"You look tired, Aemilius," Dio said.

Papinianus pinched the bridge of his aquiline nose and sighed. "Argentocoxus is getting many talents of silver, and I'm the one who has to try and find it. If the Caledonii demand much more, we may be melting down those cups you're drinking out of."

"Oh, no. Surely not!" Dio laughed uneasily.

"No. I do but jest," Papinianus said, taking a sip of wine.

"Praefectus, forgive me," Lucius began, "but we beat the Caledonii soundly in battle. Surely they can't dictate terms?"

Papinianus regarded Lucius warily, but nodded understanding. "True, to an extent. But if we want to leave this frontier secure and open to trade when we leave, then the Caledonii can dictate terms."

"But all is favourable to Rome, in the end, no?" Dio's eyebrows raised and Papinianus looked at him over the rim of his cup.

"Yes. Of course." At that moment the emperor motioned to Papinianus from his large, heavily blanketed throne. "Metellus, the emperor will see you now."

Lucius turned to see Septimius Severus looking his way. He set his cup down, and began to make his way over, greeting Julia Maesa as he passed her.

"Praefectus," the empress' sister smiled as he went by.

When Lucius came to the bottom of the emperor's dais, he saluted in the military fashion, and bowed his head.

"Imperator," Lucius said.

"Metellus," Severus said, just before a coughing fit gripped him.

Lucius noticed that his legs were heavily wrapped beneath his robes, and that there was a smell of herbs and ointments about him, only just hidden by the scent of food and incense around them.

"Sire, thank you for inviting me," Lucius said with another bow.

"You should be here after all you have done in this war," the emperor said.

Many heads turned to listen at that, and some conversations died away. The emperor continued.

"I'm told centurion Cornelius has already informed you of what is to happen, and our reasons for it?"

Lucius could see Alerio standing guard at the back of the room. "Yes, sire. The men of Ala III Britannorum Sarmatiana have fought very hard for you. As ever, we obey your commands."

Out of the corner of his eye, Lucius could see Caracalla frowning at him. Beside him, Marcus Claudius Picus was smirking again.

"And the Votadini?" Severus asked. "Are they still loyal to Rome?"

"Yes, sire. Coilus, their chieftain, was slain in the battle… But prince Afallach, his son, now leads his people. They are, as they have ever been, loyal to the Empire."

"That is good."

"What ghastly names these Britons have," Tribune Claudius muttered to Caracalla.

Lucius looked at him briefly, but held his tongue beneath the emperor's gaze.

A loud clapping went through the room then as slaves began to carry in platters of roasted venison and boar, trout stuffed with grains, an array of delicate birds, and dormice stuffed with chopped olives.

The low tables that lay in a long row flanked by couches were filled, and everyone was ushered to their assigned couches as Papinianus and Castor helped the emperor to descend the steps to his own couch at the head of the gathering.

Lucius found himself half-way down the length of couches, beside Senator Dio, and across from Nearchus Chioticus, the Coastal Praefectus.

When everyone was settled, Severus held up his golden cup of wine, and poured a libation on the floor.

"To Jupiter, Mars, and Baal, the Light of the World. To victory, and a lasting peace!"

Everyone held up their cups, poured libations, and drank. Before long, the gathering settled into conversations, each with their neighbours.

Curious as ever, Dio asked Lucius what he had learned about the Sarmatians after having lived with them for so long.

"They are the best horsemen, and toughest warriors I have ever known," Lucius said proudly. "They're fiercely loyal, disciplined, and knowledgeable about their weapons and horses."

"They have some customs that we would call barbaric, no?"

"If you mean the taking of scalps and the heads of their enemies, yes. They do. But the effects upon the enemy's morale more than make up for it. Plus, it seems to empower them. They are the stuff of nightmares, to some."

"And to you?" Nearchus asked from across the table where he had been listening.

Lucius looked at the grizzled sea-captain whose scarred, leathery face stared back.

"They are my brothers now. I admire their bravery, their fierceness, and their humility when it comes to the Gods."

"It seems, Praefectus, that you have gone Sarmatian yourself," Julia Maesa said, leaning forward from next to the empress to see Lucius' forearms and the dragon tattoos protruding from his toga's sleeves.

A titter went about the room, and Lucius could feel himself flushing.

"Metellus is Roman, through and through, my lady," Dio said good-naturedly. "After all, his family is one of the oldest here, is it not?"

"Hmph! One of!" Marcus Claudius Picus looked with disdain at Lucius from his place beside Caracalla. He was about to say more, but Caracalla whispered something to him, and he stopped.

"By all accounts," the emperor said, "Ala III Sarmatiana has been more than a match for our enemies on this campaign."

"Our enemies who are now our allies," Caracalla said suddenly, and loudly. "It's time for peace now, Metellus, don't you think?"

Lucius felt Dio tense beside him. He could also see Julia Domna staring coolly at her son.

"Yes, Caesar," Lucius said, as calmly as he could. "My men and I have fought long and hard for that."

"As have many of us," Marcus Claudius Picus said, garnering grunts of approval from the length of the tables.

Caracalla smiled and continued. "I'm surprised to hear you so amenable to peace now, Metellus. After all, it was not that long ago that you would have lopped off Argentocoxus' head, had I not been there to stop you."

Lucius looked at the emperor who was busy with another coughing fit and did not hear.

"Lopping his head off would have been just reward for the brutality he has shown, and the many thousands of Roman lives the Caledonii have taken, sire."

"Oh, is that it? And I thought you just wanted a chieftain's head to decorate the walls of your 'Dragon's Lair'."

There was some uncomfortable laughter, and several people started staring at their plates or wine cups.

"Am I wrong, Metellus?" Caracalla pushed.

"Stop this!" Julia Domna said to her son as quietly as she could, but Caracalla ignored her as the emperor began to listen, his coughing subsided.

"Yes, sire," Lucius said.

"What?" Caracalla sat up. "Did you say I am wrong?"

"In so far that I wanted Argentocoxus' head, yes. But I did believe he should have died then and there to send the Caledonii a decisive message, and deliver a crushing defeat."

"Well, Father?" Caracalla addressed the emperor. "Did you hear that? Metellus believed Argentocoxus should be killed."

"I meant at the battle, sire," Lucius protested.

"Why kill Argentocoxus when you wanted the Boar of the Selgovae to be kept safe, a prisoner?"

Marcus Claudius had chosen his moment well.

Lucius wanted to put a knife in the man, get out of that room, and back to his men, and his family. He could see Alerio watching with concern from the shadows.

"Because, Tribune, the Boar actually fought with honour on the field, meeting us in open battle. Argentocoxus fought like a coward!"

Papinianus spoke before Caracalla or Marcus Claudius could answer. "I for one have to agree with the doubt expressed by Praefectus Metellus," he said. "I wonder if the Caledonii can be trusted long-term. Rome has been fighting them in these lands for over a hundred years. That kind of defiance may not simply vanish with the capture of one chieftain, no matter how much silver we throw at them."

"I think the Praetorian Praefectus has been poring over the fine words of his treaty late into the night," the emperor chuckled.

Caracalla ignored them and continued on at Lucius. "It's a good thing you won't be dining with us tomorrow, Metellus," Caracalla said. "With Argentocoxus and Conn Venico present, I fear you may rob them both of their heads and destroy the peace you claim to have been fighting for."

"I have no quarrel with Conn Venico," Lucius protested.

"Except that you killed his servant," Claudius added.

"A man who tried to kill me," Lucius said evenly. "Not long after one of your visits, Tribune."

"Are you accusing me of something?" Claudius hissed.

"Enough!"

The emperor's voice crushed the argument, and Lucius felt Dio's hand squeeze his arm in warning.

"Events have unfolded as the Gods intended," the emperor said. "As they were meant to. I'll hear no more belittling of our allies who will swear the Sacramentum tomorrow." He stared at Papinianus a moment, but his eyes finally rested their accusing gaze on Lucius. "I've known Lucius Metellus for a long time, and seen him grow from a youth of great wisdom and discipline, to an able commander in the field." He spoke to the room at large, covering his mouth to stifle another cough.

Lucius felt affection for the aged emperor, a man he had followed to Parthia and beyond, so many years ago. Then, something happened, a change in the emperor's voice as he now spoke directly to Lucius.

"Have you become so enamoured of war, Metellus, that you seek out argument when there is none? Don't you want some peaceful days?"

Lucius felt deflated, betrayed at the words the emperor had just spoken, and it took him a moment to rally himself.

"Yes, sire. I yearn for peace more than anything. I've fought for an age, it seems, for Rome, and for you, sire."

"So have I!" Septimius Severus raised himself up on his couch and an echo of the strong man he was leapt out of the ailing body. "We all want some peaceful days now. So, I expect you to take your year's furlough and calm the fires of war that seem to have scorched your breast."

Severus lowered himself down again. "You have been fighting this campaign longer than most here. It's time for you to rest and regroup for the next fight elsewhere in the Empire. When a man can, he should look to his family, no?"

Lucius saw Julia Domna grip her husband's hand and look from him to her son.

"Do you agree, Metellus?" Severus asked.

"Yes, sire. With all my heart," Lucius replied, bowing his head slowly.

The emperor nodded, sipped his wine, and slowly conversation began to take hold again around the couches and fringes of the room.

"This isn't good, Lucius," Dio whispered.

"No. It isn't," Lucius agreed, pushing his plate away.

The rest of the banquet passed in a blur. Lucius moved about the room to speak with some of the officers of the legions who were present, but, in truth, many avoided him.

He was too angry to care. What he needed to do was attend the Sacramentum, and then go away with his family. Far away.

"The emperor needs your support, Metellus," Papinianus said to Lucius as he stood outside beneath the peristylium, looking up at the stars that appeared now that the rain had passed. The fresh air felt good, but Lucius found it hard to enjoy with the Praetorian Prefect standing next to him.

"Sir, the emperor has my loyalty, as ever."

"That is good," Julia Domna's voice surprised Lucius on his other side. "What are you thinking about out here, Praefectus Metellus?" she asked.

"A word my wife reminded me of," Lucius said, a thin smile catching on his lips.

"What word?" the empress asked, curious as ever in such matters.

"Philotimo."

"Philotimo?" she repeated, herself smiling, but not mockingly.

"Ah, yes," Papinianus' academic side came to the fore. "The idea that your every action should be for the greater good." He sighed. "A Greek notion of honour few men put into practice. It is something more for dreamy youths, lazing in the decrepit agorae of Greece."

"And yet," Julia Domna said, "a word of great importance. Wouldn't you say, Metellus?"

"Yes, my lady." Lucius took a deep breath of the night air, and looked at them both. "I should return to my quarters so that I will be rested and prepared for the ceremony tomorrow."

"So should we all," Papinianus agreed. "You're to stand in the front ranks on your horse with the other officers."

"Yes, sir."

"Do remember the peace, Metellus," the empress said, her once-lovely face more stern than he had ever seen it.

Lucius was not sure if she meant for him to keep peace with the Caledonii, or with Caracalla. He was second-guessing everything now.

"For the good of the Empire," Lucius said, bowing to her.

Julia Domna, Papinianus, and her Syrian kinsman who had been standing in the shadows, watched Lucius take his cloak from a slave and walk along the peristylium until he exited the praetorium.

"We should keep him close," Julia Domna said.

"You think he'll be trouble?" Papinianus seemed doubtful.

"Not to us. No. To himself, perhaps. But if the truce is ever broken by the Caledonii, we will need to unleash our Dragon and his warriors upon them." The empress turned and began to walk back into the golden light of the gathering. "Hmm... Philotimo," she said beneath her breath, a whimsical smile on her lips.

Back in the small cubiculum of the barracks, Lucius barred the door and checked the room again to see that all of his weapons and armour had remained untouched, that nothing else was amiss.

He knew the Praetorians and others employed poisons and venomous animals at times. He hated being paranoid, and chided himself for being so. Still, he had seen a lot, the romantic naivety of his youth having been stamped out long ago.

The room was untouched.

Lucius removed his toga, and lit a clay lamp that sat on the table across from the cot. He stood there in his breeches, his chest bare, the cold night air poking at him. The stone floor felt cold too, but rejuvenating after the stuffiness of the banquet.

It rankled that he had basically been referred to as a war-mongering barbarian.

So ungrateful...after everything we've been through!

When he thought about it, however, it was not surprising. They were rulers, and he the descendant of an ancient family fallen from grace.

He outstretched his forearms and looked at the coiled dragons, then at the polished cuirass, helmet, and greaves on the wooden stand a few feet away.

The Dragon was there for him, in him. *Ile Anguis...*

Lucius reached into his satchel for a small bag of incense, removed a chunk, lit it, and set it on the dish beside the lamp. The smoke began to snake its way upward and out to envelop him, wrap itself about his bare neck, chest, and the crown of his head where his hair fell about his face. He knelt with his hands on the edge of the table, his eyes lingering on the lamp's flame.

"Apollo, Venus, and Epona... Please guide me on the morrow. Help me to control my anger so that my family and I can leave in peace. I...I'm tired of war...of Rome. I don't know where the path will lead us, but I do know I'm eternally grateful to you." Lucius paused, about to finish, but another thought occurred to him.

"Epona, mother of our camp, when I am away, please watch over your warriors, my brothers. May they remain my friends and allies, even in my absence."

He stood and took several deep, calming breaths before lying down on the cot, his lids heavy.

XVIII

SACRAMENTUM

'The Swearing'

The legions of Emperor Septimius Severus were turned out in force on the plains to the southwest of Horea Classis.

It was a sunny, crisp, wind-swept day, the sky bright blue with whiffs of white cloud parading quickly overhead. The waters of the Tava, where the Roman fleet and an army of eager merchants bobbed up and down, glistened in the late morning sunlight.

The air echoed with the tramp of hobnails, the moan of cornui, and the voices of the legions' centurions ordering their men into position on the plain. Tens of thousands of Roman troops stood still before a massive, pine tribunal which had been constructed between them and the combined armies of the Caledonii.

Every buckle had been polished, every leather strap oiled, and every lorica and helmet brought to a brilliant shine. They stood stalk still beneath a forest of vexilla, imagines, and other insignia, waiting, watching their former enemies where they were lined up on the opposite side of the field.

In the courtyard of the principia, Septimius Severus and Caesar Caracalla had finished with the sacrifices and auguries.

The omens were favourable.

From the east wall of the courtyard, Lucius stood watching the proceedings along with the other prefects and tribunes of the legions. He was in full armour now, as brilliant to behold as any man there that day, the dragon upon his armoured chest drawing curious looks from those who had never seen him up close.

Lucius wanted to lower his face mask, but it would have been frowned upon. Besides, he knew he deserved to be there, more so than Claudius, who stood across from him with all the other Praetorian tribunes, and Papinianus. Ulpian stood by the latter, carrying a leather satchel of scrolls that were the treaties to be signed by Argentocoxus. Also present were the empress and her sister, Senator Dio, Castor, the emperor's freedman, and other ladies of the empress' circle.

Lucius felt better armed compared to the previous night, and he sought out Alerio as they all moved onto the Via Principalis where their mounts were being held by an army of grooms. He spotted Alerio escorting the empress and Julia Maesa to a covered litter. Both ladies wore stolas and brilliant jewellery, but they were covered in furs against the chill wind.

Papinianus and the emperor mounted a covered wagon that would take them to the plain. The driver snapped the reins, and the procession made its way through the southern gate.

Praetorians marched on either side of the column and at the head, where Caracalla and the Praetorian officers rode, were the aquilifers of the various legions, carrying Rome's most sacred standards.

The golden eagles seemed to fly above the emperor, divine escorts and symbols of Jupiter's favour of the men of the Tiber.

Lucius scanned the camps as they went, and noticed only a few guards at the gates of each fort. Most of the legions were on the field, standing in formation as if a titanic game board had been laid out on the plain.

His breath caught when the legions came into sight. He had not seen that many troops in one place since following Severus into Parthia, across the Euphrates and Tigris rivers. Now they had come to this northern outpost of the Empire to accept the arms of yet another defeated foe.

When the emperor's wagon stopped, he was helped down by Papinianus and Castor, who aided him in mounting his white stallion saddled with cloth of Tyrian purple.

Severus moved slowly, the pain in his feet causing him great discomfort, but all there saw him as the glorious Imperator, resplendent in rich brown leather armour chased with golden images of Jupiter and Victory, and draped in thick flowing robes of purple and white. Severus wore a crown of golden laurels which rested snuggly on the top of his curled, gray hair. Once in the saddle, he rode to the front, before Caracalla and the Aquilae, down the centre of his legions.

A hundred cornui sounded, and the troops erupted so that their voices crashed into the Caledonii on the other side of the plain.

"Severus! Severus! Severus!"

Lucius felt a chill run up his spine at the sound, and he wondered what Argentocoxus must be thinking on the other side. Lucius and all the other officers followed Severus and Caracalla in a flurry of red, black, and white crests, and billowing cloaks.

The empress' litter followed also, all the way onto the field, and was promptly surrounded by Alerio and his Praetorians.

On the great tribunal, a large chair awaited Severus, beside which was a table.

At their morning briefing, Lucius and the others had been told they were to rein in their mounts before the tribunal, to watch the emperor and Caesar Caracalla approach Argentocoxus in the middle of the plain.

The Caledonian chieftain was to swear loyalty to Severus before all the armies, and then they would mount the tribunal to observe the surrender of the Caledonian arms and the Sacramentum of all the Caledonii warriors present.

Lucius worried that the emperor would have another coughing fit in the middle of the proceedings, but, as he and the others waited on their horses before the tribunal, he was relieved to see Severus in full control, looking every bit the emperor he was.

The cornui stopped, and silence fell over the field.

A wave of muttering could be heard from the Caledonii as the tall figures of Argentocoxus and his wife came forward. The chieftain wore a brown tunic and matching breeches, fastened with a golden belt. His cloak was pinned with a massive brooch, and about his neck was a knotted torc. Beside him, his wife, who matched his height, strode confidently beside her husband. Her long red braids swayed down her back which was covered by a long bear fur.

Lucius noticed the woman's face was not delicate, but was still beautiful, if not a victim of worry and hardship.

The Caledonii had felt the war too, but Lucius wondered if they would feel it a lot less now that peace was here, helped as well by the numerous wagons laden with silver that waited to be delivered to Argentocoxus after he swore his oath.

Lucius turned in his saddle slightly to look up at the tribunal where Papinianus stood in full Praetorian regalia, along with the empress, and her sister, and attendants. Behind them rose the Aquilae of the legions which had arrived with the emperor, and off to the side of the tribunal, sat a quiet Conn Venico and his wife, watching the proceedings silently.

Julia Domna stared out at the field, a hint of concern on her face as she watched her husband and son, along with Castor, ride toward Argentocoxus and his wife.

Severus rode out front, his white stallion prancing gently as he went.

Lucius could just hear the jingle of the golden horse harness. Then, he saw Caracalla drop back a little behind his father. The Caesar looked up and about the field, at the legions behind him.

"What's he doing?" Lucius heard Papinianus say.

As everyone watched, allies and enemies alike, Caracalla drew the spatha from his side and rode faster toward his father's back.

"Sire, look out!" Lucius yelled without thinking.

Severus, without any hint of panic or surprise, halted his horse and turned to stare at his son who sat on his horse just a few feet away, panting and wild-eyed, his sword raised above his head.

"Centurion Kasen!" Papinianus called to Alerio. "Take your men to the emperor now!" he ordered.

Lucius watched Alerio run out onto the field.

"Praefectus Metellus," the empress said from the tribunal behind Lucius. "Go with him."

Lucius kneed Lunaris, and cantered out onto the field after Alerio and his men. He did not see Tribune Claudius sneering after him from where he stood with the other officers.

"Sire!" Alerio called to the emperor as they approached, Lucius galloping up near Caracalla, ready to draw his sword.

But the emperor continued to stare his son down and waived off Lucius, Alerio, and the others. After a moment, Severus turned back to Argentocoxus who had been watching the proceedings with great interest, his wife in open-mouthed shock.

Alerio formed up his men nearby with Lucius and Castor beside him.

Caracalla sheathed his sword and reined in his mount beside his father.

Lucius could feel Caracalla's eyes burning into him, but he did not look. He was not the only one on that field to be shocked by what had just happened. The only person who did not seem surprised was the Caledonian chieftain.

"Argentocoxus, Chieftain of the Caledonii," the emperor's voice rang out surprisingly loud, strong, and clear for all to hear. "You and your people have been defeated by our legions in open battle. You have proved a mighty foe that we feel could aid Rome in maintaining the Pax Romana."

Lucius watched Argentocoxus closely as he listened to Severus' words, their eyes locked on each other.

"Do you come here today to swear loyalty to Rome, and to count you and your people among our allies?"

"I do!" Argentocoxus turned to look at his massed people, and then at the ranks of the Romans.

The emperor continued. "Do you, Argentocoxus, agree to come whenever Rome has need of you, to swear never again to make war on Rome, or any of her subjects or citizens?"

"I do!" the chieftain said again.

"And do you come, this day, to surrender your arms, and those of your people, to a power that defeated you in battle, and by so doing, live under the laws of the Roman Empire?"

There was a silence as Argentocoxus mulled over the words. His wife gripped his hand, her chin up. Before he spoke, he stared at Lucius a moment, and then looked back at the emperor.

Argentocoxus removed his long sword from his scabbard and held it up for all to see as he turned once. Then, he held it sideways in both hands and approached Severus to hand it to him.

"My people and I surrender to Rome and swear loyalty to the emperor. Let it be so!"

"Let there be peace between us!" Severus called out.

The legions cheered and chanted his name again as he and Caracalla rode to the tribunal with Argentocoxus and his wife following behind.

At that moment, waves of Caledonii walked onto the field to lay down their weapons in a great pile before the tribunal on which their chieftain stood beside the emperor of Rome in his great chair.

Lucius noticed that many of the weapons were old and ill-used, no doubt because they had not wanted to surrender their good weapons of war. He could not blame them, but it cast further doubt on the validity of the Sacramentum of the Caledonii. He glanced back at the tribunal where Papinianus had Argentocoxus make his mark on the treaty he had drawn up.

Conn Venico and his wife looked on sullenly, not trying to hide their dislike of the Caledonian.

Meanwhile, the empress and Julia Maesa spoke with Argentocoxus' wife, who towered over them and seemed to be speaking with great confidence to the two Syrian women who held much sway over the Empire.

Lucius looked at Alerio who glanced up from watching the surrender of arms.

Alerio blew out a great breath of air and Lucius knew he too was puzzling over Caracalla's worrisome actions. What would happen? Would the emperor order his son executed, and make Geta his sole heir?

Their attentions were soon drawn back to the long file of Caledonii who dropped their weapons at Rome's feet. Many of the warriors looked with hatred on Lucius, the Dragon they had been fighting for so long.

He ignored them, and let his thoughts drift beyond the imperial family, humiliated foes, and sacrilegious oaths. Instead, Lucius looked forward to rejoining his family that very night, even as the clang of dropped weapons continued to ring in his ears.

When Lucius' things were packed, and he was ready to travel with a detachment from sixth legion that was headed back to the Dragon's Lair, Alerio appeared to see him off.

"You going to be all right?" Lucius asked him as he hoisted his satchel.

"I suppose. Yes. But that was mad, no?" he whispered. Alerio's eyes were wide.

"Be careful," Lucius warned. "What's the emperor going to do with him?"

"I don't know. He's ordered Caracalla to attend him shortly. Papinianus says I'm to come too."

"Might be you who has to arrest Caesar," Lucius said, his voice dark.

"That won't go over well." Alerio grasped the handle of his gladius. "You'd better get going. The men from sixth legion are waiting for you outside the west gate."

Alerio leaned in to hug Lucius, which took the latter by surprise. "Take care, and let me know when you get there," he said.

"I will." Lucius stepped into the street in front of the barracks block. "Come and see us in the South when you get a furlough. Should be warmer down there." Lucius smiled.

"I'll do that." Alerio nodded. "You'd better get going."

Lucius raised a hand and walked down the street, his helmet under one arm and his satchel over his shoulder.

Alerio watched as his friend's red cloak disappeared around the corner, then closed the door to the cubiculum. Putting his horizontally crested helmet on his head, and tucking his vinerod beneath his right arm, he made his way to the principia where the emperor waited for his son.

When Alerio arrived at the principia and passed through the double doors into the main reception room, he found the walls lined with people, all of them silent.

All legionary legates and tribunes were present, as well as several lictors, Senator Dio, Ulpianus, Papinianus, Julia Domna, Julia Maesa, and the emperor with Castor standing behind him.

Severus was on a dais in a chair, his eyes hard, his lips pursed.

Alerio bowed to the emperor then went over to stand before the other Praetorians who were present with Papinianus. He noted the Praetorians were all men loyal to Papinianus, and not to Caracalla.

Just as Caesar's name came into his thoughts, the lictors pounded their reed bundles on the cobbled floor, and the doors opened.

Caracalla entered, his face a mixture of anger, rage, and incredulity. He was escorted by a few Praetorians, including Claudius Picus.

The emperor did not speak, but pointed at an empty table that stood on the floor between them.

When Caracalla stopped and looked up, Castor stepped from behind Severus. The freedman looked nervous, as though approaching a starved beast in the arena. He held out a gladius for all to see and, with a look at Caracalla, laid it on the table, before stepping back up onto the dais.

Then the emperor stared directly at his son. All anyone could hear was the faint flickering of the torches in the brackets on the surrounding walls.

"How dare you come onto the field before all our allies and enemies to commit such sacrilege as parricide." The emperor's voice was a low, steady, menacing rumble as he spoke. Beside him, Julia Domna watched her husband intently, having pleaded for him to spare Caracalla's life. "If you really wanted to kill me, you could have. You're certainly strong enough. And I…I am old," Severus indicated his legs, savaged by disease. He coughed for the first time as if to emphasize the point. "There is a sharpened gladius before you! If you wish to be emperor now, do not be a coward about it. Strike me now!"

To Alerio's surprise, Caracalla began to move toward the table and the sword. He moved slowly, like a wild cat readying to pounce. The leather of his cuirass with the golden Nike on it creaked as he moved. There was a sound of teeth grinding too, coming from the young Caesar's mouth as he mulled over the deed he seemed to want to do.

In the background, from another room, there came the sounds of slaves hurrying about to prepare for the banquet which was supposed to start soon – a broken dish here, a call there, the sound of a lyre being tuned. But all was silent in the room as Caracalla reached out for the gladius' handle.

"Do not shrink from your wretched deed," Severus pressed his son. "Use your own hands or, if you don't have the stomach, order Papinianus to do it for you. He will obey since you are all but emperor."

Caracalla looked to his mother for the first time, and then back to the emperor. Sweat formed on his brow, and he licked his lips as if savouring the act before him, or terrified by the thought of it.

Alerio doubted whether Papinianus beside him would actually carry out such an order, but his heart raced as he wondered what to do.

In the end, Caracalla just crossed his arms and stared back at his father.

"The mood has passed me by, Father," he said.

"The mood?" Severus stood up with difficulty, and limped down the steps with Castor at his elbow. "You should mind your moods more if you are to be an emperor without a blade in his back someday. Caligula had moods!" he shouted. "What sort of emperor would you be?"

"I would -"

Severus' blow caught Caracalla across the face, and there was a collective intake of breath around the room.

Caracalla's face turned crimson, and he breathed fiercely as he stared at his father.

"Take it, coward!" Severus said. "Use it!"

Caracalla began to reach for the blade again, but pulled his hand away at the last moment.

"Finally. Some control," the emperor said. "I could have you flayed for what you almost did."

Julia Domna was on her feet then, near to protesting.

"But," the emperor continued, "you are my son, and one of my heirs, and I'll not accept that you were such a total failure." Severus turned his back on Caracalla again, and went slowly back up to his chair. "You may live," he said without turning.

Caracalla inclined his head and began to back away.

"But!" Severus continued. "If you ever show such weakness again, I shall not be so lenient." He sat down. "We will go to the banquet and show our new allies that we are united…that our empire's rulers are strong."

"Yes, Father."

"Now…get out!" Severus yelled, his voice crashing off of the walls around them.

Caracalla spun on his heel, his long, black cloak writhing about him, and stalked off with Claudius Picus in tow.

Alerio could hear Papinianus breathe a sigh of relief as the double doors shut behind them. However, he wondered if it was truly done. When Alerio had, in the past, been on personal guard duty for the emperor, he had heard Severus criticize Marcus Aurelius for not having killed his son, Commodus. Alerio now wondered if Severus was not making the same mistake, letting his love of his son outweigh the good of the Empire.

"Centurion," Papinianus said to Alerio.

"Yes, sir."

Tell Caesar Caracalla I will come to his quarters to report on Praetorian dispatches. Between us, I don't like Tribune Claudius following him everywhere," he whispered.

"Yes, sir."

"Go now."

"Yes, sir." Alerio saluted and left the stunned room which had emptied out but for the Praetorian Prefect, Castor, the empress, and the emperor who sat beside her with his head in his hands as he coughed.

Alerio did not need to ask where Caracalla had gone. From the office of Tribune Claudius across the courtyard, he could hear Caesar raging. He stopped and pretended to make notes on the wax tablet he had tucked in his cingulum, so that he could listen.

A series of loud crashes rent the air from the office.

"Hounds of Hades! I should've done it!" Caracalla said.

"Sire," came Claudius' voice. "Had you tried just now, Papinianus' men would have cut you down."

Caracalla spat. "Let them try."

"Why didn't you, then?"

There was another thump as Caracalla slammed Claudius' armoured back against the wooden door.

"Watch yourself!" Caracalla hissed. "I made you, worm. I can unmake you."

"You would have succeeded if not for-"

"Metellus!" Caracalla said Lucius' name with such disdain, such animosity, that Alerio felt a chill cut its way up his spine.

"The man thwarts you and your followers at every turn," Claudius said.

"I know! I know! But he helped take care of that bastard Plautianus."

Claudius' voice was low and even, difficult to hear beyond the door in the courtyard.

"I know he did. But all men eventually outlive their usefulness, sire."

"And don't you forget that, Claudius."

"I don't, sire. I was, however, referring to Praefectus Metellus."

There was a silence and an echo of hobnails walking across the floor among the debris of papyrus scrolls and shattered pottery.

"He has become a problem lately," Caracalla said as he sat on a stool. "I would be emperor right now if not for him."

"The troops love you too, sire."

"They do." Another pause. "Do you still have loyal men in sixth legion, inside the Dragon's Lair?" Caracalla asked.

"Yes. I do."

"Metellus is travelling south with his family soon. Have your men follow until they cross Antoninus' wall, into the land of the Selgovae."

Alerio approached the door to Claudius' office slowly, unable to hear clearly.

Caracalla continued. "I've had enough of the Metelli. When they get that far, have your men kill them."

"All of them?" Claudius smiled.

"Yes. The whole family."

"It'll be my pleasure, sire." Claudius' eyes widened as he thought of what he would do, how he would make them suffer.

"Not you," Caracalla said sharply. "You're still not fully trusted and must be above suspicion, especially if you want our favour."

"Yes, sire," Claudius conceded. "I'll send word to my men tomorrow."

Alerio felt his anger rise, and he knocked firmly on the door through which he had been listening.

The talking within stopped abruptly, and the door opened.

"What is it?" Claudius asked as he stared down at Alerio.

"I have a message for Caesar from Papinianus."

"From Papinianus 'sir'," Claudius corrected. "You are a centurion, Cornelius, and I'm a broad-striped tribune. Therefore, I out-rank you. You address me correctly or I'll have you flogged."

"Very well, sir," Alerio said through gritted teeth.

"What does Papinianus want?" Caracalla said from where he sat.

"Sire, he would like you to attend him to discuss Praetorian troop assignments."

Caracalla frowned for a moment, then smiled. "Good idea. We need to keep things fresh, and I have a few ideas."

"Yes, sire."

"One is that you should be assigned to my personal guard to stay with me at all times while the Caledonii and Venicones are in such close proximity."

"Yes, sire," Alerio said. "When, sire?"

"Beginning tonight with the banquet. If I'm to dine with Argentocoxus and Conn Venico, I'll want guaranteed protection. After all, Praefectus Metellus believes they're not trustworthy, and who better to help me than the man who helped me toss Plautianus' body from the Palatine Hill?"

Claudius' eyes went quickly to Alerio.

The latter simply bowed, his face impassive. "I am…honoured…to serve Caesar."

"Good!" Caracalla clapped his hands. "Dismissed, Centurion. Tell Papinianus I'll come when I choose."

"Sire." Alerio saluted, and went out, his heart pounding in his chest.

"Why do you want him close, sire?" Claudius asked. "He's Papinianus' man."

"Among other things. Besides, Tribune, I have my reasons. That should be enough for you."

Caracalla stood, flinging his black cloak over his shoulders. As he passed Claudius, he slowed.

"Contact your men."

As Caracalla disappeared into the courtyard, his gruff voice giving orders to the lingering guards, Claudius spat at his back, and turned to the chaotic mess of his office.

XIX

MORS ET DEA

'Death and the Goddess'

The principia of the Dragon's Lair was quiet but for the hissing of torches in the cool Caledonian night air. A full moon lit the courtyard where two loaded wagons waited for the departure of the Dragon and his family the following day.

The base was secured for the night, the troops on night watch posted at intervals along the walls and streets of the base. Though the Caledonii had taken the Sacramentum, sworn to the treaty, Lucius, Dagon, and Brencis had thought it best to keep peace-time complacency at bay. The chaos of war with the Caledonii was still too fresh for all of them.

The men of sixth legion who were posted to the Dragon's Lair were inclined to agree.

Einion paced the courtyard in the silver light, wondering where the Gods would lead them next. They were going south again, true, but for what purpose?

For weeks, Briana had not heard Etain's dream-whispers from their mist-shrouded home of Ynis Wytrin, and then suddenly, the night before, the priestess' voice had called urgently to her.

Ravens are gathering! The road, Briana! Etain's voice had urged. *Mind the road! Danger!*

Briana had woken with a start, surprised by Etain's reaching out to her after so long, but also terrified at the words. She told Einion as soon as she woke.

That was why he now paced the courtyard, hand on the handle of his father's longsword, his eyes alert to every movement and sound.

The Dragon's family had, to his great surprise, become his own family.

Einion looked across the courtyard at the door of the Sarmatian lord's quarters where his sister had spent many a night. He smiled.

Dagon was a good and honourable man, and a great warrior.

Einion was happy for his sister, that she had come to love the man, and he to love her in return. Romantic love was perhaps not for him, he thought as he continued his circuit of the courtyard. He was content to feel the touch of women during the sacred fires of Beltane and Lughnasadh. After all, his mind was often taken up with other things, not least his sacred charge to protect Lucius' family, but also vengeance for his own family's slaying, and the reclamation of their father's lands.

Einion took a hunk of bread from the baskets in the wagon, slung a skin of wine over his shoulder, and sat on the bench outside the praefectus' quarters to keep his guard.

Lucius had been relieved to return to the Dragon's Lair two days before. The strong walls and ditches were well-manned with the warriors he trusted and would miss when he went away. However, he knew he needed to step away from war for a while for his sake, and that of his family's. The relieved embrace that Adara had given him when he dismounted outside the principia had solidified the thought in his mind.

Let them have their banquets and their tenuous peace bought for a few talents of silver, he thought.

Now, the night before their departure for the South, Lucius sat on a couch with Adara, sipping wine beside the bronze brazier, watching their children play with the toy wooden horses some of his warriors had fashioned for them.

Adara leaned in against him, her long hair against his cheek and running down along his neck and chest.

Lucius, calm and content in that moment, was struck by the duality of his life, of himself.

Only two weeks before, he had been dealing death to Rome's enemies on the Caledonian plains, and among the hills. And now, he found himself reclined with his wife as they watched their innocent children play on the floor before them.

As Adara traced the lines of his left hand with the tip of her lithe fingers, he wondered that those hands that wielded both kontus and spatha, and took the lives of countless others, were also the hands that held Phoebus and Calliope close with a love that was pure. Those blood-stained extremities were also the hands that held his wife's naked body in their deepest moments of passion and tenderness.

The long months in which Lucius had been separated from his family had hardened his resolve in battle, but they had also made him more determined to love and protect them all the more, to the death.

He wondered if perhaps the two contrasting halves of himself were not mutually exclusive. They were linked within the person he had become.

Diodorus had tried to teach Lucius about self-reconciliation in order to better oneself

Perhaps I'm only now able to understand?

He felt Adara shift.

"I wonder what Britannia will be like in the South compared to here?" she mused, breaking into Lucius' thoughts.

"Hopefully warmer," he said with a chuckle.

"Briana says it's very green with wide open fields and forests leading down to the sea."

"Baba?" Calliope said as she appeared beside him. "Will we be able to ride Twilight and Shadow more often where we are going?"

"I think so. There is no war in the South," Lucius answered, his hand touching his daughter's cheek. "Just farms and villas."

"Do we have a farm?" Phoebus asked.

"No. I don't think so. Your grandfather's map shows some stables, and a spring, but no farm buildings."

"As long as there is room for our ponies," Phoebus said.

"The ponies are sleeping now," Adara sat up, "and so should you be."

"Mama's right. We leave early tomorrow, and you need to rest."

"Yes, Baba," the children said. They kissed each of their parents and went to crawl beneath the blankets of their sleeping mats, their beds having been packed for the journey.

When Adara returned to his side from tucking the children in, Lucius poured more wine into their clay cups.

"Have you finished the letters to our parents?" he asked.

"Yes. I sent them today. I told my father a while ago that we would try to see the lands he gave to us, but that we were not sure when it would happen."

"I'm curious," Lucius admitted. "It's a new adventure for us."

"It's too bad Dagon can't travel with us," Adara said, thinking of Briana.

"He'll join us later after things are in order here. I've been assured he'll get a long furlough too. Brencis can handle things while we're gone."

Adara looked hesitantly at Lucius before speaking again. "You don't mind about Dagon and Briana?"

Lucius sighed. "It's not my place. Besides, they are good for one another. I haven't seen Dagon smile so much since I met him."

"Venus has her ways," Adara smiled.

Lucius glanced over Adara's shoulder at the two soundly-sleeping forms and smiled. He took her cup and set it on the table. Then, with surprising ease, he picked Adara up and carried her to their own sleeping mat, kissing as they went.

In the days following the banquet in which the emperor had welcomed his new allies, Argentocoxus of the Caledonii, and Conn Venico, chieftain of the Venicones, Horea Classis seemed to explode with activity.

Now that there was peace, markets seemed to pop up everywhere around Rome's fortresses and the camps of the tribes. For the merchants who plied their wares about the Empire, peace-time meant profit.

Tribal warriors walked from stall to stall expressing their curiosity over Samian dishes, spices, and other things that were foreign to them, such as the bitter olives the Romans seemed to love.

In turn, off duty troops tried to haggle with native vendors over the price of thick woolen cloaks and clothing in anticipation of another bone-chilling, Caledonian winter.

The brothels were busy as well where they had popped up in the vici around the legions' encampments once the war had ended. The cries of the dead and dying had, it seemed for now, been replaced by the groans and orgasmic cries of troops thrusting away their well-earned sestercii with whores from all areas of Rome's dominions.

Amid all of this, Alerio stood watch over the six centuries of Praetorians assigned by Papinianus to guard the wagon loads of silver and gold that were to travel with Argentocoxus on the morrow.

"Get away from there!" he ordered a group of drunk troopers from second legion as they stopped to gawk at the wagons beyond the wall of Praetorians.

"Yesss…Centurion, ssir," they saluted sloppily before stumbling on.

Alerio continued to pace, under the gaze of his troops, his horizontal crest bobbing furiously as he clenched his vinerod. In truth, he could not have cared a fig for Argentocoxus' blood-money. Alerio had tried to get away several times to get a message to Lucius about what he had overheard between

Caracalla and Claudius, but each time he had tried to slip away, Caesar gave him a new order or demanded his presence.

I have to find a way to warn Lucius!

He suspected Caracalla was monitoring all messages that went out, and if he could not take it himself, the chances of something getting through were slim indeed. From what little he knew, command at the Dragon's Lair had changed yesterday, which meant that Lucius was already on the road south with his family.

As he thought of this, Tribune Claudius came riding up to him.

"Centurion!"

"Yes, sir." Alerio saluted.

"Caesar wishes you to attend him at the praetorium. The Caledonii are arriving from their camp to meet with him and collect this." He pointed to the wagons. "Get going, Centurion, unless you want a nice long leave like your friend, Metellus?"

"What's that supposed to mean, sir?" Alerio clenched his fists and thought of tearing the man down from his horse, but he knew Claudius' men would cut him down.

"Keep your fucking mouth shut, Centurion!" Claudius hissed. "Or you'll get that flogging I promised you."

Alerio saw the men looking at them. He saluted Claudius, turned, and left for the praetorium.

"Absolutely useless," Claudius said to the group as Alerio left, several of them chuckling.

As Alerio shoved his way through the crowds to the main fortress, his mind whirled with anger and rage. He stepped onto the Via Principalis where he could see a mass of horses and guards outside the praetorium walls, awaiting their imperial masters.

He began to walk toward them.

Then, he stopped.

Gods help me, he thought. *Damn Caracalla!*

Alerio calmed himself, and felt he was seeing clearly for the first time in a long while. Promises he had made long ago in the depths of his heart on lonely nights were, he realized, far more important than oaths to power-hungry tyrants.

He turned away from the praetorium and went directly to his quarters where he removed his uniform as quickly as he could, and filled his saddle bags with clothing, some food, and a pouch of coins.

From a hook on the wall, he removed a short bow and quiver of arrows which he wrapped in his spare cloak.

Lastly, from the table, he picked up the painted image of Alene, the sides of its frame worn from where he had held it tightly in his prayers. He put it in one of the saddle bags, checked his gladius and pugio were secure about his waist, and slipped out the door.

“Oi you! What are you doing?” a voice called out from behind Alerio as he stepped into the street behind the Praetorian barracks.

Alerio turned slowly to see another centurion, a man named Flacus, one of Claudius’ men.

“Centurion Cornelius? Shouldn’t you be at the praetorium right now? Caesar wants you close.”

Alerio looked at the man and then back down the empty street. He leaned the extra cloak against the wall and moved closer, nodding to Flacus.

"You're right. I'm on my way," Alerio said.

"Well get over there! Ahh! –"

Alerio caught the man's armoured weight in his left arm as he sliced and twisted his pugio into the base of Flacus' neck, above the armour.

When the man stopped twitching, Alerio withdrew the blade and kicked open the door to his quarters. He dragged the body inside, and dropped it on the floor as the smell of loosened bowels began to permeate the air.

Alerio sheathed the pugio, picked up his belongings, and made his way to the east gate, close to where the public stables were.

It was easy to get out as the guards were more interested in stopping people coming into the fortress. Luckily, the few who stopped Alerio as he made his way out were men whom he was friendly with. They clapped him on the back and congratulated him on finally getting some time off.

"Thank you, Fortuna," he whispered as he exited the fortress and walked briskly to the stables.

After some hurried negotiation with the Gaul who was renting out the horses, Alerio managed to secure a white gelding for an extortionate amount. He saddled up, strapped on his saddle bags and bow, and led the horse the long way around the camps to avoid being seen by any Praetorians, especially Claudius.

He knew he had to get away before Argentocoxus' convoy left with the silver and a whole lot of attention. When he finally cleared the legionary camps, and joined the road heading south, Alerio kicked his mount into a gallop, eager to get as far as he could before nightfall.

They would be looking for him by now.

Gods, make me not too late, he prayed as he sped away.

It was the third day of their long journey, and Lucius had just finished packing up camp with Einion and Briana as Adara was readying the children to set out.

They were close to where the engineers had bridged the Bodotria from Caledonia into Britannia Inferior.

The previous night, they had camped in a hidden copse of trees backed by a high rock formation. There was still a lack of inns this far north, but Lucius assured Adara that once they crossed the wall, they would be able to sleep in proper beds all the way to their lands near Lindinis in the South.

As he packed up, Lucius kept thinking back to the morning they had left the Dragon's Lair – the men lined up in orderly rows, their armour and horse harness gleaming in the morning light.

Dagon, Barta, and Brencis had stood there beneath the Dragon vexillum which they would care for in Lucius' absence. They wished Lucius farewell, and hoped he enjoyed his well-earned furlough. They too would get theirs, but not as long, and not yet.

With all the good wishes and the fine turnout, Lucius could not help sensing the reluctance of his brothers to be without him. He had been at their head for a long time. He had also been their bridgehead to the Roman mind, their champion in the corridors of power.

Despite his assurances that they would be well taken care of, Lucius felt something was amiss. He prayed to Epona to watch over his men, her warriors.

When the sacrifices to Apollo, Venus, Epona, and Jupiter were finished on the altar in the principia courtyard, Lucius had turned to Dagon and Barta.

"Take care, my friends. I hope to see you soon."

"Oh, you won't keep me away," Dagon said, smiling at Briana.

Lucius laughed and turned to Barta. "Take care of our lovesick princeps, Barta."

The big Sarmatian grunted. "I should be going with you, Praefectus," he said in his deep voice.

Lucius looked him in his one, remaining eye. "I'll be fine. We'll be fine." He looked at his family. "Just you all stay alive and keep me apprised of what happens."

Barta nodded, saluted, and turned to help Adara and the children into one of the wagons.

As Lucius and Einion led the wagons, driven by Briana and Adara out of the fort, the Sarmatians watched as they rolled out with the two ponies, and the women's horses in calm tow behind the wagons.

Three riders holding draco standards saluted as Lucius passed, and then rode hard about the fort so that their dragons howled farewell to their praefectus as he went.

Lucius smiled at the memory of that farewell, and the tenderness of Barta as he had quickly wiped a tear away as he lifted Phoebus and Calliope into their wagon.

As he finished his work, Lucius heard a sudden squawk that shattered the calm, morning peace. He looked up to see three ravens perched on the rocks above them, their beaks stabbing at the carcass of a hare they had fought over.

"Let's go," Lucius said suddenly, the sight and sound of the ravens oddly disconcerting.

They packed the last things, tied the horses to the wagons, and doused the flames of their cook fire.

After two hours, the dark line of the Bodotria lay before them. It had been a long time since Lucius had been in the land of the Selgovae. He looked back at Einion and Briana where they sat side-by-side in the other wagon, and sent a silent thought to the Boar, his old enemy, for without his shade, they would not have come to Lucius.

Also, Lucius knew, the Boar's words in that dark prison at Trimontium had woken something inside, though he was not sure what exactly.

At the bridge, Lucius showed the centurion on duty his imperial pass, and was waved on without incident into the lands just north of the Wall.

"What a sight!" Lucius whistled as he gazed at the open expanse of rock and bulbous green hills in the distance. The air smelled fresher, and as they continued along Dere Street, the main Roman road south, Lucius began to relax.

Behind them, Briana and Einion's eyes followed the three ravens who still followed the wagons.

Alerio had ridden hard for two days in order to reach the Bodotria. He was exhausted, his horse near to being blown, but he pushed on as if harpies were on his heels. He did not know whom Claudius had sent after Lucius, but he knew there would be a few, that they would be mounted, and well-armed.

It was evening when he reached the bridge over the Bodotria.

"Salve, Centurion," he said to the man on duty. "Have you seen a Praefectus Metellus come through here with his family and a couple of servants?"

"Who wants to know?" the centurion crossed his arms and blocked Alerio's way.

"I'm a messenger from Horea Classis. I've got an urgent message for the praefectus. Was he here?"

The centurion looked Alerio over and then nodded, having decided he was legitimate.

"Aye, they came through here. This morning."

"Thank you, Centurion." Alerio sighed

"Must be some popular officer," the centurion added.

"Why do you say that?"

"Not long ago there were three other riders looking for him. They weren't messengers though. They had a Praetorian pass, so I let them go as they pleased."

Alerio began to panic.

"Which road did they take?"

"Straight on to the South, both groups." The centurion pointed with his vinerod, through the gate house and out the south gate to where Dere Street stretched into the distance.

Without another word, Alerio kicked his horse's flanks and sped across the bridge, leaving the centurion and his men staring after him.

As he rode, Alerio could not think of anything else but going faster and faster. The terrain was not open, but slashed here and there by low hills, forests, and outcroppings of rocks.

He found a separate set of tracks that were unaccompanied by wagon ridges. When he reined in to look at them, he saw that they diverged from the main road to run on a parallel track.

He cursed the choice, for if he was wrong about the others, if they were not the assassins' tracks, he could be too late.

"You'll be too late if you debate it now!" he told himself, closing his eyes. "Gods guide me… Which way?"

He chose to go right.

It would be slow going, but with night falling, he thought he might just overrun the killers.

After a long night, when the darkness was finally cracked by the first rays of sunlight, Alerio was able to see the path ahead. Twice during the night he had nearly ridden off a precipice, but the gelding had the sense to ignore its rider's orders at the right time.

Alerio cupped his hand over his eyes to see a group of ravens in the sky. When he followed them downward, he spotted the slowly moving wagons and horses on the road.

"Lucius…" he sighed. "Made it."

He heard a horse whinny then, down the path he had been taking, and his heart jumped to see that the path was now sloping down to meet the Roman road on the plain below.

Alerio tied his horse to a tree and unrolled his bow and quiver from the back.

Gods, don't let me fail.

He began to sneak along the path, hoping surprise would be better so that he could overcome the assassins before they made their move.

With an arrow nocked on the string of his bow, he went along the path until he saw three horses tied to a log. The riders were not to be seen.

He moved past the horses where they clipped at the grass around the base of some of the trees.

Two men were crouched behind a boulder, watching the wagon roll along at a distance that was too far to shoot.

Where's the third? Alerio scanned the area quickly. He could see the two assassins readying themselves to run out and attack.

Each had hunting bows with deadly, barbed arrows, and he shuddered to think what those would do to his friends.

He approached slowly, drawing the string back and sighting along the shaft. Then, he loosed.

His arrow took one of the men in the back of the neck, slamming his face into the rock in a shower of blood. The other man whirled around before Alerio could string another arrow and fired.

Alerio felt his leg swept from under him as he ran and pitched forward with a cry as searing pain rent the bone of his thigh. When he stopped rolling he felt a kick to his head. He struggled to draw his gladius and swept it up blindly, just in time for the tip to slash the second man's chin.

With the few seconds that bought him, Alerio stabbed at the man's chest and threw his weight into it, pinning the man against the body of his companion.

Alerio cried out as the arrow shaft in his leg caught on his victim's cloak. He stood shaking, looking to see if the wagons had stopped or if they were moving on.

He forgot about the third assassin, and so, when the pain of a pugio blade in his back slashed through his senses, Alerio's eyes went wide.

Strong hands turned him and held him fast, and a gritty voice stinking of garlic suffocated him.

"Nice try, but they're all going to die anyway," the voice said.

Alerio gaped at the hateful eyes and mangled beard of the assassin.

Gods help me, he prayed.

With his last bit of strength, Alerio's forehead sprung forward to crush the man's nose, and he plunged his pugio into his guts, twisting violently. With a cry of pain, he withdrew the blade, and drove it into his neck, uncaring of the second blade that stuck out of his own side.

Alerio fell forward to the rock face, stumbling over the bodies of the men he had just killed.

His eyes were clouding over as he pulled the blade out of his side and searched the road for the Metelli. He tried to cry out, but he could not as his breath began to leave him.

Pressing his pulsing wound so that the blood flowed out between his fingers, Alerio slumped back against the rock to sit down in the sun, facing the distant road and the plain. His eyes watched the wagons continue their progress unmolested.

The ravens that had been circling suddenly broke off and came toward him. As they landed before him, they morphed into the form of a tall woman whose black hair hung in oily, matted tangles, and whose skin was as pale as death.

She laughed at him, but he could tell she was angry.

"You can't hurt them..." he muttered, spitting blood at her.

The Morrigan raised a clawed hand to strike him, but a flash of light drove her away.

Alerio's golden eyes widened, and his pupils dilated as he watched another approach.

She was barefoot, dressed in a white stola that flowed like lovely clouds, and crowned with golden hair.

As she came toward him, spring flowers sprouted from the grass at her feet.

Alerio smiled as she knelt before him.

"Alene..."

Yes, my love.

"I've...missed...you."

And I you...so much.

Alerio looked down the road to where Lucius, Adara, and the children disappeared from sight.

"I kept my promise," he said. "They're...safe..."

Yes, my love. They are.

Her hand stretched out to caress his bloody cheek, and he reached out to her, the blood now flowing freely from his side onto the grass and dirt.

You can come with me now, she said, without a trace of sadness. *It is time.*

"Yes..." Alerio sighed, relieved. He smiled. "I will follow you...my...love..."

As his eyes closed, warmth and light returned, and they left the pain and blood behind, walking away in golden fields beneath an ever warming sun.

EPILOGUS

The journey south filled the Metelli and their companions with optimism as they travelled toward their new life.

It didn't matter that it might all be fleeting. Lucius had come to realize that nothing lasted forever, and so, rather than let that thought consume him, he made a conscious effort to seize every opportunity the Gods put before him now. He knew he owed that and much more to the family he had come so close to losing as he groped in the darkness of war in Caledonia.

As he flicked the reins of their wagon team, he looked ahead to a blue sky that stretched from one end of the horizon to the other, felt the heat of Apollo's sun on his face, and reveled in the laughter of his wife and daughter as they took their turn exercising their mounts along the side of the road.

The journey had been long thus far, his nights filled with nightmarish visions that he hoped he could forget.

Briana had told him the Gods were warning him of something, but he always woke from his sleep, unable, or unwilling to carry on with the dreams. "Those are the dreams you must endure most and see through to the end," she had said.

Thankfully, the last couple of nights had been better, and so, as they passed Lindum and turned off of Ermine Street onto the Fosse Way to the southwest, Lucius began to enjoy himself. The shades of those awful dreams were pushed to the back of his mind for now.

As Briana and Einion rode with Adara and Calliope, Phoebus sat beside his father on the bench, silent, his young eyes taking in the vast countryside before them.

After several miles on the Fosse Way, the boy turned to his father.

"Baba?"

"Yes," Lucius answered, smiling at his son and ruffling his hair. He had not tired of hearing his children call him, for he felt as though he had not heard that music for an age. "What are you thinking about?"

"Well…" Phoebus looked away for a moment, suddenly unable to look at his father.

The shame began to creep up on Lucius again. He could hear his angry voice ringing in his ears and it took all he had to block it out, like the sounds of war the night after a battle.

Then Phoebus spoke, his courage plucked up.

"I was curious about a word Mama said the night that…I mean…when you…"

"That night I was not myself?" Lucius finished, hating that part of himself.

"Yes."

"What word, was it?"

"I think it was…Philoti?"

"Philotimo?"

"Yes. That's it!" Phoebus seemed happy that part was done, his curiosity overcoming the dread of asking.

My children should never dread speaking to me, Lucius told himself.

"What does that mean?" Phoebus continued. "It's not Latin, is it?"

"No," Lucius smiled, a little sadly. "It's not. It's a Greek word." He flicked the reins again and urged the team up a slope. The click of the horses' hooves behind them echoed on the paving slabs. "Before I answer you, I need to tell you about a lesson my tutor gave me when I was a little older than you."

"You mean your Greek tutor, Diodorus?"

"Yes. Oftentimes, he would take me outside into the Forum for my lessons, or the markets, the temples and other places about Rome. He wanted me to see and learn from the world around me. Well, the night before this particular lesson, there was a terrible storm. The Gods, everyone said, were very angry and they had lashed the city all through the night."

He could still hear the crack of Jupiter's thunder over the Seven Hills, and he flinched at the memory of screaming throughout the night, the crackle of fires, the hooting of thieves as they plundered the Subura, and the ravings of people driven mad by the Gods' wrath.

"What was your lesson about?" Phoebus asked.

"When day finally dawned, life seemed to come back into the world. People who had been terrified the night before emerged from their homes to help others, or to clean up the detritus of the previous night."

"Weren't they scared to come out after?"

"Surely. I know I was," Lucius answered. "But Diodorus was adamant that we go out for our lesson. He told me that sometimes the Gods threaten us so that we see the world differently. So, we sat on the steps of the Temple of Antoninus and Faustina in the Forum to watch people sweeping, picking up things, and caring for the wounded. Many were made to feel smaller after so much violence, after having lost their businesses or homes. Many had to start all over."

"And that's probably not easy," Phoebus observed.

"No. It's not. But it's important to do so. Diodorus wanted me to look past all the rubbish littering the streets to the hard work that was going on. He wanted me to think about the action people were taking, whether it was a Suburan peasant cleaning his stoop, or the emperor himself who instituted a program to help the citizens of Rome get back on their feet."

"Everyone must have been very busy."

"Well, not everyone, but many were. Some people just don't care about others or even themselves. But those who took action made the world a better place that day. Only through action could good come out of the chaos. It was the people who had the eyes, mind, and heart to see what was needed who improved things. Do you understand?"

"I think so."

"Rome became better because of the goodness people had put into it, even after so much destruction and fear."

The boy nodded, and Lucius wondered if he wasn't complicating things more. Being the teacher was new to him. It was strange, but he had been mulling over those very same events on the journey south, as he lost himself in thought.

Was I ever so young and full of wonder? he thought as he looked sideways at his son and nudged him playfully.

"So…Philotimo," Lucius continued, and Phoebus perked up and repeated the word.

"Philotimo. You said it is a Greek word?"

"Yes. And Diodorus told me that there is no word like it in Latin, Hebrew, Aramaic, Egyptian, or any other language. Only Greek."

"What does it mean?"

"It refers to the love of honour."

"Like honour on the battlefield?" Phoebus asked.

"Not exactly, though that can be a part of it. Philotimo refers to how you live. It's the honour and goodness you insert into your actions and decisions the length of your days."

"I'm not sure I understand." Phoebus slouched on the bench, a quizzical look on his face, and Lucius thought him a mirror image of his younger self.

"Philotimo is, at it its heart, the reason for a person's decisions or actions. It is living with goodness and honourable intent." Lucius waited and watched, then asked, "Why might a good man go to war?"

"To defend what he loves?"

"Yes," Lucius answered. He was secretly very proud, for his own answer when Diodorus had put the question to him referred more to plunder and wealth. His son was better than him, and that was a relief.

Phoebus continued. "A man should go to war to because he loves his country and wants to defend it."

"Yes. And what else?"

"To defend a weaker being? Someone who has done nothing wrong."

"Good. You see, Philotimo is not about personal glory or reward. It is about the greater good of your family, your city, your society, and your world. It is true civility. The more people who act with Philotimo in their hearts, the better our world will be."

Lucius felt like a hypocrite as he spoke, but he knew the importance of this lesson for both of them.

He pointed at the horizon, the world before them. "Think about the world you've seen on your travels to Britannia. Think of everyone, including yourself. Did everyone act with Philotimo?"

"No."

"Do you think everyone with Philotimo is remembered, or showered with honours?"

"No."

"It's true. Most are forgotten, but it is the good that arises from their actions that remains in this world. And that is pleasing to the Gods."

The wind picked up then, and white clouds skittered across the vast sky, casting shadows on the green hills that swept southward.

"By acting with honour and good intent…with Philotimo...we do not only elevate ourselves, but also, and perhaps more importantly, the people around us - our families, our friends and colleagues, and our brothers-in-arms."

Phoebus nodded, but hung his head.

"What is wrong, my boy?" Lucius asked.

"Did you forget the word, Baba? Did you forget Philotimo?"

The words were like a gladius through the heart, but Lucius knew that his son was right, that it took great courage to say what he had just said, especially after Lucius' betrayal.

He nodded silently then stopped the wagon and turned to his son. He looked him in the eyes and for a moment was worried Phoebus would recoil in fear.

But the boy did not look fearful. He stared back at his father, and his young hand reached out and grabbed Lucius' scarred fist.

"I'm so sorry, Phoebus. Yes, I did forget Philotimo. Your mama was right." He looked down at their hands, the one large and battle-worn, the other young and vulnerable. "But I swear to you and the Gods of our ancestors that I will never again forget that word and what it means. I love you, my son. With all my heart and soul, I do." Lucius gripped Phoebus and pulled him close to his chest, his young face buried in the black wool of his cloak. He felt the thinly-muscled arms grip him tightly.

When Phoebus sat straight again, wiping his eyes quickly, he seemed to sit a little taller, as if the question had been weighing him down for weeks.

"And what do you fight for, Baba?" he asked.

Without hesitating, Lucius answered, "I fight for you, for Calliope, and for Mama. I fight for the world that surrounds you."

"And that is Rome?"

Lucius did not answer this time. He nodded to Einion who had stopped beside them to see if all was well, and the wagon lurched forward once more.

Phoebus reached out and held the handle of Lucius' sword then, felt the thick grip, and gazed at the dragons on the hilt.

"What happens when we fail, Baba? When we forget Philotimo?"

Lucius put his hand on his son's shoulder and squeezed gently.

"When we fall, Phoebus, we have to pick ourselves back up again…and again…and again. We never give up on goodness or hope. If we preserve that in ourselves, then the Gods will forever be our allies."

Phoebus nodded, then smiled, and Lucius too felt an enormous weight lifted from his shoulders. He watched Adara, Briana, and Calliope racing ahead on their mounts toward the sun and sent a prayer up to his gods.

"I wonder what our new home will be like," Phoebus said, wrapping his cloak about his shoulders and leaning back, the smile still playing about his mouth.

"We're together," Lucius said. "Whatever awaits us will be a blessing."

The End

Thank you for reading!

Did you enjoy *Warriors of Epona*? Here is what you can do next.

If you enjoyed this adventure with Lucius Metellus Anguis, and if you have a minute to spare, please post a short review on the web page where you purchased the book.

Reviews are a wonderful way for new readers to find this series of books and your help in spreading the word is greatly appreciated.

The story continues in *Isle of the Blessed*, and the next Eagles and Dragons novel will be coming soon, so be sure to sign-up for e-mail updates at:

https://eaglesanddragonspublishing.com/newsletter-join-the-legions/

Newsletter subscribers get a FREE BOOK, and first access to new releases, special offers, and much more!

To read more about the history, people and places featured in this book, check out our blog series *The World of Warriors of Epona* at the following link:

https://eaglesanddragonspublishing.com/the-world-of-warriors-of-epona/

Become a Patron of Eagles and Dragons Publishing!

If you enjoy the books that Eagles and Dragons Publishing puts out, our blogs about history, mythology, and archaeology, our video tours of historic sites and more, then you should consider becoming an official patron.

We love our regular visitors to the website, and of course our wonderful newsletter subscribers, but we want to offer more to our 'super fans', those readers and history-lovers who enjoy everything we do and create.

You can become a patron for as little as $1 per month. For your support, you will also get loads of fantastic rewards as tokens of our appreciation.

If you are interested, just visit the website below to go to the Eagles and Dragons Publishing Patreon page to watch the introductory video and check out the patronage levels and exciting rewards.

https://www.patreon.com/EaglesandDragonsPublishing

Join us for an exciting future as we bring the past to life!

AUTHOR'S NOTE

Quite a bit of time elapsed from when I finished *Killing the Hydra* and then started *Warriors of Epona*, so much so that I had to go back over my research and get to know the characters all over again.

The funny thing is that, because I had spent so much time with Lucius Metellus and his family, when I started writing again, it was like catching up with old friends – we picked up right where we left off, without awkwardness, but with a genuine sense of familiarity.

However, I had aged and changed with the experiences life had thrown at me, as had my characters, and so it was with a fresh perspective that I set out on this new campaign. And make no mistake, writing an historical novel is a campaign, complete with preparation, strategies, logistics and much more!

Readers will notice the absence of some of the secondary characters from the previous novels, but also the larger role played by others such as Dagon and Barta of the Sarmatian contingent. I loved writing about the Sarmatians and their culture in *Killing the Hydra*, and had been looking forward to exploring it further in this book.

I first came across the Sarmatians in my research for my Masters dissertation several years ago in relation to Roman cavalry auxiliaries active in Britain and elsewhere, so it was a nice fit to make them a part of Severus' Caledonian campaign. They are a fascinating people! To read more about them, check out part four of *The World of Killing the Hydra* blog series on the Eagles and Dragons Publishing website.

Starting a new novel in a new setting also allows a writer to introduce some new characters. This is something I really enjoyed. The Druid, Weylyn, the priestess, Etain, and the Christian priest, Father Gilmore, were a joy to write, and helped me to explore the hearts and minds of some very different characters. We've only met them briefly in *Warriors of Epona*, but they will be back in the next book.

I have to say that Briana and Einion are my favourite new characters in this book, and they, along with Weylyn, Etain, and Father Gilmore, are the first steps of this series into the Celtic world which I have always been drawn to.

As the title of this book implies, new gods have been thrown into the mix too, highlighting the emerging Celtic theme.

Epona was originally a Celtic horse goddess, but she came to be worshiped by Romans as well. This was a truly unique circumstance for a Celtic goddess, for worship of such deities was usually local in nature. However, the worship of Epona spread across the Roman Empire, especially among cavalrymen.

I have always been drawn to Epona since I read the *Mabinogion*, the compilation of early Welsh tales, or 'Triads'. In the tale *Pwyll, Prince of Dyfed* (my favourite!), the otherworldly woman, Rhiannon, is a reflection of the Goddess Epona, riding a brilliant white horse, followed by three white, red-eared hounds, and of course the birds of Rhiannon. In *Warriors of Epona*, I chose to portray the goddess who is Lucius' new protector as Rhiannon is portrayed in the Welsh Triads. If you have never read *Pwyll, Prince of Dyfed*, I highly recommend it as it beautifully portrays some of the strongest archetypes of ancient Celtic myth.

Of course, I had to have a dark goddess to pit against Epona in this story, someone to whom the Caledonii could turn in their fight against Rome. The Morrigan fit this perfectly, and though I took some liberties in having the Caledonii worship her so strongly, I think it was suitable. Whereas Epona is brilliant and white, the Morrigan is traditionally a dark goddess, followed by carrion crows and representing doom and death in battle.

I first came across the Morrigan in my Celtic studies courses when reading the Irish epic the *Táin Bó Cuailnge* in which even the fearless hero, Cú Chulainn, thinks twice about insulting her. She is a nightmarish force to be dealt with in mythology.

The locales in *Warriors of Epona* are, of course, places which I have researched, visited, and lived in or near. When I was doing research for *Children of Apollo*, and reading up on the campaigns of Septimius Severus, I knew Lucius' path would eventually lead him to Britannia, and I knew which places I wanted to feature.

Ynis Wytrin is, of course, Glastonbury, in Somerset, England. For those of you who don't know it, Glastonbury is a very special place. Having lived there myself for several years, I got to know it intimately, to cherish the gentle curve of Wearyall Hill, where Weylyn and Morvran dock their boat, and where archaeologists found the remains of an ancient dock. I enjoyed my weekly walks up the spine of the Tor to watch the crows dive in the wind, and marvel at the setting sun over the Somerset levels.

I even had to find alternate routes in and out of town when the dykes and rivers broke their banks and Avalon flooded once more. Many only think of Glastonbury as a medieval place of legend, but settlement here is far older than that. It was a sacred pagan site for ages, the Tor believed to be a gateway to Annwn, the Celtic Otherworld. The first Christian settlement and church in Britain was said to have been established there by Joseph of Arimathea, and his Christian followers lived peacefully with the pagan Britons in that place. This peaceful co-existence of faiths is something I tried to explore in *Warriors of Epona*, for it is one of the things that made Glastonbury so special.

As far as Roman sites in *Warriors of Epona*, there are of course too many to go into detail here – Hadrian's Wall and Coria will be familiar to many, as will Eburacum (York), and parts of the Antonine Wall stretching roughly between the Forth and Clyde estuaries in Scotland.

Newstead, or rather Trimontium, is a place that is not usually on the beaten tourist path. It is located near Melrose, in the Scottish Borders, north of Hadrian's Wall. Again, my Masters research led me there and I found it to be a magnificent site. The remains of the legionary base are no longer there, but the outlines of it can be seen on aerial photographs. The site is marked by a large Roman-style stone with an inscription.

Trimontium was first built by the troops of Agricola in the first century A.D. and then later rebuilt during Severus's campaign into Caledonia. The site has yielded some amazing artifacts, including horse harness and ornate cavalry helmets. If you ever go to Trimontium, be sure to walk to the top of

Eildon Hill North (one of the three peaks). The view is magnificent and it is, of course, where Lucius climbs at night in *Warriors of Epona*, when he succumbs to the stresses of his command.

Probably the most interesting sites that are featured in this novel, however, are part of what has become known as the Gask Ridge (a modern name I decided to use in the novel). Around the time I began research for *Warriors of Epona*, some ground breaking work on the Gask Ridge frontier came to light.

A fellow-historian and good friend of mine who worked on various digs and field walking expeditions along the Gask Ridge, gave me a copy of *Rome's First Frontier: The Flavian Occupation of Northern Scotland* by B. Hoffman and D.J. Woolliscroft.

The timing couldn't have been more perfect.

I read the book with great interest and discovered that the Gask Ridge was actually the oldest Roman defensive frontier in Britain. Basically, it comprised a chain of fortlets, watchtowers, and signal stations stretching from Drumquhassle and Camelon along the Antonine Wall, diagonally along the border of Fife, northeast all the way to Stracathro in Angus, north of the Tay estuary. It also included the legionary fortress of Inchtuthil.

The Gask Ridge was built A.D. 70-80, and was basically intended to cut off the Highlands from the lowlands to the East. Many of the forts and other structures were re-used during the Antonine period as well as the Severan invasion of Caledonia.

In *Warriors of Epona*, I have tried to focus on Gask Ridge sites where the archaeological finds have indicated activity during the Severan campaign of the early third century A.D. – sites such as Bertha, Carpow, Doune and Strageath. With some other sites, such as Ardoch and Alauna, I took some liberties. However, just because Severan finds have not been recovered from all Gask Ridge sites, does not necessarily mean they were not used. The Ridge was an important defensive network. The Romans knew a good site when they saw it, and made use of it. The Severan campaign was big, and so it would not be surprising if most, if not all, the sites were re-used at that time. From my time in St. Andrews, I remember field walking in the area and being blown away by the beauty of that landscape with the Highlands looming in the distance.

The major legionary base of Carpow, along the Tay in Perth and Kinross, was the main military and naval base for the Severan invasion of Scotland. In *Warriors of Epona*, it is known as 'Horea Classis', a name from an eighth century text of place names that some believe refers to the fort at Carpow.

If anyone would like to read more about the Gask Ridge frontier, be sure to check out the book mentioned above, or visit the website of the Roman Gask Project at: www.theromangaskproject.org.

As ever, Cassius Dio's *Roman History* has been my primary source of choice for the period – as I've mentioned before, the contemporary sources for this period of Rome's history are few and far between. Thankfully, Dio is as interesting as ever when it comes to the Severan invasion of Caledonia.

Dio does indeed write about the Caledonian leader, Argentocoxus, in his history, as well as the incident in which Caracalla, drew his sword and made to kill his father during the treaty ceremony with the Caledonians. Yes, that did happen, according to Dio. I don't know if Dio was actually on the campaign with Severus, so I took some poetic licence in placing him there since he wrote an account of the events of the Caledonian campaign. His insights into the personalities of the imperial court helped to add some flavour to the story. To read the text for Cassius Dio, you can download a free copy from the Project Gutenberg website.

As Cassius Dio and other ancient writers often show us, the history of the Roman Empire is always entertaining!

Thank you for reading.

Adam Alexander Haviaras
Toronto, December 2016

Glossary

aedes – a temple; sometimes a room

aedituus – a keeper of a temple

aestivus – relating to summer; a summer camp or pasture

agora – Greek word for the central gathering place of a city or settlement

ala – an auxiliary cavalry unit

amita – an aunt

amphitheatre – an oval or round arena where people enjoyed gladiatorial combat and other spectacles

anguis – a dragon, serpent or hydra; also used to refer to the 'Draco' constellation

angusticlavius – 'narrow stripe' on a tunic; Lucius Metellus Anguis is a *tribunus angusticlavius*

apodyterium – the changing room of a bath house

aquila – a legion's eagle standard which was made of gold during the Principate

aquilifer – senior standard bearer in a Roman legion who carried the legion's eagle

ara – an altar

armilla – an arm band that served as a military decoration

augur – a priest who observes natural occurrences to determine if omens are good or bad; a soothsayer

aureus – a Roman gold coin; worth twenty-five silver *denarii*

auriga – a charioteer

ballista – an ancient missile-firing weapon that fired either heavy 'bolts' or rocks

bireme – a galley with two banks of oars on either side

bracae – knee or full-length breeches originally worn by barbarians but adopted by the Romans

caldarium – the 'hot' room of a bath house; from the Latin *calidus*

caligae – military shoes or boots with or without hobnail soles

cardo – a hinge-point or central, north-south thoroughfare in a fort or settlement, the *cardo maximus*

castrum – a Roman fort

cataphract – a heavy cavalryman; both horse and rider were armoured

cena - the principal, afternoon meal of the Romans

chiton – a long woollen tunic of Greek fashion

chryselephantine – ancient Greek sculptural medium using gold and ivory; used for cult statues

civica – relating to 'civic'; the civic crown was awarded to one who saved a Roman citizen in war

civitas – a settlement or commonwealth; an administrative centre in tribal areas of the Empire

clepsydra – a water clock

cognomen – the surname of a Roman which distinguished the branch of a *gens*

collegia – an association or guild; e.g. *collegium pontificum* means 'college of priests'

colonia – a colony; also used for a farm or estate

consul – an honorary position in the Empire; during the Republic they presided over the Senate

contubernium – a military unit of ten men within a century who shared a tent

contus – a long cavalry spear

cornicen – the horn blower in a legion

cornu – a curved military horn

cornucopia – the horn of plenty

corona – a crown; often used as a military decoration

cubiculum – a bedchamber

curule – refers to the chair upon which Roman magistrates would sit (e.g. *curule aedile*)

decumanus – refers to the tenth; the *decumanus maximus* ran east to west in a Roman fort or city

denarius – A Roman silver coin; worth one hundred brass *sestertii*
dignitas – a Roman's worth, honour and reputation
domus – a home or house
draco – a military standard in the shape of a dragon's head first used by Sarmatians and adopted by Rome
draconarius – a military standard bearer who held the draco

eques – a horseman or rider
equites – cavalry; of the order of knights in ancient Rome

fabrica – a workshop
fabula – an untrue or mythical story; a play or drama
familia – a Roman's household, including slaves
flammeum – a flame-coloured bridal veil
forum – an open square or marketplace; also a place of public business (e.g. the *Forum Romanum*)
fossa – a ditch or trench; a part of defensive earthworks
frigidarium – the 'cold room' of a bath house; a cold plunge pool
funeraticia – from *funereus* for funeral; the *collegia funeraticia* assured all received decent burial

garum – a fish sauce that was very popular in the Roman world
gladius – a Roman short sword
gorgon – a terrifying visage of a woman with snakes for hair; also known as Medusa
greaves – armoured shin and knee guards worn by high-ranking officers
groma – a surveying instrument; used for accurately marking out towns, marching camps and forts etc.

hasta – a spear or javelin
horreum – a granary
hydraulis – a water organ

hypocaust – area beneath a floor in a home or bath house that is heated by a furnace

imperator – a commander or leader; commander-in-chief
insula – a block of flats leased to the poor
intervallum – the space between two palisades
itinere – a road or itinerary; the journey

lanista – a gladiator trainer
lemure – a ghost
libellus – a little book or diary
lituus – the curved staff or wand of an augur; also a cavalry trumpet
lorica – body armour; can be made of mail, scales or metal strips; can also refer to a cuirass
lustratio – a ritual purification, usually involving a sacrifice

manica – handcuffs; also refers to the long sleeves of a tunic
mansio – an inn or hostel
marita – wife
maritus – husband
matertera – a maternal aunt
maximus – meaning great or 'of greatness'
medicus – a Roman doctor
missum – used as a call for mercy by the crowd for a gladiator who had fought bravely
murmillo – a heavily armed gladiator with a helmet, shield and sword

nomen – the *gens* of a family (as opposed to *cognomen* which was the specific branch of a wider *gens*)
nones – the fifth day of every month in the Roman calendar
novendialis – refers to the ninth day
nutrix – a wet-nurse or foster mother
nymphaeum – a pool, fountain or other monument dedicated to the nymphs

officium – an official employment; also a sense of duty or respect

onager – a powerful catapult used by the Romans; named after a wild ass because of its kick

optio – the officer beneath a centurion; second-in-command within a century

palaestra – the open space of a gymnasium where wrestling, boxing and other such events were practiced

palliatus – indicating someone clad in a *pallium* (a sort of mantle of coverlet)

pancration – a no-holds-barred sport that combined wrestling and boxing

parentalis – of parents or ancestors; (e.g. *Parentalia* was a festival in honour of the dead)

parma – a small, round shield often used by light-armed troops; also referred to as *parmula*

pater – a father

pax – peace; a state of peace as opposed to war

peregrinus – a strange or foreign person or thing

peristylum – a peristyle; a colonnade around a building; can be inside or outside of a building or home

phalerae – decorative medals or discs worn by centurions or other officers on the chest

pilum – a heavy javelin used by Roman legionaries

plebeius – of the plebeian class or the people

pontifex – a Roman high priest

popa – a junior priest or temple servant

praefectus – a high ranking Roman officer, often leading auxiliary forces

primus pilus – the senior centurion of a legion who commanded the first cohort

pronaos – the porch or entrance to a building such as a temple

protome – an adornment on a work of art, usually a frontal view of an animal

pteruges – protective leather straps used on armour; often a leather skirt for officers
pugio – a dagger

quadriga – a four-horse chariot
quingeniary ala – an auxiliary force of about five hundred men commanded by a *praefectus*
quinqueremis – a ship with five banks of oars

retiarius – a gladiator who fights with a net and trident
rosemarinus – the herb rosemary
rusticus – of the country; e.g. a *villa rustica* was a country villa

sacrum – sacred or holy; e.g. the *via sacra* or 'sacred way'
schola – a place of learning and learned discussion
scutum – the large, rectangular, curved shield of a legionary
secutor – a gladiator armed with a sword and shield; often pitted against a *retiarius*
sestertius – a Roman silver coin worth a quarter *denarius*
sica – a type of dagger
signum – a military standard or banner
signifer – a military standard bearer
spatha – an auxiliary trooper's long sword; normally used by cavalry because of its longer reach
spina – the ornamented, central median in stadiums such as the Circus Maximus in Rome
stadium – a measure of length approximately 607 feet; also refers to a race course
stibium – *antimony*, which was used for dyeing eyebrows by women in the ancient world
stoa – a columned, public walkway or portico for public use; often used by merchants to sell their wares
stola – a long outer garment worn by Roman women
strigilis – a curved scraper used at the baths to remove oil and grime from the skin

taberna – an inn or tavern
tabula – a Roman board game similar to backgammon; also a writing-tablet for keeping records
tepidarium – the 'warm room' of a bath house
tessera – a piece of mosaic paving; a die for playing; also a small wooden plaque
testudo – a tortoise formation created by troops' interlocking shields
thraex – a gladiator in Thracian armour
titulus – a title of honour or honourable designation
torques – also 'torc'; a neck band worn by Celtic peoples and adopted by Rome as a military decoration
trepidatio – trepidation, anxiety or alarm
tribunus – a senior officer in an imperial legion; there were six per legion, each commanding a cohort
triclinium – a dining room
tunica – a sleeved garment worn by both men and women

ustrinum – the site of a funeral pyre

vallum – an earthen wall or rampart with a palisade
veterinarius – a veterinary surgeon in the Roman army
vexillarius – a Roman standard bearer who carried the *vexillum* for each unit
vexillum – a standard carried in each unit of the Roman army
vicus – a settlement of civilians living outside a Roman fort (plural is *vici*)
vigiles – Roman firemen; literally 'watchmen'
vitis – the twisted 'vinerod' of a Roman centurion; a centurion's emblem of office
vittae – a ribbon or band

ACKNOWLEDGEMENTS

Whenever I get ready to put a new novel out into the world and try to recollect all the people who helped in its creation, it never ceases to amaze me how very many people did help, and how far back in time that help originates.

The genesis of *Warriors of Epona* can be traced back into the misty memories of my youth, and that is why I dedicated this book to my parents.

They planted the seeds of the book not only with the stories of knights on horseback that they told me when I was young, but also with the gift of my first sword and set of armour. I remember a Christmas when I was around five years old. My parents had given me and my brother each a set of ornate plastic armour which included a sword and shield, crested helmet, breastplate and battle axe. It was magical and familiar all at once, as if my story-induced dreams had become a reality.

At once, my brother and I armed ourselves and clashed like the titans we thought we were. The swords didn't last long, so fierce were our battles, but the memory and feeling of a sword in my hand has lasted to this day and been sustained through years of fencing practice, re-enactments, and the collection of full-size replicas.

My parents also allowed me to take horseback riding when I was old enough, and that completed the picture in my mind's eye, for there is nothing quite like sitting atop a horse and charging across an open field. All of these memories and experiences given to me, and encouraged by, my parents went to feeding the creation of this novel.

As always, the deepest of thanks goes to my wife and daughters who are as much a part of this writing journey as I am, for they inspire and encourage me at every turn. They give me the perspective I need to write of family and of the true meaning of life and love and what is truly important in this world that seems to be caught in a never-ending, chaotic race. I am a better man for the peace and perspective that they give to me.

When it comes to the new locales visited in this book, an immense debt is owed to my good friend and fellow historian, Andrew Fenwick of Dundee. When I set out doing the research for *Warriors of Epona*, it was Andrew who introduced me to the cutting edge research being carried out on the Gask Ridge. This book is much better off for Andrew's contribution and his impassioned descriptions of many of the forts included in the story.

As ever, my sincere thanks goes to the learned Kostis Diassitis of Athens for his help in reviewing my Latin translations and helping me to navigate the perilous realm of cases and declensions. Without his help, this book would be riddled with errors like a battlefield sprinkled with caltrops. Needless to say that any remaining errors are entirely my own fault.

Support for a book is not always tangible, and so I owe thanks to Dennis Tini of Detroit, a true artist and warrior, for his tireless support and encouragement of my work.

Likewise, I should thank the learned Duncan Macleod of Detroit, via the Isle of Lewis, for being the first to introduce me to the world of Latin (and his patience doing so), as well as our riveting (and challenging!) discussions of history and the nature of faith.

When it comes to the elements of Celtic myth that are introduced in *Warriors of Epona*, I owe a great deal to Professor Ann Dooley at the Celtic Studies department at St. Michael's College, University of Toronto. It was Professor Dooley who first introduced me to the world of the Mabinogion, Celtic archetypes, and the tale of Cú Chulainn and the Morrigan in the *Táin Bó Cuailnge*. Her passion for the subject grabbed hold of my imagination and held it fast like no other professor in all my years of study. When writing this book, I felt like I was back in her class discussing Pwyll, Prince of Dyfed, and Rhiannon, and the magical world of Annwn. I am truly lucky to have been taught by such a wonderful champion of Celtic lore.

To Laura Wright LaRoche at LLPIX Designs, my deepest thanks for her excellent cover designs that have breathed new life into the Eagles and Dragons series. In this day and age, people do indeed judge a book by its cover, and Laura has always managed to create covers that grab the attention of wandering eyes, helping new readers to find the series and help make it a success.

Writing can be a lonely business much of the time, so it is with gratitude that I give my thanks to the members of the various Facebook groups whose interactions and input I value, including the Roman History Reading Group, Classics International, and the Ancient and Medieval History and Archaeology Nerd Group.

Lastly, but most certainly not least, I want to thank all of my readers who have helped make the Eagles and Dragons series a magnificent success this year. Not only have the books become official 'Best Sellers', including a #1 Best Seller, but the numerous kind reviews and e-mails about the books have been truly humbling. I thank you all sincerely and promise to make the stories better and better so that I earn your following and honour the time you give out of your lives to read these books. Cheers to all of you!

Adam Alexander Haviaras
Toronto, December 2016

About the Author

Adam Alexander Haviaras is a writer and historian who has studied ancient and medieval history and archaeology in Canada and the United Kingdom. He currently resides in Toronto with his wife and children. *Warriors of Epona* is his eighth novel.

Other works by Adam Alexander Haviaras:

The Eagles and Dragons series

A Dragon among the Eagles (Prequel)

Children of Apollo (Book I)

Killing the Hydra (Book II)

Warriors of Epona (Book III)

Isle of the Blessed (Book IV)

The Stolen Throne (Book V)

The Carpathian Interlude Series

Immortui (Part I)

Lykoi (Part II)

Thanatos (Part III)

The Mythologia Series

Chariot of the Son

Heart of Fire: A Novel of the Ancient Olympics

Saturnalia: A Tale of Wickedness and Redemption in Ancient Rome

Titles in the Historia Non-fiction Series

Historia I: Celtic Literary Archetypes in *The Mabinogion*: A Study of the Ancient Tale of *Pwyll, Lord of Dyved*

Historia II: Arthurian Romance and the Knightly Ideal: A study of Medieval Romantic Literature and its Effect upon Warrior Culture in Europe

Historia III: *Y Gododdin*: The Last Stand of Three Hundred Britons - Understanding People and Events during Britain's Heroic Age

Historia IV: Camelot: The Historical, Archaeological and Toponymic Considerations for South Cadbury Castle as King Arthur's Capital

Stay Connected

To connect with Adam and learn more about the ancient world visit www.eaglesanddragonspublishing.com

Sign up for the Eagles and Dragons Publishing Newsletter at www.eaglesanddragonspublishing.com/newsletter-join-the-legions/ to receive a FREE BOOK, first access to new releases and posts on ancient history, special offers, and much more!

Readers can also connect with Adam on Twitter @AdamHaviaras and Instagram @ adam_haviaras.

On Facebook you can 'Like' the Eagles and Dragons Publishing page to get regular updates on new historical fiction and fantasy from Eagles and Dragons Publishing.